PARIS
TROUT

RANDOM HOUSE TRADE PAPERBACKS
NEW YORK

PARIS TROUT

A NOVEL

PETE DEXTER

2014 Random House Trade Paperback Edition

Copyright © 1988 by Pete Dexter

Published in the United States by Random House Trade Paperbacks, an imprint of Random House, a division of Random House LLC, a Penguin Random House Company, New York.

RANDOM HOUSE and the HOUSE colophon are registered trademarks of Random House LLC.

Originally published in hardcover in the United States by Random House, an imprint and division of Random House LLC, in 1988.

Library of Congress Cataloging-in-Publication Data

Dexter, Pete
Paris Trout.
I. Title.
ISBN 978-0-8129-8738-6
eBook ISBN 978-0-8129-8739-3
PS3554.E95P37 1988 813'.54 87-43314

Printed in the United States of America on acid-free paper

www.atrandom.com

Book design by Debbie Glasserman

*This book is for
James Maurice Quinlan
and Mickey Rosati,
two of a kind.*

ROSIE

PART ONE

In the spring of that year an epidemic of rabies broke out in Ether County, Georgia. The disease was carried principally by foxes and was reported first by farmers, who, in the months of April and May, shot more than seventy of the animals and turned them in to the county health officer in Cotton Point.

The heads were removed, wrapped in plastic, and sent to the state health department in Atlanta, where eleven were found to be rabid.

There is no record of human beings' contracting the disease—the victims for the most part were cattle—although two residents of an outlying area of Cotton Point called Damp Bottoms were reportedly bitten.

One of them, an old man known only as Woodrow, was found lying under his house a day later, dead. He was buried by the city in a bare, sun-baked corner of Horn Cemetery without medical tests and without a funeral.

The other was a fourteen-year-old girl named Rosie Sayers, who was bothered by nightmares.

Rosie Sayers was tall and delicately boned, and her front teeth lay across her lips like sleeping white babies. She was afraid of things she could not see and would not leave the house unless she was forced.

The house was flat-roofed and warped. It had five rooms, and the wallboards that defined them were uneven, so you could see through the walls from any of the rooms into the next.

She lived in this house with her mother and her brothers and sisters. There were fourteen of them in all, but Rosie had never counted the number. She had never thought to.

The brothers and sisters slept through Rosie's screams in the night— it was a part of things, like the whistling in her youngest brother's breathing—but her mother's visitors, unaccustomed to the girl's affliction, would sometimes bolt up in bed at the noise, and sometimes they would stumble into their pants in the dark and leave.

Her mother called the dreams "spells" and from time to time stuck needles in the child's back as an exorcism. Usually after one of her visitors had left in the night. Rosie would stand in front of her, bare-backed, allowing it.

On the day she was bitten by the fox, Rosie Sayers had been sent into town to buy a box of .22 caliber shells from Mr. Trout. Her mother had a visitor that week who was a sportsman.

Mr. Trout kept a store on North Main Street. There was a string on the door that tripped a bell when anyone walked in. Colored people stopped just inside the door and waited for him. White people picked out what they wanted for themselves. There was one light inside, a bare bulb, hanging from a cord in the back.

He came out of the dark, it reminded her of a ghost. He glowed tall and white. "What is it?" he said.

"Bullets," she said. The word lost itself in the darkness, the sound of the bell was still in the room.

"Speak up, girl."

"Twenty-two bullets," she said.

He turned and ran a long white finger along the shelf behind, and when he came back to her, he was holding a small box. "That's seventy cent," he said, and she reached into the tuck of her shirt and found the dollar her mother had given her. It was balled-up and damp, and she smoothed it out before she handed it over.

He took the money and made change from his own pocket. Mr. Trout didn't use a cash register. He put the box of shells in her hand, he didn't use bags much either. She had never held a box of shells before and was surprised at the weight. He crossed his arms and waited. "I ain't got forever," he said.

SHE WALKED TO THE north end of town and then followed the Georgia Pacific Railroad tracks, east and north, back to the sawmill. Damp Bottom sat behind the mill, built on rose-colored dirt, not a tree to be seen. It made sense to her that trees wouldn't dare to grow near a sawmill.

There was a storage shed between the mill and the houses, padlocked in front and back, with small, dirty windows on the side. Her brothers said there were dead men inside, but she never looked for herself. Rosie's grandmother had died in bed, her mouth open and contorted, as if that were the route her life took leaving her, and that was all the dead people she ever meant to see.

She passed the windows wide, averting her eyes, and when she was safely by and looked in front of herself again, she saw the fox. He was dull red and tired and seemed in some way to recognize her.

She stopped cold in her tracks, the fox picked up his head. She took a slow step backwards, and he followed her, keeping the same distance. Then he moved again, closer, and seemed to sway. She heard her own breathing as she backed away.

The movement only seemed to draw him; something drew him. "Please, Mr. Fox," she said, "don't poison me. I be out of your way, as quick as you seen me, I be gone."

She knew foxes had turned poisonous from her brothers. Worse than a snake. She stopped again, and he stopped with her. Her brothers said when the poison fox bit you, you were poison too.

The fox cocked his head, and she began to run. She didn't know where. Her legs were strong; but before she had gone ten steps, they seemed to tangle in each other, and she was surprised, looking down just before she fell, to see the fox between them. Then she closed her eyes and hit the ground.

She never felt the bites. The fox growled—the sound was higher-pitched than a dog, and busier—and then she kicked out with her heels and felt his coat and the bones beneath it. He cried out, and when she kicked again nothing was there.

She opened her eyes, and as fast as he had come he was gone.

She stood up slowly, collecting her breath, and dusted herself off.

She was thorough about it, she didn't like to be dirty, and it was only when her hand touched the inside of her calf and felt blood that she knew that he had opened her up.

She saw the bites then, two small openings on the same leg, closer to her ankle than her knee. The blood wasn't much and had already dried everywhere except near the tears in the skin. She sat back down on the ground and began to cry. The clay was scorched, but she didn't feel that either.

She cried because she was poisoned.

In a few minutes the crying began to hurt her head, and she stood up again, shaky-legged now, afraid her mother would know what had happened. Afraid of what her mother would do.

She spit in the palm of her hand and wiped at the blood on her leg, over and over, until her mouth was too dry to spit. Then she rubbed both her hands on the ground, picking up orange-colored dust, and covered her legs and her knees, not to draw attention to the one that was injured.

She put dust on her elbows and some on her cheeks and neck. Her mother would be angry, to have her walk into the house dirty when she had a visitor, but she wouldn't know about the fox.

She remembered the visitor.

She turned a circle, looking for the box of shells. It was a present for him because he was a sportsman. Her mother said he might shoot them rabbits for supper.

The box was gone. She looked all around her and then back toward the shed. She traced her steps past the shed to the spot she had been when she looked up and saw the fox. She searched the ground and the weeds growing around the shed, looking up every few seconds because she was afraid the fox would be there again.

The fox was gone, though, and so were the bullets.

She stood still and waited, she didn't know for what. The sun moved in the sky. She stopped crying; the scared feeling passed and left her calm. She wondered if her mother would allow the visitor to whip her.

She had done that before.

Her thoughts turned again to the bullets and then from the bullets to the place she had gotten them. Mr. Trout wasn't as frightening now;

6

it felt like he might be glad to see her again. And when she finally moved away, feeling a tightness at first in the leg where the fox had bitten her, it was back in the direction of the store.

ROSIE SAYERS COULD NOT tell time, and her sense of it was that it belonged to some people and not to others. All the white people had it, and all the colored people who owned cars. Her mother's visitors had it, they would mention it when they left. "Lordy, look at the time. . . ."

She worried now that the time had run out for the stores to be open. She hurried her walk, following the railroad tracks. The tracks curved and then fed themselves into a bridge on the edge of town. A train was stopped there, car after car of lumber as far as she could see. The smell of fresh-cut pine.

She climbed the embankment to the bridge, using her hands, and when she came to the top the whistle blew, and the cars banged against each other as the slack in their couplings was pulled from the front, and then, together, they began to move slowly up the track.

And she watched the train from the top of the hill, standing on the bridge that led to town, and she thought of jumping, down into the dark places between the cars, and being taken in that way to the end of the tracks. And for a moment there seemed to be another person inside her too, someone who wanted to jump.

She remembered time then, and the stores and walked away from the train and back into town. She wondered if other people had another person inside them too.

SHE THOUGHT SHE WAS too late. The stores on the lower part of Main Street were half dark inside, and still. White people had gone home. She thought of her mother again and hurried. It felt like her mother was watching.

Mr. Trout's store was as dark as the others, but it had been dark earlier too. She tried the door. The handle turned, she pushed it open. She heard the bell ring and stepped inside and waited. The air was heavy and hard to breathe. She felt herself suspended in it, with the smell of everything there for sale.

There was a fussing in the back, someone was angry. She reached for the door, afraid now that it had somehow locked and that she was trapped inside. Then there was a voice, closer.

"May I help you, miss?"

Rosie turned and saw a lady, as ghostlike as Mr. Trout himself but pretty. The lady straightened and wiped at her eyes with the back of her hand, getting herself right.

Rosie had never seen a white person cry before—none except the little ones—and it surprised her that they had those feelings too, and that the lady would allow herself to be seen in that condition.

"What is it, child?" the lady said. She had a sweet voice, as if in the darkness of the store she couldn't see who it was she was talking to.

"Twenty-two bullets," she said.

The lady turned and looked on the shelves behind her. The girl knew where Mr. Trout found the bullets before, but she was reluctant to speak. The lady's finger moved along the goods stacked into the shelves and passed right over them.

"That's them," Rosie said, and the lady jumped at the sound of the voice behind her and something fell off the shelf. The child backed away from the counter, covering her mouth.

The lady turned around, though, and smiled. "I'm afraid I'm not used to finding bullets," she said.

"No, ma'am, me neither."

And it was like they were in the same mess, and for a moment it was like the fox had never bitten her.

The lady knelt to pick up the things on the floor. Rosie would have helped; but there was a counter between them, and she knew without being told to stay on her own side. Even if they were in the same mess, white people would think she was stealing.

The lady came back up slowly, flushed and serious. Rosie heard her bones pop. "Now," she said, "where were we?"

"I ain't moved," Rosie said, and showed the lady her hands.

The lady did not look at her hands. She smiled, so small it might

8

have been something that hurt. "That's an expression," she said. "It means, What were we doing?"

"We was huntin' .22 bullets," she said.

Before the lady could return to the shelves, Mr. Trout appeared from the back of the store. Just like before, he was suddenly there. He stood behind the lady, staring at the girl.

"What is it now?" he said.

The girl looked at the floor, and when she tried to speak, everything was real again. The fox and the bullets and her mother.

"She wants some bullets, Paris," the lady said.

"More bullets?" he said, to her, not the lady.

Rosie nodded, without looking up.

"You have another dollar?"

She reached into the pocket of her shorts and came out with the three dimes he had given her in change when she paid before.

"That ain't enough for a box of shells," he said.

She stood still. "It ain't enough money," he said, louder, as if she couldn't hear.

She felt herself turn weak inside and knew the fox had poisoned her. "What happened to them shells you got before?" he asked.

She shook her head. "The fox got them," she said. Without knowing why, she reached down and touched the torn places in her skin.

The lady saw the bites from behind the counter and came around for a closer look. Mr. Trout didn't move. The lady said, "She's been bitten."

"A fox?" he said. "You sure it was a fox?"

"She's been bitten for certain," the lady said.

"It might be a dog," Mr. Trout said. "You know the difference between a fox and a dog, miss?"

It took the girl a moment to realize he was talking to her. "Yessir," she said. "I know dogs."

"You need to go home, tell your mammy what happened," he said.

The lady spoke up again. "She needs to see a doctor," she said.

"Her people got doctors," he said.

The lady put her hands on the girl's shoulders and looked into her eyes. The girl could smell the lady's soap and the shampoo she used to wash her hair. It was sweet, but not as sweet as the toilet water her mother used. "Does your momma take you to the doctor when you're sick?" she said.

"My momma don't know when I'm sick."

And the lady turned and looked at Mr. Trout, her hands still on the girl's shoulders. "I'm going to take her to a doctor," she said.

"In hell," he said.

"She's bitten."

"Probably a damn dog," he said.

"I won't listen to that language in front of a child," the lady said.

"You listen to any goddamn thing I say."

The lady received that as if he'd boxed her ears. She took Rosie by the hand and led her out of the store. Mr. Trout stood where he was and watched them leave. Rosie heard the bell ring as the door closed.

They walked across the street and then to the end of the block. The lady still held on to her hand, but she walked ahead, pulling her now as they turned the corner toward Thomas Cornell Clinic.

The clinic sat across the street from the campus of Georgia Officer Academy, and the girl saw soldier boys in their uniforms over there, some of them younger than herself, hurrying in cross directions into the gray buildings. It seemed to her that soldier boys were always hurrying—that the same time that belonged to white people crawled all over them.

She thought she would rather not know anything about time than to have it crawling all over her.

They crossed another street, and the girl noticed the faces in the windows of cars. She guessed it was not every day that a white lady walked up the street toting somebody's colored girl that wasn't her own.

The lady suddenly turned left, pulling her along. They climbed four steps and then walked through a glass door. A nurse was sitting at a desk at the far end of the room, and the lady left Rosie just inside the door while she told the nurse what happened. The nurse listened and wrote things on a paper.

Every few seconds she looked around the lady to see Rosie for herself. She did it so often that the thought came to the child that the nurse was drawing her picture.

When they had finished talking and writing, the nurse stood up and came across the room after her. The girl backed away. "It's all right," the lady said. "Dr. Braver just wants to take a look."

And the girl looked at the lady and believed her and allowed herself to be taken down a hallway and then into a small room in the back. "Doctor be with you directly," the nurse said. She put the papers she had been writing on a glass cabinet, and then she frowned, and then she shut the door.

The room was white and bare. There was a narrow bed against one wall, a wood chair against the other. Between them were the cabinet and a sink. The girl could see inside, cotton and little jars of pills. She could not read what was written about her on the paper.

She sat down in the chair and waited. There was a picture on the wall, a white boy and his granddaddy fishing in a river. She studied the picture a minute and saw neither one of them knew how to fish.

She was still thinking about fishing when the door opened and the doctor came in, frowning the same way as the nurse, white hair and white shoes, wearing some loose doctor's instrument around his neck like he didn't even know it was there.

He did not speak to her at first. He went to the cabinet and looked at the paper the nurse left. He was still looking at it when he spoke. "You been bit?"

She did not know if he was talking to her or the paper.

He turned around and stared into her face. "You hear what I asked you?"

"Yessir," she said.

"Well? Did you get bit or was it a story?"

"No sir, I don't tell no stories."

"So you been bit."

She pointed to the place on her leg. He looked at it, without trying to get closer. "How long since you had a bath?" he said a minute later.

"Saturday," she said.

He frowned; he looked as unhappy as she was. "You got this dirty since Saturday?"

She looked down at her legs too. "I must of did," she said.

Without another word he left the room, and in a moment the nurse was back. She washed the spot where the fox had bitten her with water

11

and soap from the sink. She was rough and did not touch the skin except with the rag. Rosie could see from her expression that she did not enjoy to wash a colored girl's leg.

When she finished, there was a circle cleaned around the bites, and streaks of dirty water ran down the girl's calf and over her ankles. The nurse threw the washrag into a pail and then scrubbed her hands. It took her longer to scrub her hands than it had to clean the bites.

When the doctor came back into the room, he was carrying a needle. The needle was long enough to go in one side of her and out the other. "What that for?" she said.

The doctor looked tired. "Rabies shots," he said. She shook her head no and edged farther back into the chair. "If you got bit by a fox," he said, "you got to have shots." He held the needle up for her to see. "They go in your stomach."

"I don't want nothin' like that inside my stomach less I swallow it," she said.

"Now, you're sure it wasn't some dog," he said. "If it was a dog, the police just take you home, maybe ask what it looked like. As simple as pie, if it was a dog." She saw him looking at her; she couldn't see what he wanted.

"The police doesn't know where I live," she said.

"They take you where I tell them," he said.

"I never heard of that," she said.

"It's for when you get bit," he said. "Once somebody brought you here, the police got to take you home."

The girl sat still a moment, looking at the needle. "I believe I take the ride home," she said.

The doctor laid the needle down on the glass counter. "Then it wasn't no fox," he said. He looked at her as he said that and shook his head no.

"No sir," she said.

"A lot of them dogs," he said, "they look like a fox, don't they?" And then he was gone from the room again, and a minute later the nurse led her out the back of the clinic and waited there with her until a police came to pick her up.

He put her in the back seat and then got in himself behind the wheel. "Where to, miss?" he said.

She did not answer at first.

He turned in his seat. "Where's your house at?"

"The Bottoms," she said.

He put the car into gear and started out of the alley. "I heard that's a nice neighborhood," he said. She saw him smile.

He turned left at the end of the alley, and they drove back through town. The girl pressed her face into the window, and as they passed Main Street she saw the lady again, heading back in the direction of the store. The lady had lost the purpose in her walk, though, as if she hadn't made up her mind where to go.

THE POLICE FOLLOWED THE road that followed the railroad. The ride was smooth until they were out of town, and then the car slowed and began to bounce. The window bumped against the girl's forehead and her teeth until she moved away, leaving wet marks on the glass.

The road passed through brush and then separated two large pine trees. The back seat of the car was suddenly darker, and she heard the branches scrape the sides. Then they were back in the open, and she saw the railroad tracks again, and then the sawmill, and beyond that Damp Bottom.

She was excited, as if she had been away a long time, and she wondered what the neighbors would think to see her coming home in a police car.

The car stopped, and the police turned again in his seat. "Home sweet home," he said.

"Yessir," she said.

"This is it?"

She looked out the window. Half the Bottoms were standing out on their porches, to see what the police was up to now. It was an out-of-the-way thing, to see a single police car in the Bottoms. When they came, they brought everybody but Baby Jesus.

The police got out, the car dipped and rose, and then he opened her door. "Which is your house?" he said.

She nodded to the tar-roof shack just ahead of the car. Most of her brothers and sisters were outside; there was no sign of her mother. No sign of the visitor. The police began to walk in that direction, and suddenly she did not want him near the house. She didn't know why. He was smiling, enjoying something she did not understand. He was a big man, not old at all, and where his neck came out of his collar, it looked swollen up. He walked ahead of her all the way to the porch steps.

"I be home now," she said quietly.

He smiled and shook his head. "I got to deliver you to your mammy," he said. "It's a city law."

Rosie felt it again, that the police should not be near the house. She felt it and stopped. He walked ahead, forgetting her, up two steps to the porch and through her brothers and sisters to the door. When he was there, he turned to her and winked.

He knocked, and she saw the visitor in the side window.

He was standing against the wall, a shadow in a shadow, his chest rising and falling as if something had chased him a long ways. The police knocked again, and the girl's mother answered the door. At the same time the visitor climbed into the window frame, squatting, and the girl saw he was holding a knife in his teeth.

It resembled a smile.

"Miz Sayers," the police was saying, "I am Officer Andrews, and I brung you something home."

The girl's mother looked around the police until she saw her. "What's she did?"

The police's head moved back until a roll of skin formed over his collar. "Nothin'," he said. "But a white lady fetched her to the clinic onaccount she said she been bit by something."

The visitor's eyes were scared and crazy. He perched on the ledge of the window without moving, not even a finger, but the girl could see everything inside him was jumping one side to the other.

"I ain't got no money for foolishlessness," her mother said to the police. "That girl got no bi'nis in no clinic."

The police said, "I don't know nothin' about that. I just brung her home." He looked around the porch as he said that, smiling, and then he looked into the house. The visitor jumped from the ledge and hit the ground running. The knife was still in his teeth.

A changing number of children had collected along the side of the house to watch the police talk to Rosie Sayers's mother, and when the visitor jumped, one of them shouted, and then all of them shouted, and the police took two quick steps to the side of the porch and saw the visitor for himself.

"Sonofabitch," he said, and he took off his hat and his shoes and socks and set out after him.

When he was gone some of the children moved in for a closer look at the police's shoes. Rosie Sayers stood where she was and her mother went to the side of the porch, her hands on her rump, and shouted after the police. "You ain't got no call to chase that man," she said. "That man ain't did nothin'."

But even the children knew that was a story. If you run away, the police was supposed to chase you.

The visitor disappeared into the sawmill, and a minute later he came out the other side and started up a long, grassy pasture that led to a place called Sleepy Heights. Some of the girls who lived in the Bottoms were maids in Sleepy Heights, and it was a bad-luck place for an out-of-town nigger to be running away from a police.

The police stayed on the visitor's trail, running about the same speed, and then seemed to make up ground going uphill through the pasture.

The girl's mother watched until the visitor had disappeared and the police had disappeared after him, and then she turned and laid her eyes on Rosie. The girl stepped backwards, stumbling. And a second later, before she knew she was talking, she heard words coming out of her mouth.

And the words said that she was bit by a poisonous fox.

Her mother's look changed then. She seemed to forget the visitor and the police and all the pickaninnies in the yard. She seemed to forget the child herself. "The devil got you for his own, don't he?" she said finally.

"No, ma'am," the girl said.

Her mother closed her eyes, listening to God. She always closed her eyes to listen to God, and she nodded as He gave her the words. She opened her eyes again and spoke what He had told her. "You wasn't born of love," she said. "You was the child of Satan."

"It might been a dog," she said, but it was too late.

Her mother was scowling at the sky. "The Lord told me all along," she said, "and now I listened."

The girl looked down at herself to see if anything had changed, but she was the same, except for the bandage covering the places where the fox had torn her skin. Two shots went off, somewhere in the distance.

Her mother had just spoken to the Lord and was not concerned with the affairs of humans in Sleepy Heights. "I will not have Satan's child under my roof," she said, sounding something like the Lord herself.

The girl could not find an answer. She waited to see if her mother would change her mind.

AN HOUR PASSED, AND the police came out of Sleepy Heights. Rosie watched him, walking downhill through the pasture, barefoot. He crossed the creek and then the railroad tracks. He passed wide around the sawmill yard.

By the time he reached the Bottoms, the children had scattered back into their houses, or under their houses. Rosie stood by herself, with no place to go when the police came to collect his shoes and hat, no place to hide if he was mad.

The police's hair was cut so close she could see his head through it, and when he got into the yard she noticed the beads of sweat there, and running every direction down his face and neck into his uniform. The dust had collected in the sweat and streaked. His shoes lay together on the ground where he had left them, untouched. His hat was a few feet away.

She stood still, hoping he wouldn't see her. He picked up his things and opened the door to his car. He sat half in and half out to put on his socks and shoes, and then he stood up to check that it was comfortable. And when he had done all that, he suddenly looked up, right at her, and winked again.

"That rascal was tricky," he said.

"Yessir."

He slapped some of the dust off his pants and shirt sleeves. "What's the boy's name?"

"He ain't nobody I know," she said.

The police smiled at her. "He ain't your brother, is he?"

"No sir, he ain't nobody."

"Well," the police said, "he can run, I'll say that."

"Yessir," she said, and looked at her feet.

"I don't know what he was running for, but I expect he had his reasons." Then he laughed out loud, but it wasn't much of a laugh. If it was funny to him, he wouldn't have walked out of his way around the sawmill, where the men would think it was funny too.

He said, "That boy about led me into a yard had a police dog that don't like police." The police looked her over, and she stood still as the air. "Your mammy ain't going to tell me who it was either, is she?"

"No sir."

And he laughed again, but it didn't mean it was funny. She believed he was going to take somebody into town and crack open his head. But then he said, "Well, if he comes back, you tell him for me that him and me will have another time. You tell him that, hear?"

"Yessir," she said.

And he looked around once, not another soul in sight, and then got into his car and drove out to the end of the Bottoms. He stopped there a minute, still looking, and then the car moved again, back in the direction of town, leaving a cloud of orange dust to settle after he was gone.

THE VISITOR'S NAME WAS Alvin Crooms, and he came back at dusk. He climbed in the same window he had jumped out of that afternoon, and Rosie heard him later inside with her mother, telling the story. The story was like liquor, and she heard them go back to it again and again, until it had made them drunk.

She sat outside, her back against a neighbor's bricks, where she could watch the house. The night turned cold; she didn't move. She waited for her mother to change her mind.

Once, when they were all asleep inside, a nightmare started while she was still awake. She bit her hand and stopped it.

A rooster woke her in the morning. She jumped at the sound, not knowing where she was. The sky was pink over Sleepy Heights, the rooster crowed again, and she was wide-awake.

It was a long time before there were stirring noises inside the house. Her mother liked to stay in bed when she had visitors, she liked people to see the good-looking ones when they left her house.

The girl ached and changed her position on the ground.

THE SUN BROKE THE line of the sky, and she heard them inside, talking. One of her sisters looked out a window at her, then disappeared. The next person in the window was the visitor himself, and he noticed her in a certain way that caused her to press herself into the bricks.

There was the smell of fires in the air, people cooking breakfast. She heard voices she knew, but in some way they were unfamiliar. Her bottom ached, and there was a throbbing in the place where the fox had bitten her leg. She looked down at the bandage and saw that she had swollen all around it.

The sun gathered itself in the sky, smaller and hotter, and presently the girl's mother and the visitor came out onto the porch. Her mother did not look in her direction. The visitor leaned into her mother's shoulder and told her a secret. She laughed out loud, putting her hand on the visitor's arm as if to hold herself up.

Her mother wanted the neighbors to notice that her visitor had come back. He patted her bottom and then left the porch, taking the two steps down with one stride. He pointed his finger at the girl and motioned for her to get up.

She stayed where she was.

"Come on, girl," he said.

"No sir," she said.

He took a step toward her and she scooted that far away. "Your momma said for me to tote you along," he said.

The girl shook her head. The visitor looked back toward the porch, and the girl looked there too. Her mother would not meet her eyes. "I get you the strap," she said to him. "She do what you said then."

Her mother disappeared into the house and came out a moment later with a thick black belt. The girl didn't move until she handed it to the visitor. It looked different in his hand, and she got to her feet, pushing off the ground from behind, suddenly dizzy to be standing up.

"You keep that as long as you need," her mother said.

The visitor fixed on how fast the strap had gotten the girl off the ground. "The girl surely don't like this here," he said. He seemed to test the weight of it in his hand. Then he moved behind her, keeping a certain distance, and she backed out of the yard.

"That's right," he said. "Now you walk up that road where we goin'."

"I ain't never been nowhere," she said. She recalled he was from Macon, and she knew she would never get back from there after her mother changed her mind.

"Whatever I tell you," he said, "that's where you go."

IT TURNED OUT THE visitor wasn't from Macon.

He was from Indian Heights, near the river and the asylum. He walked her through the middle of town, past the college and the bank, then turned out toward the cemetery. The girl was afraid he would take off her clothes, but whatever interest he had in that, her mother had used it up. He wanted to lay the strap across her back, she could tell that, but once they got into Cotton Point, there were people everywhere on the street, and the chance was gone.

It took most of the morning to get from the Bottoms to Indian Heights. The visitor talked some; the girl did not answer. She had never been to Indian Heights before, but she had heard of the place and knew where she was when she saw the river.

The houses in the Heights were nicer than in the Bottoms, and there were more of them. There were no weeds in the road, and there were babies everywhere. She wondered how many of them belonged to the visitor. They walked to the end of the road and then turned left, away from the river, to another road.

The people in the porches spoke to the man, asked him what did he have with him now. She heard his name when they called him. It was Alvin. "I got me a maid," he said back. "Her momma give her to me for my sweetness."

The visitor moved ahead of her once they were in the Heights, and she followed him. She did not know anything else to do.

His house was hidden behind a larger house, about twenty feet off the road. It sat on stacked bricks. There was a rocker on the porch, and the front door was laid from there to the ground, in place of steps.

She followed him up onto the porch and then inside the house. There were two rooms. One of them had a wood stove, the other one had a narrow bed. There was a rope hung from one wall to the other, crossing both rooms, and the visitor had hung his clothes from it on hangers. He had more clothes than all her brothers put together.

He moved behind her while she looked at his clothes, and when he spoke, it was close to her ear. "This here is what you 'posed to maid," he said.

She looked around the room, wondering what was in his head.

"You got to keep it right," he said.

She nodded her head, more afraid of him inside than outside. He seemed bigger here in the room. "I ain't brought no broom," she said.

"My, my," he said, "then what good is you to me?"

The girl looked at the ceiling. The slats had warped, and she could see pieces of blue sky where the tar paper had torn. She did not think the man had lived here long. She took a step farther in, and the floor creaked and seemed to move.

"You like it here?" he said. He was still behind her, and he was still holding the strap.

"No sir."

She saw that she'd given him the wrong answer. "Your momma said you was a smarty," he said. He took her arm then—the first time he'd touched her—just above the elbow. He twisted it, and she bent the way he twisted. He slapped at her legs with the strap, and she yelled.

She turned her head to the side and saw him looking at her. She was afraid he would take her clothes off now, but it wasn't what he wanted. He brought the strap across her legs again, and then her bottom.

And she yelled for real, to be with someone who liked to hurt her. He stopped, still holding her arm. The blood buzzed in her head and her vision blurred. The back of her legs felt burned. She tried to be good to him. "Oh, please," she said.

He seemed to like that, but he came down with the strap again anyway. She held the yell inside this time, hoping it would make him stop. Her eyes began to tear. And he hit her again, lower, across the back of the knees. Her legs buckled, and she cried out without meaning to.

She looked at him one more time and saw no mercy. "Yell all you care to," he said, "ain't nobody gone come in this house 'less I tell them they invited."

He held the strap where she could see it. "This is my house," he said. "I bought it."

And those words were still as real as the strap when a figure appeared in the door. A woman twice as big as Rosie Sayers's mother walked into Alvin Crooms's house. He heard the noise behind him and spun to see who it was.

The girl lost her balance and fell. The woman stepped across the room, and the floorboards sagged under her feet. Alvin Crooms's posture changed, but he stood his ground. "A person might get cut comin' into a man's house," he said.

The woman was next to him now, breathing hard, sweating. She folded her arms and he gave her room. "I heard you was in here with a child," she said.

"Her mother give her to me," he said, stepping back now. The girl noticed that when Alvin Crooms moved backwards, the woman took the space for herself. She was a head taller than he was, and her arms were huge and shook when she moved them. He said, "She been took over by the devil, her momma don't want her under the roof."

The woman looked at her carefully, but only for a second. "They ain't no such thing, a child took by the devil," the woman said.

"And she been bit by a fox," he said. "Poisoned her, lookit yourself."

The woman looked again. The girl drew her knees up under her chin and averted her eyes. The woman stepped nearer, until the girl could feel the heat of her body. "Let Miss Mary see, baby," she said.

The girl moved herself in a way that exposed the bandage. The woman touched her. Her fingers were thick and white-tipped, and she pushed gently into the swollen skin around the bites. It set off a deep ache in the girl's leg. Alvin Crooms watched, over the woman's shoulder.

"See there?" he said.

"The child been bit," she said, straightening up. "It don't make her poisoned."

"It was a fox," he said.

The woman looked into Rosie's eyes and saw it was so. "It don't make her poisoned," she said again. "Now git out the way, 'less I take that strap to your neck."

THE WOMAN TOOK THE girl into her care.

Mary McNutt worked as a maid in the homes of two white families and needed someone to help clean her own. Her house stood in the far corner of Indian Heights, at the bottom of Spine Road, where it curved and crossed the other road, which had no name.

The house had two front doors and a center wall running front to back, dividing it into two apartments. The woman lived on one side with her husband—a grounds keeper at the asylum named Lyle McNutt, Jr.—and her two daughters, Linda and Jane Ray.

Linda was eleven and Jane Ray was nine.

The sons had the other side of the house. Thomas was nineteen, Henry Ray was twenty-one and had just started work at the asylum. Henry Ray didn't cut grass like his stepfather, though. He worked inside.

Mary McNutt's previous husband, Mr. James Boxer, had left them five years before, on Easter Sunday. The children all kept the last name.

Mary McNutt walked the girl through both sides of the house, showing her where to clean. "Mr. Boxer was a Christian man," she said, "but he had boilin' blood in him, could not let go of an unkindness done him by nobody." She was standing in the boys' side of the house then. She said the oldest boy, Henry Ray, was just like him.

"His daddy cut a man owned a farm up in Gray," she said.

"A white man?"

Mary McNutt nodded. "Done him in his own house over a two-dollar ham."

Rosie tried to imagine that, but it wouldn't come. The things that frightened her worst never came to her in a way she could see them. "Lord have mercy," she said.

The woman put her hand on the girl's shoulder; it was as heavy and shapeless as the dead man in the story. "Don't worry 'bout that now," she said. "That's all past times." The woman was still thinking of it, though.

"Mr. McNutt ain't nothing like Mr. Boxer," she said a little later. "Mr. McNutt don't take offense at nothin'."

And the girl could not see if that made her happy or sad.

ALTHOUGH THE TOWN OF Cotton Point, Georgia, claimed more than six thousand residents, not counting the asylum—which they didn't— there was only one person there that a twenty-one-year-old colored man could see to borrow enough money to buy a car. Paris Trout.

Trout ran a bank for colored people out of his store on North Main Street, and Henry Ray went to see him Friday morning, over his mother's objections. She saw the boy's father in him and did not like him doing business with whites.

He had started work at the asylum on the second Tuesday in June, though—cleaning crazy people's shit off the walls and ceiling and sometimes out of their own hair—and by Wednesday he knew he needed a car to keep his dignity.

"I got to work at the state," he said to his mother. "Ain't got no time now to be foolin' around walking."

And a day later he walked into town, and into the front door of the half-lit store on Main Street, and waited there until Paris Trout appeared from the back.

Trout looked at him, cold and tired. "You need twenty dollars, Henry Ray?" he said. That was what he usually borrowed.

"I need a car."

"You can't pay for no car."

"I got took on at the state," he said. "Begun this Tuesday."

"What doing?" Trout didn't believe him, and in one way it made Henry Ray angry, and in another way it scared him.

"Work," he said. "I do general work."

Trout nodded, looking him over. "All right," he said.

They walked through the store, past some canned vegetables and then a row of work gloves and then five safes sitting in a line against the wall. Henry Ray expected the money for the car was in the safes and moved slower, thinking Trout would stop and open one of them up.

He didn't, though. He went past them and then out the back. There was an alley there, and three cars were parked against the side of the building.

"Which one you like?" he said.

Henry Ray stood still, staring at them. He hadn't expected Mr. Trout to have cars for sale. Trout walked ahead of him and looked in the window of an old Plymouth. "Come on," he said. "You can't buy no car from the steps."

Henry Ray walked around the cars once. Two of them were banged up one way or another—cracked glass and missing lights. He pictured himself driving them and it made him ashamed.

The third one was a black two-door 1949 Chevrolet, he saw his face in the shine. "That one there is more than the others," Trout said. "Onaccount it's in showroom shape."

Henry Ray touched the door handle, stopping himself before he got in. "Go on ahead," Mr. Trout said. "See how it feels."

Henry Ray sat down behind the wheel. The dashboard was as shiny as the paint outside, and he saw his face in the glass that covered the speedometer. A hundred miles an hour, it said. He pictured himself riding a hundred miles an hour in a car, smiling at his own face in the speedometer.

When he looked up, Mr. Trout was leaning against the window near him, looking in too. "Now that I look at this here," he said, "I ain't sure I can sell it after all."

Henry Ray looked up, panicked.

Mr. Trout shook his head. "Might be too nice to let it go," he said. "I ought keep it for myself." Henry Ray let his hand touch the steering wheel. "Besides," Trout said, "I ain't sure you make enough money to afford it. A car like this ain't cheap."

"I got a job," he said.

"How much you make?"

Henry Ray stared at the dashboard. "Thirty dollars," he said. He hadn't been paid yet, but that was what his stepfather got.

Mr. Trout hit the roof of the car with his hand, right over Henry Ray's head. It caused him to jump and shamed him. "I didn't know you made that," Mr. Trout said. He paused, as if he were figuring something out. "Yessir," he said a moment later, "you make enough, and you seen it first out here. I guess it's rightfully yours. . . ."

They walked back into the store, and Mr. Trout held the office door open while Henry Ray walked in. They signed the papers. The car was $800. Mr. Trout charged $227 more for insurance. Then he added some and subtracted some, and when he came out with the real number, it was $17.50 a week.

"You sure you want to do this, boy?" Trout said. "Onct you made a deal with me, I get my money."

Henry Ray was standing up over the desk, and from there he could see the car out the open door. He pictured himself again, his face in the speedometer.

"Onct you made a deal with me, you get your money too," he said.

ROSIE SAYERS HAD BEEN living with Mary McNutt three days when Henry Ray came home with the car. She had not spoken to him yet, waiting to be spoken to first. It was in the morning, and she had just made the beds in Miss Mary's side of the house. All the beds but Mr. McNutt's. Miss Mary made that herself.

Rosie's own bed was in that part of the house, against the wall in the first room. She was fourteen years old, and it was the first bed she'd ever had—at least the first one that sleeping in it didn't depend on getting to it before her brothers and sisters.

She made her own bed last, tearing it up twice to get the sheets to lie even, the way Miss Mary had shown her, and then walked out on the porch to rest before she began on the floors. Miss Mary told her to rest whenever she wanted. She'd said, "Take your time, child. The faster you go, the less you gain."

Rosie did everything Miss Mary told her, the way Miss Mary said to do it. She had just settled into a porch chair when she saw the car. It was black and shiny, and a trail of dust followed it as it came up the road. It reminded her of a snake. She sat up and watched it come, and before long it was close enough that she could hear the engine.

She saw Henry Ray behind the wheel then. There and leaning half out of the window. Henry Ray was coal black and evil-looking even sitting still. She wished it was Thomas coming home instead. Thomas was lighter-colored and quieter, like herself.

Henry Ray pulled the Chevrolet into the yard and chased off the neighbor children before they could touch it. Then he walked around to the back, wiping at little spots of dirt with the leg of his pants. Once or twice he glanced in the direction of the porch. Rosie sat still and watched, and when he looked up again, he smiled.

"You like young Henry Ray better now, doesn't you?"

She folded her hands in her lap and studied her knuckles. "I like everybody the same," she said.

She heard him laugh; she did not look up. "You can't like nobody you ain't spoke to yet," he said.

"I like Jesus," she said quietly.

"What's that?"

She couldn't think with him watching her. She felt him looking and was afraid to look back. "You want a ride, Rosie Sayers?" he said. She shook her head no.

"Ain't got time for no rides," she said.

He said, "I see you busy."

"I be busy soon as I stand up."

He left the car and climbed the steps to the porch. He sat on the railing and stared at her, up and down. "I ain't gone to hurt you," he said in a minute.

She looked at her knuckles.

"You think young Henry means to hurt your pretty self?" She shook her head again. "What then?"

"They is some people that gets hurt by accident," she said.

He seemed to think that over. "I bet you ain't never been in no car," he said. "That's what you scared of."

She brought her eyes up then and looked at the automobile. Henry Ray squatted next to her and put his hand on her leg. It looked like a spider. She saw herself connected to the car in that spider web way too. Every time she pushed away, she was caught that much tighter.

He moved his hand up until it could touch both her legs at once, and she felt the heat of it through her dress. "You ain't never been with no man either," he said. "I see that for myself."

She looked at the car, looking for a way out. "How long you going to ride me?" she said.

That made him laugh out loud, and he moved his hand off her and stood up. She felt her lap cool and crossed her legs, so he couldn't get back to that place even if he changed his mind. "I bring you right back, as soon as you want," he said.

She followed him down the steps to the car. He opened the door for her and held it, smiling. She ducked under his arm, moving between Henry Ray and the door without touching either one, and then sat down in the seat. It was softer than the seat in the police car. He slammed the door hard, as if he were mad, but when he walked around the front he smiled at her through the windshield, and then he was next to her in the seat.

He turned the key and touched the starter button. The engine took, and the car began to shake in a regular way.

He pushed the clutch to the floor and studied the gearshift and finally pulled it toward himself and then up. Two different movements, two different thoughts. He turned in his seat to back out into the road.

They drove slowly out of Indian Heights. Henry Ray winced as he steered the car through the place in the road where the trees from either side grew almost together, as if he could feel the branches on his own skin. It already seemed to the girl that a car was more worry than it was worth.

In a few minutes, though, Henry Ray turned out onto Route 27, going south, and she saw his troubles were all behind. They crossed the bridge over the Indian River and then headed away from town. Henry Ray's expression relaxed when they were on the highway, relaxed until he looked like he'd gone simple. His foot pressed the gas pedal to the floor, and she counted the telephone poles as they went past, it seemed like there was hardly enough time to count one before the next was there.

"Lookit here," he said a little later. "Spring is sprung . . . Grass is riz . . ."

It took her a moment to realize he was reading the words off the signs along the road.

"Where last year's . . . Careless drivers is . . . Burma Shave."

He laughed out loud, she stared at him. "How come you know how to read?" she said.

And that made him laugh too. "All Momma's children got to read," he said. "She wouldn't let none of us out the house unless we could. You see them little babies, Linda and Jane Ray? They already learnt too." He was shouting over the wind and the engine. "Sometimes I think that woman's crazy."

Saying that seemed to change Henry Ray's driving. He slowed down, and she watched the needle of the speedometer drop back into the middle of the numbers. "She ain't crazy," he said suddenly.

"I never said she was."

"Well," he said, "I never said it neither."

She looked out the window. The prettiest thing she saw was a mare in foal, which wasn't anything special. "How far you going to drive us?" she said.

"Where you want to go?"

"Home."

He slowed down, looking for a place. The more they slowed, the more she realized how fast they'd been going. He pulled into a field, following some tire tracks through the weeds until they ended. He turned off the engine, and in the absence of its sound she heard the noises of the field. It felt peaceful to be stopped, and she wished she was alone.

He slid across the car seat for her. She sat still. He put his hands on her legs and then on her chest; she did not move. He lay back in the seat, pulling her after him. She didn't fight him, she didn't help him. He touched the waist of her dress and then followed the line of her legs on both sides until he got to the hem. Then he came back up, and the dress came up with him. Her underpants were fastened with a safety pin.

"Well, well," he said.

She did not move or answer. He unfastened his own trousers then, and she saw what he intended to put inside her. "I never done nothing before," she said.

"That's all right," he said.

She said, "Nobody told me so."

28

He put himself between her legs and took her safety pin. She felt herself exposed. "Please," she said, "I gone bleed all over your new car. I bleed bad when it comes."

It stopped him, that fast. "You ain't bled nowhere yet?" he said. "No."

He lifted himself off her, carefully, as if he were afraid to wake her up. He opened the door behind him and slipped outside backwards. She thought he would pull her after him, but he left her there and buttoned his trousers. She found the safety pin in the crack between the cushions of the seats and put herself back together.

Henry Ray did not speak when he got back in the car. He turned in a slow, careful circle, sticking his head out the window to see where the wheels were going. He drove that same slow speed back over the tire tracks. She did not know if he was mad or not; she wished she were there with Thomas. Thomas didn't take a temper.

Henry Ray stopped the car at the highway and pulled on the hand brake. "They ain't nothing to tell about this," he said. She didn't answer. "I let you go, so you ain't got nothing to tell."

She looked down at herself and wondered what it would have been like, to have that inside her. She wondered if there would be a baby there now. She wondered if it would be as black as Henry Ray. "If you tell, Miss Mary prob'ly send you out of the house," he said.

"I ain't said nothing."

"She don't like stories on her boys."

Rosie wished he would turn the engine off so she could hear the sounds of the country. She wanted to feel peaceful. "I don't tell no stories," she said.

He made no reply. He pushed the clutch to the floor and put the car into gear and then killed the engine. When he saw that he'd forgotten to take off the hand brake, he cussed her.

Then he said, "Ain't nothing gone right in this world since I seen you and tried to be nice."

And she sat still, thinking of things she could say back.

He drove back to Cotton Point slower than he had come out. Twice she felt him begin to talk and then quit before the first word. She looked out the window for the mare in foal, but she didn't see it again. Nothing looked the same on the way back.

THEY CAME OVER THE bridge and stopped at the crossroad. Indian Heights was left; the town itself was straight on. Henry Ray spoke to her then. "You want a Popsicle?" he said. He wasn't in a temper now.

"You ain't got no Popsicle," she said.

"I got money. What color you like?"

"Purple," she said. She'd had only one Popsicle in her life, and it was purple.

He seemed to be deciding something again. "You ain't gone tell stories to Miss Mary?" he said.

"I already said I don't tell no stories."

He drove across the road that led to the Heights and into town. He turned right on Main Street, and Rosie studied the people on the sidewalk, thinking she might see the lady who had taken her to Thomas Cornell Clinic. She thought she might wave. The woman wasn't there, though; none of the white people she saw were pretty.

Rosie guessed Mr. Trout kept her inside.

Henry Ray continued east, crossed into Bloodtown, and pulled into a gas station. The man who pumped the gas smiled at Rosie as he washed the windshield. He had a uniform with letters over the pocket. ROY. He was skinny and light-skinned, and she liked his looks better than Henry Ray's, maybe better than Thomas's.

She did not acknowledge his smile, even when he waved at her with his pinkie finger right up against the windshield. She thought about it later, though.

The man stopped the pump at one dollar. Henry Ray came out of the station, carrying a Popsicle, and held it in his teeth while he opened his wallet to find his dollar bill. Once he was inside the car he broke the Popsicle in half, and then slid one side out of the paper and handed it to her.

It was purple, just like he promised.

She put it in her mouth carefully, not wanting it to break, and held it there a moment, tasting just the cold at first and then the flavor beneath it. She slid it out as carefully as she'd put it in, wishing there was some way to make it last.

Henry Ray was chewing his, taking it in bites. He started the car and began to back out. She put the Popsicle back in her mouth, feeling the edges turn smooth, and suddenly there was a bump, and it was broken in half.

She did not realize until Henry Ray screamed that they had been hit. Then he was sitting up off his seat, looking through the rearview mirror. He screamed again and got out of the car.

She turned to watch him, half the Popsicle still in her mouth, and saw the truck. It was a lumber truck, just like the ones that carried cut boards out of the sawmill near Damp Bottom. The back end was up against the back end of the car, and a few of the boards had slid off onto the trunk.

Henry Ray was a crazy man.

He held his head and flapped his arms and jumped up and down and screamed. The driver of the truck got out slower; he looked half as heavy as his truck. He watched Henry Ray a few minutes, then he walked over to the car and had a look. He said, "Be quiet, nigger, so I can see what's did."

Henry Ray said, "Who you callin' nigger, nigger?"

Rosie had heard this before, it meant they were fixing to fight. She looked at the man who had climbed out of the truck and did not think Henry Ray ought to fight him. She had seen enough fighting now to know who would win.

The man in the uniform came out of the station and stood with his hands on his hips while Henry Ray and the man from the truck cussed. He studied the back end of the car, and then he studied the back end of the truck. He pushed the lumber that had slid off back onto the truck.

Henry Ray and the truck driver stood one on each side, watching. Rosie opened her door, and when nobody yelled at her to mind her business, she walked around to the back and had a look for herself.

The truck had knocked one shiny piece of the car off—it was lying on the ground—and tore a hole in another piece, about big enough that Henry Ray could have fit through it.

That thought came to her because of what the driver said to him. "I stick your skinny ass through there and back up some more, you don't shut up."

The driver said that, and then he bent down and touched the edge of the tear. His finger crumbled the metal there, and then he moved it a couple of inches farther away, and pushed straight through.

Rosie was sure Henry Ray oughtn't to fight him.

"Ain't nothing but paint and rust anyways," the truck driver said. He stood up, looking at his finger. Henry Ray was staring at the hole he'd poked in the car. He bent himself almost in half and looked underneath.

"Ooo-e," the man from the station said.

Henry Ray stayed underneath the car a long time, longer than it took to see the other side of a hole. The truck driver said time was money and he didn't have any more to spend looking at this skinny nigger's ass, and he left.

Henry Ray came out from under just as the truck driver shut his door. He started the engine, blowing smoke over the accident scene, and ground his gears. Rosie heard something familiar in the noise, the sound things made when they were forced. She looked on the ground and saw Henry Ray's Popsicle lying beside the fender, half melted, showing the ice underneath the purple.

She wished she could pick it up.

The gas man spoke then, startling her. "You ain't got no insurest, do you?"

Henry Ray looked at him. "Insurest," the man said. "You got that, they got to fix your car for you."

Henry Ray began to nod. "I got that."

"Then all you need do is to call them up," the gas man said, "and they fix it up like new."

"That do that, for sure?"

"I swear."

Henry Ray laughed. He picked the fender up off the ground and tossed it onto the back seat. "Get in, girl," he said to her. He waited until she had pulled the door shut to start the engine. The tail pipe scraped the ground when they moved, but he didn't seem to care.

She took a chance that it was all right to talk. "Where you drivin' now, Henry Ray?"

In a way she couldn't quite understand, the question decided the answer. "Takin' this here right back to Mr. Trout," he said.

She sat dead still.

He began to nod. "I paid the man his insurest, he got to fix the car."

"You gone tell Mr. Trout *that*?"

And then she was sorry that she'd asked, because that question decided the answer too. He drove up Main Street, dragging his tail pipe. White people stopped in their tracks to see what kind of racket it was. Henry Ray looked straight ahead.

He drove past Mr. Trout's store, around the block, and back up the alley. He left the car there and pulled her after him up the steps to the store.

"They ain't nothing in here for us," she said, holding back. "I been in here before."

"You just tell him what you seen," he said.

"He don't care what I seen."

Henry Ray paid no attention. He was holding her by the wrist. He touched the handle of the door, then had a different thought and knocked. Soft at first, then harder.

Mr. Trout came to the back of the store the same way he came to the front, which was he didn't come at all, he was just suddenly there. He stood behind the screen door, looking down at them, and didn't speak a word.

Henry Ray's hold on her wrist went soft. He dropped his head. For a long time nobody spoke.

"Sir," he said finally.

Henry Ray changed and went soft one part at a time.

Mr. Trout got his face closer to the screen. "What the hell you doin' that for, beatin' on a man's door like that?"

Rosie turned and started down the stairs, but Henry Ray's grip on her wrist tightened and hurt her. "I didn't intended to cause you no disturbance," he said, "but I got to talk to you about fixin' my car."

Mr. Trout said, "You got to talk to me about paying for it, is all."

Her knees began to shake like they had after the fox bit her, and she swooned in the sun.

"I brung the car back onaccount of a lumber truck run into it and tore it all up."

"That ain't my obligation, to teach you to drive."

"I can drive," Henry Ray said, but so soft Mr. Trout couldn't hear.

"Did you say something?"

Rosie could feel it building to something bad.

"I can drive," he said, louder. Still looking at the ground.

"Then how come you busted up your Chevrolet? You gone three hours and come back here with your property all busted up."

"I never tore it up," Henry Ray said. "A lumber truck run into it."

"Then the lumber company got to fix it."

"No sir."

Rosie pulled herself as far away from the screen as she could get. "No sir," Henry Ray said again. "I bought insurest from you, cost me two hundred some dollars, so you got to fix it right."

Behind the screen Mr. Trout seemed to grow taller. "You ain't paid a cent," he said. "All you done was sign a note and drove off with my car."

"Then it's your car still," Henry Ray said. His words were so soft now it took Rosie a moment to understand what he had said. Mr. Trout never moved, but when he spoke again, he was half out of breath.

"Listen to me," he said. "You signed the note, and that makes it yours. It don't matter to me if lightning tore it up, you still got to pay. I told you before, I get my money."

But Henry Ray had something in his head now, and the more Mr. Trout said one thing, the harder he believed the other. "I got insurest," he said.

"Not for that," Mr. Trout said. "It ain't that kind of insurance."

Henry Ray turned away from the screen, meaning to leave. "It ain't so bad anyway," Mr. Trout said, looking past him at the car. "It don't hurt nothing to drive around in a car that ain't perfect. Help a person to remember to be more careful next time."

Henry Ray walked down the steps and then up the alley, away from the car. Rosie was at his side, sometimes a step in front. She heard the screen door open and Mr. Trout coming down the steps.

"Hey, there," he said.

Henry Ray did not stop or turn around. "You forgot your car, mister. You don't want to leave it in the alley, something else come along and bust it up worst."

Henry turned around, still walking away. "It ain't none of my affair," he said.

"It's your own car," Mr. Trout said. He was yelling now. "You and me done business. Now come get this and take it with you." Mr. Trout pointed down the alley at them with his finger, but Henry Ray had turned back around and was walking away. Rosie saw him point, though, and a few seconds later, at the end of the alley, she looked again and he was still at it.

"I think he's gone get a police after us," she said.

"Don't make no nevermind to me," he said.

They walked to the corner—Henry Ray had let go of her wrist now—and suddenly Mr. Trout was there again; she saw that he must have gone out the front of the store to head them off. He was breathing hard and had screaming eyeballs, and he stepped right in front of Henry Ray. "Seventeen dollars and fifty cent a week," he said. "You leave the car or drive it into the river, it's still the same payment."

Henry Ray stepped around Mr. Trout and crossed the street. Rosie followed him, and when they'd got to the sidewalk, Mr. Trout began to yell. Called them niggers. "You and me got bi'nis," he yelled. "It ain't over till that car's paid for, one hundred percent."

Henry Ray turned and shouted back, "You and me ain't got no bi'nis." Rosie saw some of the white people on the street begin to laugh.

"You just ask your people about that," Mr. Trout yelled. "You ask what happens if you don't pay Mr. Trout."

Henry Ray held his ground a long time and then turned without another word and began the long walk back to Indian Heights. The girl followed him. The cement was hot on her feet, and where there was grass she walked in it. "I wished we'd took the car home," she said, somewhere near the highway.

"Henry Ray Boxer don't drive no tore-up car," he said.

"Mr. Trout gone want his money," she said, a few hundred yards later.

"It don't matter to me what a white man want."

"What if he come to get it himself?" she said.

"What if he do?"

They had just turned and were coming back into the Heights again. She didn't think he would of said that anywhere else.

THE CAR STAYED IN the alley behind Mr. Trout's store. Rosie saw it there a month later, on the day Miss Mary walked her to town to get her a dress for church. Rosie had picked the first one she touched, it was white with little blue sashes all over, from a shop in Bloodtown.

On the way back Miss Mary bought her a Coca-Cola. She would not let the girl thank her. "Hush, now," she said, "you make Miss Mary feel ashamed."

They walked back through town, drinking Cokes and looking in the windows of the stores, and suddenly they were in the alley behind Mr. Trout's store. Rosie recognized the car and realized where she was. It was sitting right where Henry Ray had left it, still tore up from the lumber truck. It looked just like it had, except it was dirty.

She stopped in her tracks, afraid Mr. Trout would come out and find her. Miss Mary walked ahead, through the alley. The girl caught up. She didn't think Miss Mary had noticed her stop.

At the end of the alley, though, without ever looking back, Miss Mary said, "That's Henry Ray's car, ain't it?"

"Yes, ma'am," she said. Henry Ray had warned her not to tell, but she never thought of lying to Miss Mary.

"That boy remindful of his father," she said.

Rosie didn't reply, but when she sipped at the Coke-Cola again, it had lost its taste. They walked past the officer academy and beyond. Rosie wondered if Miss Mary knew Henry Ray had rode her out of town in the car. If she knew what they had done. She began to feel ashamed herself.

"What I heard," Miss Mary said, "was Henry Ray had Paris Trout yellin' in the street, shaming himself in front of white people."

"Yes, ma'am."

Miss Mary closed her eyes as she walked. "He told you not to tell," she said.

"Yes, ma'am."

Miss Mary stopped under a shade tree and sat down. The girl sat down with her. For a long time Miss Mary seemed to forget Rosie was there. "The problem with Henry Ray is partly in his blood," she said finally, "and partly that he believe he got to be more than he is."

The girl did not understand and was not even sure the woman was speaking to her at all.

"They's some people walk around all the time taller than they is," Miss Mary said. "They fool you and me, and sometime they fooled themself, and then one day a thing can happen and they try and catch up all at once to what they pretend to be. They go off blind to the world. . . ." She closed her eyes and grabbed at things that wasn't there.

"Henry Ray don't know how to look at nobody else and understand them," she said, "because he don't know what he look like himself."

Rosie did not interrupt—it seemed to her that Miss Mary was thinking something out—but if Henry Ray didn't know what he looked like, she didn't know who did. He spent more time in front of mirrors than anybody alive.

Miss Mary took it a different direction. "Paris Trout is a weak man," she said.

"Mr. Trout?"

"Inside," she said, and tapped herself on the chest. "Inside, he's as weak as Henry Ray."

"He scart me," the girl said.

Miss Mary nodded and looked over at her in a slow, tired way. "That's your common sense talkin'," she said. "That man scare anybody got common sense."

Miss Mary closed her eyes and rested against the trunk of the tree. She did not seem afraid of Mr. Trout or anything else.

"You stronger than Mr. Trout," the girl said after a while.

The woman smiled without opening her eyes. "Yes I am," she said.

"You ain't scart of him."

"Oh, yes," she said, "I am that too."

Time passed, and the woman opened her eyes. She put her hands underneath her bottom and began to push herself up off the ground. The girl did not want to leave yet.

"I'll tell you what I'm scart of if you want," she said.

Miss Mary settled back into the tree, but she was awake now, and in some way she was pleased. "I brung you into my house," she said, "and now you allow me into yours."

Rosie said, "I'm scart my momma will come get me back."

"You don't have them dreams with me, do you?"

"No, ma'am."

The woman bit the corner of her lip. "I tell you what," she said, "whenever you get scart, you come to me."

"You keep me away from my momma?"

"I don't know," she said, "but I will be there with you when she come."

TWO WEEKS LATER ROSIE Sayers was sitting on the porch in her new dress when she saw the car coming up Spine Road. She'd worn the dress every day since Miss Mary bought it for her. It had rained that morning, and the car threw a steady curtain of water and mud into the air as it came.

Some of the mud landed on the car itself and blistered there in the sun. The windows were open—it had turned steamy that afternoon—and she could see Mr. Trout behind the wheel. He had pulled his hat down over most of his face, but she recognized him. From the store and from somewhere else.

Thomas was sitting on the porch too, in the chair, with his feet crossed on the railing. Thomas was sweeter than Henry Ray, but he was lazy.

The children, Jane Ray and Linda, were playing inside. Rosie Sayers stood still and watched the car come.

"Who would that be now?" Thomas said.

"Mr. Trout," she said. "Send the children after Miss Mary." They minded Thomas and wouldn't listen to her. She wouldn't hit them.

Thomas sat up straight without taking his feet off the rail. "Who he comin' to see?" he said.

"Us," she said.

He called into the house for Linda. "Go fetch your momma," he said, but she never answered.

There was another man in the car with Mr. Trout, and they looked at each other and spoke before they got out.

"Look out, Jesus," Thomas said.

"Who is that with him?"

"Mr. Buster Devonne," he said. "Used to be a police, but he treated folks too mean, had to let him go."

The men got out of the car. Mr. Trout was wearing rimless glasses and had pulled his hat down almost to cover them. The other one, Buster Devonne, was bigger than anyone the girl knew except Miss Mary. She saw he was bothered.

The men walked up the steps to the porch without a word. Rosie stood still, and they passed her by like she wasn't at home. Thomas did not get up or move. Mr. Trout found a place directly in back of him and waited. Buster Devonne stood to one side.

Thomas began to talk. He said, "The little money I owe you, sir, I pay it on the tenth. Just to the agreement we made." His voice was quicker than she remembered it.

"I ain't here about no twenty dollars," Mr. Trout said. "Your family bought a car off me, ain't paid me a cent. I come out here to find out what you mean to do about it."

Thomas shook his head. "I don't mean to do nothing, sir," he said. "It ain't my business, it's my brother's."

"Where is he?"

"He over to work at the state. Ain't that right, Rosie?"

She stood frozen. The man named Buster Devonne watched her close.

"Buster Devonne's got a blank here for you to sign," Mr. Trout said to Thomas.

Buster Devonne pulled a piece of folded white paper out of his back pocket and handed it to Mr. Trout, who reached over Thomas's shoulder and dropped it into his lap.

"I ain't gone to sign no blank," Thomas said.

He opened the paper and began to read it. Mr. Trout grabbed him then, by the collar, and lifted him out of his seat. Rosie heard a little cry come out of herself, and she saw Buster Devonne's hand go into his jacket pocket.

Mr. Trout went to his pocket too. He was holding Thomas with one hand, shaking him now, and the other hand came out sparkling in the sun.

Rosie heard herself again. "Lord have mercy," she said, "He's got brass knucks." She had seen the uses of brass knucks back in the Bottoms, they were as bad as a knife.

And then Miss Mary was there, on the first step to the porch, looking up at Mr. Trout. "There's no call to hurt nobody here," she said.

"Lord a mercy," Rosie said again, and her voice distracted Mr. Trout. He stared at her a minute, and then she saw that screaming look in his eyes.

"What the hell you got to do with it?" he said suddenly. He let go of Thomas and came after her, and she ran into the house. She heard him behind her, tearing up the furniture. The shades were drawn over the windows in the first room, and coming in out of the sunlight, she was suddenly blind.

She cried out for Miss Mary.

Mr. Trout stumbled behind her, he broke a piece of glass. She heard him curse as she passed into the second room. It was lighter in there, and she could see the details of the walls and floor, she could see her own feet. It seemed to her that things had slowed down.

And then she heard him behind her again. It surprised her in some way that he was still there. "What the goddamn hell does it got to do with you?" he said again. And she saw his face without turning to see it, and then his arm had gone around her throat, and he was shaking her from behind.

She reached in back of herself to slap him away, and then there was a cracking noise on the side of her head, and he let her go. And in that moment things went dark and she felt the beginnings of a nightmare.

And she bit her hand, to make it stop, and then she heard another noise, louder and farther away, and something hit her in the side and spun her down. Then she smelled the smoke in the air and knew that she'd been shot.

"Miss Mary . . ."

She heard the woman somewhere behind. "Coming," she said, "I'm coming now." And then there was another shot and then another.

She heard the breath go out of Miss Mary, and then she heard the words again. "I'm coming now."

Rosie lay on the floor and looked up, and Miss Mary walked past without seeing her. She was bleeding from her shoulder and her back. "Where you goin'?" the child asked.

Miss Mary stood still to speak. "I got to go into the stove room," she said. "I got to lie on the table."

Miss Mary walked slowly through the second room and into the

40

third. She dropped to her knees just before she reached the last room of the house, the kitchen.

Rosie watched her from the floor, feeling sick and dizzy. When the dizziness passed, she pulled herself up and walked into the kitchen too. She was wrong in the side, she couldn't say exactly how. She heard the men talking, she could not make out the words. The smell of gunpowder was thicker when she stood than it had been on the floor, and the voices seemed to come out of it.

She touched the wall for her balance and got into the kitchen. Miss Mary was on her hands and knees. The child wanted to help her, but she turned sick again and sat down on the trunk against the wall.

Miss Mary climbed off the floor then and laid herself across the table. For a moment it was still, and then Mr. Trout appeared in the doorway, holding his gun. He took a step in, raising his arm, and Rosie raised her eyes to meet it. The first shot hit her in the arm, a little above the elbow. The second shot took her breath.

"Lord have mercy," she said to Miss Mary, "the man has shot me in the stomach."

Miss Mary twisted up off the table at that and turned to stare at Paris Trout. He shot her in the breast. She pushed off the table.

"Come on, child," she said, and held out her hand.

Rosie Sayers took the hand and got to her feet, and she and Miss Mary walked together out the back door into the yard. They sat together on the back steps and then lay together on the ground. They heard the car engine race as Buster Devonne and Mr. Trout left.

Rosie closed her eyes. She opened them once and saw the children, Jane Ray and Linda, standing over her as still as pictures. Thomas Boxer had left to call the police.

She called out to Miss Mary.

"I'm right here next to you," Miss Mary said.

"It's so cold," she said.

"You ain't afraid, child, you been saved."

"Yes I am."

"You been saved," Miss Mary said. "And I am here with you now to wait for Jesus."

"I'm so cold," the child said.

She said, "Jesus will be here soon, cover you with a blanket."

SEAGRAVES
PART TWO

The news that Paris Trout had shot two colored females in Indian Heights came to Harry Seagraves from the police chief, Hubert Norland. Seagraves kept Chief Norland on a small retainer for just that sort of information.

The call came at supper. The maid brought the telephone to the table, but when Seagraves heard the chief's voice, he excused himself and used the phone in his study. He did not like to discuss matters of blood or violence in front of his wife, who had an interest in other people's troubles which he tried not to feed.

"Mr. Seagraves," the chief said, "I'm over to Cornell Clinic, and there's a couple of negras here got shot up by Paris Trout."

Harry Seagraves had taken the call standing up. Now he sat down. The police chief did not add to what he'd said or explain it. Seagraves liked to find things out in his own order.

"Who are they?" he said.

"Females," said the chief.

Seagraves tried to picture it, Paris Trout with colored women, but it would not come. He didn't think Paris Trout had an appetite for women, colored or white. He was one of those people who did not like to be touched.

"One of them's named Mary McNutt," the chief said, reading now from the report. "Thirty-eight years old Negress, employed by the Markham family as a maid . . . shot three, four times. The other would be Rosie Sayers, and that one ain't going to live."

Harry Seagraves sat still and tried to think of a way of removing himself from this before it began. His law firm, Seagraves, DuBois, Clatterfield & Spudd, represented most of the old and the rich families in Cotton Point, the families that lived in the houses on Draft Street, families like his own. He was part of their safety. Paris Trout was not of that group socially—he had no social affiliations—but he owned property and lumber interests and the store and was known to have money. His sister was a court clerk. His mother, until her stroke, had run the family store and been the most visible and outspoken woman in Cotton Point.

Seagraves had represented him before, in half a dozen civil suits, and did not see how he could turn him away now. The obligation was not so much to Trout as to the families on Draft Street, who counted his protection as a constant.

"The one that ain't going to live isn't but a child," the chief said.

"How old?"

"It ain't written down," the chief said, "but she could be thirteen, fourteen years old."

"You have the name?" He opened the drawer of his desk and found a piece of paper. He dipped his desk pen in the inkwell. The chief spelled out Sayers. It was not a name Seagraves had heard before.

"Is she native?"

"Not to me," the chief said. "They ain't related, but the girl lived with the woman. Sometime they take each other in like that."

"What was Paris Trout doing in Indian Heights?" Seagraves said.

"Collecting for a car, he says."

Without realizing he was doing it, Harry Seagraves drew a cross on the paper, above Rosie Sayers's name. When he saw what it was, he changed it to a dollar sign. "Paris Trout doesn't make loans to women," he said.

"Well, that's what he told me," the chief said. "Him and Buster Devonne was out there to collect for a Chevrolet."

"Buster Devonne was there?"

"Yessir," the chief said. "He done some of it too. I don't know how much. Their story is that the negras had guns."

The line was quiet while Harry Seagraves thought. Buster Devonne had been a policeman, and he'd hurt a number of colored people

46

without reason. "Are you sure the girl's going to die?" he said finally.

"That's what Doc Braver said."

The line was quiet again, and it was the chief who finally spoke. "Mr. Seagraves?" he said. "What do you want me to do about this?"

"Have you talked to Ward Townes?"

"No sir, I called you first thing after I'd finished with Mr. Trout."

"And he told you he'd shot the girl."

"Yessir, him and Buster Devonne."

Seagraves leaned back in his chair and stared at the ceiling, picturing the conversation. "Did you take it down?"

"No sir, it was on the phone. I bring them in to my girl to take it down."

Paris Trout would refuse to see it, that it was wrong to shoot a girl and a woman. There was a contract he'd made with himself a long time ago that overrode the law, and being the only interested party, he lived by it. He was principled in the truest way. His right and wrong were completely private.

Harry Seagraves had been around the law long enough to hold a certain affection for those who did not respect it, but his affection, as a rule, was in proportion to the distance they kept from his practice.

A man like Paris Trout could rub his right and wrong up against the written law for ten minutes and occupy half a year of Harry Seagraves's time straightening it out. And a man as important as Paris Trout, it was difficult to pass the case to a junior partner. Draft Street would watch what happened to him and fear for itself.

"Mr. Seagraves?" The chief sounded worried now.

"Yessir," Seagraves said. "I appreciate your courtesy, Chief. My advice to you now would be to call Ward Townes and inform him of the situation. He may want to wait, see if the girl dies. Sometimes young folks are resilient beyond medical expectations, and if that is the case with Miss Sayers, then we may be interrupting supper for no cause."

"I hate to bothered you at supper," he said, "but I thought you'd want a head start on this."

"It's no bother. . . . Listen, you come by soon and sit at the table with us. Lucy was asking on you and your family just recently."

"Thank you, sir. Y'all have to come over to see us too."

The line went quiet again, both of them out of manners. "There's one other thing," Seagraves said.

"Yessir?"

"As long as it's not taken down anywhere, I'd just as soon Paris never talked to you at all. That way me and Mr. Townes start fresh and fair." Seagraves waited while the police chief thought it over. Then he said, "Of course, if that compromises you in some way . . ."

"No sir, that'd be all right."

"Good."

"Yessir, I can do that. . . ."

"Is there something else?"

"If the girl dies," the chief said, "I'd likely have to come get Mr. Trout." Seagraves heard the worry in his voice.

"You just give me a call at the office, I'll bring him to you."

"Thank you, Mr. Seagraves. And I'd likely have to come for Buster Devonne too."

"That would be up to you," Seagraves said, "Mr. Devonne is no concern of mine." And then he hung up. Paris Trout was principled, in his way, but Buster Devonne was a dog off his leash.

The door to the study opened a few inches and his wife looked in. "Harry?" she said. He looked up without answering. He did not like her in this room, her or anyone else.

"Is something wrong?" she said.

He rubbed the front of his face with his hands, feeling tired. "I'll be out directly," he said. She did not move, though. She wanted him to apologize for leaving supper. He said, "I've got to make a call."

"Now?"

He nodded and picked up the telephone, waiting for her to close the door. She stood where she was. "What is it?" she said.

"Paris Trout gone took a damn gun and shot two colored women."

Her pretty white face turned soft, opening to the news. "Did they work for anybody we know?" she said.

"Charley Markham's maid is one of them," he said, "but that doesn't make it our business."

Her face, suddenly hurt, stayed in the opening a minute longer and then disappeared. The room took a peaceful feeling the minute she was gone.

He decided to visit Trout instead of calling. It wasn't that the man was less remote in person—he was one of the few clients Harry Seagraves had who were actually easier to talk to on the telephone—but that the news of what he had done was disquieting in a way that made him want to get out of his own house.

Lucy watched him come into the dining room and saw he was carrying the keys to the car. She was angry and did not speak. He saw she had put her glasses on, and they were fogged from the steam of the boiled potatoes on her plate.

PARIS TROUT LIVED IN a hundred-year-old white house at the corner of Draft Street and Samuel. There were eight bedrooms and four baths, servants' quarters, long hallways, and high ceilings. Seagraves had been told he kept the whole house dark.

His wife answered the doorbell. She did not seem to recognize him and stood in the door waiting for him to explain what he wanted. "Mrs. Trout?" he said. "I am Harry Seagraves."

Her look did not change. "I know you, Mr. Seagraves," she said. "What may I do for you this evening?"

He had seen more of Hanna Trout before she married than since. She had grown up in Cotton Point, taught third and fourth grades at Fuller Laboratory School, and then worked herself into a position with the state department of schools in Atlanta.

She had been plainspoken all her life, a trait which, in spite of her good looks, had scared off all the men who noticed her until Paris Trout. The town psychologists said that he'd married her to replace his mother, who had not spoken a word since her stroke.

Hanna was forty-six years old and had been married two years.

"I was wondering if I might see Paris," he said.

She stood where she was, looking into his eyes. He hadn't told her. "It's a matter of some urgency," he said, "or I would not inconvenience you like this at home."

She held herself a moment longer at the door and then stepped to one side. "Come in," she said. "I'll tell him you're here."

Seagraves stood in the hallway, and Hanna Trout went upstairs. He noticed the curve of her bottom as she climbed the steps, the movement pulled her dress against her skin first on one side, then the other. From behind she looked younger than his own wife.

The hallway itself was bare. The paint over the staircase was spotted and beginning to peel. The windows were dirty. The house felt empty, as if no one lived there, and hadn't for a long time.

In a few moments Hanna Trout was back on the stairs. She held herself straight coming down, her fingers barely touching the banister. There was a calmness about her that struck Seagraves as practiced. "Paris will be down when he dresses," she said.

Seagraves looked at his watch; it was seven-thirty.

He followed her into the living room and sat on a davenport with frayed cushions. The wallpaper was a pattern of green, blistered here and there, and torn. There were spider webs in the corners of the ceiling. Hanna Trout took a seat in a straight-back chair across the room and crossed her legs. He thought of his own wife and her legs—no better than the ones in front of him now—and the house she kept. Lucy would reburn Georgia before she let someone see her house like this.

There was a noise on the stairs, slow and heavy, and then Paris Trout came through the threshold of the door in his robe and slippers. His hair was slicked straight back and emphasized the angles of his head. He nodded at Seagraves and then looked at his wife in an unfriendly way.

Seagraves watched her change under that look. "Would you like some coffee?" she said.

Trout did not answer. "You read my mind," Seagraves said, and she stood up, walking within a foot of her husband on the way to the kitchen. He did not look at her again.

"Hubert Norland called me a little bit ago," Seagraves said when she was gone.

Trout sat down in the chair his wife had left. His arms were long and thin, and his pale hands spilled over the ends of the armrests and hung in the air. "Hubert Norland knows me," he said. "I answered him what he asked, and that's all there is to it."

Seagraves felt tired. "You told him you shot two colored people," he said. "That doesn't mean it ends."

Trout shrugged, his hands kept still. "What they gone do, arrest me for collecting legal debts? I told that boy when he took the car, I get my money. You ask any people I lent to, I told them all the same thing."

Seagraves held up his hand for Trout to stop. "You told too many people too much already today," he said.

Trout stared at him, deciding something. "You worried about this, ain't you?"

"There wasn't anybody owed you money that was shot this afternoon," Seagraves said.

"The same family."

Seagraves shook his head. "The one that's going to die," he said, "her name's different, and she isn't but thirteen, fourteen years old."

Paris Trout squinted, looking at things from a new angle. "I recognized that girl from before," he said. "She was with Henry Ray Boxer on the day he tore up the car."

Seagraves shook his head. "Her name's Sayers," he said.

"Ain't a jury in the state that could expect a white man to keep track of family lines amongst the dark aspect," Trout said. He was sitting up in the chair now, paying attention. Seagraves took it for a positive sign that he had the man's interest.

He said, "There's all kinds of juries, and now days you don't know what they expect." And he saw that Paris Trout had paid attention to that too.

Trout shrugged again, but the problem had settled on him now. He said, "Well, Mr. Seagraves, God's will be done."

Seagraves closed his eyes and let his head fall back into the cushion. "There's more men than you can count gone to prison in this state, leaving things in God's hands," he said.

His eyes were still closed when Hanna Trout came into the living room, carrying a silver tray. He heard her and sat up, smiling, and accepted a cup of coffee. She poured it without returning his smile and then turned to her husband. He ignored her.

When she had gone back to the kitchen, Trout said, "I had a legal debt to collect. I am within my rights to make the collection."

"That was two women in their own house," Seagraves said. "One of them was a child, and if she dies, Ward Townes is legally bound to come after the person that shot her."

Trout considered Ward Townes. "He got to live here just like anybody else," he said finally.

Seagraves did not answer that, he had been weighing the same thought. You could never be sure what Ward Townes would do. He had gone to the war, for instance, the only lawyer in Cotton Point except Seagraves himself who had. Seagraves knew the prosecutor could have got an exemption like anybody else with money. He knew he had forgiven legal fees when he was in private practice.

On the other hand, Seagraves had seen the deals he cut to get what he wanted.

Seagraves thought the source of the contradiction was that Ward Townes did not come from the substantial side of the Townes family and could not be depended on to side with anybody. There had been a split in the family a long time before anybody alive now could remember, and one branch established the manufacture of bricks in central Georgia and got rich, and the other side laid the bricks and waited their turn.

The substantial Towneses lived on Draft Street with Seagraves. Ward Townes's side of the family had settled in town later, on Park Street with the car dealers and dentists.

"I wouldn't count on anything from Ward Townes," he said finally. "There's some people you can't predict."

"He's got to live here," Trout said again.

"I do not want to leave your house tonight," Seagraves said, "without an agreement between us on the serious nature of the events that have occurred. Ward Townes can't be taken for granted."

"What would he go and make trouble for himself for?"

"Principle," Seagraves said. "He might do it on principle."

"The principle in this is on my side," Trout said. "You're a businessman, I ain't got to explain it to you."

Hanna Trout came back into the room again, and this time she sat down. "I would like to know what this is about," she said. Seagraves waited for Trout to answer, but he gave no sign that he'd even noticed her.

When he spoke again, it was to Seagraves. "Besides, Buster Devonne was there too. He did as much as me, and that makes two witnesses on our side."

"I think you ought to stay away from Buster Devonne awhile," Seagraves said. "You aren't in this together now, and if that girl dies, you don't want to be in it together then."

"What girl?" Hanna Trout said quietly.

Seagraves turned to her, acknowledging her. She looked clean and strong, he could not imagine her neglecting her house in the way it had been neglected. Seagraves waited for Trout to tell her what had happened, but it was as if she were not in the room.

Trout drew a long breath. "Buster Devonne is in my employment," he said, "and he will say any damn thing I tell him."

"You pay him enough to spend the next five years killing snakes for the state?"

Trout thought it over. "He would if I told him."

Seagraves caught another look at Mrs. Trout. He wished she would go back into the kitchen, it was hard to watch her husband insult her in this way. He wondered what kept her in the chair. He thought again about the condition of the house and was curious if it was connected to her stubbornness.

"People don't go to prison for other people," Seagraves said, returning to Trout. "Things look different to him than they do to you, and they look different sitting in the living room than they will in front of Judge Taylor."

"Things look different ways when they ain't clear," Trout said.

Seagraves put the cup on the table beside the davenport and stood up to leave. Trout stood up with him, and the sudden movement startled his wife. She recovered herself and smoothed her skirt.

"You be at the store tomorrow?" Seagraves said.

"Business as usual," Trout said. "All day."

"I expect you'll hear from Ward Townes in the morning," Seagraves said. "He'll likely send Hubert Norland over to pick you up, to interrogate you on what happened."

Trout considered that.

"If that in fact occurs," Seagraves said, "you have somebody call me, and I'll meet you at the courthouse. I don't want you telling Ward Townes the time of day without me there in the room."

He started for the door and then stopped. "Don't count on Buster Devonne to get you off." he said. "Or Ward Townes, or anybody or anything. The only people you can count on right now are your lawyer and your family, and that is what I came over here tonight to impress on you. We'll begin on the rest tomorrow, when there's more time. . . ." He stole a look at Mrs. Trout and then smiled because she'd caught him.

"I'm sorry to push my way into your house at this hour," he said to her, "and I hope you will forgive the abrupt nature of this business."

Trout looked off in another direction while Seagraves spoke to her, as if he were waiting for him to finish tinkling in the bushes.

"What is the nature of this business?" she said, studying his face.

Seagraves considered her again, noticing her eyes. They were as dark as the coffee she'd brought him. He found himself attracted. He said, "I think perhaps that is something you'd better discuss with your husband, Mrs. Trout." He saw that did not satisfy her.

"If you like, you could come with Paris to my office tomorrow and we'll go over it in detail." He looked at Trout for help, but Trout was still focused a long way off.

"The details are not my interest, Mr. Seagraves," she said, looking right into his face. "My interest right now is what act has brought you to this house tonight. There is a girl involved. What has happened to her?"

"It isn't scandalous," Seagraves said. "I can assure you it isn't that." He shook her hand and then let himself out the front door. Trout had not moved or changed attitude.

Seagraves walked a few steps toward the street and then stopped to light a cigar. He felt relieved to be out of the house. He thought of her bottom as she climbed the stairs and tried to remember the oldest woman he had ever taken to bed. There had been a whore in Atlanta during his first term in the state legislature—she had seemed old to him then, but that was a long time ago, when he didn't know what old was.

It came to him slowly that the oldest woman he had ever had was his wife.

And that was a long time ago too.

IN THE MORNING HARRY Seagraves walked to work. He followed the sidewalks to the college, speaking to everyone he met, and crossed the campus on a diagonal to Davis Street. His office was half a block up, on the second floor of the Dixie Theater Building, and you would never know, looking at the building or the offices inside it, that his was one of the richest and most successful law practices in the state.

He kept it that way intentionally, resisting changes. The people he represented—in the legislature as well as the courts—liked the way things were and worried in an unfocused way that they were somehow losing what they had, mostly to the federal government.

His secretary was a middle-aged woman named Emma Grandy. She looked up as he came through the doorway. "Mr. Townes has called twice," she said.

Seagraves looked at his watch, it was twenty minutes after nine. He had known Townes would call, but he had expected him to take more time to think it through. "Would you call Cornell Clinic for me," he said to her. "Inquire to the condition of one Rosie Sayers."

"Yessir," she said.

He walked into his private office and took off his coat and his shoes. His feet hurt from the walk; he determined to have someone look them over. He couldn't decide between a doctor and a shoe salesman; they didn't bother him at all after he ran.

The office was filled with old furniture and pictures. Lucy as Miss Ether County, 1935. His brother's children as babies. There was a diploma from Georgia Officers Academy on the wall, along with his law degree from the University of Georgia. Class of 1934.

Mrs. Grandy knocked on the door and looked in. She had a child's face and took everything he said seriously. She understood the law as well as most of his partners but kept it to herself.

"I called the clinic," she said. "Rosie Sayers is quite grave. . . ."

Seagraves nodded. "Did you talk to Dr. Braver himself?"

"No sir, Dr. Braver was busy. I talked to his girl."

"If you get a moment later," he said, "you might try to get the doctor on the phone for me. I'd like to speak to him myself."

"The girl said he was in surgery," she said, "some little boy that cut himself this morning on the rocks at the church—"

"Whenever he's finished," Seagraves said. "It's no hurry."

She closed the door, and Seagraves picked up his telephone. Ward Townes answered the other end himself. "County prosecutor's office," he said, "good morning."

Seagraves said, "Mr. Prosecutor? This is Harry Seagraves."

"Thank you for getting back to me," he said. "There was a problem yesterday afternoon down to Indian Heights. . . ."

"I heard that," Seagraves said.

"I thought you might. You still represent the Trout family?"

"As far as I know."

"Then let me suggest that you bring your client by my office this afternoon, save us getting Chief Norland upset, having to pick him up."

"Charges been pressed?"

"Not yet," Townes said. "But people been shot."

"We might could settle this between the parties, save everybody some aggravation."

"I think it's too late," Townes said.

"Does this mean you aren't in a settling mood today, Mr. Prosecutor? We could come in some other time."

"That girl he shot in the stomach, she's fourteen years old," he said.

There was no anger in the words, it sounded more like an argument you might have with yourself, trying to decide what to do.

"That *somebody* shot," Seagraves said. "There was more than one gun. Buster Devonne had a gun, maybe some of them had guns too."

"Buster Devonne's already told me who did the shooting," Townes said. "He came in yesterday afternoon after it happened."

"Buster Devonne is a known liar."

There was a pause, Townes considering Buster Devonne. "He said Paris shot the girl. Followed her into the kitchen to finish it, and then both of them lit out the back like thieves."

"You believe him?"

"You don't?" Townes said.

Seagraves measured his answer. "I believe Paris Trout's been a businessman in Ether County a long time," he said. "His sister's a court clerk. People know him, they traded with him. Not just whites. He's got loans out all over the county. Indian Heights, some in the Bottoms too, and there isn't anybody either color ever heard of this Sayers girl or her people."

"Obscurity isn't grounds to shoot children in the state of Georgia," Townes said, and there was something in his voice now. "The law doesn't say anything about the social station of the deceased."

Seagraves saw the conversation had somehow turned personal and moved it a different direction. He said, "Buster Devonne, he cracked so many burrheads they had to take him off the police. The first man in the history of Cotton Point, Georgia, they took off the police for assaulting Negroes. He went from that to cotton stealing, you brought him in this office yourself for that.

"He got off on cotton stealing, and the next thing you know, he's got a death grudge against a man, all he did was catch Buster stealing his cotton. Bragging all over town he's going to do this and that to some dirt farmer—hell, I think he was a Methodist—and then sneaks out one night and sets his chicken coop on fire.

"You couldn't find a jury in Ether County that is going to believe the testimony of a man that settles his grudges by setting chickens on fire—not over Paris Trout."

Townes said, "The man was there. It's what he said. The clinic reports the girl made the night, but she won't make another. The nurse said isn't a thing left to do for her but dig a hole."

"That isn't up to the nurse, to say that she's gone."

"That's so," Townes said, "but she's shot, four, five times, and I want to see Paris Trout about that at one o'clock in my office this afternoon. If he isn't here, I'll send Chief Norland to get him."

"No need for that," Seagraves said. "I think we'd both be served to keep this as uncomplicated as possible."

"Thank you, Mr. Seagraves, and we'll see you at one."

Seagraves put the phone back in its cradle, surprised at Ward Townes's sudden anger—which wasn't noticeable unless you knew him—and opened one of the lower drawers in his desk. He put his feet in the drawer, resting them on somebody's papers. He didn't look to see whose. He thought of Buster Devonne on the witness stand testifying against Paris Trout. Confused and undignified and scared.

He thought of Buster Devonne, and then he thought of the witnesses from Indian Heights. Paris Trout would be sitting beside him all the time in a blue suit, where the jury could compare him to his accusers. He might not need to say a word.

Still, something in it tugged at him. He called Mrs. Grandy in the outside office. "Did you locate Dr. Braver yet?"

"No sir, they said he's having a time with that boy."

"Keep trying him for me," he said. "Meantime, get me Paris Trout. He'll be at the store."

"Yessir," she said. A minute later she knocked and put her head inside. "There's no answer at the store," she said.

"Did you try the house?"

"Yessir, I got his wife, but she said Mr. Trout wasn't there." Harry Seagraves took his feet out of the drawer and slipped them into his shoes. "You want me to keep trying?" she said.

"No," he said. "I'll go over there myself. I need the exercise."

She said, "What if Dr. Braver calls?"

He said, "Tell him I'll be over to see him directly."

SEAGRAVES FOUND PARIS TROUT in the back office of his store. The front entrance was still locked—it was after ten o'clock—so Seagraves had walked around the block to the alley and found the door there open.

Trout was holding his head in his hands when Seagraves caught him, gray hair spilling out between his fingers, his elbows resting on the table. He was focused on a bill of sale in front of him. There was a bottle of mineral water next to the paper and a strong body odor in the air.

Seagraves said, "Mr. Trout?"

Trout looked up slowly. His eyes were blood red, and the front of his shirt was wrinkled, as if he'd slept in it. "It's here in black-and-white," he said.

A light bulb hung from the ceiling, a little behind the table, and when Trout took his finger off the bill of sale, the shadow faded and grew until it covered most of the document.

"Right here," Trout said. "Account payable, Henry Ray Boxer. One thousand and twenty-seven dollars for a 1949 Chevrolet. Neither God nor man can say that debt wasn't legal. I have the proof." He pushed the paper at Seagraves, Seagraves did not move. "Look for yourself."

The bill of sale was written in a tiny, neat handwriting, the signatures were scrawled and unreadable. Seagraves did not try to read it. "Ward Townes called, like we thought," he said quietly. "He wants to see us this afternoon at one o'clock."

"Does he care to see the bill of sale?"

Seagraves said, "We can bring the bill of sale."

"It's black-and-white," Trout said again. "That car was sold as legal as the seal of Georgia." His eyes opened wider, a frightening color. Seagraves realized he had no idea whatsoever of the transformations going on in his head.

"It would be a good idea you went home and changed shirts," he said. "Shaved, cleaned yourself up."

Trout touched the bill of sale again. "He don't need me," he said. "He's got everything he needs to settle this right here."

"No," Seagraves said, "we got to see him ourselves."

Trout suddenly stood up and slammed his fist into the middle of the table. Dust stirred, it settled. "He don't believe these are the real signatures?"

Seagraves was suddenly aware of the size of Paris Trout and the size of the room, and he wished he'd used the telephone. More than that, he wished Paris Trout was somebody else's client. This had a feeling he didn't like, that he was drawn into something further than he ought to be.

"Sit down, Paris," he said, and was surprised when Trout sat down. He began to pace. Trout followed him with his eyes, back and forth. "We got a problem here between us and the prosecutor," he said. "It isn't black-and-white, at least you better hope not. It doesn't matter what's in any bill of sale, it concerns people that have been shot."

Trout stole a quick look at the paper. "It isn't in the goddamn bill of sale," Seagraves said. He leaned across the desk, smelling dried sweat, a faint odor of vomit. "It's in Cornell Clinic. There's a child in Cornell Clinic named Sayers, and she's been shot four times and is all but done living. That's all Ward Townes wants to talk to you about now, and you would be smart to prepare yourself, not to make this worse than it is."

Trout blinked his red eyes and waited. Seagraves found himself suddenly calm. "Listen, now," he said. "I want you to take yourself home, bathe, and put on something it don't look like you've been wrestling pigs. And then, at one o'clock on the dot, you be at the prosecutor's office, looking like somebody, and talk to the man about that girl. Not that you shot her—don't put yourself in as deep as you did with Hubert Nordland—but talk about the girl, acknowledge her."

Trout patted the paper on the desk. "This is the proof," he said.

"Don't use that word this afternoon," Seagraves said. "Don't try to tell Ward Townes what proof is." He thought for a moment and put it a different way. "I'll be with you," he said. "I can stop you from saying the wrong thing, but I can't make up the right words and whisper them in your ear. I believe this thing is . . . an *affront* to Ward Townes. Something in it is personal, like you had insulted him. Treat it like that, like he was offended."

Trout sat still. "How much is this gone cost me?" he said finally.

"I don't know," Seagraves said. "Some of it's up to Ward Townes, some of it's up to you."

Trout took a mechanical pencil out of his shirt pocket and handed it to Seagraves. "I want you to write it down," he said.

"Christ Almighty, Paris . . ."

The pencil was green and translucent, he could see little specks floating around inside. The eraser was worn smooth at the corners, and the word SCRIPTO was worn half off the side. It was a nineteen-cent pencil, and Trout had kept it probably five years.

"The price to represent my legal case. I want you to put it right here on a piece of paper, so we both know where it is."

Seagraves put the pencil on the table, beside the mineral water. He noticed spit floating on top. "The price depends on the time," he said, "you know that as well as anybody." It was part of the enigma of Paris

60

Trout that he had graduated from law school himself, someplace up in North Carolina, but never practiced law.

Trout shook his head. "I want one price," he said.

"I don't discuss price," Seagraves said. "I got a girl that prepares the billings, but she can't tell you a thing until we determine what that child in Cornell Clinic's going to do and what Ward Townes intends to do about it."

"I want a number wrote down, right now at the start," Trout said. "That's how I do business." He was smiling now, as if he had Seagraves trapped. Trout's teeth were yellow and gapped, and against his will, Seagraves imagined the way it would have looked when he shot the girl.

"All right," he said, "you tell me what you did, and I'll tell you how much it costs."

Seagraves took the chair in the corner and moved it to the table. He did not want to be in the room with Trout and what he had done—he had wanted it softened first, to read it, have one of his clerks take the statement—but there was something in Trout that pushed things farther than they were intended to go.

Trout sat still. His face was changed, but it held the smile. "What did you want to know?" he said.

"Everything you did in that girl's house."

Trout rubbed his ears and pushed the hair back off his face. "The family owed me a debt," he said. "A legal debt . . ."

Seagraves did not try to guide him now. He waited to see where the story would go on its own.

"It was eight hundret dollars, I sold him that Chevrolet, and I told him I get my money. It was eight hundret for the car, another two hundret and twenty-seven for the insurance. I always tell them I get my money. You can ask any coloreds in Cotton Point, they'll tell you the same thing."

Seagraves stared at Trout and waited.

"I warned that boy when he brought the car back," he said. "He busted it up, wanted me to forgive the debt." Trout shook his head. "I don't forgive debts," he said. "I pay my obligations, and I am paid in return."

Seagraves sat still.

"And I went out there, to Indian Heights where this family is, to collect my money."

Seagraves stopped him. "You thought they had eight hundred dollars in the cookie jar?"

"I never said so. I went out to get them to sign me a note to have it took from their pay. That's all that was intended, to get my note signed."

"You brought Buster Devonne," Seagraves said.

"That debt was legal. That's all anybody's got to do, lookit the bill of sale. I am a businessman, I don't make nothing up." Trout moved in his chair, looking uncomfortable. "I don't have a cruel heart," he said.

Seagraves smiled at the phrase.

"We drove out to the house," Trout said. "This boy Thomas Boxer was on the porch. Buster Devonne had the note, and Thomas Boxer wouldn't sign it. He had his feet on the rail. I shook him by the collar. There was people behind their curtains now, and you forgive one debt, ain't none of them going to pay you ever.

"Then the boy rose up like nobody's business, made to grab me, and I went to sit him back down. The girl got in the midst of it—she put herself in the midst—and then the woman. The ruckus moved into the house, where the girl and the woman was shot. The boy run off, and I wouldn't want his conscience to live with."

Seagraves said, "Who shot the girl and the woman? Was it Buster Devonne or was it you?"

"Don't know," Trout said. "It was cloudy in the house, and it's still cloudy when I think about it."

"Cloudy?"

"Smoky," he said.

"You told Hurbert Norland they had guns?"

Trout thought for a moment and then said, "Yessir."

Seagraves heard the lie in that. "You got your gun?"

Trout opened the drawer to the table and came out with an ivory-handled Colt automatic. He laid it on the table between them, with the barrel pointed at the bottle of mineral water. "That's the one I carry," he said. "You can take it if you need, I got spares here in the store."

With the gun on the desk, Seagraves imagined the scene again, how it might have looked to the girl. "Did you clean it when you got back?" He was going slower now, thinking better.

Trout nodded and said, "That gun cost two hundret and forty dollars, you damn right I cleaned it."

"Did you look at the clip, see how many rounds you'd fired?" Seagraves studied the gun, there was something out of the ordinary. "What is that, a thirty-eight?"

Trout smiled. "No sir," he said, and he picked it up in his open hand, as if he were weighing it. "This is a forty-five. A lot of people make the same mistake; it don't look like what it is."

"How many times was it fired?"

Trout shrugged. "Didn't count," he said.

"You removed the clip when you cleaned it."

"I loaded it back up," he said. "I didn't count the rounds."

"What did Buster have?" Seagraves said. "Did he have a forty-five too?"

Trout shook his head. "He got a thirty-eight. The same one from when he was on the police. Buster gets a gun he likes and sticks with it."

Trout put the automatic back on the table and Seagraves picked it up. He thought of the girl in Cornell Clinic and the accidental nature of her associations. What would she make of a rich white man, holding the gun that shot her? He wondered suddenly if she could read. If somebody had somehow shown her the story in the newspaper beforehand—the story that she'd been shot—would she have known what it was?

"And there were guns in the house," Seagraves said.

Trout did not answer, did not seem to understand what Seagraves meant.

"Did you see guns? You said they had guns too."

"I might," he said.

"Did anybody touch them?"

It went slow, with Trout taking his time to consider the answers. "I would say so, yes, sir."

"This girl might of touched a gun?"

"Might of."

"And the woman might of touched a gun?"

Trout shrugged. "It got smoky," he said. "You couldn't tell who was shooting. . . ."

Seagraves heard the false sound in that, and Ward Townes would hear it too. What he would do about it Seagraves didn't know. On the whole, Townes was sweet-dispositioned—some days you couldn't tell he was even a prosecutor—but there was something in him that wasn't sweet too, and Seagraves saw no reason to bring it out.

He stood up, and Trout stood up with him, making the room crowded. "If a man were to come in here today," Seagraves said, in an offhanded way, "and told you this or that was the way to run your business, would you listen?"

"What man?" Trout said.

"I don't care, President Eisenhower. Would you listen?"

"Not to that sonofabitch."

"Then Marvin Griffin. Would you listen to Governor Griffin?"

"To run my business?"

"That's right."

"Marvin Griffin ain't been in a business like this."

"What if he was? What if Mr. Griffin had a business like yours up in Atlanta, and he came in here tomorrow and said this or that was the way things ought to be done."

Trout took it to heart. "I would tell him to get the hell out," he said.

"Hold that thought," Seagraves said. "Hold that one thought when you see Ward Townes this afternoon. That you're coming into his store."

Trout started to answer, but then he stopped. Seagraves said, "Leave your bill of sale here. Let him ask for what he wants to see." Seagraves looked at the paper on the table. The gun was there too. "All except that," he said. "Let me have the weapon, he'll need that, and I'd just as soon as it wasn't on your person when it changed hands."

Trout picked up the gun and handed it to Seagraves. Seagraves put it in the pocket of his coat. "I'll want that back," Trout said. "You tell Mr. Townes I want my property returned."

"It's his store," Seagraves said.

"It's my property."

"Not now," Seagraves said. "There is nothing connected to you and that girl that's yours, and there is nothing you want to claim."

"I ain't ashamed," Trout said.

Seagraves was on the way out but those words stopped him, and for a moment he fought an urge to quit Trout on the spot. "I know you aren't," he said, "but I want you to try."

"You ain't told me what it's going to cost," Trout said.

"You haven't told me what you did."

SEAGRAVES LEFT THE STORE the way he had come in, walked up the alley to the street, and turned left. A dozen people spoke to him in the two blocks to Cornell Clinic, most of them he recognized from Homewood Community, where the state hospital was. During his tenure in the state legislature Seagraves had gotten city water for Homewood, and controlled every Democratic vote there since. And there weren't any Republicans, not even in the asylum.

People in Homewood named their children after Harry Seagraves, some of them even believed he lived there.

He took his time, speaking to everyone who spoke to him, commenting on the weather a dozen times between Trout's alley and the glass door to Thomas Cornell Clinic. There had been no winter that year, and people wanted him to reassure them the seasons weren't gone forever.

He stepped through the doors of the clinic, smiled at the nurse sitting at the desk and then at the patients waiting in chairs around the room.

The nurse straightened herself and smiled. "Mr. Seagraves," she said.

"Miss Thompson," he said, reading the name off her blouse. She was a small-boned woman, somewhere between thirty and forty, and her hair hung in a ponytail over one shoulder. She put in time on her looks, and Seagraves imagined her ponytail matted against his own shoulder, wet from the bath. He put it out of his mind.

"I wonder if I might see Dr. Braver when he has a minute," he said.

She went for the doctor, and he took a seat against the wall with the patients. He signed the cast on a boy's foot and gave him a quarter to buy a Moon Pie and a Dr Pepper after he was finished with Dr. Braver.

The doctor came through the door a moment later, and Seagraves left his seat. Dr. Braver was wearing white shoes with pink soles, a white belt, rimless spectacles. He did not smile when he shook hands, but then, Seagraves had never seen him smile.

He noticed an intimate look pass between the doctor and his nurse as they came into the room, however, and surmised that she was doing what she could in that direction.

"What may I do for you today, Mr. Seagraves?"

There were specks of blood on one of the doctor's sleeves and a spot of red on the gold watch he wore under it. He had snow-white hair and had been that way since he was twenty-five years old.

"I wonder if we could have a moment in private," Seagraves said.

"We could," Braver said. He looked quickly behind Seagraves at the waiting patients and then spoke to his nurse. "Ain't nobody dying on us, is there?" he said.

"No sir," she said.

"Good," he said. He held the door to the back rooms open, and as Seagraves walked through, the doctor spoke again to his nurse. "Call Dr. Bonner for me," he said. "Tell him I said to do something about the rocks out to front of the church."

"Yessir," she said.

P. P. Bonner was not a medical doctor, but the pastor of the First Presbyterian Church. Seagraves recalled his boy, Carl, the youngest Eagle Scout in the history of the state, had gone off to Tufts University in Massachusetts when he was only sixteen years old. Won medals in Korea and was getting ready to graduate law school himself.

Seagraves did not remember the boy well, only that he was famous in Cotton Point and had always seemed too polite. As if he wanted something from you.

Dr. Braver followed Seagraves through the door and then led him down a long hallway to his office. He did not sit down or offer him a seat.

He removed his glasses and cleaned them with a corner of his coat. "Yessir," he said, "what can I do for you today?"

Seagraves was direct, anything else was wasted on Braver. "A prognosis on Miss Rosie Sayers," he said.

Braver blinked at the lawyer. "To what specific purpose?" he said.

"I represent an interested party," he said.

"What party would that be?"

"Paris Trout," he said.

Dr. Braver scratched the side of his ear and then studied the end of his finger. "Prognosis," he said.

Seagraves nodded.

"Tell you what," Dr. Braver said, "I'll leave you make your own." He walked back out of the office and then up two flights of stairs. He seemed in more of a hurry now, and Seagraves's feet began to hurt, keeping up.

At the top of the second flight of stairs the doctor opened the door, and Seagraves walked through it, pleased to hear the doctor breathing hard, and found himself at the end of a long, narrow hall. The hall was dark, lit only by the sunlight from the rooms. All the way down, the doorways seemed to glow.

Dr. Braver walked ahead again, first to the nurse's station, where a woman as white-haired and serious as the doctor himself was sitting, reading the *Saturday Evening Post*. There was a painting of a doctor's office on the cover, a red-headed boy with freckles in a sling. It reminded Seagraves of Carl Bonner. He thought it must be a sign, to think of the boy twice in the same day.

The woman looked up from the magazine, saw it was Braver, and straightened herself to look alert. "You're early for your rounds, Doctor?" she said.

Braver nodded at Seagraves. "This is the famous attorney Harry Seagraves," he said. "He wants to look in on Miss Rosie Sayers on a legal matter."

If the woman knew the name Harry Seagraves, she did not show it. "Well," she said, without ever looking at Seagraves, "she's right where you left her."

Braver walked past the nurse and almost to the end of the hall. He went slower now, as if the reason to hurry were gone. The last door on the left was closed to the hall, and that was the one. Seagraves could read the number, 313. Braver turned the handle and stepped aside.

There were eight beds in the room, all but one occupied. An orderly sat at the far end, his chair against the window, his feet resting on one of the beds. His chin was tucked into his shoulder, and his arms were laid across his stomach.

"That there is Miss Sayers," the doctor said. His voice seemed too loud for the room, and at the sound of it the orderly stirred and then scrambled.

Seagraves looked in the direction Braver had indicated and saw the girl. Her eyes were closed, and her teeth protruded and lay across her bottom lip. The pillow rose up around her face and softened it, she looked like some dark-centered flower.

Somebody in another bed coughed and then moaned. The orderly was on his feet now, smoothing his hair. Braver paid him no attention. He walked to the girl's bed and looked at the chart hung at the foot. Seagraves stayed where he was.

"You want to see the girl, Mr. Seagraves, here she is."

Seagraves walked as quietly as he could across the floor. He kept his eyes in front of him, not wanting to look into any of the beds he didn't have to. Seagraves had an aversion to illness. Braver handed him the girl's chart and moved closer. He held her eyelids open, each side, he checked the needle going into her arm. He seemed rough with the girl, but it was less in the way he touched her than the way he let go.

"That line across the top of the chart is the times," Braver said, laying his fingers along the girl's neck for a pulse. "All the patients in this room are in jeopardy. We keep an orderly in here day and night, and he carefully checks each patient's life signs on the hour, and that way we know when they have passed on."

He looked at the orderly over the word "carefully."

Then he let go of the orderly, in a way that was related to the way he let go of the girl, and returned to Seagraves. "You can see from the blood pressure notations on Miss Sayers's chart that at seven o'clock this morning she was nearly expired." Seagraves looked at the chart but could not read it. "By eight," Braver said, "she rallied back, and by nine she regained consciousness and complained of pain."

The doctor pulled the sheet back and Seagraves realized the girl was naked. It took a moment because of the bandages. They had wrapped her arms and covered her whole stomach, from the little tuft of pubic hair to her chest.

It was the undamaged parts that touched Seagraves, though. Her shoulders and legs were no bigger than the bones underneath them. He could have wrapped his hand all the way around her neck.

The doctor looked at the orderly and said, "Scissors."

The orderly produced a pair of scissors. They had long handles and took a small bite. Braver accepted them and began to cut the wrapping off the girl's stomach, starting at the bottom and working up. The orderly stood by, waiting to be of use.

Braver finished the cut and opened the dressing. The hole was almost perfect, crusted around the edge, smaller than Seagraves had imagined. "This right here is the approximate angle of penetration," Braver said. He moved farther up the bed and pointed slightly down. "It perforated her stomach and liver and ended up in her right buttocks."

Braver removed his finger and stepped away. "You want a closer look, Mr. Seagraves?" he said.

"The bullet's still in her?" he said.

"One of them is," he said. "The others passed through her append-ages. Her arm's broke in two places. Come get a good look if you want, it ain't catching."

Seagraves said, "I never asked to see this."

Braver took off his glasses again and cleaned them against the corner of his coat. He put them back on and then pulled the sheet back over the girl. It fell half across her still, narrow face, covering half her mouth, part of her cheek. It fell like the first shovel of dirt. Seagraves felt a panic loose somewhere inside himself.

"All I asked for was a prognosis, Dr. Braver," he said, and the sound of his own voice quieted the feeling.

Braver looked at the orderly, who still hadn't washed himself of sleep. "The orderly here excepted, Mr. Seagraves, I believe that you will find an agreement among the medical community that Miss Rosie Sayers is dead." He picked up an edge of the sheet and dropped it over the rest of her face, covering everything but the fuzz on top of her head.

Someone moaned, someone coughed. Braver was fastened on the

orderly again, the orderly was looking at his watch. "It must of only happened," the orderly said.

Braver held him a minute longer and then said, "Have it cleaned up," and walked out the door.

Seagraves followed him, making no effort to keep up, picturing the small, perfect hole in the girl's stomach. He felt the gun then, a secret in his pocket. And the secret settled on him with a weight, distinct from the gun.

SEAGRAVES LEFT THE CLINIC without speaking another word to Dr. Braver. He crossed the street to the campus of the officers' academy, stepped into a cluster of trees, and got sick.

He collected himself there and then returned to his office. He borrowed a car from Dick Spudd and drove out to Indian Heights. He did not tell Spudd, the junior partner in the firm, where he was going. The car was a new Cadillac, and he was fussy where it went.

Seagraves found the house almost without trying. He stopped the car when he saw it at the end of the road. There were youngsters in the yard, a man sitting on a chair in the porch. The house had two front doors, both of them were open. A pair of chickens picked their way through a ditch, eating gravel, and there were car tracks in the clay alongside the house.

The man on the porch was watching him. Seagraves found himself out of the car, walking toward him. He stopped at the foot of the porch and looked up. The sun was behind the roof of the house, and Seagraves had to squint to see him. "Mr. Boxer?"

The man shook his head. "No sir."

"Are you Thomas Boxer?"

"No sir. You must of have the wrong house."

Seagraves looked up and down the street. "Is this where Mary McNutt lives?"

"No sir, I tol' you this ain't the right house for you."

Seagraves held out his hands. "I don't mean nobody harm," he said.

"What that in your pocket?" the man said.

Seagraves felt the weight there and shook his head. "I'm an attorney of the law," he said. "I don't shoot nobody."

70

"Uh-huh."

He took the first step to the porch, the man sat up. "I wonder if I might look inside," he said.

"Fo' how long?"

"Only a minute," Seagraves said. "I just want to see where it happened."

The man nodded at the entrance on the right. "In there is where it happened," he said.

"May I go in?"

"He'p yourself," the man said. "People been through it already, I don't see how it make no difference one more."

Seagraves stepped onto the porch and then, nodding at the man, into the house. It was cooler inside than out, the smell of gunpowder was still in the room.

He went through quickly. There were stuffed chairs in the first room, and a cot. Beds in the second and third, and a kitchen at the back of the house. A wood stove, a table, an old trunk sitting in the corner.

In the kitchen he stopped, knowing this was the place. It was the smallest room of the house, and the ceiling back here slanted down for reasons he could not discern. He imagined Trout, stooping to fit himself into this place where he did not belong.

The pots and pans were hung from nails over the stove, a line of canning jars sat empty against the far wall. The door from the kitchen outside hung half off its hinges.

Paris Trout had come into this room, where there wasn't anything, and taken a child's life.

Seagraves had accustomed himself to the gunpowder now and could not smell it, but there was something in its place, bitter and metallic. More of a taste than an odor.

He turned back toward the front of the house, meaning to leave the way he had come, but the taste got stronger, and he could hear the words the man on the porch said when he came in: "This ain't the right house for you."

Seagraves looked back through the rooms, and the taste filled his mouth. He saw that something had been stirred as he came through and was waiting for him now to come back.

He pushed open the back door and stepped outside. He was dizzy in the sudden light and steadied himself against the side of the house. He closed his eyes, feeling the shaking in his hands and legs. He remembered he had been sick earlier, he thought he needed something to eat.

When he looked again, there was a child not five yards away, barefoot in a dirty pink dress, sucking her thumb. It seemed to Seagraves he had seen the girl before. He smiled but the taste was still in his mouth, and then he was sick again, without warning, without anything in his stomach to come up. His eyes watered, and he bent in half.

And beyond the noises coming out of his body, he heard the child screaming as she ran. She was screaming that the devil was back.

He straightened himself and walked back to the Cadillac. The man on the porch sat in his chair, watching him, and people on other porches watched him too. The only sound was the child—the same child—standing in the road now, screaming it over and over, the devil was back. No one moved to hush her.

Seagraves opened the car door and sat heavily behind the steering wheel. The taste was still in his mouth. He fit the key into the starter, and then the passenger door opened—he never saw even a shadow of movement—and then a freshly decapitated chicken was spraying blood and feathers all over the front seat, pounding the air and the seat with its wings, propelled a different direction each time its feet found a hold.

Seagraves covered his face with one arm and found the door handle with the other. He spilled out of the car backwards and fell into the road. He got to his feet, opening the car door wider, and waited for the chicken to spill out too. But the chicken had lost its range now and lay on the floor between the brake and the clutch, its movements reduced to spasms.

Seagraves waited, keeping his eyes inside the car but feeling the dark faces on the porches and in the windows. The chicken stopped moving. The windows and seats were sprayed with its blood, and tiny spotted feathers hung everywhere. There were larger feathers too, one of them floated in a puddle near the chicken.

He waited, and then he reached in for the bird, and as he touched it, it jumped, as if it had been hit by a current of electricity, and

Seagraves jumped too, and yelled. And then, ashamed of himself, he took the chicken by the feet and dropped it in the road.

The chicken had turned the rearview mirror almost straight down, and as Seagraves adjusted it, driving slowly up the road and beginning to talk out loud to settle himself, he saw one of them walk into the road and retrieve it.

Dinner.

SEAGRAVES DROVE THE CADILLAC to Bud Ramsey's Sinclair filling station on Samuel Street and left it to be cleaned. He walked from there to his home and found Lucy sitting in curlers and lipstick in the kitchen while the maid vacuumed the living room.

She made a face when she saw him and closed the top of her robe. She said, "What on earth?"

He sat down heavily across the table. "Would you get me a Coke-Cola?" he said.

She reached across and picked a feather off his lapel and looked at it carefully. "Your suit's spotted," she said.

"Would you get me a Coke-Cola?" he said again.

She got him the Coke. It was a six-ounce bottle, and he took all of it at once, drinking as fast as the suction of the thing would allow, and then set the empty bottle on the table. Lucy picked it up and put it in a wooden case she kept just inside the basement steps.

"Let me take those clothes," she said. "I'll get them to the cleaner's."

Seagraves stood up and allowed himself to be helped out of his coat and then his shirt and pants. He stood in the kitchen in long socks and his underwear, and she held his clothes in her fingers and studied the spots in the material. "Are you bleeding?" she said.

"No," he said, "it's not human."

The pants hung suddenly by less fingers. "I don't think the cleaner's can get this out," she said.

He walked upstairs, she came up behind him. He washed his face in the bathroom sink and then drew a bath. She stood at the bathroom door. He would have told her what had happened—he wanted to tell what had happened—but it wasn't like a story, with a natural order

73

and reason to the events. Lucy needed things lined up in front of her before she could see them.

She took the curlers out of her hair, and it gave her a softer appearance. She picked up a brush and began to stroke her hair.

He took a breath, there was a pain deep in his throat from the vomiting. "Did you say something, Harry?" she said.

He did not answer. The bathroom felt distinctly empty. She stood on her toes in front of him, putting her face close to his, and kissed the air near his cheek. "Momma kiss," she said.

"I saw the girl Paris Trout shot," he said.

She pulled away from him, wide-eyed, as he knew she would be. She always went wide-eyed at news. "What did she say?"

He stepped out of his shorts, then his T-shirt. He climbed into the tub and turned the water off with his toes. She stood in the doorway, looking down. "Was it an affair of the heart?" she said.

Seagraves eased himself in until the water covered his shoulders. "No," he said, "it was business."

"He did business with a colored girl?"

"That would seem to be a problem," he said. He saw that his wife was disappointed that it was not an affair of the heart.

She said, "I could understand if it was love . . . I mean, you've seen his wife. She would not appear to have . . . affectionate inclinations. . . ."

"You can't tell without being in the bed," he said. "It might be the opposite, that it's Paris who isn't interested."

"I don't think so," she said. "He's old, but he looks vital."

Lucy only speculated on the "affectionate inclinations" of women who were attractive in a different way than she was herself. Mostly the ones who wore less makeup. Neither of them ever mentioned her own inclinations, which were scarce. She sat down on the edge of the tub, and he pictured Hanna Trout climbing the stairs, Nurse Thompson with her wet hair lying against his shoulder, the girls he'd seen at the college on the way to work.

But the other face came with them, with the sheet dropped half across its mouth, calm and persistent. He would look away when he saw it, but in a moment he would see it again. It was there like his own reflection, glimpsed in unexpected moments.

He sat up in the tub, trying to clear himself of her. "What is it?" she said.

He picked up the soap and washed his arms and his chest. "I don't know myself," he said. "I got to sit down with Ward Townes and Trout this afternoon, and I expect it will sort out."

"I wish you would tell me what in hell is up," she said.

She didn't swear much, and even "hell" came out of her awkward. He smiled at that and stood up. His skin had turned pink in the water. It had been sensitive like that as long as he could remember.

She said, "At least tell me what's on your clothes. That's the suit I bought for you in Macon, and if they don't know what the stains are at the cleaner's, I might have to throw it away."

Harry Seagraves looked down at himself and said, "Don't do that. If I got to argue the law without clothes, I'm finished. I was still getting boners going to the blackboard in law school. It's the fear that brings it on."

That thought hit her as funny, and he saw her smile. It was against her will, and when it passed she would be angry. He reached for a towel and fastened it around his waist, and she covered her mouth and began to laugh. It came out in little bubbles, like water starting to boil.

"I can't get that picture out of my head," she said finally. "What if everybody came to court naked? Can you imagine, 'All rise for the judge' and in walks Bear Lewis?"

Bear Lewis was the previous district judge, and he was a midget. He'd turned political after he'd taken the job—some could handle it and some couldn't—and Seagraves had brought in three thousand voters from Homewood and defeated him in the last election, replacing him with John Taylor.

The laughing stopped the same way it had started, little bursts of bubbles on the surface. When it was over she wiped her eyes. "I don't know why that hit me so funny," she said.

Seagraves moved in front of the medicine cabinet, found a jar of 5 Day deodorant pads, and used one under each arm. "I swear I don't know why, but I can't get that picture out of my mind," she said. He tossed the pads toward the wastebasket, missing them both.

"Harry?"

He turned to her and waited.

"Why is it things always stop being funny when I think they're funny too?"

"I got Paris Trout on my mind," he said, "and the man takes the edge off humor."

She was still then, and he dressed.

He kissed her at the door before he left the house and saw that all the fun was gone out of her now. Her depression was insincere, but it still made him sad in a way because he knew what that was. The fun seemed to have gone out of him too, a long time ago.

She stalled him at the door. She said, "Harry, what am I supposed to tell the cleaner's?"

He said, "Why don't you get out of the house this afternoon? Call Miz Hodges and go shopping."

"I got to tell the cleaner's something," she said.

He couldn't say what it was, he didn't know why. Somehow, little things had turned big, and it had come too far to be chicken blood.

"It's blood, isn't it?"

"Animal blood," he said. "Something ran in front of the car."

And as he walked out of the house, he heard her say, "Oh, the poor thing . . ."

SEAGRAVES RETRIEVED THE CADILLAC from the filling station and drove downtown. Bud Ramsey had vacuumed the feathers out and cleaned the pool of blood off the floor but hadn't been able to do much with the seat covers.

He parked the car on the street, left the doors open to air out the smell of chicken, and walked into the courthouse. Ward Townes's office was on the second floor, next to the desk where you got licensed. Any license you wanted in Ether County—fishing, dogs, marriage—you went to the same place.

Paris Trout was sitting on the bench outside, just beneath a sign that said GUN TOTER'S PERMITS. Seagraves saw that he had put on a dark blue suit, two inches short in the sleeves, and polished his shoes.

His hair was parted in the middle and slicked back. He legs were crossed, and he held a straw hat in his lap. He looked too big for the bench. When he saw Seagraves, he pulled the watch out of his pocket and checked the time.

"One o'clock sharp," he said. "Here I am."

"Is Ward Townes back from lunch?"

"He come in a little bit ago," Trout said, "told me to wait here for you."

Seagraves opened the door to Townes's office and put his head inside. The prosecutor was sitting at his secretary's desk with a phone against his ear. Seagraves held up a finger, getting his attention, and said, "Give me one minute, we'll be right in."

He shut the door without waiting for an answer and walked Trout to the end of the hall. There was a window there, overlooking the street. "I went to Cornell Clinic this morning," Seagraves said. Trout moved a little to one side and looked out the window.

"Did you hear? I went to Cornell Clinic to see Rosie Sayers. She's passed on."

Seagraves was watching Trout to see how it affected him. He nodded slowly, keeping his eyes on the street. "She was fourteen years old," Seagraves said.

Trout looked at him quickly and then back out the window. "I didn't have nothing to do with her birthday," he said. "I never put myself in her business, she put herself in mine."

Seagraves moved closer and spoke just above a whisper. "You put yourself in her house," he said. "You and Buster Devonne went into this child's house with a gun and shot her and Miss Mary McNutt something like eight times. Neither one of them owed you a legal cent, and one of them's dead and the other's talking a mile a minute. You can depend on that."

"I told Henry Ray Boxer before he took the car, I get what I'm owed. There is a natural order of things, and you and me and everybody down to the poorest nigger in the Bottoms is part of it, and there ain't no laws can blame anybody for the way God created the earth."

Seagraves backed away to get a different view of Trout.

"Lookit out there," Trout said, "some fool went and left his car doors open." Then he looked up at Seagraves, smiling with those yellow, gapped teeth. "People who let someone take their property is as guilty as the ones that took it."

Seagraves saw that Trout had watched him park the car and get out. He said, "Don't be sly with Ward Townes. He won't appreciate it."

Trout said, "There ain't nothing to worry about, Mr. Counselor. You'll of took care of all this by three o'clock."

When Seagraves opened the door to Townes's office again, the prosecutor was off the phone and standing at the far window with his nose in a lawbook. He did not acknowledge them at first, even when he heard the door close.

Seagraves took a seat, Trout stood near the door, holding his hat. Townes rubbed the back of his neck. He was the same age as Seagraves—they had graduated from high school together at the officer academy, anyway—but on Townes the years had worn more away. His hair was thin and gray, he was heavy on his feet, and there were collections of flesh under his chin and his belt.

He was tired today, and it showed in his movements. A sick secretary put a mortal strain on anybody. "I heard you were over to the clinic," he said to Seagraves, ignoring Trout, who was standing between them.

Seagraves nodded. "It's a shame," he said. "Little bitty thing like that, and a whole clinic can't do a thing to help her."

The phone began to ring. Townes sighed, walked to his secretary's desk and sat in her chair, and stared at it until it quit. "That's better," he said, and then he had a long look at Paris Trout, who was still in the middle of the room, holding his hat.

"Mr. Trout," Townes said, "I asked your attorney to bring you into my office as a courtesy. Technically, I should of had you arrested yesterday afternoon."

Trout did not speak.

"The reason I did you this courtesy," Townes said, "was twofold. One, out of respect for your family, and two, I wanted to see which way this went."

Trout nodded, as if those had been his thoughts too.

"Miss Rosie Sayers, however, as your attorney may have informed you, died at ten-thirty this morning at the clinic." He was speaking almost in a monotone, now, which Seagraves took for a bad sign.

"And that leaves this office with no choice but to charge you and Buster Devonne with her death."

Trout looked quickly at Seagraves, then back at Townes. Some- where in the look was another bad sign, and Seagraves realized if he didn't say something now, Trout was going to.

"If I might offer two points," Seagraves said, and he saw Trout beginning to nod his head now. "There is no argument that Paris and Buster Devonne were in the house, but there is, I think, some argument that they hold equal responsibility."

Townes nodded and made a note of that on the pad of paper in front of him. "Separate trials," he said.

"Certainly, if it comes to that. But my second point is that the circumstances of the death are not uncommon in the area of the community where they occurred, in fact occur there and in the Bot- toms and even in Bloodtown with a degree of frequency, and the fact that they occurred there on the afternoon Mr. Trout, who has never been involved in such circumstances, happened to arrive to settle a business matter may speak more to the environs than to Mr. Trout himself."

Ward Townes looked at Seagraves and smiled. "You mean, like a hunting accident?"

Seagraves held up his hands and shrugged. "It's short notice," he said. "Mr. Trout and I have not had an opportunity yet to thoroughly review the events that preceded the shooting."

Trout looked at him again and then back at Townes. "I did what was right," he said.

The words startled Seagraves. "Mr. Townes," he said, "as I men- tioned, I have not had an opportunity to thoroughly review the circumstances, and I wonder if my client and I might have some time to do that before he issues you a statement."

"I did what was right as rain," Trout said.

Townes looked up from the desk and said, "Did you want to review this with your attorney, Mr. Trout?"

Trout shook his head. "No sir," he said. "I ain't guilty of a thing. I was there to collect for a car. You know my business, you live here too. I treat everybody the same, just like they do in New York. If somebody got shot, they shot themself."

Townes consulted the notes in front of him, Seagraves closed his eyes. "Miss Mary McNutt, in that case, shot herself . . . let's see, three times in the back?" Townes said.

"Yessir," Trout said. "If they got shot, they did it themself. Just like if she jumped in front of a train, you don't fix the blame on the engineer. There is a set of rules that was here before any of us, and there's no man can hold another to account for the consequences when somebody breaks them. If it wasn't dangerous to break rules, there wouldn't be no reason to have them."

Townes put his hands behind his head and leaned back against the wall. "I have a rule for you, Mr. Trout," he said. "The State of Georgia wrote it down in the penal code. It says that you cannot enter a person's house and shoot them dead. And that's a dangerous rule to break too, sir. An eye for an eye."

Seagraves saw Trout begin to smile. Paris Trout didn't smile four times every ten years, and today he couldn't stop. "Those ain't the same kind of eyes," Trout said, "and they ain't the same kind of rules."

"The murder statutes of this state do not differentiate between races," Townes said. "To the law, one kind of eyes is as good as another. That's the way the rules are written down, and those are the rules we follow."

Trout moved then, closer to Townes, and bent until his hands were resting on the front of the desk. "Those ain't the real rules, and you know it," he said.

Seagraves saw Townes's good nature change then, and he hadn't moved a muscle. "Mr. Seagraves," he said, keeping his eyes on Trout, "if I were this man's attorney, I would come over here and collect him off this desk and instruct him to shut his mouth for the rest of eternity."

At the sound of the words Trout straightened and backed away. He was smiling again.

Seagraves said, "With the informal nature of the meeting, my client spoke more frankly than he would in a legal proceeding. It was our understanding that the nature of this meeting was informational—"

"See there?" Trout said. "That's what I mean. You got two sets of rules right here in this office. You got your lawbook rules and you got your common sense."

Townes stayed against the wall, his hands behind his head. Trout said, "Now, if you got some goddamn fine I got to pay, I wisht you'd set it and leave me go back to my store and do what I'm supposed to do."

Townes brought his chair back to the desk. He looked at the notes lying on top of it, made a calculation. He picked up the telephone and dialed a four-digit number. "Hubert?" he said, "this is Ward Townes. I've got Mr. Paris Trout here in my office to surrender in the shootings of Rosie Sayers and Miz Mary McNutt, and I wonder if you would come collect him now. . . . Yessir, thank you. We'll be here.

"Mr. Trout," Townes said, putting down the phone, "you are now under arrest for the murder of Rosie Sayers and the attempted murder of Mary McNutt. In view of your position in the community and my high regard for your sister, I am sure reasonable bail can be set, under the conditions that you remain in Ether County and that you and your attorney, Mr. Seagraves here, turn over any physical evidence relating to this matter. Any firearms, clothing, or notes of debt."

Trout turned away from Townes and looked at Seagraves. He had, at least, stopped smiling. Behind him Townes was saying, "Do we have an understanding, Mr. Seagraves? Mr. Trout? It is not my desire to send Hubert Norland to disrupt your home and your wife with a search party."

"Is tomorrow morning all right?" Seagraves said. "Mr. Trout surrendered the weapon to me earlier, and we will pick up the rest after he posts bail."

"You have the weapon now?"

"At home," Seagraves said.

"Tomorrow morning would be fine," he said. He checked his watch, then stood up and walked back to the window. "You're welcome to a seat, Mr. Trout," he said, looking outside. "Chief Norland said he would be by directly, but I expect he's on the phone right now, trying to reach Mr. Seagraves to ask him if it's all right to arrest you. He may be awhile."

Trout did not move. "That man's got more common sense than anybody in this room," he said.

Townes looked back over his shoulder then, and he was smiling. He said, "That is a profound observation, Mr. Trout."

*

CHIEF NORLAND SHOWED UP a few minutes later and was clearly startled to see Seagraves in the room. He led Trout out without touching him and took him that way the length of the hall and down the stairs. They could have been friends out for a walk, except the chief kept himself half a step in front. He did not want to give Trout a chance to begin a conversation.

Seagraves shook hands with the prosecutor and followed the police chief and Trout out of the building. He half expected Trout to run. It was as bad a day as Seagraves could remember, and it wasn't through with him yet.

The problem with the day, though, was not Paris Trout, it was the girl.

When Seagraves got back to the Cadillac, there was a skinny black dog with eyes the color of sleet inside, licking chicken blood off the seat.

The dog froze when it saw him. For two seconds the only movement was the rise and fall of his ribs, and then he bolted and ran.

HANNA
PART THREE

The story of the shootings in Indian Heights appeared Thursday morning in the lower left-hand corner of the front page of the Ether County *Plain Talk*— "The Conscience of the South"—beneath a short announcement of the birth of Estes Singletary's first grandchild. Estes Singletary owned the paper.

The *Plain Talk* account of the shooting fixed no blame. It was not until the last line, in fact—"Miss Sayers was taken to Thomas Cornell Clinic and later died of her wounds"—that a reader understood someone had been wounded at all.

Until the last line it might have been something innocent.

That was Hanna Nile Trout's thought, anyway, sitting on a counter stool at Dickey's Drug, reading the story again and again, until she could have closed the paper and recited it. There was a cup of coffee in front of her, and beside that a plate of bacon and grits, untouched.

It might have been something innocent.

She couldn't think what and began the story again. Paris and Buster Devonne were in it, but neither of them were identified beyond their names. Mary McNutt, it said, was a maid. And Rosie Sayers, fourteen, had died of her wounds.

She closed her eyes and imagined her husband inside a house, shooting colored women. It came to her right away and frightened her. She knew it was true.

She folded the paper and laid it on the counter next to her plate. She stared at the plate and finally tasted the grits. They were cold and heavy in her mouth, and she was sorry to have ordered them. She ate anyway—she believed it was sinful to waste—trying to remember if she had heard of any Negroes named Sayers.

Hanna Nile had taught public school in Ether County for almost fifteen years before she'd gone with the state. She had substituted in the Negro schools, she had been appointed by Mayor Bob Horn to head a committee on truancy. She had taken her duties seriously and wondered now if she'd had this dead girl in class or if she had gone into her house one day and asked her mother to send her to school.

She wondered if she had been inside the same house where Paris had gone with Buster Devonne.

The phrase came to her again, almost like a song. *It could have been something innocent.* She finished the grits and ate the bacon with her fingers, looking at the story's place in the paper and wondering if it was somehow connected to the weight of the event. The name Sayers was familiar, but detached from her professional life.

Something she had heard, it didn't seem to matter where.

She saw it clearer now, the size of her mistake, marrying Paris. It was the same mistake she'd made when she left Cotton Point for the job with the state: wanting what she did not have.

A principal's position had come open, but the Ether County school board had turned her application down—there were no women principals in Ether County—and she had gone to work in Atlanta. In five years she was the highest-placed woman in the state department of schools, making more money than some of the men, but what she gave up for that was the teaching itself. That was an empty place inside her now.

She accepted it as a punishment for her ambitions.

There were other empty places: her mother and father, both gone; her only brother, who had died in the Philippines, fighting the war. She had been alone so long, and she had seen so many other women alone. Her profession was where they went.

And then she'd come across Paris—she'd known him before, but only to nod to on the street—and he appealed to her after the bureaucracy in Atlanta. There was a shape to his life, she was sure of that. He was direct and willful and honest, and there was a sureness about him that was missing in her own life. He did not lie.

And yes, at the bottom of it she sensed a darker side, and it had excited her. She never loved him, she knew that, but she gave up her job in the department of schools to spend her life with him, not to end up alone, without a life at all.

But there was less love in Paris Trout than the state government.

He had never said he loved her, of course, she had never expected it. She'd thought the distance between them would narrow, though. She'd thought he needed her beyond the violent jerking inside her—in a way as urgent, but on another level.

But she had mistaken his nature, and her own.

And the spasms would shake her as hard as he shook himself, but the empty place only grew.

He'd put her to work in the store, twelve and thirteen hours a day; he would not hire a maid to clean the house.

He was hard-boiled and cold-blooded and had not brought her a present since the engagement. He had fornicated with her almost nightly for two years, pulling her legs up over his shoulders to push himself deeper or bending her over a table or the arm of the couch. He had never spent a night in her bed, though, or her room.

And she stayed, because that is what you did.

Weeks would go by with hardly a word, and then he would suddenly emerge from his office in back of the store and abuse her with the worst language, sometimes in front of people she knew from her days as a schoolteacher.

The marriage cut off her friendships.

A month into it she lent him half her money—more than four thousand dollars—for a lumber transaction, and he never repaid it.

The other half was in a bank in Atlanta, and she kept it secret.

She had been careful all her life until she met Paris Trout, and marrying him—she saw it now—was reckless, and she was punished for that, too.

The countergirl appeared in front of her, freshening her coffee. Hanna did not know the girl—there was a whole generation of Ether County children she did not recognize, it was part of the punishment—and the girl did not know her.

The child wore a perfume Hanna could taste in her grits and a beauty parlor hairdo that did not move even when the fan turned and blew the collar of her uniform into her earrings. Hanna guessed she was sixteen years old.

"Did you see this here?" the girl said. She put a pink fingernail dead in the middle of the story from Indian Heights.

"I was just on it."

"It's worst than the Civil War," she said.

Hanna looked at the child, trying to decipher what she meant.

"It's what my daddy said, that it's worst than the Civil War."

"I don't understand."

"All I know," she said, "it's got something to do with politics."

There were three other people sitting at the counter, and two of them turned to see who had spoken. The girl blushed under the attention and began to speak louder. She said, "They ought make him governor of Georgia."

"Who?"

Her finger went back to the story. "Whatshisname in the paper. My daddy said they ought run him for governor, and he would collect every vote in Ether County."

Hanna opened her purse and found a dollar bill. "Trout," the girl said, reading the paper upside down. "Mr. Paris Trout. The other one is Buster Devonne, but everybody knows him. You can't get elected when you're too familiar."

She put the dollar on the counter and waited while the girl made out the check. She was slow with her addition and labored to print the numbers. The tip of her tongue appeared between her lips.

Hanna turned on the stool and began to tremble. There was a fluttering in her throat and on her lips. She stood up, trying to stop it, trying to get out before someone noticed.

The girl looked up, her pencil still on the pad. There was lipstick on her front teeth. "Was everything good?" she said.

Hanna smiled at her. She thought for a moment there might be lipstick on her own teeth. She did not trust herself to speak now, because she knew the fluttering would be in the words too.

They ought to make him governor.

She saw how it would be then, that it would be public and that she would be part of it—part of the story and part of the legend afterward. In that moment she thought of leaving Paris Trout, but she was afraid.

Not so much of him—although that was part of it too—but of asking again for a different life. She imagined herself poor, without work or a place to stay. Without the look in his eyes the moment before he pushed himself inside her.

The girl took the check and the dollar bill to the cash register. She searched the keys as if she had never seen the machine before. The fluttering spread to Hanna's cheeks, just beneath her eyes, and she knew she was going to cry.

She nodded at the people sitting at the counter and started out the door. The girl called to her from the cash register. "Ma'am? You forgot your change."

"That's all right, dear," she said. "I left it for you."

The girl checked the money in her hand. "It's sixty cent," she said.

Hanna Trout walked into the sunshine. She paused on the sidewalk for a moment, and then, without meaning to, she looked through the glass back into the pharmacy. The girl was still watching her. The was a little flash of pink nails as she waved good-bye.

It was three blocks from the pharmacy to the store. Hanna walked with her head down, afraid she would see someone she knew. The fluttering had taken her over.

The store was locked in front, in two places. Paris Trout was the only man in Cotton Point who put two locks on his doors. She found the keys in her purse and went in and then closed and relocked the door and sat in the dark on a box of tomatoes. She needed to calm herself before she saw customers. She took deep breaths until the air went in and out of her chest without catching.

A few minutes later she stood up to open the store and suddenly heard his voice. She jumped at the noise, not expecting him here now, with the story all over town. She stood in the aisle that ran the length of the store. The office door was closed, but there was a light in the space between it and the floor.

His voice seemed to shake the cans on the shelves. "What in hell is it you want from me?"

It was quiet a moment, she waited. Then Paris again: "I will not be abused like this. No sir, not over a Negro debt. . . ."

She thought it must be Harry Seagraves in the office with him because her husband did not use the word "Negro" except in legal matters. She could not hear the attorney's reply, however, and then Paris was speaking again.

"I warn you," he said. "More blood will spilt than it already has." He was shouting now, and it frightened her. He kept guns in his office. He kept guns everywhere. The reply, if there was a reply, was so soft she could not even hear the tone of the voice. It seemed to infuriate her husband, though.

"By God, I'll finish this now!"

And she knew in that instant that Paris would shoot him, and she ran to stop it. Her skirt caught her knees, and she stumbled. She heard him again, a wordless scream, just as she got to the office. She turned the knob, expecting to find the door locked. It moved with her hand, though, and the door opened.

Her husband was sitting at his desk, pointing a heavy-looking square pistol at the ceiling. There was no one else in the room. Slowly he brought the muzzle of the gun down until it rested, together with his one open eye, in the middle of her chest. He was unshaved, and there was dried food in a corner of his mouth.

The other eye opened, blood red.

"Dear Jesus," she said. She was faint and leaned against a folding chair near the wall.

He stood up, holding the gun at his side now, and crossed the room. She thought he meant to explain himself, but he walked past, smelling of urine, and looked out the door, one way and then the other.

"There's no one in the store," she said. "I haven't opened."

He turned back into the room and looked at her like six crates of melons that showed up unordered. His pants were spotted and his zipper was open. She smoothed her skirt and brushed a piece of lint off her blouse, hoping in some way that normal motions would make things normal.

He watched her, without a hint of movement in his face. It came to her that things were changing now, right in the room, and would never be retrieved.

"Sometime ago," she said, "you borrowed a sum of money from me. In light of the circumstances, it might be prudent to return it now."

She had no idea how those words came to her or how they were received.

He walked back to his desk and sat down. "You're my wife," he said.

"I had that money before."

He shook his head. "This mess with the Negroes," he said—there was the word again—"it don't have the first thing to do with you."

She began to speak, but he interrupted her. "It don't have nothing to do with the law either. I make my deals and live by them, and Jesus save those that don't do the same."

"I don't want what's yours," she said. "I want my loan repaid."

He slammed the side of the gun against the desktop, upsetting the bottle of mineral water. Mineral water was always somewhere around, here and at home. Paris Trout would not drink from the tap. The bottle rolled across the tabletop, leaving a trail of small puddles.

He made no move to stop it.

The room was quiet except for the sound of the bottle rolling across the wood and then dropping onto the floor. She met his stare, then looked away. In that moment she saw he was afflicted.

"I am sorry for you," she said, looking at the floor.

He made a noise she understood to be a laugh. "That's a lie," he said. "You're sorry for every child ever come out of its mother's pussy barefoot, and people that's old, and all the sumbitches play with their own toes up to the asylum, but you ain't sorry for me."

She looked up again and saw he was laughing at her. "I caught you fibbing," he said.

"I want my money returned," she said.

"You know what else?" he said. "I know why you said that. You want me pitiful, so you can feel the way you're supposed to. Because if somebody ain't pitiful or sick, you don't know how to act nice."

She blushed at the words and stepped backwards toward the door. The smell of his urine was fresh in her nose again.

"Well?" he said. "Is that a fact or not?"

"I don't know," she said.

"You lied again."

She began to back out of the room. He came up off the desk, and the pistol came up with him. She stopped dead. "You lied," he said.

She said, "What do you want?" She could not anticipate him at all now.

He looked at the empty bottle on the floor. He said, "Get me a drink from the store, then clean up what's spilled."

The mineral water was sitting on a shelf at the front of the store, near the door. Her intention was just to walk out. When she got to the door, though, there was a woman waiting on the other side. A small child hung from her arm, lifting his feet to swing or tip her over, it was hard to say which.

Hanna recognized the woman—she was married to one of the deans at the college—but could not remember her name. Hanna let her in. She waited until the woman was past and then kicked the wedged stop under the door. Open for business.

"Can I help you find something?"

"Thank you," the woman said, "but I'll manage." The woman's accent was southern, but not local. She carried herself in a dignified way, even with the child swinging from her arm. Hanna straightened herself, thinking of her own dignity.

She picked a bottle of mineral water off the shelf and headed back toward the office. She did not want this woman to see Paris, she did not want to be thought of in a piteous way. Something hung on the woman's opinion.

"I'll be back directly," she said.

Paris was in the spot where she'd left him. Precisely the spot. The bottle was still on the floor near his feet, a trail of spilled water formed half an ellipse across the desk. The gun, thankfully, was back on the desktop and out of his hand. She crossed the room and handed him the mineral water.

There was a metal sink in the corner, and she found a dry sponge there, wet it and wrung it out, and wiped the desk. He opened the bottle, following every move. Neither of them spoke.

She stepped around him, bending to wipe the spilled bottle up off the floor, and then there was a slamming noise in her ear, and she was suddenly out of focus. She fell against the desk, beginning to understand that he had hit her, and then his hand was around her neck, his weight pinning her to the desktop. There was a heat in her ear and numbness somewhere inside.

Still, neither of them spoke. The only sounds she heard were his breathing and hers and the rush of blood in her head. Her cheek lay flat against the desk, and her eyes were open, but he was working from the other side, where she could not see him.

It was connected somehow to the girl he had shot.

A movement then, above her, and he set the bottle of mineral water on the desk a few inches from her nose. She wondered if she'd closed the door to the office, afraid that the woman would come back to find her when she was ready to pay for her things.

She pulled suddenly, with all her strength, but he only fastened down harder, until she cried out. Not words, only a sound. He lifted her skirt, and she felt a coolness on the back of her legs.

"Paris, please . . ." The voice did not sound like her own, it was squeezed and comic.

He brought the skirt all the way up. It bunched in front and caught against the edge of the desk. He jerked at it, lifting her off her feet. And then it was loose, and a moment later she felt the soft weight of it on her back.

"I will not tolerate this," she said.

There was no answer, and in a moment her sight blurred, and she wondered, in a dreamed sort of way, if he had somehow left. Then she felt his hand on her, running over the cheeks of her bottom. He slapped her once there, the force of it moving her head, rubbing her cheek into the wood.

Then his hand found the elastic at the top of her underpants and pulled them down her legs until they fell of their own accord around her feet. She fought him, rising an inch off the desk, but he pushed her back where she had been. She thought again of the woman outside, picking a few things up on the way home.

No one came in for more than a few things, people did their heavy shopping at the A&P.

She saw his hand. It closed around the bottle of mineral water, taking it at the bottom. There was a moment of calm then; she thought she could talk to him while was drinking.

"Paris, look at yourself. . . ."

She felt him move, she thought he meant to let her go. Then she felt him between her legs, pushing to get inside. The thought came to her in that same dreamed way that he had planned this, it was why he hadn't zipped his pants.

He pressed harder, pinching her legs against the edge of the desk, and she cried out. She heard him at the same time, the sound he'd made earlier, almost a laugh. There was something wrong with the location, though; the noise seemed to come from the side. He pressed into her and pushed a little ways inside. She kicked out behind, as high as she could, but there was nothing there.

He pushed deeper, and there was a different pain, this one tearing her and lifting her up onto her toes, and she realized then that it was not Paris inside her.

He used the bottle like a lever. One end was seated deep in her vagina, the opening to her body became the fulcrum, and he lifted her in that way until she felt the warm water running into her and out, running down her legs into her shoes.

He held her there until the bottle was empty.

He pulled it out, almost gently, and then took his hand off her neck. He had yet to speak an intelligible word. He stood over her, holding the bottle, and watched as she slowly straightened up.

She was dizzy, and as moments passed, she noticed a burning sensation growing through her neck. She touched her face, and her cheek was swollen and unfamiliar. She steadied herself against the desk and pulled her underpants up. They were soaked through.

Then she pulled her skirt down, and she was finally away from him.

She felt the wet underpants against her skin, though, and she felt what he had done to her. "Look at yourself," she said again, and when he did not answer she left the room, her shoes making wet noises as she walked.

The woman was standing at the counter. There was a box of saltine crackers and some chicken noodle soup in front of her, the child was holding a pack of Dentyne gum. She looked up when she heard Hanna coming.

Hanna stepped behind the cash register and rang the order. She accepted the woman's money, made the correct change. She put the crackers and the soup in a brown bag and thanked the woman for coming in. The woman looked at her face and then glanced back toward the office.

She leaned forward, so that the child could not hear, and said, "Are you all right, honey?"

And Hanna felt the cold underpants underneath her skirt, and her legs had turned sticky. She said, "Yes, thank you. My husband and I had a small emergency, but it's taken care of now."

The woman left, and a moment later Hanna left too. She did not close the door behind her, and as she walked along the campus of the college a few minutes later, she had the impression again that things were, at that moment, changing forever.

That Paris was gone someplace and was lost for good.

SHE DID NOT MOVE out. She stayed, because that is what you did.

The house, in some way, was hers.

By the time Paris Trout returned from work that night, however, she had taken several chairs, a lamp, a table, and the rug from the front room and carried them upstairs to her own quarters. She watched him from the window, opening the gate and walking up the sidewalk. She watched until the line of the house cut him off from her, and then she crossed the room and locked her bedroom door.

He did not force his way in. She heard him on the stairs and then in the hallway. He stopped outside, a long minute, and then she heard his steps moving back in the direction he had come, and somehow a bargain had been struck.

They did not speak, not a word, for three days. Each evening she locked herself in her bedroom, and each morning, after he left, she reclaimed her house. She read books in her room, Raymond Chandler novels she borrowed from the public library. She bought a radio. She took long baths and began a diary.

She did not clean anything but herself and her own room, she did no dishes and no cooking and took her laundry out, charging it to her husband's account. She saw him, coming and going, and was careful that he did not see her.

*

THERE WAS A SERVICE for the child on Tuesday. She called the coroner, a man named Cliff Collins, and caught him drinking. He gave her the time and place.

The following morning he called back, sober, and said, "Miz Trout, I can't have it coming back that this office was the one gave you information."

She dressed in a dark suit and walked south and east, through the college campus and into Bloodtown. The service was held in a small white chapel across the street from Horn Cemetery.

She took a seat in back—there were only four rows—sweating from the walk over, and listened to a Baptist preacher say a few words over the open coffin. There were six other people in the room, two young black men, an older black man, two children—two little girls.

The smallest child sucked her thumb, staring at Hanna over her small, wet fist all through the service. The preacher read from the Bible and then put his hand inside the box to touch Rosie Sayers. "Come down with me now," he said. "Come down and join hands with me and say good-bye to this child."

Then he leaned into the coffin and kissed her lips.

Hanna Trout stood up with the others and walked to the front of the chapel. She carried her purse under her arm. The preacher took one of her hands, the older man took the other. Her purse fell to the floor. The littlest child swayed between the two younger men, her eyes fastened on Hanna's white skin.

Hanna watched the child and then looked into the casket. There was another child inside, the one she had taken to Cornell Clinic for rabies treatment. They had laid her head on a pink satin pillow.

The preacher closed his eyes and spoke. "Jesus, thank you for sending us this little girl," he said. "We return her to You now for safekeeping and pray for You to forgive us that we didn't take better care of her here."

They all said "A-men," even the children.

The preacher closed the lid to the coffin, and he and the three men carried it across the street to a mound of freshly dug dirt. They set the box down, took off their coats, and then lowered it into the ground.

*

AN HOUR LATER HANNA walked in the door of her house and found her husband sitting in the front room with his attorney. The attorney stood up to greet her. "Mrs. Trout," he said.

"Mr. Seagraves."

Her husband had not shaved that morning and was wearing the same pants and shirt he had worn the day before. She knew he had slept—even with her door locked shut, she had heard his snoring from down the hall—but he looked as tired as she had ever seen him.

The attorney stepped closer and offered his hand. She took it for only a moment and then let go. His eyes hung on to her a long time. "I hope I am not an inconvenience on you," he said.

"Convenience is no longer among my considerations," she said.

He looked at her as if her husband were not in the room at all. "You are a forthcoming woman, Mrs. Trout," he said.

Her husband moved then, shifted himself on the davenport to look out the window. The movement caught her eyes, and when she returned her attention to the attorney, he was leaning closer, as if to take her into his confidence.

"The problem here, as I was telling your husband, is partly psychological," he said.

She stared at him, not understanding what he meant, not caring to have it explained.

"In that vein," he went on, "there are two considerations. One is the age of the deceased. She was fourteen, which as you may know is legal age of consent, and it could be argued that makes her an adult."

"Consent to what?"

He did not answer the question. "The other consideration," he said, "is the fact that your husband is perceived as a rich and powerful man, and in some ways that could be used against him now, the circumstances making the girl look more defenseless by comparison."

"Mr. Seagraves," she said, "I have just come from the child's funeral, and I have no interest in the legal problems her death has presented you or my husband, nor in the way you overcome them."

Seagraves turned to Trout, who was still staring out the window. "A service?" he said.

She looked at the davenport too. She thought of what he had done to her with the bottle, wondering how long it had been there, waiting in his mind, before the act.

"You went to the service?" the attorney said. She was pleased to note the cordiality had gone out of his voice.

She did not answer.

"Mrs. Trout," Seagraves said, "I know that you wouldn't intentionally hurt your husband's case—"

"I have no interest, Mr. Seagraves," she said. "No interest in this subject at all."

He put his fingertips against his temples, as if she had built him a headache. "I don't mean to exhaust your patience," he said a moment later. "I appreciate your abhorrence at what has happened. But please understand that whatever you do now reflects on your husband."

"Mr. Seagraves," she said, looking at Paris, "you cannot begin to appreciate my abhorrence."

And she turned away from them, pleased with the way that had sounded, and walked up the stairs and locked herself in her bedroom. She undressed, drew a bath, and sat in the tub a long time. They were downstairs another hour. She heard the drone of voices, and then, as she became accustomed to the quiet, she began to make out the words.

Much of it concerned the physical location of her husband and Buster Devonne during the firing of the shots. The attorney wanted to know their exact stations, her husband did not seem to know. She heard him say, "It was smoked all through that house. . . ." again and again.

Her husband was not a good liar, and the words came out sounding unnatural and practiced. She touched the lips of her vulva, softly, and it hurt her. She was discolored and cut.

The lawyer was asking about her. If there was a "disharmony" between them, it was better to know it now than later.

Her husband raised his voice. "She don't matter in this," he said. "She ain't a consideration."

She could not hear the lawyer's reply, but then her husband's voice was back again, louder, as clear as if he were standing there in the bathroom. "She can't accomplish nothing against me," he said. "She's my wife."

They were moving toward the front door. She heard it open and close, and then her husband's footsteps were on the stairs again and then in the hall. She sat still, looking at her fingers. Wrinkled and white from the water.

He stopped at the door to her bedroom, and she noticed that the water she had been sitting in had chilled, and she shivered.

He knocked on the door.

She reached for the hot-water tap with her toe and turned it on. Her foot was as white and wrinkled as her fingers. He knocked again, then tried the door. Even with the water running, she heard the handle rattle. It went on a long time, as if he were a child who had never encountered locked doors before and did not understand what they were.

She heard his voice suddenly, and the sound startled her. "You can't pretend I ain't here," he said.

She slid farther down, until the water covered her ears and raised almost level with the lip of the tub. Rather than turn off the faucet, she found the plug with her toe and pulled it.

His voice came to her through the water. It seemed to come from a long ways off. "Cut off the goddamn water," he said.

There was a book on the floor, one of Raymond Chandler's novels she had borrowed from the library, and she picked it up now, opened it to the bookmark, and started to read. The water drained slowly out of the tub. He kicked the door, but it was an inch thick, and it held. The noise was solid and in some way comforting.

He kicked it again, harder, and she began to whisper the words in the book out loud. When Paris spoke again he was out of breath. Even with the water running, the tub had almost drained, and the inch or two left was scalding hot on her bottom. "You got obligations to me," he said. "You best keep that in mind."

She put her toes on the faucet and turned it off. His voice filled the room. "They ain't nobody gets in trouble if they live up to their obligations, not with me. That's the cause of this whole mess now."

She put the book back on the floor, stood up in the tub, and then stepped out. She dried herself in front of the mirror, noticing the discoloration where she had been pinned against the edge of his desk.

"Hanna Nile," he said. "You can't pretend I ain't here."

She wrapped herself in a robe and crossed the bedroom to the door.

She opened it and found him leaning against the far wall, his forehead pressed into his arm. She stood in the doorway and waited. He walked past her into the room.

The smell of urine came in with him.

He sat on her bed, she stayed in the doorway. She saw that he didn't know what to say. He looked at the ceiling and then covered his eyes. "Mr. Seagraves has said you made it worst than it was," he said. "He believes it was accidental."

She squared herself but did not answer.

"He don't want you near this," he said.

"I've done all I'm going to," she said, and the sound of her voice was stronger than she felt. Stronger than his. "I paid my respects."

"You flew in my face, is what. You didn't know who they was."

She thought of the girl she had taken to Cornell Clinic and saw part of what he said was true.

"Mr. Seagraves has cautioned us to present a front," he said, "for the sake of appearances. That it would be harmful if we were perceived to be different than we were."

"How were we perceived?" she said.

He shrugged. "Married."

He looked at her in a way that had appealed to her once. Plain-spoken and out of words. There was a time when he would find himself at the end of the things he knew and then suddenly stop, in awkward places, because he could not say the things he felt.

It had appealed to her, but that was before she had glimpsed the things he felt. And the things he didn't. His dark side had fastened itself to her sexually in the abstract, and then she had seen it uncovered, and it was nothing like what she had imagined. It was only ugly.

"I will not associate myself with what you have done," she said.

"Nobody said to. You don't have to admit nothing except we're married. This is the wrong time for you to disappear."

"The store? You want me back in the store?"

"For appearances."

She felt a drop of water moving down her back, the only movement in the room. "I want you out of the house," she said.

He looked at her as if this were an old, tired argument.

She said, "I will not stay here under the same roof."

"It's my roof."

"Then I'll move," she said. "I'll sue for divorce and for the money you took. I will testify in court what you did with your bottle of mineral water."

She saw she had gone too far. He rose up and came for her across the room. She would not let herself run. There was a flat look to his face; decisions had been made over on the bed, and he was now the messenger.

He slapped her in the same place he had slapped her before. She was standing this time, offering him more leverage. It was more painful, because she understood right away what it was, but the thing she noticed most was the weight. All the things she had read in Raymond Chandler's books about being hit, he'd never mentioned how heavy it felt.

She fell backwards into the wall, and it was not over. He came at her from the same side, and she held up her hands and turned away. His hand crossed the plane of her arms and found her again, but something in the turning away took the weight off the blow. Her eyes watered and her hands dropped to her sides, and she said it again. "I want you out."

He grabbed the front of her robe and pulled her into his face. She looked into the gaps between his teeth. She thought of the places she had meant to go in her life. Los Angeles. For some reason, it felt as if it were too late to see Los Angeles now.

Without meaning to, she began to cry.

He held the front of her robe a moment longer and then pushed her a few inches away and studied her face. She tried to turn her head, but the collar of her robe was tight under her chin and ears now and prevented it.

The words came from behind the teeth, someplace in the dark. "That's better," he said.

She did not answer; she was no longer sure she could talk.

"There ain't nobody moving out of this house now," the words said, "least of all me. When this other is solved, then you're free to go where you want."

He dropped his hand and her robe fell open all the way to her knees. "Until then," he said, "what goes on in this house stays in this house."

Something in that nudged her. She covered herself, thinking that for as long as she had known him, Paris Trout had never cared for anyone's good opinion.

"I will not have this," she said. Her voice was watered and uneven. And he suddenly turned reasonable.

"You should of thought of that before," he said.

HE LEFT THE HOUSE an hour later; she watched him from her window.

Four hours later she saw him return. He arrived in a truck with the words "Mims's Hardware" written across the door. He and the Negro who drove it over got out together and opened the back end.

The driver put on gloves and then climbed in. Paris stood on the street, waiting to receive what was inside. He was wearing gloves too, although she had not seen him put them on.

In a moment he reached into the truck and then backed up slowly, pausing between his steps. He appeared to be carrying something heavy, but then he cleared the doors of the truck, and there was nothing in his hands.

He took another step back and then another. She saw the Negro's boots then beneath the truck doors, carefully finding the street. He cleared the truck, and she saw he was carrying the other end. There was nothing between them.

The thought came to her that Paris had gone to the state hospital and found himself a companion.

The men turned, keeping exactly the same distance apart. She saw it was glass a moment before it caught the reflection of the late-afternoon sun. They maneuvered themselves through he gate—the Negro opened it with his foot—and then up the walk to the porch.

The Negro backed the whole way, losing his balance once but correcting himself in time to save the window. Paris stood behind, red-faced, with his cheek pressed into the glass, grunting with each step.

The Negro arrived at the top of the stairs and stopped. "It's left open, sir?"

Paris grunted. The driver set his end of the glass on the porch floor and turned to try the door. "It ain't open," he said.

"The key's in my pocket," Paris said.

She watched the Negro step off the porch and put his hands in Paris's front pocket. He came out with a key ring, it could have weighed five pounds. She thought Paris must have saved every key he ever had. "Where does a man start?" the Negro said.

"Two square ones, right together," he said.

"These here?"

"No, square ones. One's old, one's shiny."

The Negro went through the keys slowly and finally found the ones to the front door. "Which?" he said.

"The shiny one opens the top."

He went back up the porch stairs, out of her sight. Then she heard the door open downstairs and the sounds of them coming in. "Two locks on the door," the Negro was saying. "They ain't two locks on the bank. . . . You must of got somethin' in here, all right."

At the bottom of the stairs they set the glass down again. "Heavy, ain't it?" the Negro said.

"It goes upstairs," Paris said.

The Negro came halfway up and stopped on the landing between floors. "Whoever come up first," he said, "they got to lean way over to here, let the other one to past this banister."

He came the rest of the way up and opened Paris's bedroom door, which was directly across the hall from the top step of the stairs. He returned to the glass, descending the stairs more slowly than he'd come up.

"There ain't no broke glass in that room, sir," he said.

"It ain't for now, it's for later."

Hanna sat in the chair near the window and listened to them negotiate the glass up the stairs. They set it down inside Paris's room, and when they came out, they were breathing hard and blowing. "The other seven goes up here too?" the driver said.

She did not hear Paris answer.

The driver said, "I ain't said there's nothing wrong with it, no sir. You know how much glass you need better than me."

They went back out to the truck and got the next piece of glass. And then the next. She watched for most of an hour, and when she saw none of the glass was going to be dropped, she left the window, opened a novel called *The Big Sleep*, and began to read.

Except for the grunting and their feet on the stairs, the men worked in silence. The Negro did all the backing up, Paris followed him into the house and up the stairs. When they had finished, it was almost dark.

"That be the last one," the Negro said.

Paris did not answer.

"Lawdy, look at the time," the Negro said. "I been on the job two hours plus my regular duty."

Paris did not answer.

"Mr. Mims don't pay me over the time."

"How much does he pay you, regular duty?" she heard Paris ask.

"Forty dollars."

"That's a good dollar," Paris said. "More money than that, it just get you in trouble."

It was quiet a moment, and then the Negro said, "No sir, that's spendin' money, that don't get peoples in trouble. What done that is money they saved. That's the kind make them evil."

"I'll call Mr. Mims tomorrow, tell him to divest his savings," Paris said.

"No sir, you doesn't has to do that."

"You already told him, did you?"

"No sir, I don't tell Mr. Mims nothing."

"And that right there," Paris said, "is how you stayed out of trouble."

She heard the door open and looked out her window in time to see the Negro walking to the truck. His gloves were in his back pocket. He got in without as much as a glance backwards and drove away.

Of course, all he'd lost to Paris Trout was two hours.

THIRTY MINUTES AFTER THE Negro left, Paris began the hammering. It was more of a tapping when she got used to it, and she realized he was not driving the nails all the way in. Still, it shook the floor and rattled the bottles on the dresser where she kept her perfume and jewelry.

The tapping went on late into the night, and she lay in her bed, listening, trying to imagine what he was doing.

Nothing came to mind.

She woke in the morning to the sound of the front door slamming shut and moved to her window. She saw Paris had slept in his clothes—if he'd slept at all—and hadn't changed them before he left. He walked in a stiff way to the gate and then down the sidewalk in the direction of town.

She stayed at the window a few minutes longer, making sure he was gone, and then went to the end of the hall and tried the door to his room. It was not locked—not even completely shut—and it cracked open at the first touch of her hand. She paused, suddenly afraid he was somehow inside, waiting for her. Then she pushed the rest of the way in and was momentarily blind.

The floor was covered with glass. The sun came in through the east window, gathered itself in a spot about halfway across the floor, and met her at the doorway. She squinted and moved a few steps inside. The spot seemed to move with her, keeping between her and the window.

She crossed the room carefully, testing each step, feeling the warm glass on the soles of her feet. At the window she turned back and surveyed the floor. The sheets of glass were fitted flush against the walls. Lines of tenpenny nails, spaced two to an inch, had been driven into the floor at the edges, keeping the glass in place.

The glass covered the perimeter of the floor. He had moved his bed away from the wall, and it sat in the middle of the room now, in the only space that was not covered. The legs of the bed each sat in a rubber overshoe. The hammer and a can of nails lay in the corner near the closet, beside an open, half-eaten can of cling peaches.

She looked back toward the doorway and saw her footprints on the glass.

She left the room as carefully as she had entered it and hurried downstairs into the kitchen. She found ammonia under the sink and put that and some dish powder into a small pail and filled it with water. She picked up a sponge and a dish towel and went back.

She left the pail outside his door and went to her own room for a pair of socks. The ones she found first were Christmas socks, a present from a time so far removed it could have been something she'd read about. Dark green socks with little red Santas tumbling up and down the sides.

The tops came all the way to her knees.

She returned to the room, in her nightgown and her socks, and began working on the far corner of the floor. The ammonia made her eyes water, the glare of the sun caught her from unexpected angles as she backed herself and the pail toward the door.

When she had come about halfway, she turned around, and with the sun behind her, she saw it was not ordinary glass. It was thicker than windowpanes, and it did not wipe clean. It had seemed to, but as the glass dried, the footprints reappeared.

She began again, scrubbing harder, checking her work from different sides as she moved back toward the hall.

It took most of an hour, and when she had finished, she stood in the doorway and saw that all the signs that she had been in the room were erased.

PARIS RETURNED LATE IN the afternoon and went directly upstairs. She heard him open the door and stop. She did not breathe until she heard him move again, farther into the room.

He went in. Then he came out, stopping at the doorway to look down the hall. She knew he was looking in her direction. The urine smell came back to her as fresh as if he were standing in her bedroom.

He went back down the stairs, taking them slowly, and then into the kitchen. She heard the first breaking noise two minutes later. A deep pop, perhaps a jar of mayonnaise on the floor.

Which, in fact, it was.

He dropped the mayonnaise, and then all the preserves, and then the eggs, and then two bottles of milk. The little explosions seemed to come at minute intervals, and finally, when she understood that he meant to break everything in the kitchen, she put a robe over her nightgown and went downstairs to stop him.

She found her husband bent into the open refrigerator, as if he were looking for something to eat. There were pieces of broken bottles and jars all over the floor, most of them still holding part of what had been inside. His shoes were splattered with the same things.

He stood up, holding a jar of pickles, looking carefully at the specks floating in the liquid. Then he seemed to find what he was looking for, and he dropped it from eye level and watched it all the way to the floor.

She watched it too—it broke near his feet and the juice sprayed the wall. A pickle landed on the toe of his shoe, hung there a moment, and then rolled off. When she looked up, his eyes were fastened on her, and she held herself in the entrance. An act of will.

"This is a sin," she said. If there had ever been an agreement between them, it was that waste was a sin.

"Then I expect you'll be eating it yourself."

"What has got into your mind?" she said, and as soon as she had asked the question, she knew the answer.

He said, "An ounce of prevention worth a pound of cure," and turned back into the refrigerator, coming out with the catsup. This bottle did not break when it hit the floor, and it didn't break when he stomped it with the heel of his shoe. He picked a hammer up off the cupboard and hit it three times, finally catching it square, and sprayed red all over himself and the closest wall.

When he looked at her again, he was holding the dripping hammer. "I sleep with my eyes open," he said, "and I know everything that happens in my house."

He turned back to his work, selecting the bottle of ice water. It turned the mess runnier than it had been, and little pieces of relish floated a few inches on the tide and then were set back down on the floor.

He was staring at her again. "Canned food," he said, and then he smiled.

"There's nothing wrong with the canned food," she said.

"That's right," he said. "There isn't."

This time he reached all the way into the refrigerator and swept out everything on the top shelf. Part of it landed on the floor, part was thrown into the wall. She took a step backwards, and the doorbell rang.

He straightened himself and ran his fingers through his hair. He washed off his hands in the sink, dried them with a dish towel. The bell rang again, and she moved to answer it.

"Leave it alone," he said, and she stopped. "It's just my attorney, it don't have a thing to do with you."

He walked straight through the kitchen toward the front of the house. Then he seemed to think of something, though, and stopped. "We'll have rats, you don't clean that up," he said.

She waited until she heard voices in the front room and then left the kitchen. The second step she took, she was cut. A piece of the bottle went into the first three toes of her left foot so deep it stuck. She cried out, lifting the foot to protect it, and slipped in something Paris had tracked out of the kitchen.

She fell, and for a moment she could not move. She heard them in the front room. "What now?" the attorney said.

"Housework," her husband said.

"It sounded like somebody fell."

She sat up on the floor and crossed her foot over her knee. The glass had cut through her Christmas sock and was buried so tightly into the fleshy parts of her toes that there was almost no blood.

She pulled at the glass, testing it, and felt a nerve connection all the way up her leg. She heard them coming now. She shut her eyes and pulled at the glass again, a slowly increasing pressure until the toes began to let go, one at a time, and then it was loose. She held the glass up to the light and saw it was the shape of a smile.

There was a throbbing in her toes, a deep ache somewhere in her leg. Harry Seagraves came around the corner, holding papers in one hand, and stopped in his tracks. She realized suddenly that her foot was bleeding—she could feel it coming out of her toes—and she realized at the same time how she must look to the attorney, sitting in the floor in Christmas socks, holding her foot.

"I'm afraid I've cut myself," she said.

The attorney put his papers on a daybed near the door and crossed the room. She saw her husband behind him. Seagraves knelt beside her, and she pulled her robe together at the neck while he inspected her foot.

"I'm sure it's all right," she said.

"I believe it's cut to the bone," he said. "Have you got a towel?"

He stood up, removing his suit coat, and checked around the room for towels. He stepped into the kitchen and returned a moment later with a cloth napkin. He pressed the napkin into her toes and the ball of her foot, watching her face as he worked.

His own face had changed during the visit to the kitchen. "Can you feel that?" he said.

"Certainly," she said.

Her husband was standing over them now, looking down as the attorney applied first aid. "We're going to need some tape," the attorney said, "something to stem the bleeding enough we can get you to the clinic."

She began to argue that there was no reason to bother the doctor over a cut foot, but she was suddenly aware of the blood. It had soaked through the napkin and was all over the attorney's hands and shirt. It was on her own hands—she did not know how—and had soaked the length of her Christmas sock.

She closed her eyes. "You don't have tape," Seagraves said to her husband, "get me some towels. Something to tie it with."

And then Paris had moved, gone somewhere for towels, and the attorney was helping her up, his hands under her arms and touching her bottom, telling her things were all right. "It doesn't mean a thing, Mrs. Trout," he said. "You're under a strain. Everybody in the world does things when they're under a strain."

She opened her eyes and saw that he meant the kitchen. "No," she said, "nobody would do that."

The attorney led her to the daybed and laid her down, pressing the towel into her foot. There was a line of blood on the floor leading to the spot she had fallen. She felt light-headed and panicky. The attorney patted her knee and said, "It's no consequence at all. In six months this will of all passed and things will be back how they were."

"How they were when, Mr. Seagraves?"

He looked at her, with his hand still on her knee, and said, "Before this happened."

"It didn't just happen," she said. "The day was a long time in the making."

Paris was on the stairs then, coming back down, but the attorney left his hand where it was. "What he did is one thing," he said softly, just before Paris came back into the room, "what he is, is another."

"Do you know what he is?" she said.

And finally she heard him tell her the truth. "No," he said.

There was no tape in the house, so Trout brought towels. He handed them to the attorney and stood at the door. Seagraves removed the dish towel and got a fresh look at the toes. He whistled, and in a moment she felt her blood on the underside of her foot and then spilling over the ankle.

"I don't think we ought try moving her," Seagraves said. Trout did not answer but stared at the blood. Seagraves pressed one of the towels into the ball of her foot again, then wrapped another towel around it, as tightly as it would go. The foot began to throb.

"Let me give Dr. Hatfield a call," he said, "and see if we can't interrupt his supper."

Dr. Hatfield lived on Park Street but was doctor to most of the families on Draft. He had a more cordial manner than Dr. Braver, whose house was on Draft, and kept track of patients' names. Hanna Trout had never seen him as a patient, she had not been to a physician since the physical examination which was a condition of employment for the state.

Seagraves went into the front room and dialed the doctor's house. Trout stayed where he was, staring at her foot. "I heard you talking," he said.

Suddenly she could not remember what she'd said.

"It must embarrassed him to be caught in the middle of personal matters."

"I expect he's used to it," she said.

"I expect I'm not."

She closed her eyes and dropped her head into the pillow behind her. She heard the attorney describing the nature of her injury. "It looks to be cut straight to the bone," he was saying, "all three toes. . . . Well, I did that, but I didn't have much luck yet. It's soaked through the towels. . . . Right, that's what it looked like to me. . . . All right, we'll be here."

Seagraves came back into the room and said, "Dr. Hatfield will be by directly."

Trout put his hands in his pockets and began to pace the length of the floor. He went from the door which led to the hallway entrance to the kitchen door, stopping at each end of the room to stare.

Seagraves sat quietly on the bed with his hand resting on her ankle. Every now and then he checked his watch or the bottom of her foot and told her not to worry, that the doctor would be there directly. Once he called her "honey."

And once he spoke to her husband. He said, "Paris, it wouldn't hurt none if you were to clean some of that up in the kitchen before Dr. Hatfield arrives."

Paris took a long look into the kitchen and shut the door. He resumed his pacing. "Some things don't clean up on the spot," he said. "That's what doors are for."

Dr. Hatfield was there in twenty minutes. He had a head as big as a bear's. He sat down on the foot of the bed and set his bag down next to him. Her foot had turned sensitive, and it hurt when he removed the towels and sock. He apologized for her discomfort.

He dropped the towels and the sock on the floor. They fell heavy and wet, she could hear them land. Paris and Harry Seagraves stood together off to the side. Dr. Hatfield held her foot in his hands, which were warm and soft, and bent his head for a closer look.

"We got to take some stitches," he said.

She did not answer, but at the word "stitches" she felt a renewed panic. It was no accident that Hanna Trout had not been to a doctor since she started work for the state. He set her foot back on the bed, so gently she could hardly tell when it left his hands. Then he opened his bag and found a short, hooked needle and his thread.

"I'm going to need some light," he said.

Seagraves took the shade off the lamp at the window and moved it to the foot of the bed. The doctor did not thank him or in any way move his attention from her foot. "You had stitches before, haven't you?"

She shook her head.

He said, "Well, the idea of it's gruesome—I see that's already occurred to you—but the operation itself isn't so bad."

She held on to the bedcovers and closed her eyes, and he began to work on her toes. He cleaned them with something cold and sharp-smelling, and then she felt the tugging as he began to sew.

It took him a long time, and once, near the end, she opened her eyes and saw Paris near the window. The uneven surfaces of his face cast shadows in the light from the bare bulb and darkened his eyes and his mouth and one of his cheeks until she could barely see them. It was like trying to place someone from the distance of time, someone she knew but could no longer see clearly in her mind.

When the doctor finished sewing, he pressed gauze into her toes, and between her toes, and then taped her foot all the way to the ankle. "We'll need to change that dressing day after tomorrow," he said.

"I'm not sure I know how," she said.

"I'll change the dressing," he said, "you hold on to the sheets." He looked around the room then. "You need to stay off that awhile. Is this the room where you want to be?"

"Upstairs," she said.

He picked her up, without seeming to notice the weight, and carried her up the stairs. At the top he stopped, looking directly into her husband's room. Then her husband was in front of him, shutting the door and leading him down the hall. "It's over here," he said.

Dr. Hatfield followed him to her room and then carried her to the bed. She was not as embarrassed as she would have expected. He laid her down and then checked the bandages. He pushed the hair off her face. "That's going to bother you later," he said. "I'll leave some codeine. . . ."

She had never taken codeine and had no intention of starting now.

He leaned closer and spoke in a hard voice. "If it infects, I have to put you in the clinic."

She sat up a few inches until she could see the foot.

"You understand what I said?"

"Thank you for coming," she said.

AFTER THE DOCTOR LEFT, she heard them talking again in the front room. It occurred to her that the construction of the place was peculiar, that conversations in certain rooms downstairs carried into all the other rooms in the house, but that the sounds from the other rooms could not be heard downstairs. It occurred to her that it was somehow intentional.

They were talking about Judge Taylor. Paris said he'd heard the judge secretly loved niggers.

The attorney said, "It's no consequence to you, one way or the other. You want to help, keep yourself low."

"I pay my bills. I do my work."

The men moved, and she could not make out the words. When she heard them again, her husband was saying, "She gets a temper sometimes, messes up the kitchen. . . ."

"It isn't the kitchen I'm worried about."

"Doctors can't say nothing about it anyway. It's their oath."

"What about the trial?" Seagraves said. "What if she gets a temper there?"

"She don't do it in public," her husband said.

It was quiet a moment, and then she heard her husband again. "What if we kept her away?"

"From court? Your own wife? Think how it would look."

"Maybe her foot got infected. Or she hurt herself in the fall."

She sensed his thinking then, saw it for one long, clear moment.

"No," the attorney said. "It's a bad time to be claiming accidents to happen."

Hanna sat up in bed and carefully put her feet down, one at a time. She used a straight-back chair as a crutch and limped into the bathroom and began to refill the tub. She slid herself back into it, resting her injured foot on the lip. With the noise of the running water, she could not hear them talking anymore and could no longer picture her husband's thoughts.

He came to her door later, carrying a tray. He knocked and walked in without waiting for her to answer. He set the tray on the table next to her bed, wax beans, candied potatoes, some kind of pork, iced tea. Everything he brought was canned except the tea.

He had cleaned himself up, shaved and changed clothes and parted his hair, and after he'd set the tray down, he turned the chair she had used for a crutch and sat down backwards, resting his chin on his arms.

He began to speak, then stopped himself and smiled. It was his nicest smile, the one that hid his teeth. She didn't move, not an inch.

"Have you ate?"

She looked at the tray and felt a sweet nausea balance itself in her throat. She looked away, and it moved away from the edge.

"Have you?"

"No."

"You got to eat. Doctor said so."

"He said no such thing."

He picked the fork up off the tray and cut a piece off one of the orange potatoes. A small piece. He moved it across the bed until it sat under her nose. She stared at him, seeing the fork and his hand in double vision. She moved away. "No."

He put the fork on the plate, still holding the piece of food, and closed his eyes. For a moment she could see his thoughts again, and then he spoke, and she knew she was right.

"I got to feed you then?" he said.

She shook her head and moved to the far edge of the bed.

"You think it's tainted?"

"I can't eat."

"You ain't tried."

"I took medication," she said. Which wasn't true.

"It don't matter," he said. He brought the fork back to her mouth and waited for her to accept it. She turned away, pressing herself against the wall. The chair moved. Then the bed dipped under his weight, and she felt his hand on her shoulder.

A moment passed, and the grip tightened. He turned her by the shoulder, flattened it against the bed, bringing her back toward him. Then he let go and found another hold, just under the ear that was pressed into her pillow, and brought her face around to meet him. She opened her eyes and saw he was still holding the fork. Saw that there was something in the forcing he wanted.

"Nothing is changed," he said. "I'm still here."

"Everything is changed," she said. He had tightened down on her jaw, and it affected her speech. A line of spit hung from the corner of her mouth. He shook his head, and the smile came back. His nice one, without the teeth.

"Whatever you think changed wasn't never me."

She began to speak, but his fingers pressed into her jaw on both sides, opening her mouth, and then he put the fork inside—so far inside it gagged her—and pulled it out against her upper lip. She felt the cold candied potato drop onto her tongue. She tried to spit it out, but he had her jaws.

114

"Swallow it," he said. He forced her mouth closed. "Swallow."

He watched her throat, and when she had swallowed he said, "See? It ain't tainted. It's good food."

He turned back to the tray, sticking the fork into the pile of wax beans, and she tried to run. He caught her by the hair and pulled her head backwards until it rested on his fist against the bed. He had dropped the fork, and with his fingers he reached into the plate and picked up a piece of the canned pork. He held it over her face. She clenched her teeth.

He laid the pork across her lips. Then he pushed it inside. His fingers were thick and hard and slid with the piece of meat into her cheek. She had not opened her teeth. He pulled his finger out and looked at her. "Swallow," he said.

She did not move.

He studied her a moment. He said, "Does it need salt?" and she spit the meat out of her mouth. It rested on her own chest. She felt it there but could not see it. His purchase did not offer her head an inch of movement in any direction.

"Stop it," she said. "My hair . . ."

"Hair?" he said.

He reached down, out of her line of sight, and then she felt his hand up underneath her nightgown. It followed her legs, which were tight together, to her underpants. He went in through one of the legs, his whole hand, and then, for a moment, she thought he had torn her open.

His hand came out, holding a little patch of her pubic hair between his thumb and first finger. Tiny pieces of flesh were still attached where they had been uprooted. He held it over her face, in the same way he had held the pork. "Did you want hair?"

He dropped the hair in her face and picked the pork up off her chest and put it in her mouth. She chewed it and swallowed it. He filled her mouth with a whole candied potato, choking her, and then the beans, and then the rest of the meat. She lay with her head pinned to his fist and swallowed.

"Nothing is different," he said. "You just misunderstood the way things was."

She swallowed until there was nothing left to eat. He let go of her hair, watching her, and then, gently, he leaned closer and whispered, "You understood it now, don't you?"

A numbing sensation spread across the back of her head, her injured toes pounded against the wrapping. It seemed to her he was asking if she knew he would kill her.

"I'm different now," she said.

She saw that puzzled him, and in the moment before he got off the bed, she glimpsed his apprehension.

THE FOLLOWING EVENING, HE arrived home from work and stood at the gate for nearly an hour. She watched from the bedroom window. She had planned to leave that morning, take the train to Savannah, but as she packed her things into suitcases, hobbling from her bed to the dresser, she lost her resolve.

She imagined Paris intercepting her on the way to the depot, she imagined herself in Savannah, in her sister's house. The questions. She imagined herself without a house of her own. She sat on the bed and realized that Paris had somehow stolen her direction too.

She was still on the bed, hours later, when he took his station by the gate. He looked down the street, toward the center of town, and checked his pocket watch frequently. People passed in front of him, some of them as close as the gate itself, but he did not speak to any of them. He did not look at the children.

She remembered the day—they had been married less than a week—he had forbidden her to associate with the Godseys, who were their neighbors. He said it was a business matter. And then, one by one, he found business reasons or grudges—one meant the other—against everyone she spoke to and isolated her in the same way he had isolated himself.

THE TRUCK WAS A flatbed, similar to the ones that hauled lumber, and it arrived just after seven o'clock. It was empty and seemed to come from the wrong way—at least it was not the direction Paris had been watching—but as soon as it stopped, Paris opened the passenger door

116

and climbed in. She could not be sure from the window, but it appeared to be Buster Devonne behind the wheel.

It seemed to her that Paris might intend to take him into the country and shoot him, except she did not know why he would need a truck for that.

HE WAS GONE A long time. She slept in a bothered way, dropping in and out, listening, even in her sleep, for the sound of the truck. It came deep in the night and stopped in front.

Paris got out one side, Buster Devonne got out the other. They unloaded what looked like a door, sliding it off the bed onto a two-wheel dolly. They wheeled the dolly through the gate and up the sidewalk. She heard Buster Devonne's voice as he came in the door.

"This damn thing heavier than a lead pussy, Paris."

His reputation for offensive language, even as an officer of the law, was admired all over Ether County. He would say whatever came into his head without regard to where he happened to be at the time. Those who did not admire Buster Devonne's language frequently made the observation that the man obviously had a small vocabulary.

Hanna did not know Buster Devonne at all, but she did not believe the limits of his vocabulary explained his manners.

They came up the stairs, pausing between each step, pulling the dolly. They went into Paris's room, and Buster Devonne said, "Maybe we could lie this sumbitch sideways and slide it over."

Paris did not answer, and in a moment there was a crash and the floor shook. It was quiet, and then Buster Devonne said, "Son of a bitch, Paris"—enunciating each word—"now we got to pick this fucker up."

She heard them moving around the room, and then she heard Paris counting. "One, two, three . . ." The word "three" seemed to choke and die, and then she heard Buster Devonne trying to talk, and it sounded like somebody was squeezing him lifeless.

There was another crash—softer than the first one, with more of a metal sound—and then hard breathing. "The bastard must of gone four hundret pounds," Buster Devonne said.

"It was two fifty in Macon."

"No sir, I know two fifty, and that ain't it. That there is at least three fifty. Rely on that."

It was quiet a long minute. "Are you reliable, Buster?" he said.

"They ain't nothing going to happen to us."

"It might," her husband said.

SHE PUT A SOCK over her good foot and went back into his room the next morning. He'd left his door open again. The glare of the sun off the floor caught her again, and she stopped in the doorway a moment, dizzy, and then moved to the windows and looked back. She had found a way to walk that didn't hurt her as much, keeping her weight on the outside of her foot. She had been walking on her heel, but in compensating that way, she pulled at the nerves below the cuts.

You could not walk on your heels to avoid hurting your toes.

His bed was a mess, the mattress slightly off center. It took her a moment to see it, underneath. A sheet of lead, a quarter inch thick, ran the length of the mattress and lacked only half a foot of being as wide.

She knew what it was. He was afraid of being shot from underneath. She pictured herself doing it: three muffled shots and then his hand dropping off the bed into view.

She went out of the room, not touching the door, and walked down the stairs. She sat down beside the phone and tried to call Harry Seagraves. First his office, then his home.

His wife picked up the phone at home. Hanna could not remember her name. "This is Hanna Trout," she said. "I wonder if I might speak with your husband."

"I'm sorry," she said, "Mr. Seagraves isn't in presently. May I take a message?"

She tried to think of a message. She said, "Would you tell him, please, that I need to speak to him, in confidence?"

"In regards to what matter?"

"This is Hanna Trout," she said, slowly. "My husband—"

"Oh, Mrs. Trout. Goodness, I misunderstood your name. Yes, what was the message?"

"That I need to speak to him," she said.

"Has something happened?"

Hanna found herself staring at the mantel. There was an ancient picture of Paris's family there, Paris sitting in short pants and a cap, cross-legged in front of his mother. One of her hands rested on his shoulder, some secret connection, and his father, off to the side, staring straight toward the camera.

She wondered what thoughts he'd had as a boy.

"Mrs. Trout? Should I try to locate him for you? Has something . . . *further* occurred?"

She heard the interest in the woman's voice, and she understood its pleasurable nature. Hanna fought her own interest in other people's trouble, but she knew the attraction.

She imagined telling her that she had been violated in the office with a bottle of mineral water. What would Harry Seagraves's wife tell her in return?

That she understood?

Hanna said, "No, don't trouble yourself to find him."

"It's no trouble," she said. "I told Mr. Seagraves back when this started, 'Consider the poor woman at home. . . .'" It was quiet for a moment, each of them hearing how that sounded. "I don't mean to offend you," the lawyer's wife said.

"I am not offended."

"It's just that the men don't take into account what it's like to be the woman."

Hanna could not think of a single word to say.

"I know how you feel, dear," the lawyer's wife said. "If you want to talk, here I am."

THE LAWYER DID NOT call.

She waited downstairs until five o'clock and then went back to her room. She locked the door and lay in bed and was suddenly weak. She had not eaten at all since Paris forced her. Remembering what he had done, she could suddenly smell canned pork, and she gagged.

The doorbell rang while she was in the bathroom. She stood still, the toothbrush in her mouth, listening. The bell rang again. The sound grabbed her, in the chest and throat. For a moment she seemed to forget how to breathe. She looked at herself in the mirror, afraid of her own house.

She brushed at her hair and wiped the toothpaste out of the corners of her mouth. The bell rang again as she was coming down the stairs. She saw a man's shadow through one of the windows that led to the porch.

She hurried to the door before he rang again—it seemed to matter—and a moment before she arrived, the door began to open from the other side, and then Dr. Hatfield's head poked inside, waist-high. He called, "Miz Trout?" before he saw she was there.

"Dr. Hatfield," she said, and he started at the sound of her voice.

He smiled, recovering and straightening, opening the door farther to step inside. "I hoped to save you the trip downstairs," he said.

She did not understand.

"Your foot," he said. "I was passing the house, and thought I might change your dressing and look at the stitches."

"It seems to be healing," she said.

"May I look?"

"Of course," she said, and led him into the front room. She sat on the davenport, he moved a straight-back chair and sat in front of her and took her foot into his lap. He found a pair of scissors in his bag and began to cut the tape. The scissors were cold where they touched her skin and tickled her feet as they moved.

He stopped for a moment and searched her face. "Is this causing you pain?"

"No," she said, "it's a tickling."

Without smiling, he returned to her foot. He made a single cut from her heel to her toes and then opened the dressing the way she would open a box of canned goods at the store, pulling at one side and then the other. There was a noise like opening a box too, and then her foot felt cool.

He removed the gauze he had packed into her toes more carefully, squinting to see the work he'd done. She could not tell if he was pleased or disappointed. He went into the bag again and found cotton and a bottle of disinfectant.

"Have you been on this today?"

"Not much," she said.

He began to dab at the underside of her toes with the wet cotton. It was freezing cold. Her leg jerked reflexively, but his other hand had encircled her ankle and held her there.

"You need to stay off it a few days," he said. "You don't want to end up in the clinic over a cut foot." He picked up her second toe, wincing as he looked underneath. She fixed on his collar, the hair growing all around his neck, down into his chest and back. He was round-shouldered and warm-looking, she thought again of a bear.

"Dr. Hatfield," she said, "may I speak with you on another matter?"

He looked up, over her toes, waiting.

"I have reason to believe I may indeed find myself in your clinic," she said. He waited, she framed her words. She looked out the front window, checking the walk. "My husband has become irrational."

His expression did not soften or change.

"There have been incidents which I would prefer not to discuss," she said, "which now put me in jeopardy, and perhaps my husband as well."

"It's a normal thing, missus, to feel threatened. It's threatening times," Dr. Hatfield said.

"No," she said. "His behavior may appear normal, but it is not. Events have occurred of a highly bizarre nature."

"Are you physically injured?" he said.

"I have been assaulted," she said in a quiet voice.

He did not seem to understand. "In what way?" he said.

"In ways of a private nature," she said.

He leaned back to look at her again. "I don't see marks," he said. "Not even a bruise, which is common enough even in the best households."

"He has assaulted me."

The doctor rubbed his chin. "If they went to commit everybody that assaulted his wife into the asylum, they'd be more in than out."

She saw that the doctor, for all his kindness, was no help. And it didn't feel like kindness then.

He picked a roll of gauze out of his bag and began to repack her toes.

"Dr. Hatfield," she said, but then the front door opened, and Paris was in the house.

He stood in the entranceway, looking upstairs and then noticed them sitting in the front room. He came in without a word and stopped a yard in back of the doctor, following his work. "I was on the street," the doctor said, turning to acknowledge him. "I thought I might have a look in on your wife's foot."

The doctor was afraid of him too, she heard it in his voice. His taping went faster now, and she could see it bothered his nerves to have Paris standing behind him.

"I appreciate it," Paris said, "to have a doctor drop by so late." He lifted his eyes and stared at her.

"I was on the street," Hatfield said again. "It's no trouble. I expect Mrs. Hatfield can keep dinner another five minutes."

Paris walked out of the room and into the kitchen. He reappeared a moment later, carrying his toolbox, and climbed the stairs. The doctor tightened his face against distractions. She watched his hands as he wrapped the tape. The hair on them lay in one direction, as if it had been combed. There were noises from upstairs, tapping, things falling onto the floor.

"Is Mr. Trout handy?" the doctor said. He spoke in a manner that denied what had been said between them before.

"He has been fortifying his room," she said. "He has covered the floor with glass and set the legs of his bed into overshoes." The doctor nodded, as if that were something he was thinking of doing himself.

"He sleeps with a sheet of lead under his mattress," she said.

He patted her foot, first on one side and then on the other. "How does that feel?"

She did not reply, and he said, "Is it too tight? Let me see you wiggle your toes."

She moved her toes, and a pain went all the way through her foot.

"That's good," he said. "You don't feel your pulse in there, do you?"

"No," she said quietly.

"Good. That's excellent."

The doctor moved to stand up at the same time Paris started back

122

down the stairs. He had been up there no more than five minutes. The doctor said, "Call me, that gives you any trouble," and then he shut his bag and stood up.

Paris met him in the entranceway and steered him out the door. "Her foot appears to be healing," the doctor told him. "If you can, keep her off it."

"She's lost her appetite," he said, and then they were out of the house, and she could not hear what they were saying.

She stood up slowly, getting used to the new wrapping, and walked up the stairs. On the way she saw them through the window, stopped halfway to the gate. Paris was speaking, the doctor seemed to be watching his shoes. She was unconcerned with anything Paris could say, her worry was Dr. Hatfield.

She walked into her room, listening for Paris. It was quiet. She did not think Dr. Hatfield could stand on the walk very long with Paris without telling him what she had said. The silence downstairs frightened her, and she moved into the bath and began to draw a tub of water. Wanting the noise.

And then she froze, realizing she had not locked the door to her room. She left the water and stepped back into the bedroom, expecting to see him waiting for her.

He was still outside with the doctor.

She crossed the room and shut the door. And even as it closed, she knew something was wrong—something different in the swing—and then she saw that he had taken the lock.

SHE FOUND HERSELF CRYING, without knowing when it had started. She was sitting in the tub again, the water was an inch from the top and still running. Underwater, a line of pink smoke rose from her bandaged foot. She had not bothered to rest it on the edge.

Behind her the bathroom door was shut and locked, but the lock was only a hook, with enough play so it could be opened from the outside with a pencil. It was a lock to keep the door shut, not to keep anyone out.

She heard him moving, she couldn't say where. She pressed her toes into the end of the tub, and the line of smoke darkened and billowed.

He came through the door just as the water began to spill over. He turned off the faucets and sat heavily on the commode. She covered her breasts and slid farther down, sending more water over the side.

"Dr. Hatfield said you might need a rest," he said.

She turned her head away and looked at the wall.

"He asked if there was a relative you could visit." He stood up and moved closer to the tub. He stared down into the pink water. "Did you tell the doctor you was tired?"

She did not answer because she was crying and did not trust her voice.

"Tell me what you said."

"I am tired," she said.

"That's what he said. I told him you didn't have nothing to be tired about."

She felt his hand then, on the back of her head. It moved down, gently, and rested against her neck and shoulder. She tried to sit up, but he held her where she was.

Then, slowly, the points of his fingers pressed into her and forced her down into the water. She didn't intend to fight him. He held her under until the panic took over, though, and she did fight. Clawing at his arm, trying to find his face.

His expression was unchanged when he brought her up, although his face was dripping bath water. "Is that what you told him?" he said. "That you was tired?"

He pushed her under again, with both hands this time, and held her there longer than he had before. She fought him again, raking his cheek until suddenly there was less reason to fight and then none at all. A calm took over, and she opened herself to it, without realizing what it was.

She would have stayed there forever, but something changed—a direction—and she was suddenly moving, and then her face was out of the water. Her eyes blurred, and she looked up into his face.

"Is that what you told him?" he said again.

In one moment of clarity she saw his thoughts again and understood that he was afraid. Not of the doctor—Paris had no interest in his opinion, good or bad—but of her. He believed he owned her the way he owned his own hands, and she was out of control now, working against his interests. She thought of the food spilled across the kitchen floor.

She wiped water out of her eyes and noticed that the whole tub was pink now. She lifted her foot out of the water, and fresh blood ran down the bandages. "Get out of the house, Paris," she said calmly. "You know that I'm poisoning you."

The movers were in the next day and cleared everything out of his room.

SEAGRAVES
PART FOUR

On a morning in August, two weeks and three days before the murder case against Paris Trout was scheduled for hearing in Ether County Circuit Court, Harry Seagraves woke up with the way to defend him. Seagraves was hung over, but that was when he did some of his best thinking.

Lucy was lying next to him, her features changed by the blindfold she wore to bed until she could have been someone else. They had been to a lawyer's picnic in Macon the day before, celebrating the state legislature's summer break, and he'd barely kept the car on the road getting home.

Seagraves sat up slowly, not wanting to wake her, not wanting to hear her voice until he'd had a chance to examine the idea that was lying like some perfect blue egg dead in the middle of the nest that sleep and alcohol had made of his brain.

He had been dreaming of the photographs of Rosie Sayers's dead body. Earlier that week Ward Townes had invited him to his office and laid them across the table. There were six altogether, showing the girl from every angle. His thoughts at the time had centered on how they would look to a jury. The girl appeared younger in the pictures than she had in the flesh, and her wounds had been enlarged by the instruments used to remove the bullets.

Ward Townes was almost apologetic. "I don't have a choice in this, Harry," he said.

Seagraves hadn't answered for a long time. Finally he looked up, away from the girl, and said, "You going to use these?"

"What would you do?"

Seagraves put his feet on the floor now and stood up. He was dizzy a moment, and when it passed he walked to the bathroom and drank cold water from the spigot. He brushed his teeth, shaved, and brushed his teeth again. There was a taste in his mouth that would not wash out.

He stayed in the shower a long time, starting warm and finishing cool, letting the water run over his head and into his lips. Then he shut the taps and waited, watching the water drip off the points of his body, until the idea came back to him, the way to defend Paris Trout.

When he came out of the bathroom, Lucy was sitting up in bed. Her face was white and puffed, there were red lines from the corners of his eyes back into her hair where the elastic that held the blindfold had cut into her skin. She held her head in her hands and did not acknowledge Seagraves as he walked back into the room.

"You under the weather?" he said, and sat down on a corner of the bed to dress.

"I may die," she said.

She smelled stale to him now that he was clean. He said, "Get you a cold shower, it'll put the color back in your cheeks."

"Harry . . ."

"What?"

"Get me a glass of water, honey."

He stood up in his socks and pulled on a pair of boxer shorts and his robe, then he went into the kitchen and opened the icebox. The maid was sitting at the table, drinking Coca-Cola. "Good morning, Betty," he said.

The maid said good morning.

"Mrs. Seagraves isn't feeling well," he said, "so she won't be down for a while."

"That's fine," the maid said. "Me and the broom get along just fine all by ourself."

He took the water upstairs. Lucy was settled back into her pillow. He handed her the glass and returned to his dressing. "Are you going out?" she said.

"I've got some work."

"It's Sunday. You can't do anything for Paris Trout on a Sunday."

He stood in front of the closet mirror to put a knot in his tie. He could see her in the corner of the mirror, soft and white and stale. "How do you know it's Paris Trout?" he said. Seagraves had the largest law practice in Ether County, there were hundreds of clients.

She covered her eyes and spoke through her hands. "It's him all right," she said.

He kissed the top of her head before he left, looking down the fold in her nightgown and noticing the pale blue veins beneath the skin of her breasts. It was a continuing mystery of his life that he was always most interested in what was underneath her nightgown when he had been drunk the night before and the odds were the steepest against him. Lucy was either hung over too—as she was this morning—or resentful to have been left behind.

"I won't be long," he said, and allowed his hand to fall off her shoulder, following the line of her body behind her arm until he felt the junction where her bottom met the bed. She moved a few inches, making room for his hand to slide underneath, until he felt the place things more or less came together.

"Harry," she said, "don't." Then, in a different voice, "Get me some more ice water, honey."

HE WAS OUT THE door a few minutes later and walking in the direction of Hanna Trout's house. He would see Trout himself later; first he wanted to ask her in a personal way to attend the trial. The alcohol visited him in waves, and once he stopped to sit on a brick fence until it passed.

Seagraves did not drink often, but when he did he made it count.

It was Sunday morning, and there were people on the sidewalks. Some of them he knew by name, some of them only to nod. The ones he knew by name tended to be Methodists, on the way to church. He spoke and smiled, and the women, fresh and red-lipped and perfumed, left him pounding. He thought of them in bathing suits.

And between these thoughts—or beneath them, like an undertow— he thought of Paris Trout. In the months since the girl had died, his feelings regarding his client had changed. This was partly from his closer acquaintance and partly from a growing premonition that he would lose.

Seagraves had lost before, but never a case as noticeable as Paris Trout's would be. He had gone into the matter assuming he would win, gone in with certain advantages, but as the weeks passed, Seagraves had come to see that those first advantages were all he had.

He had found some things on the colored family—Henry Ray, for instance, had driven a truck over a white man the previous year—but Trout himself belonged in the asylum—"gone to Cotton Point" was the expression—and could not be trusted to testify for himself at a trial.

A pistol had been found under a mattress in the house where the girl was killed. It was the wrong side of the house, and it hadn't been fired—or if it had, there was no evidence of it—but the pistol itself seemed to lend weight to the story Trout and Buster Devonne had told Chief Norland on the day of the shooting.

And ordinarily, those things would have been enough. But there was something resilient in the nature of what had happened—perhaps in the nature of the girl herself—that returned again and again as Seagraves prepared his case and informed him that something was headed wrong.

He had found himself avoiding Trout, seeing him once or twice a week, never for more than an hour. During the last visit Trout had threatened him. Not just the words—"I paid you to look after this, and you took the money"—but a feeling. He was always half a second from turning loose the dogs.

Seagraves had turned over all his other work to his clerks and partners and spent most of his time studying statements of the witnesses. The worst of the trouble was in the account of Mary McNutt, who had been shot four times. A jury would listen to her because of the bullets still in her body. She had refused to have the operations to take them out. She was the worst of the trouble, but in a way she was the answer, too.

Seagraves opened the gate and walked to the house. He pushed the doorbell and waited, and in a moment the door opened wide, and Hanna Trout was standing in front of him, dressed for church and holding her purse.

"Mrs. Trout."

"I thought you were my ride," she said.

He noticed both her feet were in shoes. "I see you've recovered the use of your foot," he said.

She did not answer, she did not invite him in. "That was some cut," he said. She stood motionless, looking into his face. He stared for a moment at the line of her leg inside her skirt, at her hip. He stretched to distract them both from the moment. "I saw toes caught in a lawn mower weren't as bad. . . ."

She looked at the watch on her wrist, and then checked the street behind him. She wore a shiny black belt that pressed into her waist and a silk blouse that she had buttoned all the way to her chin.

"You waiting on a ride to church?"

"Reverend Clay was supposed to pick me up," she said.

"Pardon?"

"Reverend Matthew Clay," she said.

Seagraves stepped inside the house, uninvited. He stood close to her and looked into her face. "Of the Bright Hope Baptist Church?"

She held herself erect and calm. "He may have been held up," she said. "He teaches Sunday school too. . . ." He smelled her soap and her shampoo.

He said, "I came by to ask you personally to attend your husband's trial."

"Mr. Seagraves," she said, "I have spent the last three months separating myself from what he has done."

Seagraves felt the alcohol wash over him again and sat down on the steps leading upstairs. "Excuse me," he said.

She considered him a long moment. "Can I get you something?"

His face was suddenly wet with perspiration, his shirt stuck to his sides. He shook his head. "I apologize for this," he said. "It passes in a moment. . . ."

"Do you need a drink?" she said.

He put his arms across his knees and rested his forehead against them. He considered going to sleep. "If it wouldn't be a bother," he said.

He did not watch her go into the kitchen, but in a moment he heard her open the refrigerator and then crack an ice tray. When he finally lifted his head, she was standing in front of him, holding what looked like a glass of tomato juice. He accepted it, thanked her, and felt the ice against his lips. He took a long drink and did not notice the alcohol until it was swallowed.

"You keep liquor in your home?" he said. He could not picture her breaking the law, even that one.

Immediately he felt himself improving. He took another drink. The front door was still open, and she checked the street. "What in the world are you doing with Reverend Clay?" he said.

"Going to church."

He took another drink, slower this time.

"I hope you will pardon my manners," he said. "I do not normally put myself in the middle of a family matter. But this . . . separation presents legal problems for Paris that I am sure you do not mean to inflict."

He drank again, finishing what she had brought him. It left an acid taste in his mouth, and presently he realized he was half drunk.

He looked at Hanna Trout again, staring at her belt. "I'm afraid I've come here dehydrated," he said.

"It would appear so," she said.

"Your husband . . ." Seagraves shook his head and concentrated, but he could not take his eyes off Mrs. Trout's belt. It was something about the way it led to her hips. "I know you don't mean to harm him," he said.

He looked up into her face and saw that she wasn't following his thought, so he began to explain. "In a situation like this the appearance of things is often as consequential as the facts. I'm speaking legally—"

"Do you need another?" she said.

He looked at the glass, then at Mrs. Trout. "That might do nicely," he said, and she took it back into the kitchen. A minute later, when she put it into his hand, he noticed his fingers were shaking.

She invited him into the living room, and he followed her there, sipping at the drink as he moved to keep it from spilling. She bent over the davenport, straightening a pillow, and he was poleaxed at the shape of her bottom. She straightened up, he found a chair and sat down.

He looked around the room and saw that it had changed. He did not know if she had painted or set the furniture in new places, but the room was lighter. She sat on the couch and crossed her legs. Her ankle moved, up and down, and he followed it until he felt sick again and closed his eyes.

"You were speaking of appearances," she said.

He rubbed his face and sipped at the drink. "A marriage is a thing," he said, "that people understand in the way they're married themselves. In the case of a dissolution they picture themselves in that too. They assume hurtful things about the parties, to assure themselves their own marriage is safe."

She sat still, watching him. He thought she might be fascinated.

"What I am saying is, there is a certain amount of lying that goes on between people that live with each other. Polite lying, that makes cohabitation possible. And at the time of a loss of affection there is a tendency of both parties to unburden themselves of those lies and tell things that indirectly threaten those who are still married. That threaten the institution itself—"

She squared herself and said, "My husband never afforded me the polite lying, Mr. Seagraves. He did not strike poses for me, he is not good at that."

He sipped at the drink. A piece of lemon was floating among the ice cubes, he hadn't noticed it before. "Little lies," he said, "flirtations."

She shook her head. "In the week that followed the killing of that child," she said, "Mr. Trout assaulted me three times. He forced me to eat rancid food, he attempted to drown me in my own bath, he abused me in an unmentionable way with a bottle. . . ."

Except for the shaking in his hands, Seagraves did not move. He stared into her face, trying to imagine it. He cleared his throat.

Mrs. Trout held his eyes for a moment and then looked out the window. "I expect Reverend Clay was delayed," she said. "Did you drive?"

"No," he said, and his voice seemed to belong to someone else. "I thought the exercise would . . ."

She wasn't listening. He thought of her receiving the bottle and wondered what it had been. Coca-Cola? Where had it happened? In this room? He cleared his throat again, warm-faced with liquor. "I will not break this confidence," he said.

When she looked at him again, she was smiling. "It hardly matters, does it?"

"Yes, to the appearance of things it does. To yourself and to your husband."

"What sort of appearances do you favor, Mr. Seagraves?" she said.

He thought she was teasing him now, he thought that she knew what he was thinking. He put the glass on the floor next to the chair. "The appearance of normalcy," he said.

She laughed out loud and leaned into her own lap. It crossed his mind that she herself had been drinking before he arrived.

"Mr. Seagraves," she said finally, straightening up, "that appearance is the very thing that allowed this to happen. My husband is an aberration. It is not normal to shoot children. Whatever effort is made to lend that appearance, it does not change the perversion itself but only asks that the perversion be shared. I will not be party to the shooting of children."

He said, "What if I proved that your husband was defending his life by discharging those shots?"

Her expression turned unfriendly. "You can't prove what didn't happen," she said.

"It's for a court of law to determine."

She shook her head. "There is no story you can tell in your court that will change what happened in that house." She looked around the room. "Or in this one."

"That is a misperception," he said, "that an act is, of itself, a crime or a perversion. It becomes such only after it is judged." He had no idea why he was explaining this to her.

He saw that she had begun to smile again, as if she were judging him. "The misperception," she said, "is that the law, and lawyers, decide what already happened."

Seagraves sat back into the chair. She stood up, checking the window again, and then crossed the room and took the glass out of his hand. "Another?"

He held his head, deciding.

"Mr. Seagraves?"

"One more," he said, and when she went into the kitchen, he followed her. She held her shoulders in one place as she walked, setting off all the movements below her belt. He passed through the room with the daybed and thought of her on the afternoon she had been cut.

She had seemed less substantial then. He remembered Trout's mischief, and his thoughts came back to the bottle.

He had never heard any woman outside of a courtroom acknowledge such an act before, and now Hanna Trout, whose life was as circumspect as anyone's in Ether County, had said it without so much as clearing her throat.

He realized he had stopped at the daybed, and she had stopped in the doorway to the kitchen, waiting for him. "I was remembering the afternoon you lacerated your foot," he said. She waited. "The mess on the floor . . . I never saw a worse cut. It's a miracle they saved all your toes."

It hit him then that he had no idea if they had saved her toes or not.

"There's no feeling in the ends," she said.

And that struck him as intimate too. He moved toward her, and she went the rest of the way into the kitchen.

She kept the jar in plain sight, on the cabinet beneath the glasses. The liquor inside was caramel-colored, and he saw a peach at the bottom. He recognized it as coming from Elbert Street's still. Elbert was an idiot with a gift for aging liquor.

Seagraves had been told that he stored it in kegs. He used charcoal, which purified it and gave it color. The kegs were buried in a cave somewhere on his property north of Gray for close to a year, and when it was time, he poured it into fruit jars, usually over a fresh peach.

Seagraves had measured one of the jars once and found that the liquor brought Elbert close to fifty dollars a gallon. It was commonly acknowledged as the best liquor in the state, but to Seagraves's knowledge it was sold in only one place, the Ether Hotel. You gave the boy there ten dollars and then reached into the pocket of an overcoat hung on the rack near the emergency exit and took the jar.

He could not picture Hanna Trout giving the boy ten dollars and wondered if the liquor was something her husband had left behind when he moved.

"The last time I was in this room," he said, "it looked like somebody'd blew up the icebox."

She unscrewed the lid of the jar, and he sat down at the table and stared at her while she fixed his drink. The tablecloth was plastic and stuck to his hands. She brought the glass to the table and set it in front of his nose. He was still staring at her, but she did not seem to notice. He saw her chest was not as heavy as Lucy's but seemed to be attached to her at a more favorable angle.

She sat down in the chair across the table, and for just a moment he felt the brush of her leg against his, and then he was dizzy. He recovered himself and said, "Where was I?"

"You were reminiscing over the kitchen," she said. "It looked like the icebox had blown up."

"Before that."

"The law. My misperception that a crime can happen without a lawyer there to verify it . . ."

It reminded him again of what Paris had done with the bottle.

"I'll give you the case," he said, and leaned heavily on the table. He noticed she did not move away, not even an inch. "What if a woman was to suggest, as you have, that her husband had in some way abused her with a bottle?"

He saw that she wouldn't stop him.

He said, "And that is a crime in the state of Georgia—"

"Sodomy," she said, and he felt himself humming beneath the table. The word sounded different coming from Hanna Trout in her own kitchen than it did in court. There was a sort of connection, both of them knowing what it meant.

"Sodomy," he said. "But what if it went to a court of law—which it wouldn't, because there were no witnesses—but what if it did, and all the details were revealed, where it occurred, what sort of bottle, everything that was said, and it became evident, in the course of this discovery, that the woman . . . had agreed to the act?"

She cocked her head, as if she had not understood the words.

He said, "If the woman had agreed. Or perhaps she didn't agree, not directly, but she enjoyed it. What does that say for her complaint? The act still occurred, a crime has been committed, but now we see it different. It's shaded by the woman's agreement. . . ."

He was reckless now, he had taken it too far and delivered himself into her hands. But part of being reckless was knowing you were reckless, and he was. He reached across the table and laid his hand on her arm. She did not seem to notice.

"A conspiracy," she said.

"It could be," he said. He was suddenly aware of his breathing, the feel of air over his lips and teeth. "A thing that could happen spontaneous. Who can say then that what occurred was even a crime? Law without compassion is not law at all."

She sat still a moment longer and then drew her arm from underneath his hand. He did not try to hold her. She said, "Do you believe I asked my husband to abuse me with a bottle, Mr. Seagraves?"

He did not answer at first. "It was only intended as a case for argument," he said finally. "I never meant it in a personal way. It came to mind because you had just spoken of your problem. . . ."

He was suddenly panicked.

"Do you believe the child asked to be shot?" she said. "Or the woman? Do you believe they agreed to it?"

He pulled himself back off the table and reached for his drink. He lifted it to his mouth and smiled just before it touched his lip. The smile was wrong in some way he could not identify or correct.

"I will tell you this," he said. "There wasn't anybody in that house completely innocent. Not the way you think of it. It didn't happen by itself."

It was quiet a moment, and he sipped again at the drink. He wished she had used less tomato juice.

"Do you know my husband well, Mr. Seagraves?" she said.

"As well as I need to," he said. Then: "As well as I care to."

"Can you predict what he would do if he walked in now and found us here talking on him?"

Seagraves pictured Trout coming in.

"I believe he'd bust up the kitchen."

"Would he speak?"

"You can't tell with him. He might and he might not."

"And when you left, what would he do then?"

Seagraves shook his head. "I never saw that side of him."

"You would leave. . . ."

He did not follow her now. He thought she might be asking him to stay. He thought she might be offering him something in return.

"I couldn't move in to watch him. I got a house of my own."

"Then who will watch him?"

"That's not my end of things. . . ."

Suddenly there were tears in her eyes, and he moved to touch her arm again. He said, "Perhaps you misunderstood my meaning, Mrs. Trout. . . ."

She pulled her arm away, and when she spoke again, her voice was shaking. "Who will watch him?"

He took another drink, but the tomato juice was at cross purposes with the liquor now, thick and hard to swallow.

"It's a simple question," she said. "When you and the law have decided that the child and the woman conspired to be shot, or enjoyed it, and have set my husband free, who will keep him from conspiring with another child to shoot her?"

"If he goes free, he is free," Seagraves said.

"And what then?"

He shook his head, wanting to leave now, wanting to get away from her misunderstandings and her warnings. "It's not my end," he said again.

She wiped at her eyes with the sleeve of her blouse. He tried to stand, but he was dizzy and felt himself begin to pitch onto the floor. She was speaking to him of the appearance of normalcy, he could not follow the words. She was warning him. He moved and fell into the sink.

SEAGRAVES WOKE UP ON the floor. There was a pillow beneath his head, a light blanket tucked under his chin that covered him to his knees. He sat up, exactly as sick as he had been in the morning. His tie had been loosened, and his belt. The room was darker than it had been, and he had the sudden feeling that people might be looking for him.

He found the edge of the sink with his hand and used that to pull himself to his feet. He stood still a moment, feeling the blood wash through his body. His foot was asleep, and there was a numbness in the left side of his buttocks. He waited, and those feelings passed.

The house was quiet.

He turned the faucet on and let cold water run over his face. He saw a box of baking soda on the counter and used that and his finger to wash his teeth. He combed his hair without a mirror and then pushed his shirt into his pants all the way around. He fastened his belt.

He walked carefully, not wanting to see Mrs. Trout again, and headed in the direction of the front door. He thought of putting off the visit with her husband until the morning, but if he did that, the expectation of it would be bothering him all night.

The sun had moved to the west side of the house, leaving the side he was on in a kind of dusk. He did not see her resting on the daybed until she spoke.

"I hope you're not injured," she said.

It startled him, and in the aftermath he felt his blood again, returning to places it had left. He nodded, and to calm himself, he began to speak. "It's the hours I been putting in," he said, "they catch up to you. It happened once before. I'd just got out of the courthouse, and the next thing I knew I was looking at the squirrels in the trees."

"I didn't think you'd want me to call a doctor," she said.

"No," he said, "no need. I must have cut out just as I was leaving." He looked at his watch then, but in the poor light he couldn't make out the hands.

"Have I been here long?"

"Yes."

"It's still Sunday, isn't it?" he said. He smiled, and then felt the weight of her stare, and stopped.

It was quiet.

"Are you going to get him off?"

"I can't say what will happen." He put his hand on the doorknob, telling himself to turn it, walk through and then out the front door. . . .

"If you turn my husband loose, you open the door for everything that follows."

Seagraves opened the door and paused in the threshold. "I wish you'd reconsider," he said. "Come to the trial."

SEAGRAVES CLOSED THE GATE outside the house and looked at his watch. It was nearly four o'clock. He began to walk south, into town. He straightened himself as he went, lining up the buttons of his shirt with his belt buckle, smoothing the wrinkles out of the sleeves of his coat.

A block from the house he turned east, in the direction of the college. It was one place in Cotton Point he was not likely to be recognized, and there were professors walking around the school who looked as wrinkled as he did now every day of their lives.

He crossed the street, stepped over a parking chain, and was on the campus. Feeling safer, he began to reconstruct his defense of Paris Trout. It was not as pure now as it had been in the morning; Hanna Trout was still with him, staring across the dark room, using his own words to warn him. It felt like a curse.

He wondered if she were part Gypsy.

He walked the length of the campus and came out behind the courthouse. The street beyond that was Browne, and then Main, where he turned left. The Ether Hotel stood in the middle of the block, a shade of green, it seemed to him, that nobody drunk or hung over or anywhere in between ought to have to confront.

He walked inside. The lobby was empty except for a clerk sitting behind the desk, playing solitaire. Seagraves noticed the coat hanging on the rack near the emergency exit, the side pocket heavy with a jar of liquor, and he thought for a moment he was going to be sick.

"Is Mr. Trout in?" he said.

The clerk looked up, saw who it was, and hurried to his feet. He turned and checked the mailbox. "Yessir," he said, "must be, on account his key's gone."

"What room is that?" Seagraves said.

The boy hesitated.

"I am Mr. Trout's attorney, and I am here on a matter of business."

The boy said, "Mr. Trout don't take visitors. It's in his instructions."

"Instructions . . ."

"Yessir, he wrote them down when he first moved in. Like, he takes the paper in his mailbox just so, and if it ain't there, he won't pick one up off the counter. He'll go to his room and call down to have somebody bring it."

Seagraves saw the boy was as afraid of him as he was of Trout. "What room?" he said.

"Three-ten. The honeymoon suite."

Seagraves looked up and down and could not imagine it. "Paris Trout's got the honeymoon suite?"

"Yessir," the boy said, and Seagraves thought he sounded sad. "He flat took it over."

Seagraves climbed the stairs, holding on to the rail. When he got to the third floor he stopped, right on the edge again, and waited until his stomach settled.

He walked up the hallway to the end and found the door. It was dark wood, the numbers 310 nailed in gold right at eye level.

He knocked and heard the bedsprings. "Who is it?" Right on the other side of the door.

"Harry Seagraves," he said.

The door cracked open, a few inches. He saw one of Trout's eyes. "We got to talk."

Trout offered no sign that he recognized Seagraves or even heard him. He kept his eye in the crack of the door, waiting for something else.

"Are you dressed?"

Trout looked him up and down then, as if he were comparing their clothes. Then the door opened another half foot, and Seagraves saw the gun. Trout was wearing a long-sleeve white shirt, buttoned at the neck and wrists, and in the hand Seagraves could see was a heavy foreign-looking automatic.

"Who are you fixing to shoot?" Seagraves said.

Trout still didn't answer, and the thought settled for just a moment in Seagraves's head that this man knew where he—Seagraves—had spent the day. Trout walked away from the door, leaving it open, and came back a moment later wearing his coat. He put as much of the gun as would fit into the side pocket and came out of his room.

As he opened the door, Seagraves caught a quick, blinding reflection of the sun off the floor. "We could talk here," Seagraves said, but Trout had already started toward the stairs.

At the front desk Seagraves stopped him. "Leave your gun with the boy," he said.

Trout took a step back. "It's legal. I got a right."

"You don't need a damn gun to walk up the street Sunday afternoon."

"How far?"

"As close as you want," Seagraves said. "The college, officers' academy, it doesn't matter as long as it's private. It won't help things to be seen walking the streets with a weapon two weeks before they call a jury. . . ."

Trout looked at his pocket. The mouth of the pistol peeked out of the corner like some pet snake. He took it out, the barrel moving quickly from Seagraves to himself to the door, and then handed it to the boy behind the desk. "Don't allow nobody to monkey with this," he said.

The boy took the gun, holding it with two hands, and set it behind the counter. "No sir," he said.

"Even yourself."

"No sir."

Trout stared at the boy a moment longer. "I'll know if you do," he said.

"Yessir, I know you would."

They walked down Main Street, passing Trout's store, and came to the academy. Seagraves was sick again and went through some bushes to a bench underneath an elm tree. He sat down heavily, Trout stood in front of him.

"Well?" Trout said. "It's private."

Seagraves wiped at the sweat on his neck. "I went and talked to your wife today," he said.

"It's no one's concern what's between her and me."

"It's your concern that she comes to your trial," Seagraves said quietly.

Trout stared down at him, then looked around, as if he were afraid someone were listening. "I pay you for that." Then he looked at his watch.

"Are you late somewhere? You need to get back to your hotel room?"

"What is it you come by to say?"

"The first thing," Seagraves said, "you got to talk to your wife, patch up what you can. People know you left the house, but if you could get her to the courtroom, it might help."

"I mind my own business," Trout said, "let everybody else mind theirs."

"It isn't your business until it's over," Seagraves said. "After the trial you got all the privacy you want, one way or the other."

Trout looked at him. Seagraves could see he was angry, but he held it. "Now," Seagraves said, "you and Buster Devonne been going over what happened in Indian Heights?"

Trout shrugged. "Ain't much to go over."

Trout began to pace.

Seagraves closed his eyes to keep himself from following the movement. "Buster and myself was in it together," Trout said. "We decided what we said and took a pact to stick to it."

"A pact?"

Trout nodded. "On the way back to town. That nothing happened in Indian Heights was gone turn two white men against each other."

Seagraves opened his eyes and stared at him, trying to imagine how it would have looked. He saw Trout stained with the child's blood, he and Buster Devonne shaking hands on their pact.

"Did Buster shoot the woman, or did you?"

Trout stopped pacing and studied his feet. "He works for me," he said. "He'll say what I tell him." Then, more quietly: "He thinks they'll invite us in the jury room—my trial and then his—give out party hats to celebrate."

Seagraves took a deep breath.

"Buster is a popular man in Ether County," Trout said. "They ain't going to do nothing to him. It could be their own trouble."

It was quiet a long minute, and then Seagraves heard his own voice. "If it was you who shot the woman and the girl, and they had a gun of their own, it would explain things better."

Trout stood dead still.

"If it happened that all the shots came from your weapon . . ." The words came out of him easier than he thought they would, easier than they should.

Trout still hadn't moved, but Seagraves began to notice the rise and fall of his chest. "Which one of us you think is paying you?" he said after a moment.

"It was your gun that fired the bullets into the girl," Seagraves said. "Ward Townes has got the gun and the bullets, that's the starting point. We all got to agree to it because there it is. But if it happened that the bullets inside the woman were yours too—there is no way to prove that because they're still inside her—then we've got a situation that a jury might see self-defense."

"I ain't in this alone," Trout said a little later.

Seagraves stood up, steadying himself with his hand against the back of the bench. "Either that," he said, "or you were in it together." The next time he looked at Trout, he was glad he'd made him leave the gun back at the hotel.

"There isn't going to be any party in the jury room for either of you," Seagraves said. "Buster Devonne doesn't know Cotton Point, he only knows what fits his own way of thinking about it." He saw Trout didn't believe that. "It's a mistake to take a place and say it's all one way or another, just because that's the way it's comfortable," he said.

THE TRIAL BEGAN SEVENTEEN days later on a Wednesday, at eight o'clock in the morning. Judge John Taylor was a little under five and a half feet tall and weighed 220 pounds, even without his robe, and started early because he was intolerant of late-afternoon heat.

During the summer, in fact, he was sometimes disposed to call a five-minute recess every hour, to retire to his chambers, undress, and cover himself with baby powder. Attorneys who were taken into his chambers for scolding or to argue sensitive issues were accustomed to seeing the judge sitting in his shorts behind his desk, the color of death itself.

He smiled now, at the beginning of the case, and noted the spectators. They had filled every seat and were standing in the back and sitting in the windowsills. "You-all welcome to stay, of course," he said, "but in the afternoon you ain't going to want to."

A few of the ladies looked uncomfortable at the warning.

Seagraves was sitting with Trout. There was a notepad between them on the table, for Trout to write down his thoughts or objections. He was immobile today, staring straight ahead, as he had been the day before during jury selection. He took it as an affront to be judged.

He was dressed in a pale gray suit and a yellow tie. He had been to the barber and shined his shoes.

Hanna Trout, however, was missing from the room. Seagraves had saved a place for her in the seats just behind the defense table, and it was the only empty seat in the room. He took it as a setback and as an omen.

And he was disappointed in some way that was unconnected to the trial.

Buster Devonne, whose own trial was scheduled to follow Trout's, sat behind the gate, on the aisle of the third row. Seagraves noticed he bore a certain resemblance to some of the members of the jury, a resemblance of attitude and manner which Trout, under any sort of scrutiny, did not share.

As the trial date closed in, Seagraves had spent long afternoons with Trout and Devonne, together and then one at a time. Devonne, who was an imbecile, understood immediately; Trout held some unspoken resistance. Hours went into the preparation of the statement Trout would read at the trial, and more hours into trying to coach him into some sort of ordinary civility. But each time they met, Trout was more remote than the last. It was almost as if he had removed himself from what was coming. On the last afternoon Seagraves gave up and left the instructions at this: "If you need to say something, write it down. Write slowly, so it looks thoughtful."

Trout had said, "I don't need to write things down. That's what I paid you for."

THE FIRST WITNESS WAS Henry Ray Boxer. He wore a long-sleeve shirt with cuff links at the wrists, Sunday pants, work shoes. His hand on the Bible was as narrow as a woman's. He slouched in the witness chair, afraid to look left or right, and spoke so softly he could barely be heard.

Seagraves noticed that Ward Townes's voice was lacking capacity too. It was Townes's courtroom manner to take a jury out of the reference of a courtroom, to make them comfortable, let them know it was all right to smile like ordinary people. This morning, though, there was none of that, and the thought came to Seagraves that Ward Townes didn't want to be here any more than he did.

Townes asked Henry Ray Boxer where he lived, who all lived with him. Henry Ray used his fingers, giving each one a name of a brother or sister. He didn't know ages.

Townes asked when he had bought the car, how much he paid. Henry Ray went over the arrangement, mentioning the $227 for insurance. He told about the accident at the gas station and bringing the car back to Paris Trout after it happened.

His testimony went on for most of an hour, with Seagraves objecting only once, at the end, when Henry Ray called the truck driver who had run into him a "damn nigger."

"Your Honor," Seagraves said, standing up, "we are as understanding as anyone of the great divergence of people this matter has brought together, but out of respect for the ladies I would ask the court to instruct the witness to refrain from gratuitous profanity."

"Mr. Boxer," the judge said, "do you understand the meaning of the word 'profanity'?"

"Yessir."

"Then I instruct you not to use it."

"I didn't said it, he did."

"Not the word itself," the judge said, "but the examples thereof." And Henry Ray Boxer sat still, looking at the judge as if he'd just said there was a twenty-dollar fee to be a witness.

"Thank you," Seagraves said, and sat down.

Townes smiled, the first time that morning. "That's all I have for now," he said, and turned the witness over for cross-examination.

Harry Seagraves walked toward Henry Ray Boxer slowly, scratching his head. He felt the jury watching him. He would have made them wait—he liked to build a feeling—but then he noticed Trout was staring at the witness in a way he did not want the jury to see, as if the boy had just walked in and told him all over again that he wasn't going to pay.

"Henry Ray Boxer," he said. The boy did not reply. "That is your name?"

"Yessir."

"Henry Ray, where was the last car you bought before the one from Mr. Trout?"

"Didn't have none before this."

"Didn't you buy a car from Mr. William Sutter in Eatonton?"

He shook his head. "I haven't bought no car from Mr. Sutter."

"Weren't you driving Mr. Sutter's car the time you ran into Mr. Louie Veal?"

"No sir."

"That was a different car?"

Henry Ray moved in his chair. "No sir, that was a truck."

"You weren't driving the car in question. . . ."

"What question is that?"

There was some laughter in back, Seagraves smiled and shook his head. "The car you agreed to purchase from Mr. Trout."

"No sir, a lumber truck hit that."

Ward Townes stood up then, looking tired, and objected to everything about Mr. Louie Veal, saying it was included only to prejudice the jury. Judge Taylor sustained.

Seagraves walked back to his table and picked up his notes. "Now, how much did you tell Mr. Townes there that you paid?"

"Eight hundred."

"Could it have been more?"

"Could have, I don't know."

"Don't you know what you paid for it?"

"I didn't pay for it," he said. "I was gone pay on it."

"But it was eighty-five dollars, even money, every month?"

"I don't know even money or not."

Seagraves tossed the papers back across his desk. "It looks to me, if you wanted to tell the truth about this thing, that you could tell us. You ought to remember how much you paid."

"Eight hundred," the boy said. "Assurance ran it up to thousand twenty-seven."

Seagraves sighed and then looked at the jury. Half of them came from Homewood and worked at the asylum. They had sewage and city drinking water because of him. "You bought the car from Mr. Trout," he said, without looking at the witness, "tore it up, and then refused to pay on it because Mr. Trout wouldn't fix it?"

"Yessir."

"Was it running when you brought it back?"

"Yessir, it was running, but it was tore up so."

"And you won't drive a car like that—"

"No sir, I don't drive no ragged car."

He turned away and asked the next question. "Have you got a license, Henry Ray?"

"Yessir."

"Is that the same license Chief Norland looked at the day when he arrested you for running over Mr. Veal?"

"That is the same one."

Townes stood up, making the same objection. Judge Taylor sustained.

Seagraves put his hands deep in his pants pockets and bent as if he were looking for something on the floor. "Had you done business with Mr. Trout before you bought this car?"

Henry Ray nodded.

Seagraves looked directly into the jury again. "These folks can't hear you unless you talk, Henry Ray. They come here to try and find out what really happened out to your house, and they need to hear all your answers, not just the ones you feel like giving."

Judge Taylor said, "The witness will answer the question."

"What question was it?" Henry Ray said.

Seagraves turned back slowly. "The question was, had you ever done business with Mr. Trout before you bought this car?"

"I borrowed money away from him."

"Good. Now can you tell us how much you owed?"

The boy shrugged. " 'Bout twenty-five, I expect."

"Are you sure it wasn't a hundred?"

"No, sir, it wasn't no hundred dollars."

"But you owed him something."

"Yessir, I paid him along on that too."

Seagraves went back to the table and consulted his notes again. "Now, that pistol your brother Tommy has out there, whose pistol is it?"

"Mr. Lyle's."

"Your stepfather."

"Yessir."

"So in other words, on the day of the shooting Tommy had Lyle McNutt's pistol out there?"

"I don't know, sir. I wasn't home."

"Did Tommy have your pistol out there that day too?"

"No sir, I don't have one."

Seagraves froze, as if something had reached out and touched him in the night. Then, moving only his head, he looked up at the witness. "What did you do with it?"

"I never had it to do nothing with it."

"Am I mistaken," he said, "or weren't you convicted for carrying a pistol in 1954, right in this courthouse?"

"That was Mr. Lyle's pistol, I was bringing it from Eatonton."

"But you were convicted here."

"Yessir."

"You were found guilty."

"I don't know, sir, if I was found or not."

"Didn't they give you two months' sentence?"

"No sir, not that they said."

"Didn't they fine you twenty-five dollars? You remember that, don't you?"

Ward Townes finally stood up again, Seagraves was surprised he'd allowed it to go as far as he had. "Your Honor," he said, "the attorney for Mr. Trout has exceeded the limits of fairness. This line of questioning has been employed only for prejudice, and you and I and everyone in this courtroom knows there is enough of that here already."

"Overruled," the judge said.

But as Townes spoke, Seagraves watched the jury. There were three of them he could read clearly, a couple of others that he was beginning to. He did not like what he saw.

"I'm through with this witness," he said.

TOWNES CALLED THOMAS BOXER. He was smaller than his brother, and more delicate-looking. In some ways, Seagraves thought, he resembled the pictures of Rosie Sayers. He settled into the witness chair after he was sworn and then jumped at the sound of his name.

"Thomas," Townes said, "you were at the house the day Mr. Trout and Mr. Devonne came to see your brother?"

Thomas Boxer told the story, what he had seen and heard. It took him a long time, but it came out true. Trout and Devonne on the porch with their guns, the things that were said and done.

Trout following Rosie into the house, Mary McNutt following him, and then Buster Devonne coming in behind. Thomas Boxer looked at his hands when he said he had run into the other side of the house.

"Why did you go in there, Thomas?" Townes asked.

"Went in there to get out the way."

"Do you know what else happened?"

"Shooting," he said. "Shooting started before I got to the door."

"How many shots?"

He shook his head. "You couldn't say. Seem like firecrackers. They was almost all together, all of it didn't take but four or five seconds."

"What happened after the shooting stopped?"

"After the shooting I went out to the back, there was Momma and Rosie both coming out the house. Momma holding herself here on her breast, Rosie holding her 'tomach."

"Did you see Mr. Trout or Mr. Buster back there?"

"No sir, they gone by then."

"Was there a pistol in the house at the time all this happened?"

"Yessir, on my side. Right under my mattress."

"Did you ever get that pistol?"

"No sir, I never bothered it till the next morning when they come out after it. I give it to a police."

"Did you fight Mr. Trout any? Did you put your hand on him?"

"No sir."

"Did he put his hand on you?"

"Yessir, but he didn't have his hand on me but a little while. He didn't touch nothing long, but when he left his hands off us, we was changed for good."

Townes stood quietly a moment, giving that time to sink in. Then he looked at Trout and said, "Your witness."

*

SEAGRAVES STOOD UP, UNDECIDED as to how that last remark had affected the jury. He looked at them again, trying to remember which ones were indebted to him for their city water, but in some way that would not quite come clear, they were not as familiar as they had been an hour before. He smiled, glancing down at the pad in front of Trout. He was drawing cartoons—ducks shooting guns at each other.

"He didn't touch us long, but when he left his hands off us, we was changed for good." Seagraves repeated the boy's words in a monotone as if he were reading them.

"Yessir."

"Could you tell us how things were before Mr. Trout changed them?"

"I don't know that I exactly could," the boy said.

"Well, let's see. When you needed money, where did you go to borrow?"

The boy did not answer.

"Did Mr. Trout come to you, or did you go to him?"

"He come out that day."

"I'm not talking about the day of the shooting right now," Seagraves said. "We'll talk about that later. Right now I want to know about this beatific life you-all had that Mr. Trout changed."

The boy moved in his seat. "I didn't say it was that," he said.

Seagraves closed his eyes. "What I am getting at here is that Paris Trout was part of the reason you had the good life you did. That he had been a friend to your family, loaned you money when you needed it, and would still be a friend if you hadn't tried to cheat him on this car."

The boy did not answer.

"Am I going too fast?"

"No sir."

"Then answer the question."

"I didn't hear none."

"The question I asked you was to describe the life that you say Mr. Trout changed."

The boy paused. "Rosie's life," he said.

Seagraves felt it getting away from him now. He looked again at the jury and saw the size of his mistake. "Now sir," he said, "when

Mr. Trout came up on the porch, did he do anything to threaten you?"

"He put his hand back of my collar, you know naturally that would threaten anybody."

"Were you scared?"

"No sir, I recognize they wasn't coming up there for me. I had one payment before that was overdue, and I just paid them on up."

"Why did you grab Mr. Trout by the neck then?"

"I never grabbed Mr. Trout. I never raised my hand."

"Did you try to fight Mr. Trout?"

"I didn't attempt to fight. If I did, Mr. Buster was glad to shoot me."

"That was the reason you didn't fight?"

"Nobody would fight, somebody got a pistol on them."

Seagraves held his head as if he were dizzy. "All right," he said, "you say Rosie ran into the house, then Mr. Trout, and then your mother."

"Walked," he said. "She just walk in there calm."

"You saw that? She just walked in nice and slow?"

"No sir, she was walking pert. She don't ever walk slow."

"Did you see the rest?"

"I didn't see it all," he said. "I didn't stayed out there. I saw him when he caught up to Rosie, that is the only thing."

"Did you see him hit her?"

"He grabbed her by the head. I don't know what else. He might of hit her."

"You are the gentleman who was there, and you can't say if she was hit or not?"

"Yessir, he hit her with something. I saw the place on her head."

Seagraves moved closer to the jury. "All right," he said, "and then you ducked in the house. Is that where your rifle is?"

"Yessir."

"It's a .22, single-shot rifle?"

"Yessir."

"Did you mean to get it out?"

"Don't I have a right to protect my house?"

"Awhile ago you said you ducked in there because you were scared. Why did you say that?"

"I was scared," the boy said. "I'm naturally scared when somebody is shooting."

Seagraves saw the boy's fingers were shaking. "Which is it? Were you scared or were you mad?"

"Yessir," he said.

"You were scared enough to shoot somebody with your .22 rifle, but you weren't scared enough to shoot them with a pistol?"

"I don't know how to shoot no pistol," he said.

"Then why was it under your mattress? Why take it from your stepfather in the first place?"

"I didn't have no reason, I just liked it," he said.

"Do you know what perjury is?" Seagraves asked. "Do you know it is a crime in this state to tell a lie under oath?"

"I know it."

"I'll ask again. Why did you want it on your side of the house then?"

"I could take what I wanted on my side. Mr. Lyle don't mind what I take."

Seagraves leaned closer to the boy and spoke to the jury. "The truth is," he said, "that gun wasn't there, was it? It was on the other side, and you took it out of there after the shooting, didn't you?"

"No sir, I had it before."

Seagraves shook his head. "All right, you said Mr. Devonne had a gun too."

"I saw the print of it through his coat."

"Did he say anything while this was going on?"

The boy shrugged. "He didn't say a mumbling word the whole time."

"He just walked in, without rhyme or reason, and began to shoot? Does that make sense to you?"

"I don't know," the boy said. "I never seen people act out like that before."

Seagraves walked back to the defense table and saw that Trout had filled the page. Ducks, mice, guns, pools of steaming blood. A woodpecker smoking a cigarette. He was beginning to draw walls and a window, to make the scene indoors.

"I have no further questions," he said.

Judge Taylor consulted his watch and broke for lunch. It was ten thirty-five, and Paris Trout was out the door before any of the spectators.

TROUT CROSSED TOWN ON foot, using alleys and backyards, and arrived at the Ether County Retirement Home in ten minutes.

He walked through the lobby without signing the visitors' book, without acknowledging the nurse sitting behind the reception desk. There was a rule that visitors had to sign in and residents had to sign out, but the nurse looked at Trout and decided not to make an issue.

He climbed the stairs to the second floor and walked into room 26 without knocking. His mother was sitting in a wheelchair near the sink, naked.

A fat Negro woman in a green uniform was kneeling in front of her, sponging her feet. The woman looked over her shoulder at the sound of the door, stopping for a moment, and then rinsed the sponge in a bowl of dirty water and started up the old woman's legs. She knew Trout from other visits.

Trout sat down on the unmade bed, watching. His mother's toenails were yellow and thick and had not been cut in a long time. They had not grown straight but followed along the curve of her toes, reminding him somehow of talons.

Her legs were thin and bruised, unshaved.

Her lap was hidden by the way she sat in the chair, a little tuft of gray hair showing at the top. "Miz Trout be finished here in a few minutes, you want to wait outside," the woman said.

Trout did not move.

The sponge went over his mother's knees and then moved to her chest and stomach. He saw little bumps rise on her arms, chicken skin. The woman stood and pulled her halfway out of her chair. His mother's chin rested on the woman's shoulder while she washed her back and bottom.

"There now," the woman said, "we be done in a jiffy." She dropped the old lady back into the chair and studied her work. There was a wet shine over her, top to bottom, and she had begun to shake.

156

The woman walked into the bathroom and came back with a towel and bent over the old lady, going back over what she had done. She was drying the chest when she noticed the old lady's breathing. "Lord a mercy," she said, "something got Miz Trout excited today."

He saw the rise and fall of her stomach too, it was spasmodic, as if she were crying. "I bet she knows you come to see her," the woman said. "I bet she knows you here." The woman moved until her face was in front of his mother's. "You know your sonny boy come to visit, didn't you?"

She opened the closet door and came out with a white nightgown. She fit it over the old lady's head and then her body, tugging at the arms to get them into the sleeves.

"People 'round here say Miz Trout don't realize a day has passed the last five years, but she knows more than they think."

She took the combs out of the old lady's hair and then smoothed it as it fell, the ends just touching the floor.

"You want to comb your momma's hair?" the woman said. "Sometime peoples like to comb their mothers' hair. . . ." She thought for a minute. "But I expect it's ladies like to do that, ain't it?"

Without a word Trout stood up and walked out the door.

TRIAL RESUMED AT ONE O'clock.

Seagraves approached the courthouse by himself, from the back. He'd eaten lunch at the college cafeteria, wanting time alone to think. Something was wrong with the case, the same thing was wrong with him. There was a confusion that defied order, and Paris Trout was in the middle of it, getting clearer all the time.

Seagraves saw Buster Devonne then, standing on the sidewalk where he could watch both doors to the building, and as soon as he spotted Seagraves, he crossed the lawn of newly planted grass to head him off.

"Mr. Seagraves," he said, smiling, "if I might have a minute of your time, sir . . ."

Seagraves stood where he was.

Buster Devonne stopped close enough so Seagraves could smell his sweat and lit a cigarette. He pulled the smoke deep into his body, and it came back out with the words as he spoke.

"Sir," he said, "there is some feeling among my friends that I am being used in this trial in a way that is detrimental to my own case."

Seagraves did not answer.

"On account, you know, of the conflict of my testimony with my original statement."

"You need to talk to your attorney about that," Seagraves said. "I represent Paris Trout's interests."

"That's what I mean," he said. "You see, I ain't got no Harry Seagraves to get me off. I got Bear Lewis, the midget, and he's a worst lawyer than he was a judge."

Seagraves kept still.

"And what I thought," Buster Devonne said, "was it might be to our mutual benefit if you was to represent me also."

"No," he said.

Devonne ran the palm of his hand over his head, from the forehead back to his neck. "I got to protect myself, you see. I can't afford no crackerjack lawyer."

"Bear Lewis knows the law," Seagraves said.

"No sir, not good enough. I need me a better lawyer, or I can't go saying nothing at this trial here. . . ." He smiled and pulled again on the cigarette.

"How much do you want?" Seagraves said.

Devonne left the cigarette in his lips and put his hands in his pockets. He looked at his shoes, caked with fresh dirt. "A thousand," he said. "A thousand, I ought get me a lawyer of my own. . . ."

WHEN SEAGRAVES REENTERED THE courtroom, the air was dead weight. Hot and still and dead. It was an effort to breathe. Judge Taylor came in a moment later, pulling at his collar. There was baby powder between his fingers and streaked here and there across his robe. He sat down and broke an immediate sweat. He instructed the court officer to clear the spectators out of the windows and then sent him for a fan.

Ward Townes called Mary McNutt. For half an hour Townes questioned her, uninterrupted by defense objection, leading her from her first meeting with Rosie Sayers to the moment things started on the porch.

She said, "I come up on the step, and Mr. Trout had brass knucks on his left hand. He made a rake to hit her, and she dodged.

"Rosie tore off into the house, and he tore off after her, like he was tearing down a panel. I come through the door, and they was at the foot of the bed. He had hold of her, and she had hold of him, around his waist. I saw where he hit her with the knucks. He surely bust the skin. I went in the second room door, and Mr. Buster Devonne come right on behind me and shot me in the back. I walk on, and he shot me again, a little before I got to Mr. Trout and Rosie, right there in my own house."

"And what did you do?" Townes said.

"I kept straight by them, I didn't do nothing."

"Were you hurt?"

"Sir . . . those bullets went inside."

"Could you feel them?"

"I could feel the shock, oh, yes."

Sitting at the table, Seagraves felt them too.

Townes said, "But you went on walking? Did you ever get hold of Mr. Trout?"

"No sir. I went on in there in the kitchen. I just got to the table to lay down, and then I dropped to my knees and couldn't stand up. I felt the bullets a different aspect, and I just wanted to lay down. Then Rosie come in after Mr. Trout had shot her, sat down on the trunk. He had shot her in the arm and the side."

"How many times did Mr. Trout shoot her after she sat down?"

"I know of twice, maybe more."

"And you were there when he did the shooting?"

"I was laying down," she said. "I was laying down with her to die. She said, 'Lord have mercy, Mary, he has shot me in my stomach.' I raised up, and just as I turned around Mr. Buster ran in a little piece and shot me again. I said, 'Come on, Rosie,' and she got up, and me and her went out the back door."

Ward Townes waited a moment, and then, quietly, he said, "Can you show the jury any of the places the bullets hit you?"

Seagraves came out of his chair slowly, as if he were undecided whose side he was on.

"Objection," he said, sounding tired. "The witness is not the deceased, the condition of her body, whatever it may be, is not germane to this case and is not admissible."

Townes said, "It is certainly germane to the business Paris Trout conducted that day in Indian Heights. It cannot be separated out because Mrs. McNutt did not succumb to her injuries."

Judge Taylor dropped his chin into the palm of his hand and thought. "Well, Mr. Townes," he said, "I don't think you can make an exhibition of these wounds without subjecting the witness to a certain embarrassment."

"We won't need to disrobe her," Townes said. "All she has to do is pull up her dress."

Seagraves spoke again, more deliberately. "I would further object, for the record, that any such display would be highly prejudicial and would impugn the dignity of this court."

Judge Taylor would not meet his eye. "I will let it in," he said, "if counsel can show the wounds without undue embarrassment."

Seagraves walked back to his seat and heard the first question before he had turned around.

"Now, Miss Mary, where did the initial shot hit you?"

"Right in the middle of the back," she said.

"Would you please stand for a moment?"

The woman stood up and turned around. She had worn a long cotton dress with buttons up the back. Without being asked, she unfastened the top three. Her dress separated, and the skin beneath was rolling and brown, and just to the right of her spine was a black spot the size of a half dollar. Two black lines led from it in opposite directions, as if she had been cracked.

Townes positioned her so the jury could see. Then he said, "Thank you," and she rebuttoned her dress and sat back down. She had not hesitated or fumbled over the buttons.

"Where did the next bullet go?" Townes said.

"In the side," she said. And she reached behind, without standing, unbuttoning herself again, and then pulled the dress open until another black mark appeared. It lay on the wave of flesh beneath her brassiere.

"And the next?"

She covered her side and pulled the dress down from the neck. Showing her right shoulder. The spot there was larger than the other two, and unlike them, it rose above the skin. The last mark was beneath her left breast, and she displayed it easily and without embarrassment. Unlike her sons, she was not afraid.

"All this time you were being shot," Townes said, "did any of you folks curse Mr. Trout or Mr. Devonne?"

"No sir," she said.

"Did you have any kind of weapon, any of you?"

"No sir."

"How long did it take? I mean, were the shots fired quick or slow?"

"As quick as anything is ever done," she said.

"And when it was over, what did Mr. Trout and Mr. Devonne do then?"

"When I looked," she said, "both of them was just running like rabbits. I told Rosie then to come on, and me and her made our way out the door. It didn't seem like no reason to stay in the kitchen where it happened. We had other things to do then."

He looked at her, not seeming to understand. But Seagraves did.

"To prepare ourselves," she said.

Seagraves closed his eyes; Trout looked straight ahead. Townes waited a moment, making sure everyone understood. "Did they ever get any of those bullets out of you?" he said finally.

She shook her head. "No sir. I feel them in the night."

"Thank you," Townes said, "that's all I have."

SEAGRAVES STARED AT THE woman from his seat, she stared back. "Do you own a pistol, Mrs. McNutt?" he said.

"No sir."

"There is no pistol in your house?"

"Yessir, there is one. It belongs to my husband, Mr. Lyle McNutt."

"Do you know where your husband keeps it?"

"Yessir, I know everything in my home."

"What caliber pistol is that?"

"I don't keep track of nothing like that. I just know it's there."

Seagraves stood up and began to walk toward the jury. He had found an assault charge which was filed and dropped against Mary Boxer in Daniel County seven years previous. A white veterinarian claimed she had tried to hit him with a chair in a scuffle over the rent.

He had meant to bring that into it here, he knew he ought to bring it in. Something stopped him, though, he couldn't say what. Only that things were confused enough.

"The point I'm coming to, Mrs. McNutt," Seagraves said, "our contention here is going to be that you are accusing Mr. Buster Devonne because you don't want the jury to believe him later on. I want to give you the chance to speak to that now."

For a moment she seemed to rock, as if a breeze had suddenly blown through the room. "Lord," she said, "I wouldn't say nobody shot me if they didn't."

"You know a good bit about the courthouse, don't you?"

"No sir."

"You and your family know something about how to try a case?"

"Ain't none of us lawyers," she said, and suddenly everyone in the court except Mary McNutt herself was laughing.

Seagraves smiled, and the judge wiped tears out of his eyes. "I didn't mean to accuse you being lawyers," Seagraves said. "I meant you folks have been through this procedure before."

"No sir, I never been in court."

"What about those boys of yours?"

"No sir, they never in nothing like a big court. Henry Ray been in little troubles, but never in nothing with a gun."

"Our contention, Mrs. McNutt," Seagraves said, "is going to be that Thomas came up off that chair and cursed Mr. Trout for everything in the catalog and then came in after the shooting and removed the gun. Is that the truth?"

She and Paris Trout stared at each other then, until Seagraves walked between them.

"No sir," she said. "I told the truth about it. You can make it look any which way now, but I told how it happened."

Seagraves said, "That's what we called the jury for, to decide."

She turned then, looking directly at them. "They don't decide what happened," she said. "It's already done. All they decide is if they gone do something about it."

*

162

HARRY SEAGRAVES ATE A late supper alone with Lucy. The maid had gone home ill, and the liver Lucy cooked had a metallic taste. He had no appetite anyway.

He played with his food until she had finished and then stood up, not waiting for dessert, and headed out the front door. "Harry?" she said.

"I've got some things to do," he said, without turning around.

"Are you going to be long?"

"I'm in a trial," he said.

He drove the car to Sleepy Heights, a gritty housing development that overlooked the sawmill on the edge of town. Two-bedroom houses, most of them cheap brick. Brand-new, they were forty-two hundred dollars each. Police lived there, workers from the sawmill, teachers.

The development was built on two hills, and Buster Devonne's place sat in between, at the bottom. Seagraves stopped the car in the road and turned off the lights. He checked to see the envelope was still in his coat pocket. He got out. The air was full of the smell of sawmill chemicals.

The driveway sloped downhill, and ridges of baked clay left by car tires broke under Seagraves's feet and made him unsteady as he walked toward the porch. It was screened in and ran the length of the front of the house. Seagraves knocked and then realized Buster Devonne was sitting six feet away, watching him.

Buster Devonne stood up slowly and unhooked the screen door. Behind him, inside the house, there were lights on. Somebody was playing a piano. Buster Devonne didn't wait for Seagraves to come in but turned his back as soon as the door was unlocked and sat back down and lit a cigarette. "Help yourself," he said, and nodded to the other chairs.

"I didn't come to sit with you," Seagraves said.

"This ain't personal against Paris," he said. "I got to protect my own interests. You explained that to Paris the way I intended it. . . ."

"I brought you the money," Seagraves said. "I don't run your errands."

Buster Devonne was bare-chested, thick in the neck and shoulders, turning fat. The porch smelled of tobacco and sweat.

"Help yourself," he said again.

Seagraves stayed where he was. The heel of his shoe held the door open, perhaps an inch. He took the envelope out of his coat pocket, feeling the weight. "This is from Paris Trout," he said. "It isn't connected to me."

"Whatever you say."

Buster Devonne accepted the envelope without looking inside, folded it in half, and pushed it into his pants pocket. "Mr. Trout don't have nothing to worry about," he said. "All those people looking for is a way to let him go."

Seagraves did not answer.

"I know people, and I lived in this county all my life," he said.

Seagraves walked back to his car, feeling the man on the porch watching. He got in slowly, feeling as if he'd left something behind. He stared at the porch a moment, and then, before he started the car, he saw the point of Buster Devonne's cigarette glow red and then disappear. In the moment of illumination, though, he saw him. Buster Devonne was counting his money.

HE DROVE THROUGH SLEEPY Heights and came out on the highway. He turned left, in the direction of town, and a few minutes later he passed his own house and then the college and then the courthouse. He turned right at the river, and the sound of his tires changed as he dropped off the pavement onto the dirt road that led into Indian Heights.

He stopped up the road from the house where it had happened and turned off his lights, thinking of what he had just done.

He watched the windows for most of an hour, trying somehow to weigh the place now without the girl, until a shadow moved and the lights inside went off.

He had no idea why he was there.

SEAGRAVES ARRIVED AT COURT at five minutes to eight, red-eyed and spent. He had fallen into bed exhausted and then been unable to sleep until after five. Trout was already there, staring in a murderous way across the aisle at Ward Townes. Townes ignored him, and with the jury out of the room, Seagraves ignored him too.

The first witness was Agent J. E. Smythe of the Georgia Bureau of Investigation, who referred repeatedly to a small leather notebook he took from his coat pocket.

Agent Smythe had visited Rosie Sayers at Thomas Cornell Clinic the day after she was shot and written down what she told him.

Seagraves objected before he could read it. "No grounds have been laid for this," he said. "A dying declaration is not admissible without proof that the declarer knew they were dying. There was no doctor present, no medical basis for this at all."

Ward Townes did not wait for the judge to rule. "Did Rosie Sayers know she was dying?" he said.

"She said as much."

"I'll allow it," the judge said.

"Thank you," Townes said, and then to the agent: "What exactly did Rosie Sayers say that indicated to you that she realized her condition was mortal?"

The agent went back to his notebook. "She complained of her stomach," he said. "She believed she was too young to die, that God had made a mistake."

Seagraves stood up again. "That is the statement of a delusional child, Your Honor. I ask that it not be allowed to prejudice this case any further than it already has."

"I think we'll listen to this," Judge Taylor said.

"Did she tell you what happened to her?" Townes asked the agent.

"Yessir. She said Mr. Paris Trout had arrived on the porch with brass knucks and grabbed Thomas Boxer." The agent looked at his notebook again and began to read.

"'I told Thomas the man had knucks, and he said, "Goddammit, what is it to you?" He chased me in the house and hit me on the head with his knucks. Mary come in and pulled him loose. He shot me in the arm, he shot at Mary too. I went on inside the house and sat on the trunk. He came to the door and shot me in the shoulder and stomach.'"

The agent looked up.

"Did you ask if she had a gun herself?" Townes said.

"Yessir. She said she didn't. She said she didn't even have a stick."

"Was there anything else?"

The agent shook his head. "She couldn't talk much, except to swear under oath it was true."

Townes went back to his table and pulled a folder out of his briefcase. An edge of one of the photographs lay beyond the lower edge of the folder, and Seagraves knew what it was.

"Objection."

The judge looked up, surprised. "To what, Mr. Seagraves?"

"The photographs Mr. Townes is about to offer as evidence are gruesome beyond the matter in front of this court. They show the marks of the surgery."

"Are those pictures, Mr. Townes?" the judge said.

"Yes, Your Honor." He closed the folder of pictures and delivered them to the judge. Seagraves was surprised that he had not taken the pictures out and given the jury at least a glimpse as he carried them up. The judge fit his glasses across his nose and looked them over.

"Is this the girl?" he said.

"Yessir," Townes said.

"Is she deceased here?"

"Yessir."

The judge frowned. Seagraves moved next to Townes and folded his arms. "As Your Honor can see," he said, "the wounds are enhanced by the surgical procedures necessary to remove the bullets. The woman in those pictures has not only been shot, she has been mutilated."

Townes did not reply, and it struck Seagraves that the prosecutor had reservations of his own about showing them to the jury.

Judge Taylor, however, had changed sympathies. "I believe the jury is able to see for themselves which wounds were bullets and which were surgery."

He handed the pictures to Seagraves, who took them back to the defense table and studied them, one by one. Trout looked at the first three, and then he moved in his chair until he was facing a different direction.

The pictures showed the girl on an examining table. She was naked, and even with her eyes closed, something in the flashbulbs made her appear surprised. The surgical cuts were closed with tangles of black thread. As Seagraves finished with each picture, he handed it back to Townes, who carried it to the first juror, who passed it on to the second.

It took half an hour for all the jury to see all the pictures, and then Townes showed them to Agent J. E. Smythe. "Are all these wounds consistent with her description of the wounds she suffered inside the house?"

"I would say so."

"In your experience with the Georgia Bureau of Investigation, have you had occasion to visit other victims of gunshot wounds?"

"Yessir."

"Do you have a knowledge of anatomy, Agent Smythe?"

"Yessir, I do."

"And do you have an opinion which one of these shots killed the girl?"

"I would say the one into the stomach."

"Objection," Seagraves said.

The judge said, "I'll allow it," and Seagraves stood where he was a long time, staring at him, until the judge met his eyes. "I believe the agent's opinion would be considered reliably expert in shooting matters, Mr. Seagraves." There was a conciliatory note in what he said, however. Seagraves saw he had remembered who got him elected.

Seagraves sat down and stared at the table where Trout was drawing something across the top of his pad.

When he looked again, he recognized it as a family tree.

SEAGRAVES BEGAN HIS CROSS-EXAMINATION. "Agent Smythe, in your medical opinion, how successful was the surgery to remove the bullets from Rosie Sayers's body?"

"I do not know, sir."

"But what I want to know, do you feel Dr. Braver did a good job?"

"I have no way to know that."

"You couldn't say if he might of gone in there with his knife and scissors and cut too much off this or not enough off that?"

"No sir."

"You couldn't say if he might of made it worse. . . ."

"From the direction of the shot," the agent said, "I don't believe there was a thing your doctor could do to make it worst."

"You have seen wounds like this before?"

"Yessir."

"You have seen someone who was shot in the stomach?"

"Yessir."

"You have seen someone shot in the side?"

"Yessir."

From the table Seagraves leaned toward the witness. "Have you ever heard of somebody died from an operation?"

When Seagraves had finished with the agent, he glanced again at the notepad on the table. At the top of the family tree, where his mother's name was, Trout had drawn a spider that was also a face.

It wasn't a face Seagraves recognized—he couldn't say if it was male or female, young or old—but he thought it was somebody real.

Judge Taylor recessed for lunch at ten-thirty again and did not reconvene until one, when Ward Townes called Linda Boxer.

THE LITTLE GIRL CAME out of the back of the courtroom alone, wearing a new yellow dress, her hair tied in back with ribbons. She was afraid, and when the court officer offered her the Bible, she accepted it as if it were a present. Seagraves noticed the ladies in the jury box smiling.

Judge Taylor leaned toward the child and said, "I'm afraid we need that Bible there for the court, honey, but I'll get you your own if you want."

The girl straightened her dress. "I got my own," she said, and handed it to the judge.

"Would you put your hand on top of it for me?" he said.

She put her hand on the Bible, and the court officer swore her in. When it was done, Townes leaned on the rail in front of the witness box and scratched his head.

"Linda, can you tell us how old you are?"

"Eleven."

"And you say you've got a Bible at home?"

"All us got Bibles."

"You and your sister?"

"Me and my sister and my brothers too. Everyone got us our own."

"And so, when you put your hand on top of the Bible and promise to tell the truth, you know what that means, don't you?"

The child nodded.

"Could you tell us?"

She nodded again.

"Now? Could you tell us now?"

"The devil get you if you don't tell the truth," she said. "Come and snatch you up for that."

"All right then, let me ask if you remember the day when the men shot Rosie?"

Seagraves stood up. "Objection. I am understanding of the problems with witnesses of this age, but the prosecutor is leading her here."

Judge Taylor sustained.

"Do you remember the day when the shooting happened?" Townes said. The child nodded, her braids were as stiff as wire and moved with her head.

"You have to say it out loud, honey," Townes said.

"I remember."

"Where were you when the men came?"

"Me and Jane Ray was in the house," she said.

"The boys' side?"

She nodded.

"And what did you see?"

"We seen the men come up on the porch, and then Momma come up there to argue with them."

"Did you go out on the porch too?"

"No sir."

"And did you hear them arguing?"

"They said something, and then they ran into the house and shot Rosie."

"The other side of the house?"

"Yessir."

"Did you see them shoot Rosie?"

"No sir."

"You heard them?"

"Yessir."

"Did it take a long time or a short time?"

"A long time," she said.

"And when did you see Rosie again?"

"Me and Jane Ray stayed put."

"Did you see Rosie again?" The child did not answer. "Linda? Can you tell us?"

"We seen the men," she said.

"When was that?"

The child began to search the courtroom then, looking for someone. Her thumb went into her mouth, and Seagraves saw that she was about to cry.

"Linda?"

Her eyes filled, and tears the size of marbles rolled down her cheeks. There was no sound at all. "You don't have to talk anymore," Townes said. "You want to stop now?"

"We seen them running out from the back the house," she said suddenly. "They was runnin' and fannin' their coats. When they got into the car, then we come out and saw Rosie."

"And where was she then?"

"Out the back door, on the ground."

"Did Rosie say anything?"

The child shook her head. "To Momma," she said. "We never got that close to hear it."

"Where were you, and where was your momma?"

"Me and Jane Ray come out and saw what they had did. Momma was shot on the ground too, holding Rosie."

The child's eyes filled again. She dropped her head, and Seagraves could see tears dropping into her lap. Townes said, "Did you think your momma was going to die?"

"We thought we was all going to die," she said.

"Thank you," Townes said, and then he turned and looked at Seagraves as if something had been explained.

SEAGRAVES APPROACHED THE CHILD carefully. He said, "Linda, did you know who Mr. Trout was before that day?"

At the sound of the new voice she flattened herself against the back of the chair. The judge leaned toward the child again. "Just a few more questions, honey. Can you tell us a few more things?"

She nodded.

Seagraves said, "Did you hear of Mr. Trout before he came to your house? Did you know who he was?"

She nodded.

"How was that?"

"When he lent the boys money."

"He lent Thomas and Henry Ray money?"

"Uh-huh."

Seagraves smiled at the child, trying to get her to smile back. "That was a nice thing to do, wasn't it?"

"No sir."

"It wasn't nice to give your family money when you needed it?"

"He didn't give it," she said.

"You're right. He lent it. Do you know what that means?"

She looked beyond him now, into the seats behind the railing.

"Linda," he said, bringing her back, "did you wonder how come Mr. Trout would shoot your momma and Rosie?"

She did not answer but slowly brought herself to look at Trout.

"Linda?"

"It just seem like a natural thing for him to do," she said.

Seagraves held the gate, and she went through it and then to her mother, who was sitting on the aisle in back. Mary McNutt straightened the girl's dress and wiped at her cheeks, and then she picked her up, pressing the child's face into her collar, and carried her out of the room.

Seagraves was watching her when he heard Townes's voice. "That's all for the people, Your Honor."

SEAGRAVES CALLED BUSTER DEVONNE. He stood in the witness box in a coat that looked like somebody had stolen it off an organ grinder. He put his hand on the Bible and stared right at the jury and swore to tell the truth. He stared at them, and he smiled.

"Mr. Devonne," Seagraves said, "what is your age?"

"I'm forty-four years old."

"Are you employed by Mr. Trout?"

"Yessir, I worked for Paris, off and on, eight years."

"In what capacity?" Buster Devonne narrowed his eyes. "In what position?"

"I do some collecting," he said.

"Anything else?"

"Whatever else needs to be done."

"And on the afternoon in question did Mr. Trout have occasion to use your services?"

Buster Devonne smiled and shook his head. "Excuse me," he said, "but it struck me comical. It sounded like Twenty Questions." There was some quiet laughter in back, and Buster Devonne straightened in his seat. Seagraves repeated his question.

"Yessir," Buster Devonne said. "He asked me would I drive him out to Henry Ray's, to get him to sign a note on the car."

"Why didn't Mr. Trout just go out there by himself?"

"When he thought there might be trouble, he took somebody along."

"What sort of trouble?"

Buster Devonne shrugged. "There were two pretty big Negroes there, which I had information were very bad, mean Negroes. Plus Mary McNutt and the girl."

"So you went with Mr. Trout to protect him."

"I went to keep things in hand, yessir."

"And what happened when you got to Henry Ray Boxer's house?"

"Well, let's see. Thomas Boxer and Mary Jane was on the porch with this girl that got shot. We stopped at the steps and greeted them very nicely."

"What exactly did you say?"

"Inquired for their health," he said.

"And what did they say?"

"Nothing at first. They stood up on the porch, looking down, and then Mr. Trout talked to her."

"You mean Mrs. McNutt?"

"Yessir. He said, 'We have never put a hardship on you, Mrs. McNutt. We have always done you kindnesses when you called on us, and I can't understand to save my life why you or one of the boys didn't come in and talk this over.'"

"And what did Mrs. McNutt say?"

Buster Devonne shook his head. "Nothing. Then Mr. Trout and myself assented the stairs, and he told them that they would have to sign a blank note. He said, 'You-all know this is right,' and asked me for the note."

"You had the note."

"Yessir. Mr. Trout don't tote papers. And so I handed it to him, and he give it to the boy to sign."

"Did he sign it?"

"No sir. As soon as he touched it, the woman said, 'Don't sign that thing, Tom.' And then she looked at Paris—Mr. Trout—and cussed him."

"What specifically did she say?"

Buster Devonne shrugged. "She said, 'You white sonofabitch, I will shoot your damn heart out.' You can imagine how I felt."

Before Seagraves could ask his next question, he heard Ward Townes behind him. "Objection," he said. "No one has more respect for this court than myself, Your Honor, for what it is and what it can accomplish, but everything has its reasonable limits, and asking the court to put itself into Mr. Devonne's mind exceeds them."

There was some laughter again from the back, and Seagraves smiled with it. Buster Devonne put a look on the prosecutor. When the noise had passed, the judge sustained the objection.

"All right, Mr. Devonne," Seagraves said, "would you please tell what happened next."

Buster Devonne was still staring at the prosecutor. "Thomas Boxer got up and grabbed hold of Mr. Trout by the neck," he said, "and the girl commenced to tearing at his clothes, to pull him off-balance. They tussled into the door, and then Mrs. McNutt come in there and jumped on Paris from the back. The girl had a pistol."

"What kind of pistol?"

"A thirty-two automatic," he said, and looked right into the jury box again.

"Then what happened?"

"I was tied up by the door. Thomas Boxer gone disappeared after he grabbed Mr. Trout, and there was supposed to be another Negro somewhere, who was known to be a big bad one. There was shooting then, and then the boy come in from behind to pick up the gun on the floor, and I yelled for Paris to look out, he's coming the other way. I was still waiting on the other Negro to appear and expected Paris could handle the women and Thomas until I got a fix on where he was."

"Did Mr. Trout have a gun?"

"Yessir, he did."

"Was that unusual?"

"Not that I know. I believe it was an ordinary forty-five automatic."

"Was it unusual for Mr. Trout to carry a gun along when he went for collections?"

"In Indian Heights? No sir. Paris Trout keeps a bank. He does it hisself, loans and collections, keeps it all in his head. In that business, money and guns go hand in hand."

"Did you also have a gun?"

"No sir."

"Do you own a gun?"

"Yessir, but I didn't have it with me."

"And so if someone comes in here and testifies they saw a gun in your pocket, they're mistaken."

"I'll tell you what they might of saw," he said. "I sometimes put my hand in my coat pocket and stick my finger out, looks like the same thing." Seagraves suddenly had the thought that Buster Devonne was about to wink at the jury.

"So you did not fire any shots that day?"

"No sir."

"Did you go into the house?"

"No sir, I went to the door. That's as far as I got."

"Did you see the shooting?"

"I heard it, a minute after the woman went 'round to the back. But I couldn't say this shot was fired first and then that one."

"How long did the shooting last?"

"Not long," he said. "It didn't take long."

"And what did you do when it had stopped?"

"Paris come out of there, it looked like World War One. Both of us made to the car as fast as we could get there."

"Did you drive back to town, or did Mr. Trout?"

"I did. He was anxious over what had happened. He said he'd never known a good family to turn on him like that."

"And you went directly to town?"

"I took him back to his store. I did that, and then I called Chief Norland and tol' him what happened."

"Mr. Trout asked you to do that?"

"Yessir. He would of done it himself, but he had pressing business to attend."

"Thank you, Mr. Devonne." Then, to Ward Townes: "Your witness."

WARD TOWNES FROWNED AND shook his head. For a long, dreamlike moment Seagraves thought he did not mean to cross-examine. Then he stood up, looking at his notes. "Mr. Devonne, how much do you weigh?"

"I ain't put a penny in Mr. Dickey's scale lately," he said.

"The last time you did, what did you weigh?"

"Maybe two-fifteen."

"Have you seen Thomas Boxer and Henry Ray Boxer in this courtroom? What do you estimate they weigh?"

"I couldn't," he said. "They got to weigh themselves."

"You were a member of the Cotton Point Police Department?"

"Eleven years."

"In all that time you never had occasion to estimate the height and weight of a suspect?"

"Sometimes."

"All right, as a policeman, what would you estimate Henry Ray Boxer weighed?"

"Hundret and forty."

"And Thomas Boxer? Would you say he was bigger or smaller?"

"About the same."

"Is that your idea of big Negroes, a hundred and forty pounds each?"

"It depends on the Negroes," he said. "Mrs. McNutt as big as me all by herself."

There was some laughter in the courtroom again, but Seagraves noticed there was none in the jury box. Judge Taylor pounded for quiet. "Sir," he said to Buster Devonne, "I will not have women embarrassed in my courtroom."

"All right," Townes said, "now you testified here that Thomas Boxer choked Mr. Trout and then disappeared when the scuffle started?"

"Yessir."

"Once again calling on your experience as a Cotton Point police officer, did you ever see a person disappear? See it for yourself?"

"I sure as hell looked for a bunch of them that seemed to," he said, and the judge himself laughed at that.

"But not in front of your own eyes?"

"No sir. What happened, I was distracted when he and the girl grabbed Paris, and next thing I knew he was gone."

"Where did he go?"

"Don't know."

"Into the other side of the house?"

"Inside, underneath, I don't know."

Townes stopped for a moment, changing directions. "How long did you say you were a member of the police force, Mr. Devonne? Eleven years?"

"Yessir."

"Do you recall why you left that job?"

Seagraves objected, and Judge Taylor admonished the prosecutor.

"Let me ask something else then," Townes said. "When you spoke with Chief Norland after the shooting, did you indicate then that you had been unarmed?"

"I don't recall," he said.

"You didn't tell him you were in the thick of it out there?"

"I might of left that impression."

"Why would you want to do that, Mr. Devonne?"

"We was in it together," he said. "I didn't want it to look like I was putting the blame on Paris—"

Townes turned his back on Buster Devonne and returned to his table. He sat down, and then, almost an afterthought, he said, "I think we've heard all we need to from Mr. Devonne."

UNDER THE LEGAL CODE of the state of Georgia, the defendant in a murder trial was allowed to read a statement without any accompanying obligation to face cross-examination. This privilege covered only the statement, and in the event that the defendant also chose to testify, his previous statement became part of the testimony and was opened to the prosecutor's questions.

Paris Trout left the defense table straight and dignified and took the witness stand. "Your Honor," Seagraves said, "on my advice, Mr. Trout will exercise his privilege to read into the record his statement on how this tragedy occurred. This has been an ordeal, as anyone with an ounce of compassion can see, and I do not think it would serve his interests or this court's to have him testify beyond that."

"Thank you, Mr. Seagraves," the judge said. Then he turned to Trout and said, "Whenever you're ready, sir."

Trout took a pair of glasses out of his pocket and fixed them carefully behind his ears. They softened him, Seagraves thought, and made him older. He took two pieces of paper from another pocket, unfolded them, and began to read.

" 'Your Honor, I do not honestly know how all this happened. Mr. Devonne and myself visited the home of Mary McNutt to settle a financial matter of little importance. When we had come upon the porch, Miz McNutt cussed us, and her son Thomas slapped his hands up around my neck, making to choke me.

" 'There was a girl there, and she attacked me at once with the boy. She looked to be about twenty-five years old and was strong. Stronger than the boy. We struggled for a moment on the porch. I would of just as soon left right there, but the girl broke loose and went running into the house. I heard Mrs. McNutt tell her to shoot my damn heart out. My damn white heart.

" 'I followed into the house after her, trying to keep her from getting a gun. When I caught up, she'd put her hands under the pillow where the gun was. I knew that's what was there. I didn't want to kill her, then or anytime else. I didn't have any business killing people, and it looked to me if I could knock her down, it would settle the whole matter.

" 'I never raised my fist to a woman in my life, but I did then, to stop her before things got out of hand, and you know, I didn't hit her hard enough. She staggered and dropped the pistol on the floor, but she never fell.

" 'And then she took a breath, like it was just starting, and reached to pick it up. I shot her in the shoulder right there. It could just as easy been the heart. It could of ended then, but I did not intend to kill her. I just wanted to get out without nobody getting hurt.

" 'At that moment Mary McNutt come in, slammed against me with all her weight, and tried to get her hands around my neck. When I cleared of her, the girl had got to the pistol, and it was in her hand again.

" 'I grabbed the girl's arm, and the same time I felt Miz McNutt's weight across my back, about pushed me over, and then she grabbed me around the neck, got both hands on my windpipe, and I began to shoot. I don't know how many times. Three, four, five shots, I honestly don't know.

" 'And then Miz McNutt said, "I am shot," and let loose of my neck. I saw Thomas Boxer next. He came in from behind and grabbed up the pistol. I squared to shoot him, but the girl recovered—I'm talking about Rosie Sayers now—and I shot her again. Then I called out, "Come on, Buster, let's go. There is apt to be more shooting here." And we goose-stepped it into the car and left. I asked Buster to report to the police, and that's all I know, how this came to happen.' "

He looked up then, adjusting his glasses, and he seemed to be shaken by what he had remembered. "Is that your statement, Mr. Trout?" the judge said.

"Yessir. I didn't go out there to shoot those people. I am in the business of helping people. That's what we try to do, and we expect to get paid for it, get a living out of it. Colored people aren't the only ones got a right to a living."

He folded the papers and put them back into his pocket. "I didn't want nothing like this," he said. "I had nothing against that girl or against the woman. The honest truth is, I don't have nothing against them now. We were all somebody's baby once, we all come from the same place.

"I didn't want to get killed either. That is the reason I shot them, the only reason. In defense of my own life."

He looked at the jury, a long examination. "We are all somebody's baby," he said again.

And then he folded his glasses and put them back into his pocket too, stood up, and returned to the table with Seagraves. Somewhere in the back a woman was crying.

Trout folded his hands and seemed, for a moment, to be praying.

JUDGE TAYLOR, NOTING THE courtroom was 104 degrees, gave each counsel five minutes for closing arguments, keeping the time on his wristwatch.

"What we have here," Seagraves said, "is a death and two stories how it happened. We all regret that someone was killed, no matter who was at fault. But you are not being asked to regret the loss of Rosie Sayers's life today, you are being asked to decide if Paris Trout, an honest and respected citizen of Ether County, deliberately caused that death, with malice and forethought, as the prosecution claims.

"I want you to think of the times you have seen Mr. Trout on the street or perhaps spoken to him at his store. Ask yourself if it seems possible that same man would drive out to Indian Heights to shoot a girl he did not know.

"Does it make sense, if that is what he intended, to go out there in broad daylight? Do you believe Mr. Trout, a substantial member of this community and the owner of several businesses, would intentionally jeopardize his own life over an eight-hundred-dollar debt?

"Paris Trout did not need eight hundred dollars. His concern was a principle, and the principle is what led him out to Indian Heights. He went there as a reasonable man, to talk.

"Now, the prosecution asks you to believe something else. That Mr. Trout and Mr. Buster Devonne just walked into that house and began to shoot colored people up. They say that Mr. Devonne shot Mary McNutt in the back and the shoulder and the side and the breast, while Paris Trout was shooting the girl. They ask you to believe that the colored people themselves had no guns, that the guns were all in the other side of the house.

"Is that possible?" he said. Seagraves stopped for a moment and seemed to think. "Yes. Is it likely? No. Is there proof that's the way it happened, physical evidence? No. All we have here is the words of the family against the words of Paris Trout and Buster Devonne."

He paused for a moment.

"The real proof, of course, was right in this courtroom yesterday. Not ten feet from where you're sitting. The proof is inside Mary McNutt, the bullets she has never had removed. If those bullets are anything but forty-fives, then somebody besides Paris Trout was shooting at her in that house, and she is telling the truth. But if those bullets are forty-fives, then they came from the same gun that shot Rosie Sayers, and you are obliged to believe Paris Trout."

He had been walking up and down in front of the jury as he spoke, hands in his pockets, but now he took them out and leaned against the rail of the jury box. "We are that close to the proof, and that far away. But if those bullets were inside Paris Trout," he said, "you know he would of found a way to have one of them removed and take the decision of who to believe off you. . . ."

He looked at the jurors, but the train had left the station. The foreman's face was two feet from his own, and there wasn't a sign he even understood the words. Seagraves knew to a certainty it had slipped away. It surprised him, to see it was already lost, and insulted him.

He pulled back off the rail, to keep the jury from seeing it.

"The law," he said, "is reasonable doubt. And even if you did not know who Paris Trout was, or that he had been doing honest business in Cotton Point for as long as most of us can remember, even then, you could not look at this case and make more than a guess at what happened. There is no weight of evidence here, it is one story against another. And what we are left with is a tragic death and doubts over how it occurred. Reasonable doubts."

WARD TOWNES WAS EVEN shorter in his remarks.

"Ladies and gentlemen," he said, "I am not as eloquent as Mr. Seagraves, but then I am not as expensive." There was some polite laughter from around the room, and Seagraves smiled.

"So I think what I will do now is borrow something from Mr. Seagraves's own argument and remind you of his words that the proof was right in the courtroom yesterday, in the person of Mary McNutt.

"I believe that too," he said, and pointed at the empty witness chair. "She was sitting in that seat, and I think you can weigh what she said. I think you heard Mr. Trout too, and everyone else who was there when Rosie Sayers was killed. People who were in their own house when Paris Trout and Buster Devonne came to visit.

"You have seen the pictures of the girl after Mr. Trout and Mr. Devonne left. You have seen the scars on Mary McNutt's body.

"There is no reasonable doubt. You all understand what happened out there, and all I am asking you to do now is acknowledge it. To say that it matters."

THE JURY WENT TO its deliberations at three-thirty. Seagraves took Trout out of the courthouse. They crossed the street and walked half a block to the Dixie Theater, and climbed the stairs. Seagraves's office overlooked the street, and he stood in the window, watching good Cotton Point people taking care of their business, people he knew by name. He had not spoken to Trout since they left the courtroom.

"Am I loose?" Trout said.

Seagraves did not turn around. "Not yet," he said.

"How long does it take?"

"It depends on what they're going to do."

"They ain't going to do nothing," Trout said.

Seagraves did not answer.

"What can they do?" Trout said, a little later.

"Isn't anybody safe, Paris," Seagraves said. "Not all the way. You might keep that in mind next time."

"What can they do?" Trout said again.

Seagraves shrugged. "It's a jury, they can do what they want."

Trout laughed, that barking sound. "I think you forgot where you are," he said.

Seagraves turned away from the window. "Maybe," he said.

Trout slammed his hand against the desk. "I paid you to look after this," he said. "I want more back than *maybe*."

"You should of come hired me sooner," Seagraves said, feeling the anger returning. "You should of called me up before you and Buster Devonne went over there to shoot that child and Mary McNutt. You should of called and asked my advice then, and I would of given you advice that it was murder."

"That boy owed me money," Trout said. "You ought to explained that better." He had moved halfway across the desk, and his face was so close Seagraves could see the thin red lines in his eyes.

"There's some things," Seagraves said, thinking of himself, "that business isn't an excuse."

Trout stayed where he was, leaning across the desk. "You think I don't know what a lawyer is?" he said.

It was quiet a long time, and Trout slowly sat back into his chair. His mood seemed to change, and he turned thoughtful. "Say they come back and find me guilty," he said. "What's left then?"

Seagraves shrugged. "Depends on you," he said. "File motions for a new trial. Allowing the pictures was a judicial error . . ."

"What then?"

"Then we go through appeals until we get a new trial or run out of courts."

"How long is something like that take?"

"Depends. A year or two . . . sometimes longer." He turned in his seat and looked back out the window. "It's expensive," he said.

"It's already expensive," Trout said.

"Yes, it is."

THE JURY WAS OUT a little over three hours. Seagraves had left Trout in his office, looking at a *National Geographic,* and was down the hall with a young lawyer named Walter Huff when his secretary knocked on the door and said they'd called from court.

Walter Huff's family owned the Ether Hotel, where Trout was living, and he had just told Seagraves that the maids were afraid to clean the room. "He's supposed to said he's got poison up there," the young lawyer was saying, "and there's guns everywhere."

"You allow him up there like that?"

The young lawyer smiled. "He pays his rent."

Seagraves thought of that on the way back to court. It seemed to him that the young man had good judgment for an attorney fresh out of school. And then his thoughts turned to the Bonner boy, who had graduated Tufts Law School that spring and would be opening his own law practice in the fall, and Seagraves wondered what the schooling had done to him.

Most of them came out thinking they knew something.

Seagraves and Trout walked through the courtroom's main entrance. Ward Townes was already sitting at the prosecution table, the spectator seats were close to empty. People had gone home.

The room had a hollow sound without spectators. Whispers carried, words spoken out loud seemed to hang in the air.

Judge Taylor came in buttoning his robe. There was grease on his chin, and he was sweating. When he settled, he checked the papers on the desk in front of him and then instructed the court officer to bring in the jury. Trout stared at them as they filed into their seats. Seagraves could see a pulse in his forehead. Only two of them glanced back, the foreman and a woman from Homewood.

The judge asked the foreman if the jury had reached a verdict. The air in the room smelled a hundred years old. "Yessir," he said.

Trout slowly stood up, his eyes still fixed on the jury box.

The foreman did not see him rise, he stared at the paper in his hands. " 'We find the defendant guilty of second-degree murder,' " he read. Then he looked up and found Paris Trout staring at him. A look passed over the foreman's face, and when it was gone, so was his color.

Seagraves stood up too. "We request a poll of the jury," he said.

One by one the jurors stood and pronounced the same verdict. Only one—the woman he recognized from Homewood—dared to look

Trout in the eye. Seagraves wondered if she cared anymore who it was that had got her city water.

"Mr. Trout," the judge said when the last juror had spoken, "you have been found guilty of second-degree murder in the death of Rosie Sayers. Do you have anything further to say at this time?"

Trout turned his look on the judge but did not answer.

"We have no further remarks," Seagraves said.

"In that case, gentlemen, it is the finding of this court that you are guilty of the crime prescribed in the true bill filed by the people July twenty-first of this year—namely, second-degree murder. Further, it is the decision of this court that you be incarcerated in the state work camp in Petersboro County for a period of not less than one nor more than three years."

He leaned forward then, folding his hands, and spoke informally. "It is this court's fervent hope that you will return to the community at the soonest possible time," he said, "and resume your place among its business leaders."

Judge Taylor looked at Seagraves then in an apologetic way.

"Your Honor," Seagraves said, "in light of Mr. Trout's established business, civic, and family ties to the community, we ask that he be allowed to remain free on his own recognizance until new trial motions are settled."

"Mr. Townes?"

"The people have no objection to that, Your Honor," Townes said.

Judge Taylor thanked the jury and excused them. Trout stared until the last juror was out the door. Then he stared at their empty chairs.

"Mr. Trout," the judge said, "you are free pending your appeal. You may not leave the county or change residences without notifying this court of your intention to do so. You are not to have contact with any of the witnesses or jurors involved in this trial. Do you understand the conditions of your release?"

"We understand, Your Honor," Seagraves said. But there was no sign that Trout understood at all.

They walked out of the courthouse together and then stood for a moment in front of the town monument where, if you believed the monument, the state seal of Georgia had been hidden in a privy when General Sherman came through at the end of the war.

Cotton Point had been a rich place then, the center of the state's agriculture and law. At that time "Gone to Cotton Point" did not refer to the asylum.

Trout took a pack of cigarettes out of his pants pocket and looked back at the courthouse as he smoked.

"I'll let you know where we stand," Seagraves said.

"You said the judge made an error."

"I believe he did."

Trout turned quiet, and Seagraves started to leave. He wanted to walk. "I'll be by the hotel later, when I got some idea where we are."

"Leave word," Trout said. "Don't come up on me unexpected."

A farmer passed them in his pickup, the back end loaded with coon dogs, baying at the sky. There was nothing to chase and tree, so the noise itself had become the purpose.

"How long does it take to figure this out?" Trout said.

Seagraves shook his head. "You work it out," he said. "You get an accommodation. There's no figuring, not the way you mean it."

"Is it more money?"

Seagraves blew all the air out of his chest. He wanted to move to a different place, to walk. He could still hear the dogs, fainter now, like a memory. "You missed the point, Paris."

"If a man stole from me tomorrow," Trout said, "I'd do the same thing again."

CARL BONNER

PART FIVE

On an afternoon early in December, five months beyond the trial, a woman arrived at the office of a young attorney named Carl Bonner without an appointment, knocking so tentatively on the smoked-glass window that he thought at first it was the maid.

Carl Bonner walked from his desk through the outer office and opened the door. He did not have a secretary yet and could not persuade his wife to work for him until the practice was making enough money to afford one.

The woman stood in the doorway, looking at him in a direct way. "Mr. Bonner," she said, "I am Hanna Trout. Mr. Seagraves suggested your name to me this morning, and I was just passing your office and thought I might take a chance on catching you in."

He stepped back, making room for her to come inside. "Mr. Seagraves has been very good to me," he said.

Paris Trout's wife was old, of course, but there was something in the way she carried herself that did not fit her age. He watched her a moment from behind and then shut the door. She stopped halfway across the floor and turned, waiting for him to indicate where she should go.

He led her to the smaller inner office, and when they were sitting down, he smiled in an uncomfortable way and said, "What may I do for you today, Mrs. Trout?"

"I called Mr. Seagraves this morning to initiate divorce papers against my husband," she said, "but because he continues to represent

Mr. Trout in his appeals, he was unable to handle this for me and suggested your name instead."

Bonner opened his drawer and found a pencil to take notes. "Will Mr. Seagraves be representing your husband in the divorce?"

She shook her head. "He said not. Perhaps someone from his firm, but not Mr. Seagraves himself." She looked around the room then. His degrees hung on one wall, commendations from the war on another. There was a canary in a small cage in the corner.

"Have you handled divorces before, Mr. Bonner?"

"I handle everything," he said, and then moved on, as if that had answered the question. "Is the divorce adversarial?"

"I would think so, yes."

"Has your husband been notified of your intention to proceed against him?"

She shook her head. "He stays at the Ether Hotel, and I do not see him except by chance."

Carl Bonner noted the address at the top of the paper. "How long has he resided out of your home?"

"Since late spring."

"And did he leave of his own volition—were you abandoned—or did you ask him to leave?"

"I asked him," she said. "After the girl was shot, I did not want him in the house."

He looked at her then, studying her face. She looked directly back. There was something incongruous about her appearance, but he could not find its origin. "Is that the reason for the dissolution? Moral turpitude?"

She did not answer at first, and he saw she was weighing the answer. "Is it adultery?" Bonner said. He waited to see if the word embarrassed her and saw that it had not. For a moment, in fact, he thought he saw her begin to smile at what he had said.

"I don't believe so," she said. "In any case, Mr. Trout's sexual interests are not my concern, except in that they have led to abuse."

He wrote the word "abuse" across the top of a piece of paper and underlined it twice. Beneath that he printed the Roman numeral *I*. "Physical abuse?" he said. She studied him a moment, trying to make up her mind. He wrote the word "physical" and then an *A.* beneath that, slightly indented.

"Mr. Bonner," she said, "you are a young man, and I know your time is valuable. This situation, however, is complicated in ways that will not fit into an outline form, and perhaps it would be beneficial if we spoke informally at first, to acquaint you with what has happened."

He put the pencil down and leaned away from his desk until the back of his head touched the wall. He felt as if he had been scolded. "I didn't mean to rush you," he said.

He felt the embarrassment press into his face like the summer sun.

"Do you know my husband?" she said.

"I know who he is," he said. "I have a passing knowledge of his business interests. . . ."

"Were you in Cotton Point at the time of his trial?"

"I'm afraid I wasn't," he said. "I certainly heard about it."

"Did you find it frightening?"

"In what way?" he said.

"The arbitrary nature of the act itself, did it frighten you?"

"Shooting a woman and a girl?" He shook his head and answered without thinking. "Mrs. Trout, I spent two years not long ago in a place where they shoot back."

She thought for a moment, her teeth holding the edge of her lower lip. "It frightened me," she said.

"I can appreciate that."

"In the first month of our marriage," she said, "I lent my husband a sum of money. He believed it was all I had—in fact, it was half. Mr. Trout, as you probably know, has substantial holdings, both in Ether County and eastern Georgia, and did not need the little money I could add to it. I have never been privy to the figures, but he is a wealthy man."

"That is my understanding," he said.

"At the time I made the loan," she said, "his assets were tied up in his businesses, at least that was his explanation."

"You believed Paris Trout did not have cash on hand?"

She smiled at him then, he did not understand why. "I came into marriage late, Mr. Bonner," she said. "I was forty-four years old and left a career which I had devoted myself to with some success for many years. I did not marry for security, I gave it up. It was a wager I took which I cannot begin to explain, except to say that the reason may lie in the excitement of the wager itself.

"And so, when, a few weeks after we were married, Mr. Trout asked me for the money I had in the bank, that in some way became part of the wager too." She leaned forward for the first time. "I do not do things halfway," she said.

"I see that," he said. "If I may ask, what was the amount of money involved?"

"Four thousand dollars."

"And you kept another four from him?"

"There is another five thousand dollars in an account in Atlanta, which I have been living off since he left."

"I take it your husband did not return the money."

"No, he did not."

"And is this the primary source of the discord? Four thousand dollars?"

"Not the money itself," she said. "The possession. Paris aspired to render me helpless, Mr. Bonner. It is a pattern. That's what taking the money was about. That is why the child was killed."

She paused, and he waited.

"In the weeks following the murder," she said, "Mr. Trout abused me repeatedly. All pretensions of normal behavior disappeared the moment he entered our house."

"There were no witnesses to this abuse?"

She shook her head.

"Beatings? What else?"

"He is a profoundly disturbed man," she said. "The abuse he inflicted reflected the state of his mind."

He nodded as if he understood her. Something cautioned him not to push her for the details. "Have you thought about what sort of settlement you want from the dissolution?"

"I want my house," she said, "and I want the money."

"How much of the money?" he said quietly.

"The money he took," she said. "I wouldn't touch a cent of the rest. The rest is tainted."

Bonner looked at his notebook but did not try to pick it up. "You've got to live afterwards. . . ."

"Alimony?" She relaxed against the back of her chair. "I would as soon stick up a bank."

He shrugged. "He must have assets close to half a million," he said. "You're entitled to some consideration by law."

"The house I claim," she said, "for the two years of servitude which followed my marriage. Until shortly after the killing, I worked six days a week, twelve hours a day in my husband's store. I was his bookkeeper and his secretary and his clerk. I did stockroom work and mopped the floors.

"During that time Mr. Trout treated me as an employee, without warmth or consideration, and would fly into fits of temper at the least divergence from his instructions. He would not allow me to visit my sisters in Savannah or my friends in Atlanta. He would not allow me to visit with neighbors. So I will take the house in payment for those two years, although given the choice, I would certainly have the two years back."

"You are forty-five years old now?" He would have thought she was younger, but it was hard to say. With Bonner there was a single stage women passed into when they were no longer young. He could not attach an age to it, but after women had crossed the line, he lost interest in their appearance and could not differentiate the stages beyond it.

"Forty-six," she said.

"And your husband?"

"Fifty-nine."

"Have you thought of how you will maintain yourself?"

"I have my savings," she said, "and I am not incapable of working." She thought for a minute. "I may return to teaching, I want to do something now to clean myself of this."

Bonner picked up the pencil and made a few quick notes. She didn't try to stop him. "There won't be any problem," he said, looking at what he had written. "My advice would be to ask for alimony, but if this is what you want, there should be no problem at all."

"You may want to interview my husband before you say that."

"There is one law for everyone," he said.

That remark seemed to brighten her spirits, he could not guess why. "You'll handle it then?"

"It will be my pleasure," he said, and smiled at her the way he had smiled to please adults all his life. And once again it cut her own smile in half. He wondered about Hanna Trout and what she saw in him that she did not like.

She stood up, offering him her hand. He took it, noticing the feel of the skin. She was old, but she wasn't. "How long does something like this take?" she said.

"It depends to a large extent on your husband," he said. "I'll file the papers this week, and it could be over in six months."

"Is that what you expect?"

Bonner was still holding her hand, looking right into her eyes. "I don't know. It could last a longer time if he wanted it to," he said. He watched that register and then tried to soften it.

"It shouldn't be long," he said. "This is a favorable settlement for him, his lawyer will tell him. If he knows what's good for him, this will be over in no time at all."

She said, "I do not think you can count on Mr. Trout's knowing what is in his own interest."

AT THE TIME OF this meeting with Hanna Trout, Carl Bonner had been back in Cotton Point two months. She was his first real client.

Bonner had been away eight years. He had left the town when he was sixteen to attend Tufts University in Massachusetts on a scholarship. At eighteen he interrupted his education to enlist in the U.S. Army and spent two years in Korea, operating field artillery and reaching the rank of captain. He was shot in the hand and returned to Tufts University, decorated and honored, and finished his degree in zoology.

It took two more years to complete law school.

But if he was absent in that way eight years, in another way he was never gone at all. He had been one of those children who imprint themselves on an adult society; he was a part of the way people thought about themselves and the place they lived.

Carl Bonner had been the youngest Eagle Scout in the history of the state. He was the youngest person ever known to preach a sermon in Ether County.

From the age of six on, he had played football with murderous intentions, unconcerned for his own safety. In high school he ran three distances at the state track meet. Under the supervision of his father, the Reverend P. P. Bonner of the First Presbyterian Church, he had studied three and four hours every night but Saturday, completing both his elementary and secondary education with the highest marks in his class. He won state contests in mathematics and science. His picture was in the Ether County *Plain Talk* ten times a year, often with accounts of his study habits.

His father made the *Plain Talk* too, although it was usually with people he'd just married or a story about vandalism at the church. Religion was removed somehow from the real business of the county, and the boy came to understand that his father was insulted to be left out and drove him for that reason.

And he understood that his one abiding interest—the songbirds he kept in a shelter he built in his backyard—would never be more than a hobby. He was not meant to end up teaching biology.

The boy's fascination with birds—like his grades and his Scout accomplishments—was common knowledge in town, and some years fifty or sixty mothers, hoping to influence their own children in the same direction, would empty the five-and-dime of its canaries and parakeets at Easter, only to bring them back a month or two later for refunds, feet up in the bottom of the cage.

Carl Bonner lost very few birds.

They were his only childhood friends—the birds and the friends he invented.

CARL BONNER HAD RETURNED to Cotton Point with a wife and opened an office on the second floor of the Jefferson Building, a few hundred yards up the street from Harry Seagraves's firm.

His wife's name was Leslie Morgan Bonner, and she was a sincere disappointment to the many townspeople who felt a personal stake in Carl's life. It had been assumed that he would end up with a Miss Georgia or someone outgoing.

Leslie Bonner was from Ardmore, Pennsylvania, and she kept to herself. While her husband accepted memberships to the Kiwanis Club, the Moose, and the Junior Chamber of Commerce, she eschewed the ladies' auxiliaries and stayed home. He taught Sunday school at the First Presbyterian Church, she met him in front afterward and attended regular services.

Within a year there would be rumors in town that she could not have children.

Their house sat at the end of Leisurebrook, the first development built in Cotton Point. A small brick house with two bedrooms. He mowed the lawn twice a week, and she spent afternoons under a wide straw hat, working in the flower beds. When people waved or blew a horn, she would sometimes look up from her flowers, but she would not return the wave, and she would not smile.

The birdhouse was in back. It was a circular shape, built mostly of wire, with the northern side enclosed. Canaries and lovebirds and parakeets. The birds were advertised in the American Ornithological Society's monthly publication, and from time to time a pet store in Atlanta or Macon would order a hundred at a time. More often the orders were for two or three birds.

Carl Bonner kept meticulous records and sent Christmas cards to even the smallest customers.

He was as obsessive in business as he had been in school, and as isolated. And even though he had very little, he watched the community of lawyers on Madison Street, thinking they would try to take it away—this in spite of the fact that his only work was what they sent him.

He made collections, he handled their pleas when they were out of town. He would do their research and accept indigent clients they did not want to handle themselves.

ON THE DAY HANNA Trout hired him, Carl Bonner went home early. There was a Kiwanis Club meeting at seven, things to do at home.

He found the front door of his house locked. Leslie was sitting at the window, reading. She saw him, but she didn't move. The birds began to chatter in back, knowing he was there. He let himself in, wondering if his neighbors had noticed yet how often he needed a key to get into his own house.

People in Cotton Point did not lock their homes, they went off all day without closing the front door.

She was sitting cross-legged on the couch in shorts and one of his undershirts. It hung by narrow straps from her shoulders, sleeveless, the drop of cloth under her arm showing the crease of skin at the bottom of her breast.

He wondered if she had been in the yard without her brassiere again. He walked down the hall to their bedroom and changed into dungarees and an old shirt. She followed him in, still holding the magazine, the *New Yorker*. He buttoned the shirt and tucked it carefully into his pants, checking himself in the mirror.

"You look fine," she said, "the birds will be dazzled."

He noticed she had not brushed her hair. She lit a cigarette and sat down on the bed with her knees spread wide apart. He saw that she had shaved her legs. The smell of the smoke—a different thing from the smoke itself—filled the room. "Was there any mail," he said, "besides the magazine?"

"Word from the outside world?" she said. He didn't answer, and in a moment she said, "Bird things. They're on the kitchen table."

He went down the hall into the kitchen. Last night's dishes were still in the sink. He found the monthly newsletter from the American Ornithological Society and checked to make sure it had included his advertisement. She came in behind him, bringing the smell of her cigarette, a faint odor of soap. She dropped her magazine on the table and took the newsletter out of his hand.

"I have Kiwanis tonight," he said.

She held his hand against her mouth a moment, then guided it underneath her shirt until he felt the weight of one of her breasts resting on his knuckles. She was always doing something he did not expect. The first night he asked her out, she had come back from the ladies' room and put her panties into the pocket of his coat.

Until that moment he had thought she was shy because she didn't talk much.

He did not move now. She stood in front of him, watching his face.

Another moment passed, and then she pulled away. "It's not the same here, is it?" she said.

"Everybody's different when they go back where they come from."

"Everybody hates tits in their hometown?"

He saw the windows were open and hushed her.

"I'm quiet," she said. "You couldn't hear a damn shotgun over the birds anyway."

He moved away from her to shut the window. "I wish you'd make a few friends," he said.

"It isn't that easy for me," she said. "Besides, look at you. You don't trust anyone. All this Kiwanis Club, Junior Boy Scouts of Commerce is a pose."

He got the window down just before she finished that. "You can't make everything a choice," he said. "It isn't you on one side and how I make a living on the other. That's not the way things are after you're married."

"We're not married like other people," she said.

"You do what you have to do first," he said, "and then what you like. And right now I have to take care of the birds and then go to Kiwanis."

It was quiet a little while, and then she went back into the living room and opened the magazine.

"I need to see Harry Seagraves tonight and thank him," he said. He waited, but she did not ask for what. "He sent me a client. Hanna Trout." He saw she did not recognize the name. "Married to the man that shot that Negro child this summer."

"Shot a child?" she said.

He nodded. "She's divorcing him. If you would push yourself out the front door once in a while, you'd know what he did."

"Why in the world would I want to know that?"

"It's where you live," he said. "It isn't Philadelphia, but we get a killing once in a while. If it's the noise you miss, there's some to be had."

Outside, a squall of bird sounds rose and fell. "It isn't the noise," she said.

He mixed seeds and vitamins into a bucket and started out the back door and then was suddenly filled with feelings for her.

He said, "You want to help me feed the birds?"

EARLIER THAT SAME DAY Paris Trout had come to see Harry Seagraves.

In the four and a half months following his conviction on second-degree murder, it was the third time Paris Trout had come to Seagraves's office. The first time was after Seagraves had prepared the appeal to Superior Court, the second time was the day Buster Devonne was convicted of assault and sentenced to six months, and the third visit—today's—was to ask why the appeal had been rejected.

None of those meetings lasted fifteen minutes.

The appeal was written to almost a hundred pages but centered on only two points: that the pictures of the dead child should not have been admitted as evidence and that allowing Mary McNutt to show the scars of her wounds was prejudicial and beyond the scope of the complaint against Trout.

Trout never asked to read the appeal or the opinion rejecting it. He sat in Seagraves's office both times, arms crossed, and listened. And on this morning, when Seagraves finished, he'd said, "What court next?"

Seagraves took a long breath. The papers were lying on top of his desk in an open folder, corners of the pictures showing underneath. He kept them hidden beneath the papers and would have kept them in another folder altogether except he was afraid they would be lost.

"I don't know," Seagraves said. "We ought to think about this, if it's worth your money."

Trout had not changed expression. "Is the State Supreme Court the next court?" he said.

"You know the courts as well as anybody," Seagraves said.

"Then that's where we're going."

"We need to reconsider our case," Seagraves said. "There's no hurry now, we got time."

Trout did not seem to hear him. He stood up and walked to the door. "If the court made mistakes—if it wasn't your mistakes—then you got to write it in a way that it's clear," he said. Then he left.

Seagraves pulled the pictures out then.

He was looking at the child again, the reflections of light from the flashbulbs shone on her shoulders and forehead, the places her skin lay against her bones. He knew the pictures by heart, they came back to him sometimes early in the morning—looking at Lucy asleep in her blindfold would in some way remind him of the other darkness that had fallen across Rosie Sayers's eyes—and sometimes sitting in a courtroom or when he was out to dinner or making a speech.

He spent the day in his office, avoiding calls and appointments, thinking of the child and Paris Trout.

At four o'clock Lucy called, wanting to know if he would be home for supper. He could not place her voice at first, and then, even as it became familiar, there was a long minute when he could not remember how she looked.

"I've got Kiwanis," he said.

"Oh, I had Betty get us some sirloins," she said.

"They'll keep a day."

"Then I don't know what to have tonight . . ."

It occurred to him that this same conversation, with variations for chicken or roast beef, had been going on for close to twenty years. And then, as they spoke, he noticed that the low December sun had stretched across the floor and halfway up the bookcase on the far wall, glaring off the titles, and somewhere in that moment the fact of the child's death was fresh again.

"Harry?" It was Lucy, but even the shape of her was gone now. It was as if she were lost somewhere in the dark parts of the bookcase. "Harry, are you there?"

"I've got to go," he said.

"What am I going to do about supper?"

"I've got to go," he said again, and then he hung up.

When the phone rang again, he didn't answer.

IT WAS SIX O'CLOCK before he left the office. It was beginning to rain, and the air felt cold. He walked across the street to his car, started the engine, and waited for it to warm up enough to put on the heater. In the dark he began to shake.

He put the car into reverse, backed out into Madison Street, and drove, without thinking of what he was doing, to the corner of Draft and Samuel. The lights were on inside, he saw her once, moving toward the back of the house. He found himself walking toward the door, then he was knocking.

A sudden wind almost took the hat off his head, and he held it in place and waited for her to answer. The porch light went on, the door opened. He did not move.

"Mr. Seagraves," she said, not surprised at all.

She stepped out of the doorway and he filled the empty space, dripping rain. "I was on the way to a meeting," he said, "and I saw your light."

She did not answer him.

"Did you contact Mr. Bonner?"

"Yes," she said. "He said he would accept my case."

Seagraves was still holding on to his hat, unsure if he should remove it or not. "He's a fine young man," he said. "I'm sure he can handle it."

"He seemed confident," she said.

He smiled in spite of himself. "Young lawyers are always confident. It's a failure of our law schools."

"Let me have your coat."

He let her have his coat and his hat. "Have you eaten?" she said. "I was just fixing myself a bite."

He shook his head. "I have to sit through a Kiwanis dinner in a little bit, and you cannot face that on a full stomach."

"A drink?"

And he smiled and rubbed the rain off his cheeks. "I'm surprised you would take a chance."

She offered him a seat on the couch and fixed him a drink. She made one for herself too. "Well, Mr. Seagraves," she said, "what is on your mind?"

He sipped at the drink. The room, he noticed, had been painted since his last visit. The windows had been washed, the furniture moved to new spots on the floor.

"I don't know," he said. "I happened to think of you on the way somewhere else, then I saw your lights." She watched him and waited. "I don't know why I stopped," he said.

She said, "Perhaps I reminded you of something when I called this morning."

He took another sip, and with the taste of it still in his mouth he began to tell her. "I am bothered by the case I tried for your husband," he said. "Aspects of it have transcended the courtroom and have not left me alone since."

"Which aspects?" she said.

"The girl herself." It was quiet in the room, and he drank again. "Somehow I've obligated myself to her. The meaning of what has happened will not settle one place or another. It moves, again and again, so I never know where to expect her or when she will intrude on my thoughts."

He stood up and walked to a chair that was closer to hers. "There was a moment today," he said, "when I felt a remorse as strong as if I had shot her myself."

She leaned forward, resting her chin on her hand, her elbow on her knee, and drank from her glass. He saw that she was not going to answer.

"I remembered today that you warned me."

"I warned you about my husband," she said.

Seagraves nodded. "He was in today, shortly after I spoke to you."

She reached out at that moment and touched his hand, the one holding his drink. She ran her fingers along the side of the glass and then, cool and wet, across the back of his wrist. Her fingers stopped there and settled.

"Does it affect you that way?" he said. "Do you think of her too?"

She shook her head no. He noticed her neck, the tiny wrinkles at the bottom, the smooth rise to her chin. "Not like that," she said. "I saw her alive, in the store. She'd been bitten by a fox, and I took her to the clinic. It's not the same."

It was quiet.

"During the course of the trial," he said, "Buster Devonne asked for a payment for his testimony. We gave him a thousand dollars—I gave him a thousand dollars—for what he said."

She thought a minute. "It didn't help Paris."

"No," he said, "it went against him as hard as it could." Seagraves sighed. "He was convicted, and punishment was handed down, and that ought to be it. But the child is on my mind. The law dealt with this and moved on, and I'm still tied to it."

"Cut it loose," she said.

"I don't know how."

"My husband is the connection," she said.

He thought for a moment, and she absently began to follow the line of his watch with her fingers, teasing the skin next to it. "I can't drop a client in the middle of appeals," he said.

"Why not?"

"It's unethical." He brought the glass to his mouth and took a drink this time, not a sip. "You can't just get rid of a client because you don't like what he did. Not after a guilty verdict. The time for that is before you take the case."

"I got rid of him," she said.

"That's personal, this is business."

She moved her fingers off his arm and sat back in her chair. "We're all only one person," she said. "You can't separate what you do one place from another."

"I have to," he said. "I'm a lawyer."

THE NEXT TIME SHE went into the kitchen, he followed her. There was a clock in the wall, seven-fifteen. He was already late for the Kiwanis meeting. He leaned against the sink and watched her make the drinks. The wind was picking up outside and seemed to be coming from the south.

"Is it different now?" he said. "Living alone?"

She smiled at him from the sink. "Do I miss being half drowned in my own bathtub, you mean?"

"I mean, are you still afraid of him?"

"I have more time now," she said. "I think about him."

"Has he been back?"

She shook her head. "Not once since he moved out . . ." Then: "He's afraid, too."

She handed him the glass, and at the same moment he noticed the first feelings of intoxication. It felt like his brain was waking up happy. "Of what?" he said.

She shrugged. "That he's poisoned."

"He thinks you did it?"

"That," she said, "but it's more than that."

"How long has he been believing he was poisoned?"

"I don't know when it started. You don't notice everything at once."

He thought of her new in this house, beginning to notice her husband's peculiarities. He reached out and touched her arm, about the same way she had touched his. She looked at his hand, and for a moment nothing moved. Then she drank from her glass, then she led him into the small room just off the kitchen and sat down on the daybed against the wall. The shoes dropped off her feet. She brought her knees up under her chin and hugged her legs. She took another drink.

He sat down with her, kicking off his own shoes. The only light in the room came from the kitchen and lay in a rectangle across the floor. "I was glad to see you tonight, Mr. Seagraves," she said. "You have a kind nature."

He did not answer for a moment. He heard her drink, the ice cubes falling back into the bottom of the glass. She moved her legs, and the skirt of her dress fell into her lap. She did not seem to notice.

"Somehow," he said, framing the words, "there is a connection. You and I and Rosie Sayers are tied into each other's secrets."

"I told you my secrets," she said. "You haven't told me yours."

"I paid Buster Devonne," he said. "That's a secret." It was quiet a long time. They drank and stared out the window into the branches of a black tree. The wind was blowing harder now, everything outside trembled.

"I told you about the girl," he said.

He sat farther back until he was resting against the wall. She had not moved, and from his new position he saw the outline of her legs against the light from the open kitchen door. The straight line across the top of her thighs, the roundness underneath, where the muscle lay. He thought of touching her there, underneath.

"My darkest secret," he said.

She turned then and took the glass out of his hand. She put it on the reading table beside the bed, along with her own.

"The thing he did with the bottle . . ."

She waited.

"I cannot get that out of my mind."

Still there was no answer.

"It aroused me," he said, and so it was all out.

He could see her eyes now, the rest of her features were lost in the dark. "That was hardly a secret, Mr. Seagraves," she said finally.

"Are you disappointed?"

He thought he saw her smile. Then her hand was touching his arm and then his cheek. Her face came close, and he felt the heat off her skin a moment before she pressed herself into his neck. He thought she might be crying.

He began to rock her, as you might rock a child. "I didn't mean I wanted to do that myself," he whispered. "I wouldn't inflict that on a person. . . ." He moved back and forth, smelling alcohol and shampoo, and she moved with him. For a moment they seemed to be synchronized with the tree branches outside the window, but then the wind suddenly died and the branches stopped, and Seagraves kept rocking.

In the sudden calm his voice seemed louder. "There are things like that buried in everybody," he said. "That doesn't mean you want to act on it, just that it's there. We are all flawed people."

She tugged at a button of his shirt then and laid her hand on his stomach. Her face moved against his neck and she kissed him once, softly, along the line of his jaw. His head slid against the wall, and she followed it, kissing him again, moving herself over him until his head was stopped by the bed itself. There was a sudden coolness, and he realized she had unbuttoned his shirt, top to bottom, and pulled it away from his chest.

She sat up, watching him. Her features were distinct now, his eyes were more used to the dark. Her hand moved from his stomach to his belt. There was another tug, and that was loose too. She looked up from her work without a trace of a smile. She unzipped his trousers, as practiced at it as he was himself. He began to sit up, to help her, but she put her hand against his chest and pushed him back.

Then she was not touching him at all. She reached for something out of his view. Her drink.

She brought the glass to her lips for a long minute, and then put it back on the table. She leaned toward him again and kissed the corner of his mouth. Her lips were icy at first, and he tasted the liquor, and then they moved, slippery and cold and opening, until her tongue was touching his teeth, and it was cold too. Her fingers traced the line of his jaw, following the places she had kissed, and settled behind his neck, pulling him up into her mouth.

He felt his penis pushing against the opening in his boxer shorts, and he moved a few inches against the bed, trying to realign it. The vision of his penis coming through the opening struck him as childlike and embarrassed him. And at that movement the head found the crack and poked through, perhaps half an inch.

He tried to move again, but she wouldn't let him. A hand on his stomach. She pulled back and stared at the opening in his shorts. She put the tip of her finger in her mouth and turned it as it came out, as if she were carrying something, carrying it down and out of his sight, and then her finger was circling the ridge of his penis, so softly he could not say exactly when it stopped.

She watched him growing and then touched him again, at the mouth. "It's leaking," she said. He lay absolutely still. She pulled away again, unbuttoning her dress. He did not try to help. She leaned forward, and it fell away from her shoulders. She pushed it over her hips and lifted her legs, without effort, and it was gone.

Seagraves was struck at her acrobatics.

He noticed then that her underwear was gone too, if she had been wearing any. There was no brassiere. He felt her breasts against his chest. He reached behind and touched the back of her leg, feeling the round muscle, and followed it up until he reached her bottom. The edge of his finger lay against pubic hair, and it was wet and cool too.

He whispered, "Let me out of my pants."

For a moment she did not move, and then she brought her knees up and lifted herself off him while her hands followed his ribs to his hips, and then his pants and shorts were coming off and down. His penis felt like it was caught outside the elevator door on the way to the top floor.

He whispered, "Oh," but she didn't stop, and a moment later his shorts and trousers were down around his knees. He tried to push them further, but she straddled him, holding him still. *Pay attention.* Her face began to drop toward him again, and a moment after he felt the press of her cheek, he felt her fingers around his scrotum. She used it to guide him inside her. A soft, insistent pressure that would not let him move.

She held him in that way and slowly lowered and raised herself, pulling back to watch his expression. Little bits of light from the doorway caught in her eyes—the spark—and then lightning lit the room, turning her white. The thunder that followed shook the house. He jumped at the noise, and she squeezed him sharply, stopping him, her own lowering and rising progressed without change, unattached.

"Don't move," she said. "Not even when it's time."

He started to answer, but she shook her head. There was another roll of thunder, farther off, then more lightning. Shadows danced over the walls and ceiling. A few minutes later she closed her eyes and seemed to shake inside, a long time. And in her shaking he began a shaking of his own. She held him, though—the only still thing in the room—and he spent himself without the distraction of movement, tracking its course as it came and passed, the clearest the feeling had ever been.

When it was over, she pulled his pants the rest of the way off, and his socks, and lay with him on the bed. The storm came in waves, with quiet moments in between.

"I never paid enough attention to the feeling before," he said.

She did not answer right away. Then: "What is it like?"

"It moves," he said. "It goes through you."

She reached for her glass and drank. The lightning lit her up, and he saw the muscles of her stomach. When she finished, she brought the lip of the glass to his lips, and he drank too. The ice had melted, and the drink was weaker and somehow oily in his mouth.

"Where does it begin?" she said.

"I don't know," he said. "Somewhere inside."

"Show me."

He smiled and shook his head. She took his scrotum again, softly now, and looked at his face. "Here?"

"No, further inside."

Her fingers moved behind the scrotum, perhaps an inch, and she pressed up into him. "Here?"

"It's closer there," he said. "I can't say. . . ."

Her fingers moved again, separating his cheeks, and then she put one finger directly in the middle. "Does it begin in there?" When he did not answer, she pushed her finger into him until she found a place where it seemed to him that the feeling in fact began.

He nodded, and she watched him closely, as if he were somehow remarkable or different. "And where does it go?" she said.

"You aren't going to try to follow it the rest of the way," he said.

She smiled at him and removed her finger. When it was out of him, he noticed that his penis was half erect. "Where does it go?" she said again.

He thought for a moment, trying to remember. "Somewhere," he said, "it touches a nerve that runs a message all the way to my toes. The feeling stays in the lower parts, though. There is no direct connection going up."

She did not seem to understand. "The feeling itself, I'm talking about," he said. "The actual release."

She nodded.

"The titillations that build it come from all over, but you know that."

"Yes."

He thought again. "I don't think it's a straight course," he said finally. "I think there is a little track in there like a roller coaster that it follows on the way out. . . . Little drops and then a big one at the end. That's the killer, the last drop."

She kissed him suddenly in the dark. "Is it the same for everyone?" she said. "You think it's the same?"

"It sounds the same when they talk about it," he said.

They lay still a long time. The rain and thunder stopped, the wind almost quit too. "There'll be stars out before the night's over," he said.

She put her head into the space between his shoulder and his neck, and he thought again that she might be crying.

He held her quietly, thinking of the things they had said. In the calm he saw there was something in it beyond the questions and answers, but he could not see the purpose. As he thought, he noticed the weight of her hand against his leg. It seemed to be the spot they were connected, although she was pressed against him up and down.

Her hand moved—the smallest movement—and settled again, perhaps a quarter inch closer to his groin. His penis crawled toward it, moving on its own across the distance, and touched one of her fingers. He thought she might be asleep—the steady rise and fall of her back where he held her—but then, unmistakably, he felt her finger. It moved to the underside, touching a spot just behind the head, and then slowly traced the route backwards, following it into his body at the junction of his penis and scrotum.

Once again she would not let him move. "Is this spot close to where it starts?" she said, pushing into him.

"I think so," he said.

"Closer than before?"

"I don't know."

She pushed into him further, her finger finding what felt like the drop at the end of the track, and moved against it, up and down. He tried to kiss her, she pulled herself back. "Let it come by itself," she said.

And he waited, and then the feeling came. Clearly defined, a beginning and an end. And afterward there was a deep sting in the place she had found.

She was staring at him.

He moved in the bed, feeling the cool places on his legs where he was wet. "What time is it?" he said.

"I can look." But she didn't move.

He was suddenly uncomfortable, pressed between her and the wall, and sat halfway up. "Must be after midnight," he said.

She stood up and walked to the kitchen. He heard the refrigerator door open and close, the sound of ice cubes dropping into a glass. She came back and sat on the bed, her breasts were small without being narrow. She held herself in the same way naked as she did when she was wearing clothes.

She offered him a drink from the glass, which he took. It was fresh and strong and sent a shiver through his body, as spasmodic as the other. "It's one-thirty," she said.

The liquor settled in his stomach and warmed him. He drank again, returned the glass. She swallowed as much as he had and then put it away on the table. "I was surprised you drank," he said.

"It helps me sleep. The house is full of noises."

He sat still and listened, but there was no sound at all. "You're afraid he'll come back?"

When she didn't answer, he said, "It's funny, I am affected the same way. I wake up, every morning since the trial ended, and wonder if Paris Trout is going to come into the office. I dread to see him, without knowing why."

He saw that she was feeling quiet, and it made him want to reassure her. "It's not connected to anything he might do," he said. "Paris Trout lived fifty-nine years without killing anybody, there's no reason to think he's going to go out right away and do it again. But there is a quality about him that reminds a person of something else."

It was quiet again, and he realized that he had missed what he was trying to say. Something depended on getting it right. "I hate to lose," he said. "I should never have lost that case, and your husband knows it."

"Yes," she said, "you should."

"I'm not speaking now of what's right," he said. "Just the legal issue. I'm embarrassed to have lost, and I don't know exactly how it happened. He reminds me of that whenever he comes in."

"That's not it," she said.

He reconsidered, but it came back to the same place. "Professional embarrassment," he said. "I take pleasure in the work I do, and I do it better than most."

She reached over the side of the bed for her things. She got into the dress without bothering with underclothes, then ran her fingers through her hair. He sat on the bed, watching. Presently she handed him his pants.

"All right," he said, "if it isn't professional, what is it? Not this, because I dreaded to see him before this happened."

She moved to the window and looked outside. He dressed himself quickly, the sound of his zipper filled the room. He saw that she had taken the glass with her. "Hanna?" The first time he had called her that.

"The next time he comes to your office," she said, "when he first walks into the room, put the case aside. Don't confuse my husband with what happened at his trial. Don't meet him halfway, just pull yourself back and see what is there."

The bedsprings creaked as he sat down to put on his shoes and socks. She said, "Sometimes if you hold yourself still, you can tell what something is."

She walked him to the door and opened it without checking the street. There was a formality between them that he realized had been there even when their clothes were lying in piles on the floor. She would not allow him any closer.

He patted the small of her back, wondering what she was thinking.

"I'll call you," he said.

CARL BONNER WOKE AT first light and looked out the window, remembering the storm. Leslie was lying with her knees pulled up into her stomach, her arm covering her face and head, as if she had been trying to protect herself from something in her sleep. He slid carefully out from under the covers, not wanting to wake her.

He walked in his undershorts to the bathroom and closed the door. He ran hot water into the sink and brushed his teeth in the same water that he used a moment later to shave. He combed his hair. He would not go even into his own backyard at daybreak without combing his hair.

He thought of a storm a long time ago when he had been outside all night, shining his flashlight along the floor of the birdhouse, carrying injured canaries into his kitchen.

He thought of that flashlight—three batteries, a present from the Ether County Council of Scouts at the ceremony making him an Eagle—wondering where it was.

He put on his jeans and a pair of slippers and walked from the bathroom to the kitchen and then out the back door. He took two steps in the direction of the birdhouse and stopped.

The floor of the structure was littered with dead canaries. There was a pool of water in the center, and some of them lay in it, half covered. Wings in odd positions caught the breeze and rocked the small, still bodies beneath them.

He began to count the dead birds. At least forty on the floor, two more lying, unexplainably, in the grass outside. He stepped closer, looking into the protected end of the cage, and saw that some of the birds there were injured or sick. He could not say how many.

The storm had come from the south, he thought.

He found an empty seed bag—it was heavy with rain and dripped water across the leg of his pants—and stepped into the cage. He picked up the birds one at a time, looking each of them over, and then put them carefully into the bottom. He remembered the storm from before again; he had lost eleven birds. He was fifteen years old then, and before it was over, he'd crawled over the floor of the birdhouse on his hands and knees, scraping the fingers of the hand that held the flashlight, collecting them one at a time, bringing them inside, laying them across a towel in the sink.

He'd missed school that day—the only day in eleven years he was ever marked absent—and taken care of the birds. The dead ones were heavy and wet, but things always weighed more when they were dead. He remembered standing in the kitchen that morning, trying to understand the source of a bird's weight.

He noticed it again now. The cold, wet, heavy bodies. You could not imagine, finding them like this, that a day before they could fly.

He looked up suddenly and found her on the other side of the wire, not ten feet away. She was wearing her nightgown and had pulled a sweater around her shoulders. The sun had broken the horizon, but not the line of pine trees to the east, and there was a light fog over the ground.

Tree branches were blown all over the yard, and he was holding one of the dead canaries in his hand, its head rolled off to one side at his knuckle. "It didn't seem this bad in town," he said.

She said, "We lost the lights a few minutes." He saw she was looking at the bird in his hand, and he reached into the bottom of the sack and left it with the others.

"It must have come from the south," he said. "Sometimes when it comes from that direction, you get storms within the storm." He looked at the bottom the cage again, wondering how it looked to her. "Little tornadoes," he said.

She crossed her arms, hugging herself against the morning. "You want me to help?"

"Could you dig a hole?"

She went into the garage for the spade and then began to dig at the edge of their yard. The ground was hard in spite of the rain, and he watched her work a little while, the red clay building into a pile beside her. She liked physical work, it was one of the things that attracted him to her, one of the things that was different from the girls here. She would work without rest or distraction as long as she could see a point to what she was doing. You could not waste her time.

He collected the rest of the dead birds and put the sack on the ground outside the cage. Then, carefully, he went into the protected area and began to inspect the survivors.

When he looked back at Leslie again, she had hung the sweater on the low branch of a pecan tree and was working in her nightdress. He watched the muscles in her back through the silky fabric—it was wet now with her perspiration—and thought for a moment of the neighbors, but he knew they wouldn't be awake yet.

A little later he left the cage and carried the sack to the hole. Leslie's legs were spotted with clay. Sweat ran from her hair down her face, leaving lines in the dust. She did not mind getting dirty. "That's plenty," he said. "The dogs won't dig that far."

She hitched her nightdress and stepped out. He helped her, feeling the sweat on her wrists, and then dropped the sack where she had been. He pulled it back out from the closed end, and the dead birds rolled out. Four and five at a time, they seemed to be stuck together.

"I'm sorry for them," she said. She was leaning on the spade, her chin resting on the back of her hands.

"It's not as personal as it was," he said. "It turned into a business, and that changes the way you feel about them."

"How many are there?"

"I didn't count. Forty-five or fifty, maybe a dozen more back there that won't make it. A hundred and fifty dollars . . ."

She stared into the hole. "It doesn't have to be a business this morning, Carl," she said.

"I'm not fifteen anymore," he said. He thought for a moment and said, "Although you wouldn't know it sometimes, the way people are in town."

"Let them just be what they are," she said, meaning the birds.

He took the shovel from her and began filling the hole. The clay was heavy but dry—even standing water wouldn't soak into it more than a few inches—and she winced when it first landed on the birds. In a moment, though, they were covered, and she walked back into the house without another word while he finished the job.

He found her fifteen minutes later in the tub, crying. The door was cracked open or he would not have looked inside. The water had turned dirty orange, and she was lying with her head half submerged, her face wet and streaked, not making a sound.

"Leslie?"

She shook her head, embarrassed. She did not like him to see her cry. He knelt beside the tub, finding one of her hands in the water to hold. "It's only birds," he said. "You don't care about them."

She got her hand away from him and then cupped some water with it and brought it to her face.

He found her hand again and kissed it. The sight of her digging came back to him, a direct and practical kindness. "You'll get used to it here," he said.

She slid farther down, until the waterline was right underneath her jaw. "Something is different here besides the place," she said. "It changed you to come back."

He smiled at her.

"There wasn't a purpose to everything in Massachusetts," she said. "The day we unpacked our things here, you were deciding which books we could put in the bookcase where anybody could see them." She found a washcloth somewhere under her legs and ran it over her shoulders. They were like the rest of her, muscled and soft at the same time.

"It isn't college," he said.

"No," she said, "it isn't."

"I didn't have to make a living up there. I didn't have people watching me."

She closed her eyes as if she could not stand to see him. "What is left for them to see, Carl?" she said. "You were the best Boy Scout in the world when you were eleven years old, and somehow that has obligated you to be the best Boy Scout forever."

"Eagle Scout," he said. But she did not smile. She opened her eyes, though, looking at him in a pitying way he did not like. "I was teasing," he said.

"The other thing . . ." she said. He waited, knowing what was coming. "You worry how I seem to people here."

He shook his head, knowing it was true. "There is nobody going to tell me who to marry," he said.

"We're already married," she said. "What I'm talking about is that you wish you weren't."

He dropped the few inches to the floor as if she'd hit him. He felt her watching him and knew if he said anything false, she would know it. "I worry that you don't try to fit in."

That hung in the air like the heat off the bath water.

"I worry that you try too hard," she said finally. He dropped his chin onto his chest and closed his eyes.

"Do you remember the football game?" she said a little later.

He looked up and found her staring at him. She had stared at him the same way that afternoon, sitting in a crowd of alumni waving Tufts University banners, her hand under the blanket covering their laps, it felt like ice on his cock. He had come off a moment before Holy Cross scored, and the whole side of the stadium had groaned, as if it were hoping for something else.

She groaned for the next two weeks every time he ejaculated.

"I want to be like that again," she said. "I want to have those kinds of secrets."

"People find out those kinds of secrets here," he said.

"What can they say? That I gave the first Boy Scout in Ether County a hand job at the football game? Do you think people hold you in less regard for something like that?"

"I think people might not want their lawyer having sex in public," he said.

"I would."

He felt her mood improving and took her hand again. "That's because you don't need a lawyer," he said.

And he saw the confrontation had passed. She stood up and reached behind him for a towel. The last thing he saw before she wrapped herself inside it was the water dripping off her pubic hair.

He sat behind her on the floor, his back against the toilet, while she combed out her hair. It was thick and black, cut short, and stayed exactly where the comb left it against the nape of her neck. He saw the outline of her bottom beneath the wet towel. It was a sweetheart of a bottom, but she was right. Somewhere in the move it had lost its appeal.

"Did you thank Harry Seagraves?" she said.

"No, he wasn't there."

"I thought he always came to Kiwanis."

"He probably got caught in the weather," he said. "Maybe I'll drop by his office this afternoon. I don't want him thinking I'm ungrateful." He stood up, stiff from sitting against the toilet, and undressed himself to shower.

THE LAST THING IN the world Harry Seagraves wanted to see Tuesday afternoon was Paris Trout sitting in his office. He had been thinking about Mrs. Trout all morning, the way she had held him still and focused him on the mechanics of his own release—a feeling which had been going on inside him for thirty, thirty-five years—in a different way.

He had left her place feeling, on one hand, as if it were only the start of things with her and, on the other hand, as if it were over. For all they had done, he hadn't gotten close to her at all.

He'd alternated all that morning, confused over which way he wanted it to be, then he had lunch with Mayor Horn, and then he returned to his office and found Paris Trout sitting in the leather couch against the wall, staring out at the sidewalk.

Emma Grandy—his secretary—looked up as he came in the door, plainly relieved not to be alone with Trout. Trout took his time turning away from the window. Seagraves saw the lump in his coat pocket. It was square, like a forty-five.

"We got new business," Trout said.

"What's that for?" Seagraves said, nodding at his pocket.

"Protection," he said. He stood up suddenly and walked into the inner office. Seagraves followed him and shut the door. He sat in his chair. Trout paced the length of the room, checking the street from the window each time he arrived at that end.

Seagraves watched him, holding himself still and apart, trying to see if Trout would be revealed in a new way. He was not, and in a moment Seagraves was impatient.

"What in hell are you doing, Paris?" he said. "You come in here armed, peeking out the windows like a crazy man."

Trout reached into his pocket and Seagraves froze. When his hand came out, though, it was holding an envelope from the United States government. He dropped it on the desk and went back to the window. Seagraves took the letter out and read it. Official notification from the IRS that Trout was the subject of an audit. "An audit?" Seagraves said. "You come in here like this over a notice of an audit?"

"I'm here for legal protection from my enemies."

"The Internal Revenue Service isn't just your enemy, they're everybody's. There isn't a reason in the world to take this personal. All you got to do is see your accountant, and then you both sit down with one of their people and work it out. They aren't all that unreasonable. . . ."

Trout left the window and stood on the other side of the desk. "There ain't nothing to work out," he said.

"You paid your taxes?"

"I pay my lawful bills," he said. "I don't take a thing from the government, and I don't give a thing in return."

"Never?"

Trout put his hands on the desk and leaned over until Seagraves leaned back. He smelled like tomato soup. "Sit down, Paris," he said, "so I don't need my reading glasses to see who I'm talking to."

Trout moved away but did not sit down. "How long has it been since you paid?" Seagraves said.

He shook his head. "I never started," he said.

"You been making a living in this country since World War One, and you never paid taxes?"

"I never took a cent," he said.

"You filed?"

"No."

Seagraves closed his eyes. "I heard of dirt farmers did this," he said. "The Negroes, they don't pay, they don't have Social Security numbers. I never heard of anybody ran a business of any size that ignored the government. I know plenty of them that cheated, but just to pretend like it wasn't there . . ." He scratched his head, thinking of the legalities.

"Technically," he said a minute later, "you don't have to file if you don't owe."

"That's what I told you," Trout said. "I pay what I owe."

"The government doesn't leave that to you to decide."

Seagraves looked at the letter again, then pushed it back across the desk at Trout. "They going to want to look at the books," he said.

Trout looked at the letter but did not pick it up. "I keep my books in my head."

Seagraves said, "You've got to show them your books, or they can say you're worth any damn thing they want."

"I don't have two cents in any bank in the United States," he said. "I don't keep things where just anybody can turn over a rock and find them."

"They're going to want to see what you made—"

"They're welcome to hunt it." He went to the window again, the gun in his pocket knocked against the sill as he bent.

"That's the wrong way to handle the IRS," Seagraves said. "You make it personal, and it gets personal. They know places to look. The government is like the law: It isn't exactly smart, but it's relentless."

It was quiet in the room for a moment, then Trout slapped the wall. "Everybody in the state of Georgia is after my assets," he said softly. "All over that girl."

And that fast Seagraves could see her again, lying on the sheet in the photograph. The bones under her skin.

"A person gets mixed up in your business, and then they are your business," Trout said. He spoke as he looked out the window. "We need to get this appeal settled. Get out from underneath this case."

Seagraves was affected by the memory of the pictures. "The easiest way to settle it is to serve the time," he said.

"Easiest for who?"

Seagraves waited a moment, holding himself still and watching, and then he said, "I gone over this, Paris, and I don't think we're going to win."

"You said they made a mistake."

"They did, but sometimes it isn't enough."

"I ain't going into any work camp."

"That isn't voluntary either," Seagraves said. "The government's got its hands on you now, and I can tell you it's a hell of a lot easier to avoid them in the first place than it is to get loose."

"That's what I paid you for."

Seagraves shook his head. "I've done what I can for you," he said. "I tried and I worried, but we aren't doing a thing now but putting it off."

Trout came back to the desk one more time. Seagraves saw he was shaking. "I'm the one that decides," he said.

"You been deciding this from the minute you stepped onto Mary McNutt's porch."

Trout sputtered. "That girl . . . those people brought this on themself. I didn't go out there shooting them for nothing."

A long moment passed. "That is exactly what you did," Seagraves said.

"I can do it again," he said.

"It's worn me out, Paris," Seagraves said. "You've worn me out. It's time to get away from you and your case."

"You can't quit me in the middle," Trout said.

"It isn't the middle. It's the end."

"The hell it is."

Seagraves did not answer. He looked from Trout to the letter still lying on his desk. "You like me to, I could direct you to one of the other lawyers here on this. If it was me, I'd get somebody in Atlanta that specializes in tax law."

"I had all the goddamn lawyers I can stand."

Seagraves shrugged. "You're the one that decides. I offered you my best advice, which is to drop the appeals. You can take it or not."

"It was you gave money to Buster Devonne," he said. The words stopped Seagraves, and Trout began to nod. "That don't settle so well now, does it?" he said.

"Do what you want," Seagraves said.

Trout continued to nod. "You're thinking I can't find another lawyer would bring that into court."

Seagraves held himself still, feeling cleaner now, somehow removed from the threat.

"What you have forgot," Trout said, "is that I know the law myself."

"What I overlooked with you," Seagraves said, "is what you did."

Trout put his hand back in the pocket with the gun, Seagraves did not move. "I want everything that's mine," Trout said. "The case, all the evidence, the court records . . ."

"I don't keep the evidence," he said. "Ward Townes got that."

"Give me what you got."

Seagraves called Emma Grandy and told her to bring the Trout file. She put it on his desk a minute later, keeping her eyes low in the room. The corners of the photographs still protruded beyond the file itself. Seagraves pushed it across the desk.

"I want the copies. . . ."

"That's it, everything in the world that connects us," he said.

Trout brought what looked like several thousand dollars in hundred-dollar bills out of his pocket. The money was folded once and opened with his hand. He turned it over. There were fifties on the bottom, and he took one of them off and dropped it on the desk next to the file.

"There's two visits," he said, "yesterday and today."

He picked up his folder and the letter from the Internal Revenue Service. Then he turned, without another word, opened the door and walked out.

FROM HIS DESK SEAGRAVES saw Carl Bonner standing in the outer office. Orange hair and white, smooth skin. Seagraves noticed the young lawyer bore a physical resemblance to Red Barron, the great football player from Georgia Tech.

Trout pushed past him on the way out. Carl Bonner stood still, watching him until he was gone. When he turned back into the room, Seagraves saw that he was furious.

He stood up behind his desk. "Carl Bonner," he said, "come on in here, son."

The look on Bonner's face changed in the instant he heard Seagraves's voice. The men shook hands, and Seagraves sat back down. "I can't stay a minute," Bonner said. "I wanted to thank you in person for sending me Mrs. Trout."

Seagraves nodded toward the outer office. "That right there was your adversary."

Bonner looked back in the direction the older man had pointed his chin. "That's Paris Trout? He got old."

Seagraves nodded. "Old and dangerous."

"He's rude, I'll say that." Bonner shrugged, looking again in the direction Trout had gone. "He aged thirty years since I saw him."

"He's had a lot on his mind."

The young attorney nodded. "He's about to have something more."

It was quiet a moment. Seagraves considered what he was about to say. "If I might presume to offer you a word of caution . . ."

Bonner nodded, waiting.

"Go easy in your dealings with Mr. Trout. I don't mean you oughtn't to represent your client, but at the same time keep in mind the man has lost his mind."

Carl Bonner started to smile again and then saw that Seagraves was earnest. "He isn't crazy enough to give up his money," he said.

"There's all kinds of crazy," Seagraves said. "Paris doesn't talk to himself out loud on the street or drag him a dead dog around on a leash. The way he's crazy isn't that far off center, so most of the time he seems like anybody else."

"I expect everybody's got their secrets."

Seagraves looked Carl Bonner sincerely in the eyes. "He's proved how far he'll take it," he said. "Ordinary people might consider things in the abstract, but bad intentions aren't what being crazy is about. Even if we're all on the same road, Paris Trout doesn't have any brakes."

Seagraves could not tell if the young attorney understood him or not.

"I'll keep that in mind, Mr. Seagraves," he said.

No, he hadn't understood him at all.

NEW YEAR'S EVE LESLIE Bonner put on a new black dress that she'd bought for herself in Macon, drank several glasses of Coca-Cola spiked with liquor that her husband had purchased for the holidays at the Ether Hotel, and accompanied him to a party at the home of the businessman and politician Richard Dickey.

He had been two weeks talking her into it.

The dress was cut low all the way around, passing front to back beneath her armpits, and appeared to be held up by two thin black straps running over her shoulders. There was an excitement in the straps.

A maid answered the door and led them into a room as big as the Bonners' backyard. Oil paintings on the walls, a string quartet in the corner. There was a punch bowl, and next to it a table with bottles of liquor carrying the seal of the State of New York.

The maid took Leslie Bonner's coat, and she went right to the liquor table and ordered a rum and Coke. Carl Bonner followed her through the smoke and noise, shaking hands with people he had not seen since before the Korean War. Some of the women kissed him, and by the time Leslie turned away from the table, holding the glass against her lips, his cheeks were smudged in several shades of lipstick.

She took a slow, single swallow of the drink. "Have you been raped?" she said.

He took her soft arm in his hand and leaned into her ear. He smelled her perfume and felt the heat of her skin. "We don't have to stay long," he said. "Put in an appearance, then we can do anything you want."

She pushed into him, just a moment, and then pulled back. Her lip was wet halfway to her nose, and a light flush had taken over her cheeks. Smoke was everywhere.

"No," she said, "this is nice."

You never knew.

A moment later Carl Bonner felt a hand on his arm and was introduced to a bug-eyed state legislator from Waycross, who had once seen him play football in high school. The man was smoking a cigar, he wore a class ring with a stone the size of another bug eye.

He shook hands with Bonner and then wrapped both his hands

around Leslie's, blowing cigar smoke into her hair, and told her anytime she came to Waycross, Waycross would be grateful for the change in scenery. "For some damn reason," he said, "we got the ugliest women in the state. I think it's in the water."

Leslie allowed the legislator to hold on to that hand and drank from her glass with the other one. "We got women," he said, "that could not fit one leg in that dress."

And then just such a woman emerged from one of the small gatherings nearby and pulled the legislator away.

He was replaced by others. Lawyers and businessmen from Cotton Point and Atlanta and Macon. Leslie stayed close to the liquor table, even when her husband was pulled away, and took the compliments on her appearance with no sign of embarrassment. As he watched her, it occurred to Carl Bonner that for the first time since they arrived, she was herself.

It occurred to him that she might find some friends.

At ten o'clock in the evening a Negro dressed in a tuxedo walked through the guests, announcing dinner. He went from the north end of the room to the south and opened two doors there which led to another room, as big as this one, where two long tables had been set with plates and wineglasses and candles. A chandelier as heavy as a Pontiac hung from the ceiling. There were silver ice buckets every five feet, a bottle of champagne in each one. The places were marked with name cards, and the Bonners found themselves sitting across the table from Harry and Lucy Seagraves.

Estes Singletary, editor and owner of the Ether County *Plain Talk*, and his wife were on one side, and Mayor Bob Horn and his wife were on the other. Leslie settled into her seat and reached for the champagne. Bob Horn leaned forward to smile at her. "I enjoy a woman that knows what she wants," he said.

She said, "Thank you very much," and killed everything she had poured into her glass. She refilled it and then poured one for the mayor. They toasted each other and sipped at their drinks.

"I'm afraid Carl's kept you hidden from us," the mayor said.

She stopped her glass, an inch from her lips, and looked at him. "You do this every night?" she said.

Bob Horn laughed until he began to choke. Hearing him, the rest of the table laughed too. At the other table people were straining to see what they had missed.

There were more toasts over the soup and then over the salad. It seemed to Leslie Bonner that Harry Seagraves's were the most humorous. She saw a kindness in him that was missing in the others.

The bottles at the second table—where Mr. and Mrs. Richard Dickey were seated—remained untouched, and a curious silence seemed to settle over the guests there.

Carl Bonner sat and watched his wife lead the table into a state of drunkenness he had never before seen in mixed company in Ether County, Georgia. He began to feel uncomfortable.

The maids brought in the plates. Roast beef, creamed potatoes, creamed beans. Carl Bonner watched his wife survey the food, then refill her glass. He had an unexplainable premonition that she was about to begin a food fight.

At the other table Richard Dickey stood up to offer a blessing. Carl Bonner closed his eyes and bowed his head and felt her hand on his leg at the moment Richard Dickey said, "Dear Lord . . ."

It was a light touch at first, just the weight of her fingers. He tried to listen to the words. ". . . not only for this wonderful meal but also for the life you have seen fit to give us . . ."

Her hand moved slowly up his leg, stopping in his lap. Against his will, he began to stiffen. ". . . our friends, our children, our good neighbors . . ."

She found the mouth of his penis through the material. He squirmed slightly in his chair, trying to move himself from under her hand, but she held on. Then he felt her hand change locations. Richard Dickey's voice covered the sound of the zipper.

". . . and keep us ever in thy thoughts, O Lord, and watch us through the coming year . . ."

Richard Dickey said, "In Jesus' name, a-men," and she had it out. He looked down and watched the muscles move under her skin, just at the place her forearm disappeared under the tablecloth.

Across the table Lucy Seagraves sipped at her glass and then spoke to Leslie. "What do you do with yourself, dear? Do you play cards?"

"I keep busy," Leslie said. "It seems like there aren't enough hours in the day."

She was holding the head in her fingers now, pulling down to separate the lips, then squeezing them together. He felt himself begin to throb, and then one of his legs was shaking. She pinched him at the head, stopping it. He tried to remember the last time he had been with her, and couldn't. His breathing was suddenly harder, and a line of sweat broke across his forehead. Estes Singletary was looking at him in a curious way.

Leslie reached across his plate with her free hand and picked the champagne bottle out of the bucket, filling his glass and then hers. She put the glass in his hand and said, "To the new year."

LUCY SEAGRAVES SMILED AT the young couple across the table as they toasted the new year. They sipped champagne, and then she kissed him on the cheek, lingering there only a second, perhaps long enough to whisper a few words.

Lucy Seagraves saw how much they loved each other and regretted the gossip she had repeated about Mrs. Bonner.

She was attracted to romance, it reminded her of the way she and Harry had been. She did not know if they had ever been in love like Carl and Leslie Bonner—she could not remember ever seeing Harry shaking so badly just at the touch of her lips against his cheek—but it seemed to her things might have been like that once.

TROUT
PART SIX

T hree years to the week after Rosie Sayers died in Thomas Cornell Clinic, the United States Supreme Court, voting six to three, refused to hear Paris Trout's appeal for a new trial.

The appeal was researched and prepared by Trout himself, as was his prior appeal to the State Supreme Court. It represented thirty trips to the law library at Mercer College, six months in his office at the back of the store, matching the language in his written brief to the briefs he copied at the library and brought home.

He began work every morning at twenty minutes after nine and would not quit while there was light in the sky. He ate one meal a day—canned food and ginger ale, once in a while a piece of cheese. A peg-legged woman named Charlotte Hock ran the store.

Charlotte Hock did the stock work and operated the cash register. She interrupted Trout only when Negroes came by to borrow money or make payments. She hated to see them come in. It terrified her to disturb Mr. Trout while he was composing.

She had not known Trout before he took over his own defense, but it seemed to her that the writing made him crazy. He was more normal, at least, when he came into the store in the morning than he was when he left. Of course, he visited his mother every morning at the retirement home on the way to work, and she thought that might account for his good moods early in the day.

By afternoon she would hear him in the back. Unimaginable language. Sometimes there were noises, as if furniture were being overturned. Once she thought she heard him crying.

He never cursed her, though. He never abused her at all except in the hours he forced her to keep and the low wages he paid. She never asked for less work or more money.

She knew a peg-legged woman was fortunate to have any job at all.

She could not feel relaxed in the store, if he was in it or not. She knew that he had killed someone once, and did not intend to give him reason to do it again. He carried a pistol everywhere, even when he came only a few steps out of the office to open one of the safes lined up against the wall in the hallway. The light back there was poor, and he lit matches to dial the combinations.

He visited the safes regularly, at the beginning of his day and at the end and sometimes following his afternoon meal.

THE NOTICE THAT THE Supreme Court had voted not to consider his appeal reached Paris Trout at eleven o'clock in the morning by registered mail. About the same time a similar letter arrived at the office of Judge John Taylor, who studied the document longer than he normally would, looking for some way to relinquish authority in the matter, and then—finding none—revoked Trout's bail and issued orders for his arrest.

As an afterthought he made copies of the notice and his order and sent them to Ward Townes.

Later in the day Judge Taylor took a call in his quarters from Sheriff Edward Fixx. "I got this order here to arrest Paris Trout," the sheriff said.

"That is correct."

"You want him arrested."

"I didn't send the damn thing over for you to wipe your ass."

"All right," Edward Fixx said. "I only asked. You want this done today?"

"Today, tomorrow, it's no consequence. Call him first, let him know when you're coming."

"Yessir, I'll do that."

The line went quiet for a moment. "There's no reason to make this a public spectacle," the judge said. "You might have him to come in himself."

After he had hung up, Judge Taylor pulled the notice from the Supreme Court out and looked at it again. Six to three. He thought Paris Trout must have written up an impressive application.

"The man's that smart," he said out loud, "he ought know better to get caught shooting up colored people's homes."

TEN MINUTES AFTER THE notice arrived, Paris Trout was on the telephone with a Petersboro County attorney named Rodney Dalmar, who had written him shortly after the trial, offering his services in the event Trout "exhausted ordinary legal remedies."

In the letter Dalmar said he'd had some success "arbitrating" jail terms at the state work farm, where Trout had been sentenced to serve his one to three years.

The letter had been sitting in Trout's desk, unacknowledged, for nearly three years, but Rodney Dalmar's manner was familiar, as if it were something he and Trout had talked about yesterday. "Mr. Trout," he said, "what may I do for you today?"

"Your letter," he said. "You said you might help me when the time came."

"Yessir, I might could."

"Well, the time is come."

"I see," said the attorney.

"I have just received notice that the Supreme Court has denied to review my conviction." The voice sounded flat and calm.

"Communists," Rodney Dalmar said. "But what can you do?"

It was quiet a moment. "I took it from your letter that you would know what to do," he said finally.

"Possibly," the lawyer said. "Possibly I might." There was another silence, then: "This gone run you some money, you know that."

"I never thought anything different."

"It isn't myself," the lawyer said. "It was up to me, I'd do it gratis. A man ought not to be in your situation, not over collecting a nigger debt."

There was an uncomfortable moment, and then Trout said, "It was a tampered jury."

"Sir?"

"Somebody got in my business. I know every one of their names."

"I heard that rumor," the attorney said.

"I know names, I know where they live."

"I'm sure your time will come," the attorney said.

Trout did not answer.

"Mr. Trout?"

"I am getting up a list," he said. "They're all on it."

"I don't blame you," the attorney said. "I might do the same thing in your place."

The line went quiet again, the lawyer began to wonder what Paris Trout was doing. "I can tell you got your mind on other things right now," he said, "but I might just take a minute to explain our situation down here in Pete County."

While the lawyer explained the situation, Trout took a blank piece of paper out of his desk and began to print the names and addresses of all the jurors. He knew them by heart. Beneath them he wrote Judge John Taylor, Ward Townes, Harry Seagraves, and Hanna Nile—his wife's maiden name.

He thought for a moment and added Hubert Norland, Edward Fixx, and Jack Handley—the police chief, the sheriff, and the new district attorney.

The lawyer was going over the people in Petersboro County who had to be paid. "There are legal fees to the court, of course," he said, "attorneys and the judge, but the real expense is the work farm itself. The man there is a hard man, and he can make it as steep as he wants. . . ."

"Tell me what it costs," Trout said.

"Altogether I'd say twenty thousand."

"Twenty thousand," he said.

"Yessir," the lawyer said. "Just give us a call when you're coming, and we'll be out to meet you."

Trout hung up the phone. It rang again, a few minutes later, and he sat looking at it eight or nine rings before he picked it up. He put the receiver against his ear without speaking.

"Mr. Trout?"

The voice was different, he couldn't place it at first. "Mr. Trout, this is Edward Fixx."

It was quiet a moment. Then: "I just put you on my list."

Sheriff Fixx took a moment too. "Yessir, thank you. . . . The reason I was calling is to ask you to come in."

"Come in where?"

"The sheriff department. Judge Taylor got notice from Washington that your appeal run out, and he wanted me to pick you up. I thought it might be better you just come in on your own, save you riding up Main Street in a patrol car."

Trout reached into his pocket and found the handle of the pistol. He brought it out and laid it on his desk.

"It don't have to be today," the sheriff said. "Judge Taylor indicated tomorrow would be all right, maybe a day more if you need it."

"I'll be over to see you," he said, and hung up the phone again. Then he tore the cord out of the wall.

THAT EVENING, AS WAS her habit, Charlotte Hock tapped on the office door to let Mr. Trout know she was leaving. The way she would put it was "Is there anything else you need, sir?" It made her feel less guilty about stopping work.

She tapped, but there was no answer. She tapped again. It sounded like someone was moving furniture. "Mr. Trout? Are you all right?" When he didn't answer again, she cracked the door and put her head inside and found herself looking right down the barrel of eternity itself.

The desk had been moved to the corner and set on its end, and lying right across the top, as flat as a snake, was Mr. Trout's arm. She glimpsed his face behind the gun. "Send them in," he said.

"There ain't nobody to send in," she said. "It's just me."

"Move out the way," he said, and showed her the direction with the gun. She stepped in that direction, farther into the office and away from the door. He moved the gun off her, and she saw him better from that angle. His eyes were jittery, and he'd got himself dirty moving the desk.

"I was making to inquire if there was anything else you need before I left," she said.

Without any reason she could see, he began to smile. Mr. Trout did not smile much, not even in the morning, and it would have made her uncomfortable even if he was not barricaded behind his desk, with his gun turned on the door.

"No," he said, "I don't need you anymore."

"Then I'll be going."

"I would if I was you," he said.

THE NEXT MORNING CHARLOTTE Hock pictured herself quitting her job. She stayed in bed until seven o'clock, thinking of getting up and locking the door to her house and then just lying back down and falling to sleep.

What she could not imagine doing was calling Mr. Trout and telling him that she wasn't coming in. She was afraid how he would take it. She could not imagine herself acknowledging that what had happened the night before was out of the ordinary.

And in the end, lacking imagination, she got up, attached her leg, dressed, and brushed her hair. She tried not to think about the way he had looked holding the gun, she tried not to think about the way he had looked when he smiled.

In the end what she thought about was that a peg-legged woman was fortunate to have any job at all.

She walked into the store at eight-thirty, using her key to the back door. The office door was open, and looking in, she saw that the desk was returned to its place. Mr. Trout was behind it, wearing a suit. She thought perhaps he was going up to Mercer College for the day to study lawbooks.

"Are you leaving somewhere today, Mr. Trout?"

He looked at her in an ordinary way, then he stood up. She jumped. He walked around the desk and past her, out the door, to one of the safes. He lit a match and began to move the tumbler. "I got some bi'nis out of the county," he said, "you be all right here alone today."

"Yessir." She was suddenly happy, the thought of working alone.

"I'll be down to Morganville a day or two."

"Yessir."

He stood up, holding a handful of hundred-dollar bills. He spread them once, then straightened the money on the top of the safe and put it into an envelope.

"Any colored people come in, you tell them you don't handle money," he said, and then he put the envelope in his pocket.

Which were the same instructions he left her with when he went to Mercer College. "No sir, I'll tell them to come back another time." She saw he had put his gun in a holster inside his coat; she could not think of what sort of formal occasion it might be that he would carry his gun in a holster. She knew he had no connections to church.

He looked at her more carefully now, the way he had before he hired her. "If this don't go right in Morganville," he said, "I will send you instructions how to handle the niggers."

The thought of handling the niggers terrified Charlotte Hock. Not that she was afraid of them—she felt like she was colored half the time herself—but that she would do it wrong. Keeping a store was one thing, running the bank was another. "I don't know that I could do that, Mr. Trout," she said.

He touched her then, it was the first time that she could remember. His hand was on her shoulder. "Of course you could," he said. "They ain't that different from you or me, that's the secret."

She watched him out the door that morning, wondering what had gotten into him now.

PARIS TROUT DROVE ONE of his cars—a three-year-old Ford with a cracked engine block—to the sheriff's department and asked for Edward Fixx. Sheriff Fixx came out from the back, wearing his uniform. A bone-handled thirty-eight sat on his hip at an unnatural angle, like some knot that had grown off a tree.

He seemed surprised to see Paris Trout, or perhaps just timid. "I 'preciate your coming down, Mr. Trout," he said.

Trout looked around the room. He had been in the place before, of course, but it looked different this morning. Smaller, for one thing. "You said to come in."

Sheriff Fixx opened a swinging door—it didn't reach a person's waist—and Trout walked into the back. A woman there was operating a typewriter, using all her fingers. He thought of his wife.

They passed her into the sheriff's office. It had his name on the door and was the size of a bedroom closet. There was no window. Just the desk and a file cabinet and a fan and two chairs. Edward Fixx sat down and opened the desk. He took out the papers on Trout and laid them on the desk.

"Here's my orders," he said.

Trout did not look at them.

"I don't have no choice in this," Fixx said. "Judge Taylor issues the marching orders, I got to march."

Trout sat still while the room got smaller every second.

Fixx picked the papers back up and began to read. " 'You'—meaning me—'are hereby ordered, by the authority of the circuit court of the county of Ether, the state of Georgia, to transport one Paris Trout to the county of Petersboro, the state of Georgia, and there to transfer his custody to the warden of the state work farm.' "

The sheriff did not read well and followed the words with the index finger of the hand he wasn't using to hold the order. Trout waited until he was finished and then stood up.

"Let's go if we're going," he said.

They took the new squad car, embossed with a large white star on one side and the seal of the state of Georgia on the other. It was a Ford too, but was powered by a special police interceptor engine.

Sheriff Fixx used side streets to leave the business district and then drove through Bloodtown. He did not want white people seeing him driving Paris Trout off to prison. Trout sat quietly in the seat next to him, a sawed-off shotgun stuck in the rack between them, and watched the window. It occurred to the chief that Trout might be feeling homesick. "It ain't that long to be gone," he said. "Six months, nine at the outside."

They crossed the river and started south. The sheriff stepped on the gas, and the interceptor engine pushed them back into their seats. The sheriff smiled, waiting for Trout to remark on the car.

Trout said nothing.

Sheriff Fixx took the Ford up to one hundred and then came back to seventy. One of the windows began to whistle. Trout stared at the countryside, the sheriff could not even tell if he was frightened. He rolled his window up and down, trying to get rid of the noise. Finally he left it cracked half an inch. "You can always tell a nigger worked on the assembly line in Detroit," the sheriff said; "they always whistle."

A little later the sheriff said, "I was a hot-rodding sumbitch when I was coming up. Like to end up in jail myself."

Trout turned from the window, and the sheriff saw he was never a hot rodder himself. "I done a lot of things," the sheriff said.

Trout blinked.

"That's how I come to be a peace officer. I was afraid if I wasn't, I was headed for trouble."

Somehow it wasn't working. Sheriff Fixx enjoyed transporting prisoners to the various work camps in the state, not only so he could get the car on the highway but to tell them his own story, how there was devilment inside even a police officer. It seemed to Edward Fixx that a man on the way to a work farm needed a good example. Paris Trout, however, did not appear to be making the connection between the story and himself.

"The way I look at it," the sheriff said, "there ain't nobody different. We all got to eat and sleep and hunt pussy. Time that's left over, a man ought to have to hisself. All the fine houses, fine clothes don't change that."

He realized then that Trout owned one of those fine houses and was glad he'd added the part about clothes. "What I mean is, it don't matter how much money you got . . ."

When Trout didn't answer, the sheriff lapsed into silence, watching the countryside. They passed farms a hundred years old, torn shades in the windows, endless land. Overalls on clotheslines. Every few miles there was a family plot—eight or ten graves, fenced in barbed wire to keep the animals out.

"How is Mrs. Trout's health?" the sheriff said suddenly. "I mean Mrs. Trout, your mother. . . ."

Trout had, in fact, seen her that morning before he went to work. She was sitting in the chair they put her in to eat, wrapped in a stained bathrobe, staring at something outside the window. A fat girl named Jane Penny fed her custard, catching it with the spoon under the corners of her mouth, the way you would for a baby, putting it back inside.

His mother had not spoken an intelligible word to him or anyone else in eight years. That was when the stroke had hit her, in the middle of Thanksgiving dinner. He could look at her, though, and see that she was still peeved. She saw him as clear as day and couldn't say a word about it.

Sometimes when they were alone, he would sit in front of her on the windowsill, trying to see the order of things. Where he had come from, where she was going. He did not speak to her after the help left, he was not there to cheer her up.

He thought sometimes that all the things that had happened to him were already built in the day he passed into this world from her womb.

"Some days are better than others," Trout said, which was the same thing the doctor told him whenever they met in her room. He did not know how the doctor told the better days from the worse, and he hadn't asked.

The sheriff was relieved that Trout had begun to talk. It was two hours to Petersboro County. "It tears your heart to see them age," he said. "I heard this once, that you are your parents' babies, and then they turn into yours. And damn if that ain't true."

The sheriff looked across the seat as he said that. "Mine's gone, of course," he added.

Trout stuck his fingers into the pack of Camels in his pocket and came out with a cigarette. Doing that, he moved his coat, and the chief glimpsed the gun and holster. Trout lit the cigarette and blew the smoke out of his nose.

"You can't take that there with you inside the camp," the sheriff said. His own pistol, he noticed, was wedged halfway into the crack where the seat met. He wondered what had been going on in his head, to let Paris Trout in the police cruiser without checking if he had his gun. "In fact, I ought take it for you now."

Trout studied the cigarette between his fingers. "I'll turn it over when we get there," he said. The sheriff reached into his pocket for a cigarette of his own.

"They get it from you at prison," he said, "it won't be there when you get out. Sure as hell, somebody will of misplaced it for their own."

A little later the sheriff dropped his window another inch. "How old is your mother now?" he said.

"Ninety."

He picked a piece of tobacco off his tongue, looked at it a moment, and then rolled it off his finger and out the crack in the window. "Time goes by, don't it?"

Trout didn't answer.

"Six months at the work farm," the sheriff said, "that ain't no worst than joining the army."

He looked across the seat to ask Trout if he had ever been in the army, and at that moment a liver-colored mongrel dog appeared from some trees along the road, angling for the cruiser. It crossed in front of the car, and there was a banging noise and then a bump from underneath. Sheriff Fixx stood up on the brake, panicked at the prospect that he'd torn up the new cruiser.

Trout's forehead hit the windshield, and the car came to a stop sideways in the middle of the road. Before they could get out, the front end was smoking. "Lord a mercy," the sheriff said, "what now?"

Leaving his door wide open, he walked to the front. Trout stayed where he was. A knot was growing on his forehead, under his fingers, and there was a metallic taste on the end of his tongue. What kept him in his seat, though, was the feeling that he had crossed for a minute to the other side. In the second he'd hit the windshield, he was somewhere else. He'd ridden there behind a beam of black light and seen something he had already forgotten.

The sheriff was still in front of the car. He walked back and forth, keeping his eyes the same place. Trout watched him through smoke and cracked glass. A minute passed, and he sat down heavily in the driver's seat, his feet still on the highway, and looked out over the trees.

"That sonofabitch must of come up out of the gully," he said. "I never saw him." He turned and looked at Trout. "You was right here," he said, "there wasn't a thing a body could of done. . . ." He noticed the knot in the middle of Trout's forehead. "It look like somebody laid an egg on your head."

Trout did not answer.

"You feel poorly?"

He shrugged.

"If you are, get over into the gully to do it. We made enough mess of this Ford already. . . ." He got up again and walked back to the front of the car, as if he did not trust his memory. "You ought look at this," he said. "He's tore up the radiator, broke the headlight, pushed in the bumper."

Trout got out and walked into the gully. When he returned, the sheriff pointed to a spot where the metal was crushed and said, "This is the exact spot he hit us." The dog was fifty yards north, still lying in the road.

"Probably stray," the sheriff said, looking around. "Could of belonged to somebody, but more than likely he was a stray. You wonder what gets into an animal's brain to try something like that. . . ."

There was a pine tree lying on the ground across the highway, broken two feet off the ground and still hinged to the stump. Trout walked over and sat down. He closed his eyes, feeling dizzy, and in a minute the tree branch sank and the sheriff was sitting on it too. "They'll be somebody by," the sheriff said. "They always is."

Ten minutes passed. The radiator ran out of steam, and in the building quiet Trout tried to remember what it was like when he hit the window and went away.

The sheriff stood up twice and walked back to the car, came back twice shaking his head. "Anybody can hit a dog," he said.

Time passed, nothing came along the road. The sheriff moved off the trunk and sat on the ground, with his back against the stump. "Were you ever in the armed services?" he said.

Trout looked down at him a moment, as if he did not understand.

"The armed forces," he said, "like the army or navy."

"I was in the army," he said.

"During war?"

"World War One," he said.

"Did you like it?" the sheriff said. Trout nodded and lit a fresh cigarette. The sheriff said, "The best time in a man's life, ain't it?"

"I didn't have no best time," Trout said. "I was just there."

"Tell me something," the sheriff said a little later. "Did you ever shoot somebody?"

In a minute Trout looked up the road and saw a truck.

THE DRIVER TOOK THEM back to Cotton Point, where Sheriff Fixx separated a deputy from his car, and ordered him to call the garage to pick up the one on the highway. The deputy saw the sheriff was mad, and said "Yessir" every time he paused long enough for him to get it in.

Trout and the sheriff were in sight of the wreck before either of them spoke. "That bastard's a monster, ain't he?" the sheriff said, looking at the dog.

Trout had no interest in the animal. An unfocused anger was settling over him, and dead in the middle of it was a headache. He took the watch out of his pants pocket and checked the time. Eleven-thirty. The older car smelled of cigars and urine. "Mr. Trout," the sheriff said, "you the first man I ever took to jail that worried he was gone be late."

The sheriff laughed out loud, and a moment later he reached into his pocket for a tin of Copenhagen, opened it one-handed, and then put a pinch underneath his upper lip. A little later he felt around under the seat and came out with a wide-necked bottle, which he set between his legs, lifting it to his mouth every few minutes to spit.

He was beyond the wreck now and enjoying himself. He felt suddenly charitable toward Paris Trout. "You want, I could look in on your momma until you get back. . . ."

Trout opened his coat and brought out the gun.

"Whoa, there, Mr. Trout," the sheriff said. "Don't take that thing out its holster in here. . . ."

Trout heard the fear inside the sheriff, and an anger blew through him like a scream. He put the muzzle underneath Edward Fixx's chin. He heard the right-side tires leave the pavement, then come back. The bottle between the sheriff's legs tipped, and tobacco spit spilled over his pants.

"Mr. Trout," he said, "what the world you doing?"

Trout pushed the gun up, elevating the sheriff's chin. The car began to slow. "Is it an ex-cape?" The gun barrel inhibited the movement of the sheriff's jaw and affected his speech. Trout cocked the hammer, all ready to do it now. It was loose in his head.

"You want to ex-cape, it's all right with me," the sheriff said. "I ain't got a thing in the world against you, Mr. Trout. Didn't I call you up on the phone? I told you I got this order from the judge to take you down to Pete County. That's all. I'll pull over right here. You can do what you want. . . ."

And then something stopped it, he didn't know what. It was loose in his head, and then it was gone. He put his thumb on the hammer and slowly brought it back to rest against the firing pin. He pulled the gun away, the sheriff's chin held its altitude until he was sure it was gone. The smell of fresh urine filled the car. Edward Fixx checked his lap.

The gun, still in Trout's hand, lay on the seat between them. For a long time neither of them spoke. "I want to stop we get to Petersboro County," Trout said. The sheriff nodded.

"Just tell me where."

"A phone, so I can call a man."

"Yessir."

The sheriff moved his eyes from the road to the seat and then back. The gun was still lying on the seat in Trout's hand. He had the feeling Trout had forgotten it was there.

He rolled down the window, realizing he was still alive.

THERE WAS A GAS station just across the county line, bordering Hard Labor Creek. The sheriff slowed the car and stopped without being told. Trout walked inside, carrying the gun in his hand. A fat, heavy-lipped woman appeared at the screen door, her head wrapped in a bandanna, and stared out. The sheriff lifted his hand, a gesture to reassure her, but as he moved, she was gone.

The car filled with flies, and he slapped them off his lap.

Trout was inside half an hour. He came out carrying a Dr Pepper in his hand instead of the gun and got back into the car. The sheriff considered taking the shotgun out of the rack and shooting him as he opened the door, but there was a public consideration to the Trout case: A lot of people didn't think he ought to be going to jail in the first place. He had been arrested and tried and convicted, but there was a limit to what the citizenry would tolerate.

"Let's go if we're going," Trout said.

The sheriff started the engine and backed out onto the highway, catching a glimpse of the woman again behind the screen door.

The work farm was another twenty miles. As soon as they were back on the highway, the sheriff said, "I thought that fat girl might talked you out of your britches, you was in there so long. . . ."

Trout did not reply, and neither of them spoke again until they saw the farm.

"THERE IT IS," THE sheriff said.

They had just cleared a stand of pines, and the work farm was sitting in the middle of a clearing a quarter mile off the highway. There was a chain-link fence, eight feet tall and topped with barbed wire, that went around the perimeter. The gate was wide and open, a man in prison pants and an undershirt standing at it with a shotgun.

He looked into the car, squinting, as the sheriff slowed and lowered the window. "Got one for the warden," the sheriff said. The man pointed, one finger, at a large wooden building in the middle of eight smaller buildings.

The sheriff drove past him without another word and parked the car in front of the main building. "You want me to take your gun for you?" he said.

Trout said, "I left it."

The sheriff opened his door, thinking he would stop at the gas station on the way back and find out from the lady herself what had gone on inside. They walked in. A single prisoner was mopping the hallway, which smelled of lye soap and sweat. They walked to the last door on the right. It opened as soon as the sheriff knocked. It was the warden himself, Buddy White. Behind him the sheriff saw two men he did not recognize, both of them in suits and pointy half-white shoes. A German shepherd lay with its chin on its feet, watching Trout.

"This here is Paris Trout," the sheriff said, handing the warden the papers. He did not like this particular warden, who had never as much as offered him a cold drink. The sheriff believed lawmen ought to show each other professional courtesy.

The warden took the papers without acknowledging the introduction. As he looked them over, he said, "Mr. Trout, your lawyer is over there to the desk."

He signed the acceptance form and returned it to the sheriff. "That's it?" the sheriff said.

243

"Unless you got another one in the car."

The sheriff turned to leave, and a low rattle sounded somewhere in the dog's chest. "I'll shoot that dog right here in your office," the sheriff said, "before I let him chase me out."

"Shut up, Butch," the warden said, and the dog went still.

The sheriff saw they were waiting for him to leave. It felt like he'd walked into one of Richard Dickey's fancy parties. He turned without another word, opening the door for himself, and made his way out.

When he had been gone a minute, the warden said to Trout, "I believe you have some bi'nes with these gentlemen here," and walked outside. The dog stood up, stretching one end, then the other, and followed him.

One of the men in the suits motioned Trout to the desk. "I am Mr. Dalmar," he said when Trout was closer. "This here is Judge Raymond Mims, who has come out in person to hear this matter."

The judge was sitting behind the desk with his hands behind his neck. "Your attorney informs me you have been the victim of perjured testimony, Mr. Trout," he said. He was a small man with a shined appearance. Trout saw he had never done any work in his life.

He nodded his head. "People have told things about me in court."

"I'm sure they have," the judge said. And for a minute the three men stayed where they were without speaking.

It was the attorney who broke the silence. "There is a matter of legal fees, Mr. Trout. Ourselves, we'd straighten this out gratis if we could, but Mr. White, the warden there, is not a man who appreciates the moral issues. . . ."

Trout reached into his pocket and found the envelope. It was two inches thick, and he handed it to the lawyer without looking inside. The lawyer handed it to the judge, who did look.

"Twenty thousand dollars," Trout said.

The judge paid no attention. When he had finished counting, he took papers from his inside pocket, signed his name half a dozen times, and then stood up, leaving the papers on the desk, and looked out the window at the empty yard.

Rodney Dalmar studied the papers the judge had signed and then offered Trout his hand. "The judge has issued an order freeing you on a writ of habeas corpus, citing perjured testimony at your trial," he said.

Trout looked at the attorney's hand and then at the man near the window. "I want proof he's a judge," he said.

Rodney Dalmar tried to smile, but there appeared to be something wrong with one side of his face. He put his hand on Trout's shoulder and moved to lead him toward the door. "I know you're having a joke on us, Mr. Trout," he said, "but sir, this is not the time."

Trout would not be led. "I don't make jokes about twenty thousand dollars," he said. "I never seen you before in my life, and I want proof what I paid for is legal."

The attorney held the orders open for Trout to see. "This is the seal of the Superior Court," he said. "That's as legal as it gets down here."

But Trout was looking past the document at the small man standing at the window. "I give you twenty thousand dollars," he said. "He counted it on that desk right there and put it in his pocket. I'm entitled to proof."

The attorney looked quickly at the man in the window, then back at Trout.

"You got to understand," he said, "we have a . . . *sensitive* situation here."

"I ain't asked to put it in the Atlanta *Constitution*," Trout said. "I just want proof it's a judge signed this paper."

"Mr. Trout," Rodney Dalmar said, "as your attorney I would suggest you drop this right here. If it wasn't legal, the warden wouldn't let anybody out this room. . . ."

"He ain't yet. And if he does, there's nothing to keep them from bringing me back."

The little man at the window turned slowly around. The shined look was drained out of his face. "Judge," the attorney said, "could you give us a minute? Mr. Trout is got nervous being so close to jail. . . ."

"Exactly a minute," he said, and moved to leave the room. Trout stepped in front of him.

"Nobody leaves the room till I'm satisfied," he said.

"Mr. Trout," the judge said, looking up into his face, "all I need do is to whistle, and Warden White will be back through the door with a shotgun, shoot off your legs at the knees. It has happened in this room before. The dogs come in and clean up the mess. I understand you are a man of some resources in Ether County, but it didn't save you up there, and it can't save you here. It's out of your hands now, and if me and Mr. Dalmar here wanted to rob you, you are robbed."

Then he walked around Trout and out the door. Rodney Dalmar ran his fingers through his oiled curly hair. He began to smooth feelings, but something in Trout was out of control. He saw it and left him alone. "Just have a seat there against the wall, Mr. Trout," he said.

Trout did not move. The attorney followed Judge Mims out the door. When he was gone, Trout reached behind himself and found the handle of his pistol. He pulled it out of his belt. It was a forty-five automatic, and the weight of it in his hand made him patient. He moved a chair behind the place where the door was hinged and sat down, holding the gun in his lap, and waited for the warden to come into the room with his shotgun.

The office was quiet and hot. He pictured the bullets lying in the clip in the handle of the gun, he remembered his feelings in the car again when he was right on the edge of blowing the chin off Edward Fixx. It was different from the way he'd felt shooting the girl.

When he'd gone after her, the anger blew into him from the outside.

IT WAS ANOTHER HALF hour before Trout heard the warden's steps in the hallway. He cocked the hammer, holding the gun between his knees. The warden opened the door and scolded the dog. Trout heard his voice and knew he wasn't coming in with any shotgun. He replaced the hammer against the firing pin and sat still.

In a moment he heard the dog—its nails against the cement floor— and then it came into the office, shook, and the door closed. The warden did not see Trout at first and started when he did.

"What in the world you doin' still here?" he said.

A noise began to crawl up the dog's throat, and the warden didn't hush him. "This is where I was put," Trout said, watching the animal. Something was taking it over, growing on itself, and it bared teeth and black gums.

"They supposed to take you along," the warden said. "They bust you out, they supposed to take you out. I come in here and find you playing with a gun?"

The dog was edging closer, making wet, growling noises, his eyes seemed to be fixed on Trout's, except Trout could not meet them. He leaned forward for a better look.

"Sit down," the warden said in a tired way, and in that instant the expression in the animal's face changed. He sat and looked up at the warden, his tongue jiggling happily out of one side of his mouth.

"It's my gun," Trout said.

"You brought your gun witch you to jail?"

"I wasn't going to jail."

"You could of."

"No," Trout said, "I wasn't."

The warden walked to his desk, set his hat on top of it, and sat down. "I'd like to know how in Sam hill you're fixing to get back. I don't run no bus service to Ether County, take you half a day to walk to town."

Trout waited.

"I guest I could get somebody to tote you over. . . . Might cost you some change."

Trout did not say a word.

"I expect I could get a trustee to ride you for fifteen dollars. That ain't much to somebody like you, is it?"

Trout stood up, and the dog rose halfway with him and froze. "I spent all the money in Petersboro County I'm going to," he said.

The warden shrugged. "Suit yourself," he said. "You go right out through the gate, walk to the highway and turn south. Morganville is seventeen miles. I wouldn't count on nobody picking you up around here if that's what you're thinking. The suit don't help, people know you comin' from the prison. They think everybody comes out this place is gone rob them and leave them dead in a ditch. They got no way to tell you ain't like that, Mr. Trout . . ."

Trout knew the man was laughing at him. He put the forty-five back inside his belt and walked out of the office. The prisoner was still in the same spot; he could have been mopping in his sleep. Trout walked around him, through the wet spot on the floor, and found his way outside.

He walked to the highway and turned south. Half a mile from the work farm there was a snake. She was a copperhead, as thick as a man's arm, mashed where a tire had hit her, and stuck to the highway in her own gum. She lay still, except for a twitching in the tail, until Trout was a few yards away. Then, without warning, her head came up off the asphalt, striking slowly in Trout's direction, again and again. Trout stayed where he was—a few yards away—and then the snake suddenly turned on herself and struck, three times, just in front of the spot where she was mashed.

Then she dropped against the asphalt and crawled without moving forward, stuck to the road and sliding from side to side, until some sense inside her was satisfied that she had crawled far enough, and she lay quietly against the road and waited.

Called back to the business of dying.

He saw it wasn't so bad—she just pulled further back from the world, into the safest, deepest places inside her.

THE FIRST PERSON TO see Paris Trout after he got off the bus at Cotton Point was Sheriff Edward Fixx. It was the sheriff's habit to drive from his office to the Greyhound depot after lunch and watch the passengers leaving the twelve-fifteen express. There was a bulletin board in his office filled with the faces of wanted men—faces and descriptions and methods of operation—and he required his six deputies and Arlene, the radio dispatcher, to read the board every day, not only for the wanted posters but for the admonitions he wrote on note cards and stuck there with thumbtacks.

It was a world full of rewards for those who knew what they were looking for.

Sheriff Fixx took his customary seat at the end of the bench closest to the doors and watched the faces, hoping for one that would set off a warning. There were too many pictures to memorize, so the sheriff studied them when they came in, relying on his instincts to tell him when he came across one of them in person. It was a certain feeling he got when there was trouble.

And today the feeling was suddenly on him like a stroke. A tall, gray-haired man in a suit. The sheriff caught a glimpse, less than a profile, and sat straight up, feeling for his holster. A moment later he realized who it was. The sheriff removed his hat and wiped at his forehead with a handkerchief. Paris Trout walked through the glass doors into the depot, right past him, and went to the telephone.

When Trout finished his call, Sheriff Fixx pressed the same receiver against his ear and dialed Judge Taylor. "Paris Trout just got off the twelve-fifteen," he said.

"What am I supposed to do about that?" the judge said.

"I thought you might want to know, is all."

"Shit," he said, and hung up.

Sheriff Fixx walked carefully to the front door and looked outside. Trout was standing on the curb with a Negro woman and a couple of cadets from the officers' academy. His suit was wrinkled, and there was some dirt on his shoes, but there was no other sign that he had been away. Sheriff Fixx remembered the men in suits and white shoes in the warden's office.

Lawyers.

Sheriff Fixx had walked to the depot that day because his cruiser—the new one—was being repaired, and he'd had to send deputies out in the other three cars on county calls. He thought of his new car, mangled in the drive with Paris Trout to Petersboro County, and now, with the car still in the body shop at Country Ford, Trout was back in town.

The man had put a gun against his jaw—although the sheriff decided later he never meant to use it—and then damn near beat him home. Sheriff Fixx walked through the door and stood just behind him. "I see you got time off for good behavior," he said. The sheriff had a bent for sarcasm.

Trout reached into his pocket and came out with a folded paper and handed it to him.

"What's this, a pardon from the governor?"

"Habeas corpus," Trout said.

"Hocus-pocus, you mean."

Trout took the paper out of Sheriff Fixx's hand and put it back in his pocket. "It's legal as anything else," he said. And then while Sheriff Fixx stood there thinking of an answer, a black Pontiac pulled into the curb with the peg-legged woman that worked for Trout behind the wheel, and he got in and drove away.

The sheriff watched the car until it turned, trying to remember if it was legal for a peg-legged woman to drive. Then he started the walk back to the station, smiling at people so they would think it was natural for the sheriff to be walking. By the time he got there, he had decided what he was going to do about Paris Trout, which was nothing.

If habeas corpus was good enough for Judge Taylor, it was good enough for him. He thought it had about worn Cotton Point out, taking Trout as far as it did.

He made up his mind though, to search him in the event he had to ride him back to Petersboro County. He wouldn't have a prisoner carrying any kind of weapon in an official car again and posted a notice to that effect on the bulletin board that evening.

CARL BONNER

PART SEVEN

M

onday morning of the next week some of Cotton Point's most prominent citizens and politicians gathered over breakfast at the home of Mayor Horn to begin plans for the town's sesquicentennial celebration, to be held the following spring. Among those invited to the meeting were the presidents of the Rotary, the Elks, the Order of the Moose, and the Junior Chamber of Commerce, and all those organizations' ladies' auxiliaries.

Four of the five members of the Sesquicentennial Planning Committee were present: Harry Seagraves, Carl Bonner, Ward Townes, and Dr. Hodges, who owned a furniture store. Only Walker Hargrove of the First Bank of Georgia was absent, but no one had expected him to make it. Bankers had things to do.

Estes Singletary was there too, with his wife, who took pictures for the news story she would write. Mrs. Singletary had been a cub reporter before she married.

The meeting, according to Mrs. Singletary's account in the paper the following Thursday, "went swimmingly, with ideas contributed from a great many sources, some of them delightfully unexpected."

The ideas, which Mrs. Singletary did not divulge in her newspaper account, included plans for a pageant to be held on the football field at the officers' academy, a train ride to Atlanta—although some of those present thought it was antisocial to celebrate the existence of Cotton Point by riding off to Atlanta—and a town ordinance requiring every man who could grow one to wear a beard.

A three-member subcommittee of lawyers was formed that morning to enforce the ordinance. The Keepers of the Bush. Mayor Horn appointed Harry Seagraves chairman, calling him the "finest criminal mind in Georgia."

When breakfast was over, the mayor's maid cleared the silverware, and the women, on some unspoken signal, separated into the far end of the house. When they had left, the mayor bit the end off a cigar and stuck it in his mouth. The others lit cigarettes, except for Estes Singletary, who used a pipe, and for most of an hour they discussed the pros and cons of constructing public stocks in front of the courthouse for those who showed up clean-shaven during Sesquicentennial Week.

The mayor was for it; Harry Seagraves was opposed. They talked over who all was likely to refuse to grow beards and how they would look with their ankles and wrists in stocks, laughing at some of the names, eyes watering in the smoke.

It was the newspaperman who brought up the subject of Paris Trout. He looked right at Seagraves and said, "Whatever the punishment, it ought to be worse than Paris Trout got for killing that Negro child."

Seagraves had been sitting with his hands folded across his stomach, feeling full and lazy and happy. Without having moved a muscle, everything had changed. "I didn't have any part in that," he said.

Estes Singletary shrugged. "You're the lawyer."

"My association with Mr. Trout ended with his last appeal," he said. "I would of thought you'd known that, running the Conscience of Georgia." Which was the *Plain Talk*'s motto.

Estes Singletary saw that Seagraves was angry and tried to undo what he had said. "I didn't mean it in a personal way, Harry," he said. "I only meant that Trout was convicted of a crime in this town and sentenced and then showed up loose on the street the day after he went to jail, and nobody's said a thing about it."

"You own the paper," Seagraves said. "Why don't you put something in there?"

"I might," Singletary said, but everyone at the table knew he was afraid to offend advertisers. The table was quiet, and the maid came out of the kitchen with a pot of coffee and walked from place to place, freshening the cups.

Only Carl Bonner refused more, putting his hand over the cup and shaking his head. She smiled at him and said, "You ain't had but one cup, Mr. Bonner," but he did not answer. His attention was at the other end of the table. After she poured coffee for the mayor, she looked over all the cups again to make sure no one had been missed and then smiled. "All right, I'll go see the ladies need something and leave y'all go back to your discussions."

But the discussions were over. Five minutes passed. Ward Townes checked his pocket watch and remembered he was due in court. Seagraves stood up with him, thanking the mayor for breakfast, and said he would think about the stocks. Then Dr. Hodges and the Singletarys. They left one by one until only the mayor and Carl Bonner were there in the dining room.

"You know somebody in Petersboro County who could tell me how Paris Trout got out?" Bonner said.

Mayor Horn took two cigars from his coat pocket, offered one to the young attorney, and bit the end off the other. Bonner bit the end off his and allowed the mayor to light it.

"You don't want nothing to do with Pete County," the mayor said finally. "You don't need nothing to do with Paris Trout either. Estes Singletary there, he's got a mouth on him, but he won't say nothing when he's out of this room. The lesson is don't ever invite a newspaperman anyplace there's people with manners. . . ."

The mayor stopped for a moment, considering his words. He said, "Cotton Point did as much as it could about Paris Trout already, Mr. Bonner. You don't do yourself or your law practice any favors bringing it back up."

"I don't intend to bring it up," he said. "It might be useful, is all. I represent Mrs. Trout in her suit for dissolution, and Paris Trout has stalled her every way there is."

The mayor frowned. He had known and admired Hanna Nile most of his life. He had heard of her trouble getting loose of Paris.

"There is a man that will know who got paid," he said finally. "Most likely he got part of it."

Carl Bonner sat up in his chair and waited.

"You don't need me to tell you who," the mayor said, suddenly angry. "The writ's a public document, you're supposed to be eastern educated, all you got to do is go down there and read the damn name."

Carl Bonner stood up then, the mayor stayed where he was. Very slowly he ground the lighted end of his cigar into the scrambled eggs left on his plate, twisting until the end flattened out and began to shred.

"I assure you I'll be discreet," Bonner said.

"Let me ask you something," the mayor said. "If there was something discreet to do about Paris Trout, you think that the people in this room this morning wouldn't of done it already?"

IT TOOK CARL BONNER five minutes to find the name of the judge who had released Paris Trout. Raymond Mims. He sat in the Petersboro County Courthouse the rest of the afternoon, finding other writs of habeas corpus that Mims had signed for prisoners at the work camp.

There were eight by the time the clerk shut off the lights.

Bonner decided to stay in town that night, in the best hotel room he could find, and charge the bill to Hanna Trout's account, to be paid by her husband as part of the eventual divorce settlement. He intended to hurt Paris Trout as badly as he could.

For two and a half years he'd been filing every kind of legal paper he could file, but each time Trout filed papers of his own, delaying hearings, arguing against producing whatever documents Bonner had requested. Trout was familiar with the soft places in the law, where things got lost or slowed or misplaced.

Carl Bonner's practice had grown in that time, but not in the way he had expected. The money he made was still from other attorneys' referrals, he had no big accounts, no important clients.

And Hanna Trout's divorce was waiting for him every morning when he woke up and still nagging him when he went home at night. Some nights, in fact, he felt as if Trout were in his home. Behind one of the closet doors in back, working against him.

He found a hotel with phones in the rooms and called his secretary just before six and asked her to call his wife and tell her he would not be home. He spoke to his wife through his secretary two or three times a day now. Sometimes he called them by each other's names.

And after he had called his office, he called Hanna Trout.

*

256

SEAGRAVES WAS LYING IN the daybed with her when the phone rang. She was in a slip, he had kicked off his shoes and loosened his tie. He held a glass of iced tea on his stomach, and it spilled as she got up to answer the phone. He came here once or twice a week, there was a way in through the alley in back.

She was gone less than five minutes.

"That was Carl Bonner," she said, sitting back down on the bed. He touched her shoulder.

"He was in Petersboro County."

"What for?"

"On Paris," she said. "He said he got what we need."

Seagraves lay still. "Did he say what?"

"The names of the people Paris paid to get out."

Seagraves sat up a few inches and sipped at the iced tea. "Everybody in the state knows who he paid," he said. He saw she was upset and reached out to touch her again. She did not respond. There was a part of her he could not reach, and it was the part he wanted. He thought it might still belong to Paris Trout.

She turned and looked at him. Her side was a straight line under the slip all the way to her waist, and he followed it from beneath her arm until he touched her hip. "Then why didn't somebody put him back in?"

"He won't come around here," he said.

"He is around here," she said.

And he understood what she meant and did not try to answer. "Carl Bonner said he found eight others that had gotten out the same way," she said a little later.

"That sounds right."

She pulled away and stared out the window. "There is an aspect of you that doesn't fit," she said.

He smiled. "What aspect is that?"

"Your character," she said. "You are fair with me, more than anybody else has been. You tell the truth. But there is a whole other side that comes out sometimes and makes me wonder what world you live in."

"The same world as everybody else," he said. "There's good and bad, and it's no sense getting upset over it. You take things as you find them."

She pulled her feet up onto the bed and studied them, her chin on her knees. If he moved now, he would catch her crying.

"What do you expect?" he said quietly.

"Something else."

He waited a few minutes and then touched her behind the ears, moving from there down her neck to her shoulders. She sat very still. He moved his hands back to her neck, then around, touching her cheeks and her eyes, pulling her lower lip down and running the tip of his finger inside. She shook under his fingers.

"HE JUST BOUGHT HIS way out," she said later.

He propped himself up, resting his head against the flat part of his hand, and stared down at her face. He felt a coolness in his lap and on his legs, everywhere he was up against her she left him wet. "It doesn't matter now," he said. "It's not our business."

"Is that where it settles? He's nobody's business?"

He dropped back into the pillow and thought of what she had said before: that he was fair with her and told her the truth. He tried to do that now.

"There comes a time," he said, "when it's best just to leave something alone."

TWO DAYS LATER CARL Bonner walked into the store on Main Street. The peg-legged woman frowned at him from behind the counter. He pointed to a pack of Dentyne gum and gave the woman a dollar bill. When she turned to make change, he asked if Trout was in.

"I believe he's back in his office with a Negro," she said. "He's been very busy and don't have time to see you." She counted the ninety-five cents out, putting the coins in his palm one at a time.

He started toward the back of the store.

"'Cuse me," she said, but he kept walking. He heard her behind him, the steps alternating hard and soft as she hurried to catch up. "Just hold on your britches there," she said.

She caught him at the office door, which was closed. He heard a voice inside, she grabbed at the arm of his coat. She was heavier than he would have thought and pulled him off-balance. "I already told you," she said, "Mr. Trout don't have time for you today."

He put his hands on her shoulders and moved her out of the way and then opened the door. He walked into the office. Trout was perched, bare-chested, on a chair over the sink. The mirror behind it had been broken, all except for a piece in an upper corner. His suspenders hung loose to his knees, his cheeks and chin were covered with shaving cream. There was a straight razor in his hand, and he changed the way he held it as Bonner came in.

Bonner heard the woman behind him. "I told you," she said, but he put an arm out as she grabbed him, and she fell across the floor. The peg clattered, the rest of her landed soft. Bonner moved to help her up.

"Are you hurt?" he said.

"Some Boy Scout," she said. "You knocked down a crippled lady."

Trout hadn't moved. Bonner tried to get her up. Half of her seemed to take the help, the other half seemed to fight him off. "You slipped," he said.

"I never slipped in my life," she said, getting back upright. She brushed herself off and straightened her clothes, and then, without any warning, she began to cry.

Bonner walked her to the door and closed it when she was through. Then he turned and looked at Trout. "Mr. Trout," he said, "none of this would have been necessary—"

Trout stepped off the chair and moved a foot in his direction, holding the razor. Carl Bonner picked an empty mineral water bottle up off the floor and waited. Trout stopped, and Bonner had the sudden thought that Trout didn't know who he was. "I am Carl Bonner," he said. "I represent your wife in her suit for dissolution of the marriage."

"Lawyers," Trout said, and moved back to the sink and began to shave. He did not climb back up the chair to use the mirror, and in a moment he was bleeding.

Bonner watched, determined to wait him out. He crossed his arms and spread his feet and looked around the room. Bottles, empty cans, it was like someone lived there. Trout wiped the soap off his face, leaving red stains on the towel. He put on his shirt and replaced his suspenders, making popping noises as he let them go. He left the towel on the floor.

"Mr. Trout, I am here about your wife."

"Don't have one," he said. He passed in front of Bonner and sat down behind his desk.

"Legally, sir, you do."

Trout pointed a crooked finger at him and said, "I've took as much abuse as I'm going to, pretty boy. A woman throws you out, she loses her claim. . . ."

"The only thing she wants is deed to her house and the money you took from her when you married," he said. "That, and the attorney fees. There's nothing else, except to rid herself of the name Trout."

Trout did not answer.

"I have general information on the state of your finances. The bank you run and the holding company is worth half a million dollars. There's eight hundred sixty-six acres of land in the eastern part of the state with sawmill timber, worth a hundred thousand, and you have deed to an apartment house which, along with your store, is valued at thirty thousand dollars. Then there is whatever you've got in the safes."

Bonner paused for a moment. "All Mrs. Trout wants," he repeated, "is her four thousand dollars, the house, and my fees."

Trout laughed out loud.

"This goes to court, it will cost you more than that," Bonner said. "There's judgments where the wife gets a third of the property. . . ."

"Find it," Trout said. "Collect all the niggers together in court and ask what they owe me. Show me the lumber deed. Show me where the store makes a profit. . . ." Without any warning, he began to laugh again. Bonner waited him out.

"There's always a way," he said when the older man was quiet. "You step in mud, you leave a footprint."

"I don't keep things where just anybody can find them." He tapped the side of his head and then settled back into his chair. It occurred to Bonner that the man was having fun with him. He felt his face go numb with anger.

"I expect that's true," he said, "but there is another matter." Trout put his hands flat on the desktop and stared. "The matter of Petersboro County."

"There ain't no matter of Petersboro County. That's over."

Bonner turned the chair and sat down. "Judge Raymond Mims," he said. The man did not seem to hear him. "You paid Judge Raymond Mims to get you out on a writ of habeas corpus, a move unheard of before in any court in this state."

Trout leaned closer. "You think I wrote him a check, son?"

"You bribed him, all right. Him and the warden."

"The judge here had one opinion, the judge down there had another. With judges, it's seeing the one you agree with last. Just stay loose until you found the right one."

Bonner spoke as if he hadn't heard him. "A man as tight as yourself, Mr. Trout, somebody willing to shoot children and women over a busted car, he doesn't throw real money away on a lark." He looked around the room again. "You afraid to be closed in? Eat at the same table with Negroes, sleep at night in the same room with them? You afraid to breathe the same air?"

He stopped a moment and looked around the office. "It sure as hell isn't creature comforts you're scared to lose, so it must be something else. . . ."

Trout had changed expressions, something new coming over his face. He opened one of the drawers in his desk. Bonner thought he was going to show him the writ from Petersboro County, but what he put on his desk was a gun. He laid it there, the muzzle pointing in Bonner's direction, his palm resting on the handle.

"You don't need that, Mr. Trout. All you need is to give your wife her four thousand dollars and sign the papers."

On reflection, Bonner realized that the older man had meant to shoot him. The thought was there, and then it passed. "If you come back in here, Mr. Lawyer, I'll use it," Trout said.

Carl Bonner stood at the door. "You can't shoot the thing you're scared of," he said. He walked out then, right into the peg-legged woman standing on the other side.

She stared up at him, her mouth half open, the dimmest light at work behind her eyes. "You're an educated man," she said. "You ought know better than that."

THERE WAS ONE OTHER warning.

On an evening a month later, following the second meeting of the Sesquicentennial Planning Committee, Carl Bonner found himself sitting in a cloud of after-dinner smoke at the home of Harry Seagraves when Trout's name came into the conversation again.

And it was Estes Singletary who again brought it up. Trout had been indicted that week by a federal grand jury in Atlanta on charges that he had attempted to bribe two Internal Revenue Service agents.

"It looks like our friend Mr. Trout tried to buy the federal government this time," Singletary said.

For a moment no one spoke. The newspaperman took this for a sign of encouragement and said, "The federal boys must come higher than the crowd in Petersboro County."

Someone said, "They probably charge the same and then arrest you anyway."

Walker Hargrove, the banker, excused himself and left the meeting. "Don't pay no attention to Walker," Singletary said when he was gone. "He's had dealings this year with Internal Revenue himself and can't be in the same room with anybody mentions the name."

But a minute or two later the president of the Junior Chamber of Commerce also left, remembering some Junior Chamber of Commerce business, and he was accompanied by the president of the Rotary, and then Mayor Bob Horn, and then Estes Singletary, and then almost everybody else.

In ten minutes all that was left in Harry Seagraves's living room was Seagraves, Carl Bonner, and Ward Townes. The Keepers of the Bush. Bonner stretched and looked around the room. "Paris Trout isn't much in the way of a topic of conversation, is he?" he said.

Seagraves stirred his coffee with his index finger. "The problem is working to a conclusion," he said. "What he is has about caught up with him now. The thing now is not to push, just to let things take their natural course. Enjoy the celebration, ride the train to Atlanta, put a little distance between all of us and Mr. Trout."

He pulled his finger out and frowned into the coffee. "We're never going to get nothing planned for this celebration if we keep inviting Estes Singletary to the meetings."

Carl Bonner let that sit for a moment, gradually realizing what Seagraves said was somehow intended for him too. "I been trying to get Paris Trout into court for two years," he said, keeping the anger out of his voice. "Sometimes you don't push, nothing moves."

Seagraves looked across a table full of dirty plates at Ward Townes. "The trick is knowing when that is," he said.

It seemed to Carl Bonner that Townes and Seagraves were in some sort of secret accord on this, as if they had talked about it before. It was Townes who spoke. "Don't push too hard, Mr. Bonner," he said quietly.

"I've yet to push him at all."

"The man is out of balance," Townes said.

"Because he carries a shooter? I can accommodate him if that's what he wants. I can take this matter any direction he'd like to go."

It was quiet a moment, and then Seagraves said, "No, you can't." He saw that he'd insulted the younger man, it couldn't be helped.

He said, "Paris Trout knows directions you never imagined were there."

THE CELEBRATION BEGAN OFFICIALLY at nine o'clock the following Saturday morning.

The Georgia Pacific left the Cotton Point depot at its regular hour, headed north for Atlanta, pulling a specially decorated railroad car loaded with one hundred members of the town's proudest families. The Cotton Point One Hundred.

Many of the lawyers had firecrackers.

Mayor Bob Horn carried a whip and had dressed himself in a costume recalling Alex McHandy, the slave trader who had founded the town, and looked, to Seagraves at least, like a New Orleans pimp. Every man on the car wore whiskers of some kind, most of them having started their beards weeks before the celebration began, in order to set a good example.

Very few of the men came without hard liquor, although it was

263

their wives, for the most part, who carried it in their picnic baskets. The plan was to hold the party on the lawn of the State Capitol, under a town banner: COTTON POINT—GEORGIA'S ANTEBELLUM TOWN.

The car was busy in a quiet way, there were as many people in the aisle as were in the seats, and the smell of coffee and cigarettes hung in the air.

Carl Bonner was sitting next to a window, leaning from time to time across his wife to speak to someone in the aisle. Leslie would pull back, giving him room. She had not wanted to come on the train. He put his hand on her leg once, squeezing a moment, getting no response at all.

Forty minutes out of Cotton Point, a few miles from Montclair on a long bend of track, the train passed through a tunnel. The car went black, and before it was returned to the sunshine, the engineer braked hard and half the people in the aisle were suddenly on the floor.

There was screaming—the brakes and the ladies—and laughing. A woman smelling of lilacs fell across Bonner's head from behind, hugging him for a moment before pushing herself off. Leslie stared straight ahead.

The car left the tunnel, still braking.

Bonner leaned across his wife again and saw Harry Seagraves sitting in the aisle, holding a cigar between his teeth, smiling at the confusion. A woman leaned over Seagraves, kissing him squarely in the middle of the head. He offered her his cigar, which she took.

It was nine forty-two in the morning, Carl Bonner checked his watch. The train bucked to a stop, blowing steam.

Minutes passed, and then a conductor came through the car from behind, stepping around passengers who were still helping each other up and swatting the dirt off their bottoms and sleeves. "Ain't nothing to alarm yourself, folks," he said. "Just some hillbilly decided to park himself in front of a train."

A few minutes later Bonner saw him, walking back along the tracks.

Somewhere toward the front a woman shouted, "God as my witness, it's Paris Trout!" And one whole side of the car got up and moved to the other side to see him.

Trout stopped at mid-car and stood still, in a gray, wrinkled suit,

264

arms crossed, staring up at the windows. Someone opened a window and said, "You gone come along with us, Paris?"

Trout stayed where he was. A conductor appeared from behind, shouting at him. "You get that piece of rusted shit out of the way, mister, or we'll sure as hell do it for you."

Trout paid no attention at all and a moment later the train shuddered and began to move. A cheer went up from the Cotton Point One Hundred, to be moving again.

Bonner watched Trout slowly disappear to the back. A moment later he saw Trout's Henry J—the driver's door was wide open, and the whole side was dented where the train had pushed it out of the way—and then it was gone from sight too.

On some signal, drinking began in the aisle, and the hushed, busy feeling was gone.

Bonner stood up and squeezed past Leslie into the aisle, leaving her there in the seat. The aisle filled with the celebration. The woman who had kissed Harry Seagraves's head kissed his nose and then his cheeks. Before long, other ladies were kissing him, and perfect red imprints of lips lay like blisters over as much of Harry Seagraves's face as wasn't covered by whiskers.

Leslie watched her husband. He accepted a paper cup of liquor, he accepted kisses from Cotton Point ladies who could not reach Seagraves, he put his hands on everyone he saw.

She slid to the seat next to the window and closed her eyes.

The party moved up and down the aisle. Someone threw a roll of toilet paper the length of the car. Someone else had a banjo. Men and women were crawling over seats, wearing each other's hats. A roll of toilet paper landed in the seat behind Leslie Bonner. Her husband came out of a tangle of people a moment later and sat down heavily in the next seat.

"You want some coffee?" he said.

She shook her head. She would have liked some of the liquor, but Carl did not allow her to drink now outside the house. He was afraid of the things she would do.

"I can get you a coffee," he said. "Find you a Coke-Cola."

"No," she said.

He said, "If you change your mind . . ."

He stood up and headed back into the aisle. Someone at the front of the car was blowing a bugle; the noise confused her. She covered herself with a Georgia Pacific Railroad blanket that she found in the compartment overhead and put her fingers in her ears. The sound of the party faded, and she heard the noises of the train coming up out of the floor.

Time passed, she could not say how much. She felt someone in the next seat. She moved half her face over the blanket and found herself blinking into the eyes of Harry Seagraves. Seagraves sipped at his drink but did not speak. There were lipstick smudges on his silk collar and his neck, his hair was mussed, and his tie had been turned backwards and hung down his back.

She realized her fingers were still in her ears and took them out. "Mr. Seagraves," she said.

Seagraves squinted, studying her. It seemed sexual, but it was not impolite. She came farther up in her seat. She straightened her blouse and touched her hair. It was less uncomfortable than she would have thought, to have him stare at her.

The car shook and leaned, it felt like the party itself was tipping it one way and then another. "Mr. Trout's appearance seemed to have made an impression," she said.

"It often does," he said. Then: "It isn't often that easy to put him behind you."

He finished what was in the cup and refilled it from his flask. Without a word, he handed the cup to Leslie Bonner, and she took it.

The liquor ran a spasm through her, top to bottom. She held on to the cup, looking over it at Harry Seagraves's hair. And then she put it against her lips again. "My husband does not approve of my imbibing in public," she said.

He took the cup from her hand and hid it between her leg and the seat cushion under the blanket. His movements were clumsy in a thick-fingered way. "There," he said.

She smiled at him, affected by his kindness. She felt like kissing him too. "He believes I change personalities," she said.

Harry Seagraves took the flask from his pocket, touched it to his lower lip, then seemed to change his mind. "Your husband is very young," he said.

She waited, but that was all. She found the cup under the blanket and sipped from it again. The liquor was strong, and she felt warm from her throat to her stomach. While the cup was still in her hand, he refilled it. She looked quickly at the crowd in the aisle but did not see her husband.

The bugle was blowing again, and someone threw another roll of toilet paper. The noise was not as confusing now, with half a cup of Harry Seagraves's liquor in her stomach. "Do you believe it's possible to change personalities, Mr. Seagraves?" she said.

He thought for a moment. "You can change moods," he said, "but you knock on the door, it's never somebody brand-new that answers . . . not in my experience."

He thought of Paris Trout. "I think there's some people that keep themselves private to cover up who they are, however."

"That's it exactly," she said, the liquor oiling all the gates. "There are some who seem to have a talent to hold back what they are, like it isn't good enough."

She took the cup out from under the blanket and drank half of what was inside. "Or," she said, "they try to hide their wife. They get ashamed of the people they love."

He saw that the conversation had turned and that they were talking about Carl Bonner. "It's a hard thing to build a law practice," he said. "Your husband wants things done before they are ready." He paused then and seemed to forget his thread. Then he said, "You can't be the youngest Eagle Scout in the history of Georgia all your life."

"He hates how that follows him around," she said.

"Then he oughtn't to aspire to it."

She stared at the cup in her hands, and he began to regret his words. "I didn't mean that as harsh as it sounded," he said. "Your husband is a fine young attorney, knows as much about the law as anybody. And in time he'll mellow. Everybody's got to give a little here and there, or they burn up."

"It's partly this business with Paris Trout," she said, and it startled him to hear the name out loud—he had just thought of the man again himself. "He's frustrated that Mr. Trout won't give his wife a divorce."

"I can appreciate that," Seagraves said. "Mr. Trout is a frustrating man to deal with."

"You referred him."

He looked past her, out the window. A road ran parallel to the tracks, an old woman and her mule and wagon were the only things that moved. He picked up the blanket where it was bunched next to his leg and draped it over his own lap.

"It didn't seem like a three-year job," he said. "Mrs. Trout is a friend of mine, and I knew your husband would pay attention to her case. . . . I never knew it would turn into a test of endurance."

Up in front they had begun singing. "Happy Birthday to Cotton Point." A glass broke, people laughed. The mayor cracked his whip. Leslie Bonner finished what was in her cup.

"If I could do it over," Seagraves said, "I'd send Mrs. Trout to Walter Huff. He isn't as sharp as Carl, and he won't work as long into the night, but he's got more common sense. He don't push when something won't move."

He refilled her cup, shaking the last few drops out of the flask. "I hope I haven't left you empty," she said.

He nodded his head in the direction of the party in the aisle. "Somewhere in that crowd of patriots," he said, "my wife is holding on to a thirty-pound picnic basket like it was her firstborn."

"Your wife is so beautiful," she said.

"Miss Ether County, 1934. They crowned her in the middle of the Great Depression." He looked at Leslie closely. "As far as I know," he said, "it didn't help at all."

She looked up in time to see her husband making his way back. His beard was red and uneven, and his eyes were glazed. She put the cup back under the blanket.

Carl Bonner stood in the aisle, swaying, looking down at her. "I see you found company," he said.

Harry Seagraves began to smile, but Leslie Bonner's expression stopped him. She stared up at her husband without answering.

"What are you doing back here?" Bonner said to his wife.

"I'm afraid she was minding her own business until I sat down," Seagraves said. "She never encouraged me a bit."

A smile passed over Bonner's face, but he never took his eyes off his wife. "What are you doing?" he said again. A slight trembling shook him, and his cheeks paled.

"Are you feeling poorly?" Seagraves said, but Bonner did not answer.

"I asked you a question," he said to her. "I want an answer."

Seagraves saw the girl was stupefied. "I asked her to toast with me," he said, keeping his voice reasonable. "It's not every day a town celebrates its hundred and fiftieth anniversary, and I asked her to join the celebration."

Bonner looked away from his wife for half a second, checking the blanket. She moved, perhaps two inches, but his stare returned and pinned her to the spot. "Here I am in the same car." he said.

"Wait a minute here," Seagraves said.

Carl Bonner checked his watch. "Thirty-five minutes I been up in the front end of the railroad car," he said. "That's how long I turned my back."

She slowly began to shake her head. "You don't mean to do this," she said. "You're drinking."

"I'm not blind," he said. "I can still see."

"You don't see anything," she said.

Carl Bonner looked again at the blanket. Seagraves's hands were lying on top of it, one of hers was underneath holding the glass. "Then let's pull off the blanket," he said.

"Stop this," she said.

Harry Seagraves was just focusing on the nature of the quarrel. "Son," he said, "Mayor Horn has put some work in this—dressed up in ridiculous clothing, carrying a whip and calling people niggers. It took thought and effort to ensure that he would make a bigger ass of himself than anyone else on this train, and in two minutes you have eclipsed a whole morning's work."

"I'm tired of talk," he said to Seagraves. The words were clear and loud, but they went unnoticed in the sound of breaking glass and laughter. Someone had thrown his shoes out the window, and now everybody was throwing shoes out the window.

He was glaring at her again, the paper cup he had been holding was crushed in his fist. Leslie Bonner was meeting his look now, she had asked him for as much as she was going to.

"Pull off the blanket," she said.

It stopped him. "Pull it off," she said. He took a step back, looking uncertain. "Pull off the goddamn blanket, Carl, and see if his peter's out of his pants."

Carl Bonner covered his eyes and sat heavily on the arm rest across the aisle. The squashed cup dropped from his hand. Harry Seagraves, who was about ten seconds behind the conversation, was suddenly sorry for the boy, before he'd even gotten mad.

He stood up, the blanket dropping on the floor at his feet, and put his hand behind Carl Bonner's neck. "When I was young," he said, "I once accused Lucy of sleeping with my own brother." It wasn't true—he'd thought it, but he'd never said it out loud—but it was true enough for now. He stepped closer, so only Bonner could hear. "Said it out loud at a family picnic. The plain fact is, son, pussy makes you stupid. . . ." He considered that a moment and said, "That or picnics."

Carl Bonner sat still, the understanding of what he had done washing over him in slow, regular waves.

Seagraves patted the back of his neck, his hand coming away wet with Bonner's perspiration. Leslie Bonner was right where she had been before, holding the drink he'd given her. "I'll be back directly to freshen that for you," he said. "I'll come back, and we'll all have a toast."

THE PUBLIC STOCKS WENT up Monday morning, on the sidewalk in front of the courthouse. A long table was carried out of the prosecutor's office and set to one side, along with the chair that had been used by former Superior Court Judge Bear Lewis, the midget. Even out here on the sidewalk, the occupant of the chair would sit higher than those he judged.

The Keepers of the Bush oversaw this construction and the theft of the chair. Harry Seagraves, Ward Townes, and Carl Bonner. They gave instructions to the carpenter, an elderly man named Lloyd Rose, as if they had been supervising the building of stocks all their lives. At one point Seagraves took the coping saw out of the carpenter's hand to show him how to cut lumber and broke the blade.

Seagraves, who had not slept or stopped drinking for more than two hours since Saturday morning, gave Mr. Rose a ten-dollar bill and warned him not to be caught without whiskers, or he would lose the money back to the court.

"I been wearing whiskers in this town forty years," the old man said.

Ward Townes sat on the courthouse steps while this was going on, smiling into the morning sun.

Carl Bonner made himself busy. He helped carry the table out of the prosecutor's office, he tested the carpenter's work, checking that the stocks lay flat against each other where they met. He told Mr. Rose the boards needed to be sanded.

Mr. Rose gave him a look when he said that.

For the most part, however, Bonner kept silent. And he stayed away from Seagraves and Townes. Townes judged him to be hung over. There were some, he thought, like Harry Seagraves, who could drink all night and hide it, and there were some who couldn't.

Except for the sanding, the stocks were finished by eleven o'clock. Ward Townes went into the courthouse to the Coke machine. It took a dime, and the lever was ice-cold. He bought four Cokes and then walked outside and passed them around to Seagraves and Bonner and the carpenter. Carl Bonner tried to repay him the ten cents.

Harry Seagraves sat down on the prosecutor's table and wiped at his forehead with a hankie. He looked at the Coke—there were little crystals of ice in the neck—and then drank it all in four noisy swallows, never taking his mouth off the bottle.

"You'd think he'd done the work," Ward Townes said to Bonner. Bonner looked off and did not reply.

Seagraves set the bottle on the table and hiccuped. He put his hand against his chest and waited, and a moment later he hiccuped again.

"Hold your breath," the carpenter said.

Seagraves held his breath. Ward Townes looked around at the courtyard. "You ever notice how peaceful this town seems," he said to Carl Bonner, "when Harry there is holding his breath?"

Bonner smiled in a sickly way, and the prosecutor wondered if he'd had words with Seagraves, perhaps last night at the Moose.

In fact, Bonner had been at home, having words with his wife.

Seagraves's breath came out in a rush, and he sat still a moment, waiting.

"See there? I told you," the carpenter said.

Seagraves hiccuped.

The carpenter looked into the trees. "Didn't hold it long enough," he said.

Seagraves took a deep breath and blew this one out. "All right, gentlemen," he said, "we got us an inquisition, let's decide on some rules."

"Rules?" Ward Townes said.

"You got to have penalties," the carpenter explained. "If a man breaks the rules, he's got to pay the price."

"What price?" Townes said.

"Half-dollar," the carpenter said.

"That's all right with me," Townes said, "except we already spent the morning building a public stocks. We ought to use it."

Harry Seagraves said, "Are we gone throw somebody into the stocks because they don't have a half-dollar on them?"

"We could if we don't like them," Townes said.

Seagraves thought it over. "That's fair," he said. "Half a dollar for a clean-shaven face, or an hour in the stocks if we don't like you."

"Good," Townes said, and looked at Bonner.

Carl Bonner shrugged. "Son," Seagraves said, talking to him directly for the first time that morning, "you going to sit in judgment on this court, you've got to be assertive. Think of Judge Taylor on his bench, the most ignorant man in the State of Georgia, handing down decisions like it was direct from the mouth of God. He isn't afraid to make an ass of hisself, and when he does it, it's written down in public records."

Ward Townes saw that Seagraves was talking to the young attorney in a private way and stood to excuse himself. He said he had work to finish back at his office.

"Whoa, there, Mr. Prosecutor," Seagraves said. Townes stopped. "We got to decide on a schedule. We can't be bringing these miscreants by at all hours of the day and night. We need a regular time, every day, so the public can witness for itself the fair administration of justice."

"Five o'clock?" the carpenter said.

"Mr. Rose," Seagraves said to the carpenter, "you may well possess the finest legal mind in the State of Georgia."

A few minutes later Seagraves and Carl Bonner were alone. Seagraves was sitting on the courthouse steps, eyes closed, his head resting against one of the white pillars that rose half the height of the building. He was holding his third Coca-Cola of the morning between his legs.

Carl Bonner was standing on the other side of the steps. He almost spoke once, and stopped. The words caught, and there was no place for them to go. "Thank you," he said finally, "for not pressing your advantage on me."

Harry Seagraves opened his eyes.

"On the train," Bonner said. "I had no call. . . ."

Seagraves took a drink from the bottle, then held it up in front of himself to judge how much was gone. He pointed at the spot behind Bonner where the men had left their coats. "If you would," he said, and hiccuped.

Carl Bonner handed him the coat, which felt weighted. Harry Seagraves found his flask in an inside pocket, removed the lid, and brought the Coke bottle back up to full. Then he covered the top with his thumb and turned the bottle upside down. "You and me don't have any apologizing to do to each other," he said.

When the drink was mixed, he returned the flask to his coat pocket and offered the bottle to Carl Bonner. Bonner declined. "That's what got me in trouble Saturday," he said.

Seagraves tasted the mixture, coughed, and tears came to his eyes. "Then you ought take a bottle of Coke-Cola here every morning," he said, meaning the kind he was holding, "and drink it to remind yourself what a good life you have, that what happened Saturday is your idea of trouble."

"I accused innocent people," he said.

"I can't speak for your missus," Seagraves said, "but I've put some distance between myself and innocent."

He tried the mixture again, but it tasted as bad as it had before. Carl Bonner began to say something else, but Seagraves stopped him. "You want to know the truth," he said, pointing at the bottle, "it wasn't this got you into anything on the train. It was impatience. If everybody in Georgia learned tomorrow to keep their mouth shut when they think they got something that can't wait, there wouldn't be work but for maybe eleven lawyers in the state."

THE SCHEDULE WAS POSTED on the pillars outside the courthouse and in the windows of most of the businesses in town. The Keepers of the Bush held court every evening from five to seven. The stocks were moved under a tree so that prisoners would not have to serve their sentences in the sun.

The three judges—Seagraves, Townes, and Carl Bonner—sat two at a time behind the long table outside the courthouse, one of them in Judge Bear Lewis's special chair and the other in a smaller chair to the side. The judge who was not sitting in Bear Lewis's special chair acted as a bailiff.

Two youngsters from the high school dressed in police uniforms from the 1890s stood by to operate the stocks.

The defendants, for the most part, were ticketed by police during the day and ordered to appear that afternoon. One of the first was former Judge Bear Lewis himself, who was practicing law now in a fleabag office in Bloodtown. Harry Seagraves was sitting in Lewis's old chair, Ward Townes was acting bailiff. Bear Lewis had shaved himself that morning and tried to pass off his sideburns as whiskers.

"Your Honors," he said, in a voice that seemed to come from deeper pipes than he could have had, "as I read the town ordinance, I see no specific reference to how much facial hair a citizen is required to wear, only that he must not shave clean. I would put it to the court that my sideburns constitute facial hair and ask for a directed verdict."

Several hundred people had collected on the courthouse lawn that evening for the first session of court, mostly to watch Harry Seagraves.

Seagraves looked down at Bear Lewis and cleared his throat. The courthouse lawn went quiet. "Do I understand you to say that you have found a loophole in the city ordinance?"

"I believe I have," the former judge said.

"Do I understand you to say that the author of this ordinance is incompetent?"

Bear Lewis scratched his oversize head. "That would depend," he said, "on who the author of the ordinance is."

Harry Seagraves conferred with Ward Townes while the crowd laughed. There was some hooting and calls of "Sic 'em, Bear."

Bear Lewis had been a popular judge, and there was always talk of putting him back on the ballot for the next election. It had been his habit to begin court in the morning with the following words: "All you niggers with lawyers on that side of the room, and all you niggers without lawyers on t'other."

Judge Taylor, on the other hand, had presided at the trial of Paris Trout.

"Mr. Lewis," Seagraves said when he had finished talking with Ward Townes, "it is the opinion of this court that your claim is without merit. However, noting your respectful regard for the authors of this ordinance, it has been decided not to remit you to custody, but to fine you the prescribed fifty cents."

The truth was, Seagraves could not stand to see a midget in the stocks.

TROUT

PART EIGHT

Late in the afternoon of Wednesday, the fifth day of the official week of the sesquicentennial, Paris Trout stepped out the door of the Ether Hotel and was arrested on the spot by a twenty-two-year-old police officer named Bo Andrews.

"Sir," the officer said, "you are under arrest."

Trout noticed the man had not shaved. It seemed to be the fashion. The policeman touched Trout's arm, not in an unfriendly way. Trout pulled away. He had been convicted Friday of attempting to bribe a federal officer and was scheduled for sentencing the following month.

"Get the hell away from me," he said. "It ain't my time yet."

The young policeman reached for Trout's arm again. "Yessir, it is," he said. The policeman did not know who Paris Trout was, but he hoped the old man would try to escape. In four years on the Cotton Point Police Department Bo Andrews had been outrun only once, by a colored man who had jumped out a window of a house in the Bottoms and hidden someplace up the hill in Sleepy Heights.

He tugged, and Trout tugged back. "I've got cuffs if I've got to use them," the policeman said. The old man was stronger than he looked.

Trout suddenly stopped his struggling and looked up and down the street. It was five-thirty in the afternoon, he was on his way to the rest home to see his mother. There was a nine-millimeter automatic in his coat pocket. The police officer moved slightly behind him and took out his ticket book.

"I'll need your name, sir," he said.

Trout did not answer.

"Sir?"

Trout reached into his pocket, felt the comfortable, cool weight of the handle. It occurred to him that he should write a note of explanation soon. He was not sure what the note ought to say or whom it was for.

"If you won't give your name," the policeman said, "I'll have to take you down myself."

And Trout, still thinking of the note, began to walk with him. When they had gone a block, the policeman began to talk. "You know, I thought you might run on me back there," he said. "In a way, I wisht you had. Would of made the papers, I bet."

Trout stopped, and the policeman stopped with him. "You want to make the papers, is that it?"

Bo Andrews blushed. "Not for me," he said. "Just something for my parents, you know, to see their sonny boy in print." They crossed a street and headed toward the courthouse. "I don't want the glory," he said. "It's like a souvenir of the celebration. . . ."

Trout did not know what celebration the policeman meant.

THE PRESIDING JUDGE OF the court Wednesday night was Carl Bonner. Harry Seagraves sat at his side, acting as bailiff. As Carl Bonner was not as humorous as the older attorney in his questioning of the accused, Seagraves interjected remarks when he saw an appropriate opening. It was almost six o'clock, and the court was hearing its last case.

It was Seagraves who saw Paris Trout first. The policeman—he didn't look old enough to be out of high school—was walking a step behind him, proud as a colored boy in new tennis shoes.

Trout himself was wearing a passive expression that was familiar to Seagraves from the days they had spent together in trial.

Seagraves saw Trout had shaved himself pink-cheeked, he saw the weight in his coat pocket.

The policeman had ears that stuck straight out under his hat. He stopped Trout at the edge of the circle of spectators and waited while Carl Bonner weighed the case against a science teacher at the officers' academy. The science teacher pleaded a skin condition, which Carl Bonner disregarded for a lack of expert medical testimony.

The spectators were laughing at the exchange between the science teacher and the court, and Seagraves was hoping Carl Bonner would let him off. Fifty cents might mean something to a teacher. Seagraves couldn't say that, though, without embarrassing the man worse than he already was.

"Fifty cents," Bonner said, and pounded the table with the claw hammer they were using for a gavel. Then he sat up higher in Judge Lewis's old chair and looked over the spectators. "Is that all?" he said.

"One more, Your Honor. . . ." It was the young policeman. He stepped in front of Trout and bowed.

"Well, bring him on," Carl Bonner said.

There was some hooting and whistles when the crowd saw who the officer had brought in, but more of the spectators went quiet. The antique policemen—seniors from the high school—led him the rest of the way. Carl Bonner looked down at Paris Trout and smiled. "What have we here?" he said.

"An unidentified suspect," the policeman said. "Arrested on North Main Street, cheeks as smooth as a baby's behind. Suspect has refused to provide identification or proof of residency."

Carl Bonner was still smiling. "The court is able to identify this suspect," he said.

Harry Seagraves saw Bonner's intention. He stood halfway up and whispered in his ear, "Don't fool with this."

Bonner bent to listen, and then he straightened back up. "Paris Trout," he said, "you have been charged by this court of violating city ordinance 404A in that you have appeared in public shaved during the week constituting the hundred and fiftieth anniversary of the founding of this city. How do you plead?"

Trout stood beneath Bonner, with no intention of answering.

"Mr. Trout?"

Seagraves got up again and cupped his hand in front of Carl Bonner's ear. "Let him the hell go," he said. "I'm not clowning with you, let him out." As he dropped back into his chair, Trout followed his movement. That familiar flat, murderous look on his face.

Carl Bonner seemed to be thinking something over. Then he cleared his throat and spoke. "Mr. Trout," he said, "seeing how it is a well-established fact in the city of Cotton Point that you still possess the first nickel you made, this court has little hope of recovering any fine it might impose. Mr. Trout?"

Trout was still staring at Seagraves. He turned his head now and fastened his look on Bonner.

Bonner returned the look, calm-faced. "It is the decision of this court that you be remanded to the stocks for a period of time not to exceed one hour and that your sentence begin immediately."

There was more whistling, but it was all from the youngsters. The old-timers, the courthouse secretaries, the businessmen celebrating on the way home—they all had gone quiet. Some of them began to walk away even before the antique policemen led Trout to the stocks.

He went with them at first, and then, seeing what they meant to do, he stopped dead in his tracks and would not be moved. The antique policemen took an arm each, but they could not pull Trout any closer to the stocks. As they tried, he turned his head and looked at Harry Seagraves one more time. The antique policemen dipped, taking his legs, and carried him the rest of the way.

Trout began to struggle sincerely. He got an arm loose and punched one of the boys in the neck, knocking off his hat. The crowd was quiet, and the sounds of the hissing and grunts and curses were clear all over the courthouse lawn.

The antique policeman who had been punched got one of Trout's arms in up behind his back, bending him over.

And in that space, suddenly cleared, Seagraves saw her, framed in the crowd. Frozen in what was happening. He saw that for all her words to the contrary, she and Paris were still connected. Seagraves raised up out of his seat. "Here, now," he said, "there's no need for that."

Carl Bonner sat still. The antique policemen got Trout's wrists into place. One of them brought the upper piece of the mechanism down and held it there while the other secured it with a wooden bolt. Trout cursed them and stood, bringing the stocks up off the ground with him. One of the antique policemen tripped and fell, the other took the full force of a kick from the old man high on the leg.

The one on the ground tackled Trout's legs and brought him and the stocks down. The one who had been kicked jumped on top, his elbow landing across the top of Trout's nose. When Seagraves pulled the boy on top off, Trout was bleeding.

"Leave go," Seagraves said.

The antique policeman holding on to his legs would not let go. "This here's a live one," he said.

"Leave him go," Seagraves said again, and lifted the boy by the front of his uniform. The material tore. Trout lay on the ground, his hands still caught in the stocks, his blood-splattered shirt rising and falling as he breathed. Seagraves began to loosen the bolt, but then, remembering the pistol, he knelt in such a way to cover what he did from view and reached into Trout's coat pocket and removed it, dropping it into his own.

"I'll leave this for you at the hotel in the morning," he said.

Trout wiped at his nose with his shoulder. Seagraves pulled the bolt free of the stocks. Trout sat up, rubbing his wrists, then dabbing at his nose. He looked behind him at the spectators and then pointed his index finger at them, moving in a deliberate way from one end to the other.

"He's still sentenced to one hour," one of the antique policemen said.

"Be still," Seagraves said.

Trout got to his feet—no one tried to help—and tucked his shirt into his pants and straightened his coat. In no hurry. He stepped over the stocks lying at his feet and then walked through the spectators who were still there to the street. He made a left turn, in the direction of the nursing home.

"The old sumbitch was strong," one of the antique policemen said to the other. " 'Bout broke my leg where he kicked me."

The other one was wiping at some grass that had stuck to the front of his coat. "I got him for you," he said. "I got him good in the nose."

Seagraves walked back to the judges' table, where Carl Bonner was sitting in his black robe, looking vaguely pleased. The crowd broke and headed different directions. He looked for Hanna, but she was gone. Some of the women were unnerved, Seagraves could see it in their faces. He reassured them as they passed, smiling, as if what had happened were all some part of the festivities.

They knew about Paris Trout, though, and knew he wasn't part of any celebration.

In a few minutes Seagraves took the flask out of his pocket and offered Carl Bonner a drink.

"He went crazy, didn't he?" Bonner said. He drank and returned the flask.

"He was already crazy," Seagraves said.

Bonner shrugged. "Everybody's got to obey the same law."

"No," Seagraves said, "they don't." He put the flask back in his pocket without drinking; the good feeling was gone.

"Well, nobody was hurt," Bonner said.

Seagraves reached into another pocket and came out with the pistol. He laid it on the table in front of the young attorney without a word. Carl Bonner shrugged. "Paris Trout isn't the only one that owns a pistol," he said.

"He's going off to jail, probably next month," Seagraves said. "He can't file his motions at the courthouse then. In one week you can refile your petitions, and you and your client can have any kind of divorce you want."

Carl Bonner shook his head. "There's no satisfaction, is there?" he said. "All the trouble I've been through on this, and in the end I beat him because he goes to jail." He pushed the gun away, back toward Seagraves. "All that effort, he never bent. . . ."

"Bent to what?" Seagraves said.

Carl Bonner did not answer.

"I SAW YOU AT the courthouse today," he said.

She was lying on her back, and the light from the moon lay across her stomach and shoulders. He was close to the wall, watching her muscles in the dark. Somewhere firecrackers were going off.

"It doesn't matter," she said.

"You never think of something like that," he said, "that a policeman is going to bring Paris Trout to kangaroo court. You give people credit for more sense. . . ."

She put a hand out in the dark, finding his face, and then rested a finger across his lips. He dropped deeper into his pillow.

"You looked stricken," he said a little later.

He lifted his head to see if she was looking stricken now. A small, perfect breast in silhouette against the window. She blinked, and he saw a tear roll over her eyelid. It came to him again that she still had feelings for Paris Trout. "What were you thinking," he said, "when they wrestled him to the ground?"

"Nothing," she said, "I just saw it."

"Did you remember what he'd done to you?"

It was quiet a moment. Then: "No. It seems like someone else he did that to."

He kissed the palm of her hand and then her cheek. It was wet. "You felt sorry for him," he said. His head was right over hers now, but she looked past him toward the ceiling.

"It's like watching someone die," she said. "The distance . . ."

He pushed himself up, arm's length, and moved his head until he was directly in her line of sight. She said, "Sometimes, when a person is dying, you wonder who it is that's wandering away and who is left behind."

It was still in the room, and Seagraves lay back on his pillow. He'd had similar thoughts himself, about the people he'd loved.

"At the bottom of things," she said, "he might be stumbling around in the dark."

"You believe that?" he said.

She said she didn't know. "I don't think he's come to the bottom of things yet," she said.

Seagraves pulled her into him then, one of his hands resting in the small of her back, the other in her hair. "In a month he'll be gone," he said. "He can't buy himself out of any federal penitentiary. Carl Bonner will file the divorce papers, and he's out of your mind."

She was pressed into his shoulder and did not answer.

"You could teach again," he said. "Go into business, whatever you want. This thing today, it shouldn't of happened. . . ."

He was trying to find her now, but he couldn't. "It's what you want," he said, "to be loose of him."

"What I think," she said, pulling away, "at the bottom of things, I may be stumbling in the dark too, and he might be down there with me."

"You want me to let you alone?" he said.

She said, "I don't know."

THE PAGEANT WAS SCHEDULED to run three performances. Friday and Saturday night, Sunday afternoon. Admission was free, and Charlotte Hock intended to see all of it, unless Mr. Trout kept her late Saturday evening. She could not read his mood and was afraid to ask his schedule.

On one hand, he was talking to himself more, sitting in his office with his face in his hands, mumbling words she could not understand. On the other hand, when he spoke to her, he sounded unnaturally cheerful, a condition she attributed to the town celebration.

He had seen his mother every morning that week and twice had gone back to visit her in the afternoon. Charlotte Hock had never seen Mrs. Trout and was curious if there was a family resemblance.

He came into the office late Saturday morning, about nine-thirty, and reported that he had been in an accident. A produce truck had run into his Ford and bent the door so it wouldn't open. He was soaked through from the rain.

"My goodness," she said, "are you injured?" She could see he wasn't.

He disappeared into his office and spent the next hour at his desk composing a letter. At least that is what he was doing the times she passed the open door and looked in.

She went by several times, waiting for him to notice her so that she could ask about leaving early. He never took his eyes off his work, though, not even when she stomped her wooden peg against the floor, pretending to trip. She decided to wait until he was finished and ask him then.

He came out of the office at ten-thirty, wearing his coat and hat. He was still soaking wet. She thought he might be going to see his mother again. "Charlotte," he said, "did you drive today?"

"Yessir," she said, "I always drive." She was proud of the fact that a peg leg didn't stop her.

"Let me borrow your car a little while," he said.

It took her a moment to understand what he wanted. He had never asked to use her car before; he had several of his own parked in the alley with signs stuck to their windows. "My car?" she said.

"Mine's tore up," he said.

She thought of the other cars in the alley but did not dare to ask why he didn't drive one of those. She found her purse behind the counter and looked through it for her keys. He didn't seem to be in any hurry, which was out of the ordinary too. She thought it would be a good time to ask about leaving early.

"Here we are," she said, and took the keys out of her purse. She had owned the car a year, drove it up into her backyard every night, and locked it there, out of sight. No one else had driven it, no one else had even ridden in it. She pictured it running into a produce truck.

"I'll be back before lunch," he said.

"Yessir." And then, as he was walking out, she said, "Mr. Trout, you think I might could leave an hour early today?"

He didn't say yes, he didn't say no. He heard her, though, because she saw him deciding. He stopped a moment and cocked his head. And then it was decided, but he never told her the answer.

He slammed the door on the way out, but it didn't mean anything. She thought it was probably because he was hurrying. She could hear the rain lacing the front window. She didn't think he would borrow her car if she was fired.

The office door was still open. She waited until she heard the car turn from the alley into the street and then went inside. She had never been in the office alone before, she thought he might have kept pictures of his mother in his drawers. She walked farther in, listening for the car—the muffler was bad, so she would hear it—and then saw that he'd left what he was writing on top of the desk.

It was a note card, not a letter. She could not read it from there. She listened again, making sure the car was gone, and then stepped behind the desk. She did not pick the card up for fear he had memorized where it was.

It was printed in pencil, dated Sunday, which was incorrect. It was the Saturday. She thought the celebration might have confused him.

To whom it may concern: I just do not care to continue this the way it is going.

In this connection, I will not be able to do my full duty.

I can do only the best that I can.

Paris Trout

—I was convicted by the highpocket boys and the courthouse gang who went tampering with the jury.

Charlotte Hock, no longer listening for her car, sat down in the desk chair, put her face in her hands, and began to cry.

Mr. Trout, she thought, had gone and stolen her car and run for the state line.

HE DROVE BACK TO the hotel in the rain and got out without turning off the engine. The clerk seemed surprised in some way to see him there. He thought it showed, what he intended to do.

He locked the door when he was in his room and studied himself in the bathroom mirror. He ran a comb through his hair. Water flew off and splattered against his cheeks and his neck. He straightened his tie and studied his teeth; then he pulled back his lips with his fingers until he saw the face that he recognized, a family resemblance.

It satisfied him, and he left the mirror and moved to his dresser. There was a cocked double-barrel shotgun lying across the top along with several pistols, most of them revolvers. The ones he chose were automatics: a .45 caliber Commander, which he stuck into his belt, and a smaller .38 caliber Colt, which he put in his coat pocket.

He opened the top drawer of the dresser, where he kept his ammunition. The maid had put his socks and undershorts on top, and he dumped them all on the glass floor, hearing the shells hit and scatter. The full clips made a heavier sound and did not roll away.

He kicked the socks and underwear to the side and picked up the clips: two for the forty-five, one for the thirty-eight. He put them in the empty pocket of his coat. He went back to the mirror, and then he walked out of the room, feeling the weight in his pockets. His own true weight.

The rain had stopped, the car was still running, idling high. The windshield wipers rubbed and stuck, steam rose off the hood. There were horses in the street, a few young girls with batons. The beginnings of a parade. He watched a timid girl approaching a horse, wanting to put her hand against its nose. She inched closer and then the horse threw its head, and she jumped back. She collapsed, laughing, in the arms of the other girls.

Then, untangling herself, she turned and her eyes caught Trout sitting behind the car window, and what was in her face changed. He knew he had caught her at something. He rolled down his window, and she took a step in his direction and stopped.

"You want to come with me?" he said.

"No sir," she said. "I'm in the parade."

He pushed the clutch to the floor and forced the car into first gear. The transmission ground, and the child covered her ears. He turned in front of the horse and drove across town. The streets were half hidden by long puddles, some of them a foot deep. The engine coughed and caught but did not stop.

There was an empty parking spot directly in front of the nursing home, marked DIRECTOR, and Trout took it. His brakes were gone from running through the standing water, and the front tires of Charlotte Hock's car hit the curb and bounced back.

Somewhere in the distance there was a band.

He stepped out of the car, leaving the keys in the ignition, and walked up the steps into the front door. The lobby was empty, save the one woman sitting at the reception desk. Trout did not know the woman and walked past her.

The stairway to the second floor was wide and empty. Someone had been painting that morning and stopped halfway up. Probably to watch the parade.

He took the stairs slowly, his wet shoes slippery against the waxed wood, and then paused at the top to survey the hall. He had been in this spot before, but it was brand-new.

He walked to room 26 and opened the door. The window inside had not been closed. The curtains billowed, and Trout felt himself shake, the cool air against his wet clothes. She was sitting in her wheelchair, dressed in slippers and a robe, her long hair fell over her shoulders uncombed.

"It's time for us to go now," he said.

He straightened the old woman's robe over her chest, studying her as he worked. Her breathing was quicker now, he saw that she understood he was taking her.

He took the wheelchair down the steps backwards, watching her head bob with each small drop. He stopped once to untangle her hair from a wheel.

The woman from the reception desk was standing at the bottom of the stairs, looking up. "Sir?" she said.

He did not answer.

"Sir? Nobody told me Mrs. Trout was going out today. I'm only a volunteer, and they told me I'm not supposed to let anyone—"

He reached the bottom step and turned the wheelchair around, so he and the old woman were facing forward. The woman saw that something was wrong with him and stepped into his path. "Sir," she said, "could you wait one moment while I go in back and get you some visit papers to sign?"

She saw he was not going to stop and moved just before the chair hit her. The old woman went by, and then the man. He pushed her through the front door, and she followed them, intending to get the number of the license plate.

As she watched from the door, the wind blew the old woman's hair straight back, and she looked for a long moment like some ancient child on a carnival ride, frozen in speed.

Then the man picked her up and put her in the front seat.

THE STREETS DOWNTOWN HAD been closed for the parade, so Trout drove along a service road through the campus, coming out just behind the courthouse. He turned the car off, left the keys in the front seat, and carried her inside.

There was a crowd in front, its noises rose and fell.

He was between the second floor and the third, carrying her in his arms, when he encountered one of the courthouse regulars, an older woman who watched trials as entertainment. She was wearing a straw hat today and a bow tie. Carrying a paper cup. She recognized him and smiled.

"Mr. Trout," she said, "you taking your momma upstairs to watch the parade?" She studied the package in Trout's arms, smiling. "It's a lucky mother whose children don't forget her when they're grown."

He had stopped for a moment, now he climbed the rest of the way up. He heard her behind him. "It's chilly up there, Mr. Trout, you might want get her a shawl. . . ."

There was a small room on the south side of the courthouse with a window that overlooked the street. He carried her inside and put her in a corner on the floor.

Her robe rose up over her knees, her legs lay in front of her at rag-doll angles. Her head tilted to the left, and her mouth was opened wide at the lower side, as if by its own weight. She watched him, though, he could see that she understood everything he did.

He took the gun out of his belt and laid it across the windowsill, then the one from his pocket. He put the ammunition on the floor, next to her. He checked the line to the stairway. No one could approach him from there without offering him a shot.

He walked across the hall and tried the bathroom door. It was locked. There was a note in the corner: "Please see Miss Emma in records for key!"

A moment later he heard her on the steps, slowly climbing. He heard her breathing. He went to the stairway and saw the white straw hat coming up to him; he saw that she was carrying a blanket. "Mr. Trout?" she called.

He walked back into the room with his mother and picked up the forty-five. The woman emerged from the stairway and padded into the room. "I brought Mrs. Trout a light blanket," she said, and then she saw what was in his hand.

"Dear God," she said, "you don't want to hurt nobody today, Mr. Trout. Not with your mother right here watching. . . ."

She began to back up, saying things he did not listen to, until she was even again with the stairs. Then, dropping the blanket, she started back down the stairs. He followed the sound of her feet down to the landing between the second and third floors, and then he heard her begin to yell.

He looked at his mother, she looked back. He put the muzzle of the forty-five against the top of her head. "I end my connections with everything that come before," he said.

THE KEEPERS OF THE Bush were moving their courtroom inside at the time Wilma Dunn came down the stairs. The last session was scheduled for that afternoon, and none of them intended to sit out in the rain.

Carl Bonner, in fact, wanted to cancel court—Paris Trout had broken the stocks anyway—but Seagraves and Ward Townes felt an obligation to finish.

At the moment Wilma Dunn appeared on the stairs, Harry Seagraves and Ward Townes were fitting the table against the outside of the main courtroom door, being careful not to spill the drinks sitting on top. Carl Bonner was in the men's room down the hallway, the third time since the parade began.

Wilma Dunn was a heavy woman, and shrill, and came down the stairs at them, holding on to the banister with both hands. None of them had ever seen her hurry anywhere before. She saw them and changed the pitch of her scream. "Murder," she said, "God as my witness, he's going to murder his own mother. . . ."

Seagraves walked to the bottom of the steps to catch her if she fell. He did not understand the words at first, and then, a moment before she reached the bottom step, there was a single shot fired somewhere upstairs. Wilma Dunn fell into Seagraves's arms and began to cry.

"He's done shot that poor old woman," she said.

He pushed her far enough away to look in her face. "Slow down," he said. "Tell us slower."

"It's Mr. Paris Trout, up there with his mother," she said. "He got a gun and made to shoot her. . . ."

Seagraves looked up the stairway.

"Shot dead by her own sonny boy," the woman said, and began to wail.

Seagraves turned to Ward Townes. "Can you call somebody?" he said.

Townes was looking upstairs too. "I'll try," he said, "but there isn't anybody at the police station, I know that. And Edward Fixx and his deputies all been drunk for two days." He rubbed his face, trying to sober himself up.

"There's bound to be some sort of police outside," Seagraves said. He still had the woman's shoulders, and she was still crying. Carl Bonner came out of the bathroom, zipping his trousers, holding his cup.

"The poor thing," she said.

"Where are they?" Seagraves asked her.

"He's got her up there to the little room on the south side," she said.

"Who?" Bonner said, more to Seagraves than the woman.

There was a sudden cheering outside, something in the parade. "Paris Trout," she cried. "Paris Trout done shot his own mother upstairs. . . ."

She let go of Seagraves and clung to Carl Bonner. "Please help that old woman," she said.

Carl Bonner finished what was in the cup and started up the stairs. Seagraves tried to stop him. "Hold on, Carl," he said. "The man's got a gun."

"He's shot his own mother," Bonner said.

"If he shot her, she's shot," Seagraves said. "We'll get the law to take care of it."

"It's still somebody's mother," Bonner said, and went on up.

Seagraves tried again. "You think it's *Boys' Life* up there? Take a damn minute and think what it means."

Bonner straightened and walked up the middle of the staircase. Seagraves watched him as far as the first landing, where he turned and followed the stairs up. Wilma Dunn dabbed at her eyes with a hankie. "He always been the bravest of the brave," she said.

TROUT WAS SITTING ON the floor, not far from his mother. She had fallen on her side, head tucked into her chest; her long hair was soaked in blood, a mop left in the middle of the job.

He heard the steps on the stairs. They reached the landing below, stopped for a moment, and then continued up. He laid the forty-five across his knees and sighted over her body to the stairway.

Bonner called out once, "Mr. Trout? This is Carl Bonner. . . ."

Trout did not answer. He waited, and listened, and in a moment the man came to him, crossing into his line of sight and reason.

Carl Bonner stood still at the top of the stairs, then slowly turned and offered himself fully. "Mr. Trout," he said, walking forward, "I am not here to hurt you, sir. I only want to help your mother."

Trout shot him an inch above the belt, and the force of it blew him back beyond the stairs. He lay still a moment and then began to curl. The recoil kicked the gun up into the air. Trout let it fall back where it had been, and when it was settled he shot him again, in the ankle.

In a few moments Trout heard him cry. Little noises. The room smelled like firecrackers. Trout waited for what would come, watching the man he had shot over the sights of the pistol.

SEAGRAVES HEARD THE SHOTS upstairs, he heard Bonner fall. Then the noises settled, and Ward Townes came through the entrance, towing Dr. Hatfield. "I think he's shot Carl Bonner," Seagraves said. He looked up the stairs, and in a moment there were sounds from that direction.

One of them—Bonner's voice—was as clear as a whisper in his ear. "Please, Jesus . . ."

"What in creation?" Ward Townes said. "He just went up there to him? Without a gun?"

Bonner cried out then, as if something had caught him by surprise.

"Is there a gun somewhere we can get to it?" Seagraves said.

He and Townes looked at each other a minute. "Not that I know," Townes said.

The sounds of Carl Bonner's breathing carried down the staircase, the catches and sighs. Then another cry. The woman covered her mouth and ran for the door. No one tried to stop her.

It was the doctor who finally spoke. "I got to get to a telephone," he said, "call an ambulance down here." Ward Townes took a key ring from his pocket and opened the door to one of the offices.

"I gave a boy a dollar to find us a policeman," Townes said to Seagraves. "I don't see there's any choice but to wait this out."

As if he'd heard that, Bonner cried out again.

They stood together, listening to Dr. Hatfield on the phone. "What the hell you mean, the ambulance is in the parade? . . . Then get somebody over here in a car. . . . Yes, right now, people been shot."

And the next time Carl Bonner cried for help, Seagraves went up the stairs.

He saw Bonner from the landing between the second and third floor, pressed facefirst into the wood railing, eyes open and fixed, as if he were watching something a long ways off. Seagraves took the next steps one at a time, as close to the wall as he could get.

When Seagraves's head was level with the top step, he saw the stain under Carl Bonner's stomach and then, with the next step, he saw that his foot had been blown halfway off at the ankle.

A cry came out of the body, but nothing moved. There was a noise behind him, and Seagraves turned and saw Ward Townes on the landing.

Seagraves took another step up and leaned forward until his chin almost rested on the top stair. He saw that the oak door leading into the south room opened out, the knob rested against the wall leading to the staircase.

There was something on the floor in the room, but from the stairs he could not see Trout.

He took a deep breath, checked that Townes was behind him on the landing, and then, still watching Townes, he reached around the corner of the staircase until he felt the door and slammed it shut.

He took the last three steps in one stride and threw himself against the bottom of the door. He had meant to call for Townes to get Carl Bonner and then to hold the door shut until there was help, but even before he was started, he was stopped.

Something moving at the very edge of his vision.

The shot caught him in the shoulder, just as he hit the door. It threw him sideways and turned him toward the movement he had seen, and there was Paris Trout.

He had moved to a different room and was standing in the doorway, only a few yards from Bonner. His open eye dropped to meet him over the sight of the gun.

Seagraves got to his feet and Trout shot him again. The bullet hit him in the side and passed through his body.

Seagraves closed the distance.

Paris Trout stood with his feet spread and his shooting arm straight out in front, and pulled the trigger four more times as Seagraves came across the hall. Two of the shots missed, the other two hit him in the leg and the groin, but they did not knock him down.

He staggered and surged.

The next time Trout pulled the trigger, the hammer fell on an empty chamber. He reached into his pocket and found one of the spare clips just as Seagraves's hand attached itself to his shirt. Trout tried to pull himself free, but Seagraves would not let go.

Trout stumbled backwards, trying to get the fresh clip into the forty-five. Then Seagraves had one of his fingers and was pushing it back. Trout heard the clip fall against the floor, he felt the life surge in the man he'd shot. The finger snapped at the knuckle, a crippling pain traveled the length of Trout's arm, and then the attorney let go of his shirt and dropped to the floor.

The forty-five and the clip were both somehow underneath him. A phone was ringing downstairs, over and over. No one answered. Trout reached into his pocket and found the other gun.

He walked to the north end of the hallway, noticing that his trousers were sticking to his legs. He'd wet himself. Cradle to cradle.

There was a fire escape at the end of the hallway. He thought for a moment of climbing down and looking for the rest of the people he'd put on his list, but he'd lost his purpose.

He stopped at the end of the hall and took his hand and the pistol out of his coat. He checked the safety—it was off—and put the gun in his mouth. Then he turned back in the direction of the staircase and waited until Ward Townes's face appeared there, waited until Townes found him, and on that signal pulled the trigger.

BY THE TIME DR. Hatfield arrived on the third floor, there was only a faint stirring in Carl Bonner's chest. Ward Townes had put a lawbook under his head and then gone to tend Harry Seagraves.

Dr. Hatfield knelt at the body. He felt for a pulse and then opened Carl Bonner's eyes to see if they would dilate. The doctor was shaking. There were sirens outside now, feet on the steps.

"I think he's gone," he said.

He opened Carl Bonner's shirt and studied the wound. He shook his head.

Dr. Hatfield stood up slowly and moved to Seagraves. Ward Townes held his head in his lap. The doctor searched for a pulse, but there was none.

Then he moved to the small room at the south end of the hall, opened the door, and from there saw the top of the old woman's head. He turned back to the landing without going in.

People had reached the third floor now, some of them police, some of them lawyers. A woman was crying, the police were issuing orders.

"There's another one over here," somebody said.

Dr. Hatfield stepped away from the door and saw it for himself. Paris Trout lay alone, beneath the splash on the wall. At the corner of the ceiling, bits of him hung in a spider web.

"Somebody get a boy in here," the doctor said. "Clean that mess up after we take care of the dead."

HANNA
PART NINE

A month to the day after her husband killed his mother, Carl Bonner, Harry Seagraves, and then himself, Hanna Trout signed a legal order authorizing Ether County to open the five safes that still stood in the hallway of the store.

Agents of the Internal Revenue Service had visited her twice, and Estes Singletary had written a signed editorial calling for reparations to be made from the Trout estate. Not only to the Seagraves family and Leslie Bonner but to the city of Cotton Point as well.

"Paris Trout was never a contributor to this community," he wrote. "All he did was take. And in the end he took his own mother and two of our finest citizens, and he owes a debt for that. The repugnance one feels in this matter is not lessened by the fact that the killer ought to have been in jail at the time this grievous act was committed for another act of murder, which was overlooked because the girl was colored. . . ."

The editorial went on to the bottom of the page. Hanna Trout read the first two paragraphs and put the paper aside. She did not need the Ether County *Plain Talk* to tell her about Paris Trout.

And when Sheriff Edward Fixx called her that same week about opening the safes, she said that he and the federal government could do what they wanted.

It did not seem to her that what was inside belonged to her anyway.

On an order from the coroner, the sheriff and two of his deputies had already searched Paris's room at the Ether Hotel and found nine pistols, loaded and cocked, two shotguns, and a .30 caliber lever-action carbine. They had found a steel plate beneath his mattress, stacks of canned food, and several sheets of glass fitted to cover the floor.

There was no money, no indication of where it was.

An investigation by officers of the Southern Bankers Directory showed that Trout had sold 866 acres of timber in February for $117,000, and had liquidated Trout & Co. the month before, receiving a payment slightly in excess of $170,000 from an Atlanta investment firm.

The assets of his bank, which were estimated at $400,000, had vanished.

All that was left were the house and the store and the five safes inside. Hanna Trout signed the authorization without reading it. She had put her house up for sale. She sensed she was an embarrassment now, much as her husband had been before that Saturday morning.

There were stories, of course: that she had the money herself, that her husband had gone crazy when she threw him out.

There was a story that she and Harry Seagraves were lovers, but that one died early, out of respect for his wife.

Hanna Trout had gone to the funerals—Harry Seagraves and Carl Bonner were buried the same day—and no one had offered her an arm or a kind word. Of course, there had been no offers in that direction before, when Paris Trout was only an embarrassment.

Before what he was and what he did had changed the place he lived.

HARRY SEAGRAVES WAS BURIED in the family plot in the oldest and shadiest part of Ether County Memorial Park. His stone read:

HARRY SEAGRAVES
HE WAS OUR BEST AND OUR KINDEST

Carl Bonner lay in a newer part of the cemetery, near the street. His marker was flat on the ground and carried only his name and the dates of his birth and death. You would never guess, looking at it, that he had been the youngest Eagle Scout in the history of Georgia or that a generation of Cotton Point children had suffered in the comparison with his example.

You would never guess that a perception of the future died with him.

Paris Trout and his mother were buried a day later, in separate parts of the cemetery.

There had been no church funeral for him, and only Hanna and a few of his blood relations came to the graveside. He went into the ground in a section of the cemetery where no one visiting the graves of Harry Seagraves or Carl Bonner or his mother would accidentally stumble over his name on the way in or out. The ground there was hard, and there were spots where grass would not grow.

The place looked poisoned.

There were no trees, and there was no shade, although in some seasons the late-afternoon sun dropped behind the Monument to the Unknown Confederate Dead in such a way as to cast a shadow across his grave.

A LOCKSMITH WAS BROUGHT in from Macon at county expense. He spent two days in the hallway of the store, going from one safe to another, and was unable to open any of them. By the second afternoon his curses were audible on the street.

At the end of the second day he told Sheriff Fixx, "Those ain't ordinary," and returned to Macon.

Edward Fixx informed all interested parties—including agents of the Internal Revenue Service—that the safes were not ordinary and the locksmith from Macon had left. A week later two federal agents stepped off the train from Atlanta, escorting one Ralph Guthrie, of Leavenworth, Kansas.

Mr. Guthrie was in handcuffs and was taken to the Ether Hotel and given the best room available.

In the morning he ate steak and eggs at Richard Dickey's drugstore and then walked between the agents from the restaurant to Paris Trout's store, smiling in a boyish way at the women—it did not matter if they were young or old—and did not seem even slightly embarrassed by the circumstances or the handcuffs.

Once inside, Ralph Guthrie looked at the safes and began to laugh.

Edward Fixx did not appreciate a man in handcuffs laughing at his situation. "Can he do it or not?" he said.

One of the agents considered Fixx in a Yankee sort of way and said, "Let him finish laughing, and we'll find out. It's a professional courtesy."

When Ralph Guthrie had finished laughing, he spoke directly to the sheriff. "Edward," he said, "you got yourself a problem. These here safes are Belgian."

The sheriff also did not appreciate being called Edward by somebody in handcuffs.

Ralph Guthrie looked around at the walls and said, "You wonder, don't you, how safes like that end up someplace like this."

"Can you do it?" one of the agents said.

Ralph Guthrie shrugged. "I can get in. There ain't no safe you can't get inside, but I got to blow it."

"Here?" Edward Fixx said. "Downtown Cotton Point?"

The safecracker shrugged. "You can move these somewhere else, I'll be glad to wait. They might weigh a thousand pounds. . . ."

Edward Fixx did not like the idea of a safecracker setting off an explosion in Cotton Point, but the federal agents assured him that Mr. Guthrie was as careful as a surgeon, and if it were not for his weakness to brag and spend money, he could never have been caught.

The sheriff had one of the agents write that down and then agreed to the plan, and the safe blowing was set for Sunday afternoon. The police blocked off Main Street for two blocks on either side of the store and pushed the crowd back that gathered along the edge of Georgia Officers' Academy's campus to watch until none of them could see anything.

Ralph Guthrie and the federal agents were in the store most of the afternoon, setting the charges. Edward Fixx sat in his cruiser on a side street a block and a half from the store. The cruiser was fresh out of the body shop—he'd smashed it one way or another four times in the last year—and had that new-car feeling again, and Edward Fixx wasn't about to expose it to a brick shower because some Leavenworth safecracker used too much nitroglycerin.

A few minutes after six o'clock Ralph Guthrie and the federal agents walked out of the front of the store, in no hurry at all, crossed the empty street, and sat down on the curb. A minute or two later there was a muffled explosion, followed by a cloud of smoke that rose from behind the store.

The explosion shook the ground but did not as much as crack the front windows of the store.

The men waited a few minutes more and walked back inside.

Edward Fixx drove his cruiser to the corner and got out, leaving the door open. He did not like a professional safecracker inside with no one local to watch him. He found them in the back, coughing in the dust and smoke. The five safes sat exactly where they had been, but the doors were ajar, a few inches each.

"Sheriff Fixx," one of the agents said, "if you would get a pencil and paper, we can itemize the contents as we take them out."

It took them half an hour, but Edward Fixx stopped writing a long time before that. There were more than ninety bottles, each one filled approximately a third of the way to the top with urine. Each bottle was labeled, date and time. "Urine passed from the body of Paris Trout, eleven o'clock A.M., this eleventh day of March 1954. To be used in the event of my death for evidence I have been poisoned."

Edward Fixx was not about to write them down one at a time.

There was also a sealed white envelope which held several hundred pieces of clipped fingernails and another envelope—this one light brown and containing a single sheet of paper full of columns of numbers that seemed to be a code or a map.

After several months in the hands of U.S. Army decoding experts, however, the numbers were discovered to be the combinations to the five safes themselves.

THAT WAS AS CLOSE as anyone came to Paris Trout's money, it was as much of an explanation as he ever gave.

Hanna Trout sold the house and moved to Savannah, where she taught school as long as she lived. Sometimes, looking out over the playground from her office window, a child would catch her eye, someone awkward and dark with legs as thin as bones, and she would think of Rosie Sayers.

The child was never in her dreams, though. She had no claim on Hanna Trout.

In her dreams everything was dark. She could never see the walls or the floor or her own hands. She would stumble, catching herself a moment before she fell, and then stumble again. Always moving toward a voice that called for help.

The tripping frightened her—she remembered there was glass on the floor—but in the dark, at the bottom of things, she always kept on. In her dreams she knew the voice.

And when she woke from that other place, grabbing at the roll of the mattress for some purchase to break her fall, she would hold herself still for as long as the dream was fresh, trying to hear the voice again, but the fear would pass before she could bring it back.

And then it was gone.

And she would lie in the dark until morning sometimes, wondering which one of them it was.

August 16, 1987
Sacramento, California

ABOUT THE AUTHOR

PETE DEXTER is the author of the National Book Award–winning novel *Paris Trout* as well as *The Paperboy, Spooner, Paper Trails, God's Pocket, Deadwood, Brotherly Love,* and *Train.* He has been a columnist for the *Philadelphia Daily News* and the *Sacramento Bee,* and has contributed to many magazines, including *Esquire, Sports Illustrated,* and *Playboy.* His screenplays include *Rush* and *Mulholland Falls.* Dexter was born in Michigan and raised in Georgia, Illinois, and eastern South Dakota. He lives on an island off the coast of Washington.